THE BURIAL PLACE

THE BURIAL PLACE

A ROB SOLIZ & FRANK PIERCE MYSTERY

Larry Enmon

CROOKED
LANE

NEW YORK

Published in the United States by Crooked Lane Books, an imprint of The Quick Brown Fox & Company LLC.

Crooked Lane Books and its logo are trademarks of The Quick Brown Fox & Company LLC.

Library of Congress Catalog-in-Publication data available upon request.

ISBN (hardcover): 978-1-68331-553-7
ISBN (ePub): 978-1-68331-554-4
ISBN (ePDF): 978-1-68331-555-1

Cover design by Matthew Kalamidas/StoneHouse Creative
Book design by Jennifer Canzone

Printed in the United States.

www.crookedlanebooks.com

Crooked Lane Books
34 West 27th St., 10th Floor
New York, NY 10001

First Edition: April 2018

10 9 8 7 6 5 4 3 2 1

This book is dedicated to all of my fallen brothers and sisters of the Houston Police Department (1975–1981). Some died from violence, some from accidents, and some from their own hands. You were the heroes. The rest of us—just survivors.

1

Katrina's terror grew with each passing hour. There was no way to tell how far they'd traveled or in which direction. She struggled with the tape that bound her hands behind her back. Her left shoulder ached from the strain.

The tape over her mouth and eyes had at first sent her into rounds of wild panic—hyperventilating to the point of almost passing out—but she'd gotten control of her senses and begun to study her predicament. The long, smooth road probably meant they were on a freeway. They had stopped only once, for less than a minute, not long after taking her. It still had to be dark. They'd snatched her out of her car a little after eleven o'clock. It had been no more than two or three hours since then.

Where were they going? To a place they could torture, rape, and eventually kill her? She shook uncontrollably, dread building. The diesel engine's growl decreased and the motion of the truck slowed. They'd stopped—no, they'd just turned right. They kept moving, but more slowly. If she could just shout or make some noise, this might be her best chance for rescue. But she couldn't. The one lying beside her made sure of that.

He hadn't uttered a sound since they'd thrown her in the back of the old brown pickup with the camper shell. He'd held her down for the first few minutes, as if he expected her to bounce up and try to run. After they made the quick stop and got on the long smooth road, he'd lessened his grip, but his hands still moved over her body. His coarse fingers stroked one breast under her T-shirt until her nipple was raw.

A couple of times his hand drifted down to her shorts. The jagged fingernails stroked the waistband, and once explored just below the elastic, but then withdrew. As if he was waiting for permission from someone.

Her biggest worry, the one she couldn't shake, was the odor. They lay on an old mattress or quilt that reeked of mildew, urine, and vomit. Others had lain there, gone where she was going. Her stomach churned, and she fought the urge to puke. With her mouth taped, she'd choke to death. But the other overpowering smell that sent chills up her back was an old one.

As a young girl, she'd once gone deer hunting with her dad. After the day's hunt, all the deer were dressed and the meat shared among the hunters at the camp. She'd watched the tall man with the sharp knife haul the deer up by its antlers in the tree. She'd stood a little too close as he gutted it, and when the intestines spilled into the five-gallon bucket, the odor had hit her like a hammer. The smell of blood and death. That same stench that filled her nostrils now.

2

Franklin Pierce leaned against the boxing ring in the Dallas police gym and watched Roberto Soliz pummel his sparring opponent. Roberto always sparred on Mondays. The ringing of free weights slamming onto a bar and the whine of exercise bikes and treadmills along the far wall reminded Frank of why he hated gyms. The smell of body odor and people grunting had never enlivened him. His last trip here had been for in-service self-defense training fourteen months before. *Way too soon to return.*

Roberto and his partner danced more than fought. Each bounced around the ring, probing the other guy's weak side. This was a predictable story. The officer was ten years younger than Roberto but not as experienced. He kept falling for the fake jabs. Frank lifted his jacket sleeve and checked his watch. When he looked up, Roberto's eyes met his. Frank tapped his wrist and motioned toward the door.

Sweat dripped from Roberto's twice-broken nose and ran down the sides of his short black hair. He'd worn that high and tight haircut since his Marine days. Frank shifted from one foot to the other and gazed around. This whole exercise thing was a waste of time. He looked back at the ring in time to see Roberto fake with a right hook and nail the guy hard with a left uppercut. He fell straight on his butt and looked up with a "Where did that come from?" expression. Roberto tucked his right glove under his left armpit and jerked his hand out. He strolled to the defeated man and helped him up.

"That was good. You're getting better, Randy. Same time next Monday?"

The guy wiggled his jaw, testing it. "Sure. See you then."

Roberto marched to Frank's corner, slipping off the other glove, mouth guard, and headgear. He dropped everything in a pile and accepted a bottle of water from Frank.

"You're faster than most Mexicans," Frank said.

With sweat dripping off his chin, Rob downed a couple of long swallows and screwed the cap back on an empty bottle. He tucked his Saint Michael medal back inside his T-shirt. Still breathing hard, he asked, "What's going on, cracker?"

"Terry wants to see us in his office at nine, and we all have a meeting with Edna five minutes after that."

Rob ran his hand down his face and wiped it on his trunks. "What's the deal?"

"No idea. I got the call ten minutes ago. Figured I'd find you here."

Rob checked the oversize clock on the wall and twisted his neck a couple of times. "Forty-five minutes then. Okay, I'll meet you there."

Frank turned to leave, but looked back. He sniffed in Rob's direction. "Use extra soap today."

Walking to the door, Frank wondered what this meeting was about. He and Rob hadn't crossed the line in weeks.

Besides, working criminal intelligence wasn't real police work. More about spying on criminals. Frank enjoyed it because of the mental exercise and the fact that Rob was his partner. They worked well together, and he counted him as one of his best friends. One of his best friends? *Hell, I don't really have any other friends.* Lots of coworkers and acquaintances, but no friends.

No two people could have been less alike. They both had over fifteen years in the department, but that's where the similarities ended. Rob was short and stocky with a weightlifter's physique, Frank tall and skinny with light brown hair worn a little too long. Rob, married for over twenty years with a son and daughter; Frank, forty-one and unmarried. Yeah, they were the Mutt and Jeff of the department.

He took the elevator up one floor and stepped inside the Criminal Intelligence Unit, which greeted him with its usual hum. Familiar voices, phones ringing, and detectives typing always relaxed Frank. Other than his home, this was his favorite place. He drew in a long breath, happy to breathe fresh air again. *How do people stand those nasty gyms?* Other than yoga, he got no exercise at all. People probably thought him odd, but he didn't care. He was comfortable in his skin. Everyone in the department got a reputation sooner or later. Rob was the golden gloves champion for the boxing team. Frank held the record for the cadet having the highest academic score in the history of the Dallas Police Academy. He was proud of that.

He had one other record. The most decorated officer still alive. The Nelson Park incident had given him that one. And he wished it had never happened.

* * *

Forty minutes later, Rob checked his reflection in the shiny elevator door on the way to the fourth floor. He tucked his white dress shirt tighter into his gray Western-cut pants and adjusted the blue blazer on his shoulders. Rubbing the top of each cowboy boot on the calf of the opposite leg wasn't exactly a spit shine, but good enough. When the doors opened, he marched into the CIU area. He scanned the cubicles and found Frank typing, as usual.

Rob dropped his jacket over the back of his chair and slid into the adjoining cubicle. He lifted his head toward Sergeant Terry Andrews's glass office. Few supervisors measured up to Terry. A twenty-one-year veteran, he held the respect of all his detectives. When he gave you an assignment, you felt you were working with him, not for him.

The door was open and Terry had the phone snugged to his ear. Terry glanced at Rob, his customary smile missing. *That can't be good.* Terry nodded in agreement to something the caller said and scribbled on a notepad.

Rob swung his chair to Frank, who was still typing away. He had to be the most laid-back guy on the force. Never dressed up. Still looked as if he worked the Vice Unit. His standard polo and Dockers were his idea of business formal.

"We in trouble?" Rob asked.

Frank stopped typing and peered in his direction. "Dunno. Maybe."

Frank was being Frank again. About as gabby as a deaf-mute. Rob shifted in his chair and tried recalling what they'd done lately—nothing. They'd worked a visiting foreign dignitary with State Department Security last week, and the week before had been part of a surveillance team on a biker gang. Their "We'd rather beg for forgiveness than ask permission" attitude sometimes led to misunderstandings. They considered department regulations more as suggestions, never to interfere with a good investigation. *If this stupid meeting is about that food court thing . . .*

Rob caught another glimpse of Terry. He had stopped writing and was massaging his brow and temple with his free hand.

"Hey, Frank."

"Huh?"

Rob leaned closer to the short cubical wall. "Terry has the look."

Frank never missed a key as he asked, "What look?"

"You know, the 'time for an ass-chewing' look."

Frank craned his neck in Terry's direction. "Probably just has gas."

Rob glanced over his shoulder in time to see Terry hang up and motion them to his office. "Okay, show time," Rob whispered. He put his coat on and got up.

Frank yawned and stood. He left his gold jacket hanging on the back of the chair and followed. He always got a pass from supervisors. Medal of Valor officers in Dallas PD got the same respect as Medal of Honor recipients in the military.

The comforting aroma of fresh-brewed coffee welcomed them when they strolled into Terry's office. Terry always kept a small pot going. He poured a little into his mug and held it up. "Coffee?"

"Yeah, thanks," Rob said.

Frank shook his head.

"Grab a seat." Terry handed Rob a steaming cup before closing the door.

Rob liked Terry's office. It felt like home. The standard family photos were on display, as well as the commendations and decorations you'd expect. What you didn't expect was what gave it character. A half dozen oil paintings depicted rural central Texas vistas, the most prominent being a huge canvas behind Terry's desk featuring an ancient live oak in a field of bluebonnets.

Terry sat down and looked from one to the other. He had that nervous smirk that meant there was something uncomfortable to discuss. Rob called it his shit-eating grin.

"So . . . what have you guys been up to?"

Frank didn't acknowledge the question. He slid into his slouch position.

Rob cleared his throat. "Not much, just work—you know."

Terry lowered his head and ran fingers through his thinning hair. He looked up. "Do you know who's in Edna's office?"

"No," Rob said.

"The major and deputy chief. And Edna wants to see us after they leave." Terry's eyebrows rose as he leaned closer to the pair. "What's going on?"

Rob sipped his coffee. "Honest, we haven't a clue. Thought you knew."

Terry's gaze shifted to Frank. "Is that the story you're staying with?"

Frank sat up and returned the stare. "For once we're innocent."

Terry blew out a breath and leaned back in his chair, setting his coffee mug on his slim midsection. "That's a relief." He craned his head to the left and frowned, staring out the glass past them. They both looked around as the division major and deputy chief stalked out of Edna's office toward the elevator. She stood in the doorway and gazed across the open cubicle area toward them. Edna beckoned with her index finger; she wasn't wearing her happy face.

Terry stood. "Let's go. You know that if there's anything you need to say, it's better for all of us to tell her before she lays out her case against you, right?"

Rob had a final sip and stood. "We got nothing."

Terry turned to Frank. He only shrugged.

They wormed their way around the cubicles to Edna's office. Frank brought up the rear. About halfway there, he began reciting Psalm 23:4. "Even though I walk through the valley of the shadow of death, I fear no evil . . ."

The back of Terry's neck glowed red.

"You're a real funny guy, Frank. Real funny," he said. He stopped at Edna's door and allowed them to enter first, giving Frank the stink eye.

Lieutenant Edna Crawford stood as they entered, her hair up in her signature tight bun. Edna's five-foot-ten-inch frame put her at at least eye level with most officers, and she towered over Rob. She held the distinction of being the best-liked supervisor in the department. The fact that she'd made lieutenant after only ten years had less to do with her gender and race and everything to do with her competence and management abilities. She was the first black female lieutenant to lead criminal intelligence at Dallas PD. Unlike Terry's office, which had a relaxed, homey feel, her space was all business. Decorations, commendations, and awards hung in tight formation on the walls, as did her diploma from Texas A&M in criminal justice. The only indication that she might have a private life was a five-by-seven photo on the desk of her, her husband, and two young daughters at Jackson Square in New Orleans. Edna's light-brown complexion seemed better suited to the Mediterranean than Texas.

She motioned Rob and Frank to the sofa on her right.

"Terry, close that door, please."

Terry shut the door and sat in the chair across from her. Edna dropped into her executive seat, her wrinkled brow and pained gaze an ominous sign. Rob's gut tightened when she began reviewing pages of handwritten notes, probably from the previous meeting. Her expression twisted into a frown.

Rob glanced at Frank, who looked as if he might drop off at any time. Finally, Edna raised her head.

"We have a little problem."

Terry sucked in a long breath and held it while she continued.

She dropped the papers on the desk and eyed him. "The mayor's daughter is missing and we've been instructed to find her."

Terry exhaled. "That's it?"

Edna's brow furrowed and she pursed her lips. "What, that's not enough?"

Terry flashed his shit-eating grin. "No, what I meant was—never mind."

She scanned the notes again. "Apparently there was a big row at the mayor's house last Thursday night. He, his wife, and their teenage daughter really got into it over her boyfriend. It seems they don't approve of him. Anyway, she stormed out saying she was driving to Austin the next day to spend the weekend with him and to not bother calling, because she wouldn't answer."

"How did we get all this information?" Terry asked.

Edna laid the notes on her desk and picked up her stress ball, giving it a long squeeze. "When she didn't show up Sunday night, they got worried. She didn't answer calls or text, and her apartment looks like no one's been there for several days. The mayor met with the chief and asked him to look into it."

Terry crossed his legs and interlaced his fingers. "I'm still not clear on why CIU's handling this. This is a Missing Persons case."

Edna bit her lip. "That's where things get complicated. It's the mayor's congressional race. He's slightly ahead in the polls—wants to stay there. Better-than-average chance he'll be the next congressman from this district. The chief feels keeping him in our corner is in the department's best interest."

Frank spoke up for the first time. "And the mayor doesn't want this to become a distraction to wreck his family-values platform."

Edna cocked her head. "Something like that."

"I'm still not following what this has to do with us," Rob said.

Her eyes narrowed and her lips stretched into a tight line. "The mayor wants to keep this quiet and discreet, at least until they know whether there's a real problem or if she's just laid up somewhere with a friend, sulking. I guess he's not willing to bet his future political career on the whims of a flaky teenage girl." She eyed Rob and Frank. "You two have to find her."

The tension had begun building between Rob's shoulders as soon as he heard the word *mayor*. By the time he heard the words *flaky teenage girl*, that tension had become a hammer. If there was one thing he hated, it was family drama. He rubbed his face and closed his eyes. "Why us?"

Edna rolled the ball between her palms. "Your background in Homicide and SWAT, and Frank's in Missing Persons and Vice, provides the right combination of investigative experience. Also, you're in CIU. We're keeping this in-house for now." Edna had that smug look that indicated she didn't want any arguments.

When Frank said, "You didn't choose us, did you?" her expression changed. She'd been found out.

She scowled. "No, I didn't select you. That came from the sixth floor."

"The chief?" Terry asked.

She nodded. "According to the deputy chief, he wants fast results and figured you'd get them."

"I assume she was driving a car. Has it been entered in NCIC as stolen or wanted?" Terry asked.

"Not yet. The mayor doesn't want to raise a hue and cry until he's sure she's really missing. Notifying the National Crime Information Center is off the table for now."

"Some father he is," Rob mumbled. If it had been his daughter, he'd already have had a search party looking for her.

Edna had her mouth open to answer, but quickly recovered. She stood to make major in the next couple of years, so she mostly kept her opinions to herself. She cleared her throat and said, "We all know how teenage daughters are." Her gaze shifted to Frank. "Well, most of us. They're on top of the world one minute and in the lowest canyons of the ocean the next. He's probably right. She's still pissed off and at a friend's. But that doesn't mean we can't check it out."

Edna directed her gaze at Terry. "Call me daily before five with an update. I'll pass it directly to the chief's office." She pointed at Rob and Frank. "And you two, call in your day's progress to Terry before five."

She picked up one of the pieces of paper and stood. The men all rose at the same time. She handed it to Rob. "This is a description of the vehicle and the address and home phone of the mayor. His wife can see you anytime before noon. Call before you come. Any questions?"

"What do we do when we locate her?" Rob asked. He knew what he'd do, but it didn't sound as if the mayor and his wife had that good of a relationship with their own daughter.

Edna paused. "Put her in contact with her father."

Rob said, "Yes, ma'am," and opened the door. He hated these assignments. Anytime the mayor or city council was involved, it was usually screwed up.

She smiled for the first time. "Let's do this, then."

Terry led Rob and Frank back to his office. Once inside, he leaned against his desk and folded his arms. "I know what you're going to say, so save your breath. It sucks, and it's not your job to keep up with the mayor's kid—I get that."

"Jeez, Terry, this is worse than sitting on a foreign dig for a week," Rob said.

"Hell, I know, and I'm sorry you got stuck with it, but it wasn't our call. Look, go out and visit Ms. Mayor, make it look good, and the girl will probably turn up on her own. Just don't step on your cranks." Terry eyed Frank. "You've been pretty quiet. Any bitches?"

Frank showed a curious half smile. Rob knew that expression and didn't like it. It usually meant Frank was up to something.

"On the contrary," Frank said. "It seems extremely interesting."

3

Ten minutes later, Rob wheeled out of the employee parking lot onto McKee Street with Frank riding shotgun. Frank punched Ms. Mayor's phone number into his cell, and a young woman's voice answered on the second ring. Frank's spirits rose. Had the girl returned home? Was this her?

"Yes, this is Detective Pierce, Dallas PD. Is Mrs. Wallace there?"

"I'm her personal assistant. May I help you?"

Holy crap, a personal assistant. Do all mayors' wives have personal assistants? "We were told we could interview her this morning regarding an investigation."

"Oh, yes. She's been expecting your call. When would you like to come over?"

Frank glanced at the paper. "You're in Highland Park, right?"

"Yes, do you need the address?"

"We've got it. We'll be there in about twenty minutes."

"I'll inform Mrs. Wallace. Thank you." The line went dead.

Frank pulled the phone from his ear and shook his head.

"What?" Rob asked.

"She has a personal assistant."

"So?"

Frank dropped the phone in his pocket. "Just seems strange, that's all."

"Busy people have personal assistants. Makes them more productive."

12

Frank slid lower in the seat and leaned against the headrest. "That's what we need—personal assistants." He stared at Rob, who smiled back at him before returning his eyes to the road. No matter how crappy the job, Rob wore that perpetual smile. He was probably the cheeriest guy Frank had ever met.

"I guess when we have as much money as the mayor, we can get a couple," Rob said.

"Not working for the city."

Rob slowed and flipped on his right blinker. "He made his millions in real estate, right?"

"Not working for the city," Frank repeated. "Besides, this mayor gig is just a stepping stone."

"You think he always had his sights on Congress?"

Frank tore a piece of Spearmint in half and offered it to Rob, who unwrapped it and folded it once before slipping it between his lips. He placed the wrapper in the ashtray. Frank popped his piece in his mouth, wadded the half wrapper, and flicked it onto the floor.

"No, Congress is another stepping stone. I think the guy wants to be president."

"You think?" Rob asked.

"He's set up for it. If he wins this race in the fall, he's on the glide path for bigger and better things."

Rob followed the other traffic onto the freeway entry ramp. "That's what Carmen said when he was elected mayor."

Frank hadn't asked about Rob's wife for some time. The news was seldom good. "How's Carmen doing?"

Rob's perpetual smile faded. "You know, she has good days and bad." He shot Frank a half grin.

"Yeah, I know. Sorry, buddy."

Clinical depression was a terrible thing. Particularly when it affected someone you loved, especially your spouse. It stole the personalities of its victims as surely as Alzheimer's. The stigma of a serious mental disease didn't make it any easier for someone like Carmen. Most people couldn't deal with the stress as well as Rob.

"You believe what Edna said? About the chief personally selecting us?" Rob asked.

Frank scratched his ear. "Sure, why not. The guy knows talent when he sees it."

Rob's bright smile returned. Frank had known it would. Rob always hit the reset button when he received a compliment. Frank made a mental note: *Don't ask about Carmen again for a while.* They drove for the next fifteen minutes in silence.

Rob exited the freeway and stopped at the light on the service road. A tall brunette in a short skirt and low-cut top waited at the crosswalk of the side street. Frank pulled his sunglasses down with his index finger. She looked, and he waved. She smiled before turning back to the light.

Frank settled back into his slouch riding position. "I do love April in Dallas. Skirts go up and blouses go down."

The light changed, and Rob rolled through. "You know half the department thinks you're gay, right?"

Frank looked at him. "Why, because I'm not married, or because they never see me with a woman?"

"I think you just answered your own question."

Frank chuckled. "Yeah, I know."

"That doesn't bother you, man?"

"Naw."

"Why?"

Frank pushed the sunglasses back up on his nose. " 'Cause only the gay ones think that."

* * *

Terry relaxed in his office chair and reread the paragraph of the report. He always had trouble following this detective's writing. Lynch would spend five pages talking around a subject when he could have said the same thing in less than one. It was aggravating. Terry reached for his mug and glimpsed movement at the entrance to his office. Edna leaned against the doorframe, smiling.

"You're really into that, aren't you?" she asked.

He tossed the papers on his desk. "It's that organized crime thing Lynch is working."

She glanced over her shoulder before whispering, "He's the worst. His investigations are an inch deep and a mile long."

They laughed, and she stepped a little farther into his office. "Got a minute?"

He pulled his chair closer to the desk. "Sure. Whatcha got?"

Edna took a seat. "I need your advice." She glanced at the floor for a second. "Actually, I should have asked for it earlier. I may have made a mistake."

"I don't understand, Edna."

"You know Pierce and Soliz better than most, and you have twice as much time on the job as I do. Before our meeting, I spent fifteen minutes assuring the major that the chief had made a good decision selecting those two. Higgins had his doubts. He was for recommending someone else." She wrung her hands, and a nervous frown traced across her lips. "Did I screw up not siding with him on this?"

Terry reached for the mug and took a sip. "That depends."

She grimaced. "On what?"

"On whether that girl's in real trouble, or if she's just screwing around with her parents. 'Cause I'll tell you this. If I was in a bad place and needed help sooner than later, I'd only want those two looking for me."

She grinned and nodded as she stood. "Thanks, Terry. I needed that."

He grabbed the report off the desk and lounged back in his chair, giving her a wink. "Anytime. That's what sergeants are for."

* * *

"You've got to be frigging joking," Rob yelled when he pulled up to the gate of the mayor's house. He scanned the two-story, English country–style home on the corner lot. "This isn't a house; it's a hotel. Is that real stone? It looks like real stone."

Frank stared at the house and wall surrounding it. "It's real."

"I knew he was rich, but this is ridiculous." Rob had been to rich people's homes before, but nothing like this. Way over the top for a politician. "Whatcha figure, a couple million?"

"Higher. The real estate's worth a million. This is two lots at least."

Rob rolled down the window, and a formal male voice spoke through the speaker on the pole. "Your business?"

"I double dog dare you to say 'Jehovah Witnesses,'" Frank whispered.

Rob shook his head and leaned out. "Police to see Mrs. Wallace."

The voice didn't answer, but seconds later hinges groaned and the eight-foot metal gate opened. Rob drove in as soon as he could squeeze the car through. They parked in the paved circular drive near the door. In the center was a statue fountain depicting a woman pouring water from a jug with two young children clinging to the hem of her dress. Short, well-manicured hedges and colorful flowers outlined the sculpture. Rob took in the slate roof and Boston ivy cascading down the wall as they strolled to the massive wooden door. Any minute, he expected a British butler to step out, look down his nose, and ask them both to leave.

Frank had his knuckles poised to knock when the door swung open.

A petite young woman, no more than four eleven, greeted them. "Detective Pierce?"

"That's me." Frank displayed his credentials.

Rob also flipped out his creds. "Detective Soliz."

She didn't bother shaking hands. "How do you do. I'm Dora, Mrs. Wallace's personal assistant." She said "personal assistant" like you'd say "secretary of state."

Frank smirked. "Of course you are."

A look of confusion momentarily swept across her pixie face. "Would you follow me, please?" She swung around and led them inside. "Mrs. Wallace will greet you in the visitor's room." She took a sharp left as they entered.

16

While her back was turned, Frank mouthed the words "visitor's room," raising his brow.

Dora was a cute girl, but the close-cropped dark hair with the aquiline nose wasn't a good look. Rob felt as if he were talking to a bird. Whether intentional or not, her condescending manner was irritating. She directed them to a small office with a desk and two chairs.

"I shall inform Mrs. Wallace you've arrived." She swung around and marched into the great hall, the click, click, click of high heels echoing in the distance. A vase with fresh-cut flowers in the corner gave the place a spring smell. Frank sauntered over and pulled in a long breath. He sneezed, wiped his nose, and took a seat.

Rob dropped into a chair and opened his notebook. It was his day to take notes. Frank would ask the questions. Rob scanned the area. "This is nicer than my visitor's room."

Frank gazed around and crossed his legs. "Yeah, mine too."

Pointing to the tiny painting behind the desk, Rob said, "That's a small picture for that wall."

The sounds of click, click, click drifted down the hall.

Frank leaned forward, studying the painting. "Yeah, but it's a nice one—a Matisse, I think."

Rob didn't know who Matisse was, but he guessed that the tiny painting had cost its owner a cool million.

Dora rounded the corner followed by an older, larger woman. Rob and Frank rose.

"Gentlemen, allow me to introduce Mrs. Wallace."

The lady nodded hello and sat behind the desk.

She wasn't an attractive woman. She was probably in her late fifties, early sixties—hard to tell. She'd had work done that had left her cheeks a little too tight and her lips a little too small. Her short red hair was colored and not coiffed into a very complementary style. She wore a long, quilted robe with a rose design. Rob imagined her as the First Lady and shivered.

Dora stood slightly behind and to the left of the woman, pen and notepad at the ready.

Frank spoke. "Mrs. Wallace, we wanted to ask a few questions about your daughter. It might help us find her."

Ms. Mayor relaxed into the soft leather and steepled her fingers. "Ask away."

"We understand there was some kind of disturbance that led up to her leaving?"

"Yes, we asked her to stop seeing a young man who's attending the University of Texas. We don't approve of him."

"Could he have had anything to do with her disappearance?"

Ms. Mayor gave Frank a patronizing smile. "Oh, I think not. He's not a bad sort, just not one of our people."

Rob paused in his note taking and looked up. *Not one of our people"? What the hell does that mean?*

Frank also hesitated before saying, "So Thursday was the last time you saw or spoke to her?"

"Yes, we knew better than to call. When Trina gets in one of those moods, there's no reasoning with her." Ms. Mayor dropped her hands in her lap. "We thought that by the time she turned nineteen she'd out-grow this kind of behavior, but we've been proven wrong."

Frank leaned in. "So you don't believe she's missing, just hiding?"

The woman grinned and chuckled. "I know my daughter. She's with a friend, refusing to answer the phone."

"Have you contacted her friends?" Frank asked.

"Of course, all we know. But she could be sitting right beside them and they'd lie."

"I see," Frank mumbled. He thumbed through his notebook and laid a form on the desk. "I'd like your daughter's cell phone number and provider information."

She glared at him. "Why?"

"Because if you'll sign this release"—he tapped the paper—"we'll request the cell provider to track her through her phone."

Her eyes widened. "They can do that?"

"Yes, ma'am."

"I'll be honest, I don't know for sure. AT&T, I think." Ms. Mayor looked around to Dora.

"That's correct, ma'am. I'll get them all the necessary information," Dora said, scribbling on her notepad.

Frank slid the form across the desk. "Also, we understand someone checked her place a day or two ago. Is that correct?"

"I drove there myself," Ms. Mayor said. "Looks as though she hasn't been around in several days."

"May we borrow your key to her apartment? We'd also like to take a look."

She frowned and opened her mouth to speak, but Frank cut her off. "We might find something that'll give us a clue to her whereabouts."

She exhaled. "Very well. Dora, please give them the extra key."

"And the address, also," Frank added.

Dora stopped taking notes and cut her eyes from Frank to her employer.

Ms. Mayor nodded.

"Yes, ma'am," Dora said.

She'd been writing since they'd started talking. Rob's gut tightened. *Is she recording this meeting? Did Frank know?*

"If we strike out on the phone thing, we might also request her credit card information. You know, to see if she's using it." Frank removed another form from his notebook and placed it on the desk. "If you'll sign this release, the credit card company will provide that information without a subpoena. Might give us a starting point."

Dora picked up the form and shot a look at Mrs. Wallace. She nodded again and Dora added another item to her growing list. "I'll take care of it," she said.

The regal lady stood. "Gentlemen, I must apologize, but I have a luncheon. Will there be anything else?"

Rob bounced up, and Frank rose at a snail's pace. "Just one last thing. If we find it necessary to interview the young man attending UT, we'll need his name, address, and phone number."

The queen rolled her eyes. "I'm sure I don't know anything except his name. Dora, do you have the other information?"

"Yes, ma'am." She added it to her list. "I'll get it."

Mrs. Wallace stepped from behind the desk and promenaded toward the door. "We've already contacted him. He said she left Austin at eight o'clock Sunday evening driving to Dallas. Call him if you like, but Mr. Ruiz is like the rest of Trina's friends. He lies."

Rob finally made the connection. *Ruiz—not one of our people.*

Dora pranced to the threshold. "Would you like to wait here or in your car?"

Before Rob could answer, Frank said, "We'll be in the car. Also, we could use a recent photo, if there's one available."

Dora added it to the list.

They strolled outside and the door closed. Rob looked at the mansion. "She's a cold one."

Frank kept walking. "Which one, Dora or Ms. Mayor?"

"Both."

They eased into their seats and left the doors open. Frank slid lower and propped a foot on the doorframe. "Yeah, I have to agree. That bitch is no good."

"Which one?"

"Both."

"If I ever had any ideas about voting the mayor into Congress, they're gone now," Rob muttered.

Frank leaned his head on the rest and closed his eyes. "Oh, I don't know. I'm more inclined to vote for him now that I've visited his home."

"You're kidding, right?"

He glanced at Rob. "No. Being this rich makes him less likely to take a bribe."

Dora took her time getting everything they'd requested. Frank's soft snoring, mixed with traffic sounds and water falling from the fountain, almost caused Rob to doze off. When the door opened, he punched Frank, who sprang awake.

Dora walked to the car and handed Frank an envelope. "I've completed the forms."

Frank peeked in the envelope and pulled out a key and wallet-size photo. There was a catch in his breath and he stared at the picture a little too long, his eyes wider than usual.

"Thanks," Frank finally said.

Dora didn't reply but whirled around and stalked toward the door.

Rob drove out the gate and looked in the rear mirror. "Well, now I can say I've visited an English castle."

Frank still held the photo, eyeing it as he mumbled, "You mean a Scottish castle."

"Huh?"

"Wallace is Scottish, not English. Remember William Wallace? *Braveheart*?"

"Whatever. You hungry?"

"Yeah, let's stop at Sarge's for a bite."

Rob grunted. "We can't go there. You're banished for that remark about his food."

"Sure we can. It's already been more than a week. Besides, he was only joking," Frank said.

"Joking about you being banished, or joking about kicking your ass if you set foot in there the next seven days?"

Frank lowered his head in thought. He touched the tip of each finger with the tip of his thumb, counting to himself. He looked up and grinned. "We're good. Let's go."

Sarge, whose downtown bar was a cop hangout, still held a place of respect in the department even though he'd been retired for three years. A sergeant in the Vice Unit, he'd supervised Frank for several years and had been the first one to roll up on the scene when Frank had been stabbed during the Nelson Park incident. Sarge said he'd waded through a pile of bloody bodies and found Frank collapsed by the truck with a dead whore lying in the seat. If Sarge hadn't given him immediate first aid and called an ambulance, Frank would have bled out then and there.

Frank pretty much ignored what supervisors said most of the time. He just didn't care. He wasn't rude to Terry or Edna, but he never got in a hurry to complete their commands. But when Sarge issued him an order, he promptly followed it to the letter.

On the way downtown, Frank didn't talk. Just kept gazing at the photo of the girl, studying it for a long time. The look on his face seemed strange—not a Frank look at all. Instead of dropping it back in the envelope, he slipped it into his pocket.

4

Katrina awoke in a haze. She shifted her head from side to side and focused, realizing they'd removed her bindings and blindfold. Objects spun and blurred but began to take shape. She couldn't sit up, and the room whirled a couple of times as she collapsed on the pillow. *Where am I?*

The last thing she recalled—the truck ride. They'd stopped and the tailgate had opened. With her eyes covered, she hadn't seen a thing, but it was still dark. The sounds of crickets and frogs sounded in the distance. The air smelled good, like those air fresheners you hang from a rearview mirror. Muffled voices whispered around her as the men dragged her out and leaned her against the tailgate. Strong hands held her as a sharp sting punched her hip. More muffled voices, and they half led, half carried her to a place with soft music playing.

She didn't recall the song, but it relaxed her. Her legs weakened as she shuffled into a warmer area. Doors opened and closed, and the warmth flowed through her like a wonderful sauna. Her head felt heavy, lolling from side to side with each step. The sound of one last door opening, and the floor dropped out from under her. No—going down stairs. Her legs weren't working at all now. Her toes dragged across each step as she tried to regain her footing. She was so tired. More muffled voices as they laid her on a soft object. And that was where the memory ended.

She focused again and rolled to her right side. *She'd had a dream*—a weird one. In the dream, women undressed her, and a warm soapy thing lightly brushed over her whole body. It felt good. She'd stared at the overhead light fixture while they bathed her. The bare bulb, twisted into the ceiling, kept her full attention. The women sang softly, some religious song she couldn't remember. They dried her and pulled a nightshirt over her head, all the time speaking in lyrical voices about how she would be okay. They lifted her and fitted something over her hips and between her legs, then smoothed the long gown past her knees.

One of them sat behind her, propping her up, as the other spoon-fed her a thick soup. She ate, but just wanted to go to sleep. Someone wiped her mouth and chin with a wet washcloth, and a cup touched her lips. She drank several swallows of cold water.

One of the women said, "That's good, missy. Y'all should get some rest now."

They gently laid her on the bed, and footsteps echoed up the stairs. The bare bulb flicked off, but a small table lamp still burned in the corner.

Katrina had never had such a strange dream. She pushed to a seated position, dangling her legs off the bed. Steadying herself with both hands until the spinning stopped, she drew in a long breath. Something pinched her crotch. She slipped her hand under the white cotton gown to readjust her underwear. It was gone. Instead she wore a diaper.

*   *   *

Sarge's bar was long and narrow and a little too close to the Greyhound bus terminal, which meant that parking was always a bitch. It wasn't a fancy place, but most cops didn't want fancy anyhow. Who you were drinking with was more important than where you were.

By the time Sergeant Jimmy Bielstein had retired after forty-one years on the force, he had been a sergeant for thirty-five years in six different divisions. Half the department, from patrol officers all the way to the chief, had served under his tutelage. He had wanted to open a bar after retirement and envisioned a Cheers-like place with plenty of room in a nice downtown location. That's not what he got, but he still made lemonade out of lemons.

24

By the time he'd worked on it almost a year, it had sucked up half his retirement. In the end, though, he'd succeeded in creating a police haven—a bar where law enforcement and others in the criminal justice community could relax in a friendly, nonthreatening environment. Cops from dozens of agencies, as well as jailers and court bailiffs, frequented the place because it was close to work. Defense attorneys could be found begging prosecutors for plea deals over a beer most days. It was a good location to grab lunch or a drink on the way home. It had a stellar reputation and—except for that one ugly episode with Billy Ray Moore a couple of months after opening—few problems with customers.

Billy Ray was from Etowah, Oklahoma. He'd decided that the state had gotten too hot for him—a couple of outstanding warrants for hijacking liquor stores and a third for aggravated assault, just because he'd pistol-whipped a woman who was taking too long emptying the register.

Billy Ray needed a vacation, so it made sense to head for the beach. Every cop in Oklahoma knew his car, so he kept it hidden in his little brother's garage. He gathered his loot, bought a bus ticket to Corpus Christi, and set out for a week of sun and surf. No one would look for him in a Greyhound speeding south. He congratulated himself on a well-thought-out plan. And it was well thought out, until he reached Dallas. The bus came limping in on a half-flat tire, and the passengers were informed it would take an hour to change.

Billy Ray, always an entrepreneur, must have seen this as a godsend. He had just enough time to knock over a place, flee to the terminal, and get lost in the dozens of passengers waiting for their bus. The perfect getaway, courtesy of Greyhound.

Not knowing Dallas, he strolled in increasingly larger circles for several minutes until he happened upon Sarge's. It looked perfect—a quiet place, with well-dressed customers and a cash register near the door. He lit a cigarette and sauntered inside. Sarge rushed over to help him.

With the cigarette dangling from his lips, Billy Ray grinned. "Need a pack of smokes. What brands you got?"

"Sorry, but we don't sell cigarettes," Sarge said.

"Then I'll just take what's in the register," Billy Ray whispered, brandishing a pistol.

Several patrons watched the holdup in progress. As their conversations died away, the rest of the customers stopped talking and gawked. Billy Ray didn't help matters when he swung the weapon away from Sarge and pointed it at the assembled group. In his defense, no one was in uniform—just a bunch of off-duty cops and plainclothes detectives grabbing lunch.

He waved the gun and said, "You sons of bitches just keep your seats and no one gets—"

And those were his last words. Sarge had opened the register with one hand; his other gripped the short, double-barreled shotgun he kept under the counter, loaded with double-ought buck. He pulled both triggers. The blast tore through the quarter-inch veneer counter paneling and blew Billy Ray against the opposite wall. But that only started the excitement. Likely already dead, Billy Ray leaned against the wall for a few seconds, loosely holding the revolver.

The patrons later used this as justification for what happened next. Seven customers stood and fired. Forty-two shots rang out in seconds. Those present described it as sounding like a prolonged firing squad. Billy Ray got hit another thirty-six times as he slid down the wall, leaving a bloody trail in his wake.

"An amazing demonstration of marksmanship," one officer later stated. No exaggeration there. That many shots fired, with that many hits, under stress, in a small area—remarkable. Perhaps having a drink under the belt settled their nerves, improving their accuracy.

Forensics later determined a big sheriff's deputy scored the best. All five rounds from the .44 bulldog hit her target. Not an easy task, because the damn thing kicked like a horse. Sarge noted that after shooting, the deputy ejected the spent casings, reloaded, and holstered her weapon. She reclaimed her seat and then waited for the patrol units to arrive as she calmly finished her beer.

No one at the scene could hear very well for the next week, but all recovered and none held it against Sarge. Officers from four different police agencies were involved, so the subsequent investigation was a mess. Sarge had to shut down for three days because of the investigation and to make repairs.

Meanwhile, newspapers in New England had a field day with the story, which confirmed their collective opinion of Texas. With everyone exonerated, the Dallas police chief made a heartfelt plea to Sarge.

"Please, do something to avoid this in the future."

Sarge agreed, and a week later posted a simple sign on his new glass door: "Police Welcome." Not exactly what the chief had in mind, but what could he say? Sarge had broken him in as a rookie twenty-eight years earlier.

All of this did have one positive effect. Ne'er-do-wells went blocks out of their way to avoid the bar where the crazy, gun-happy cops drank.

When Rob and Frank walked through the door, the familiar bar scent welcomed them. Mostly the place smelled like beer. Rob sucked in a lungful and headed toward the twenty-five-foot bar that dominated the space. A well-stocked, mirrored wall displayed the liquor bottles behind the bartender and provided the joint with the illusion of width it only dreamed of. There was plenty of standing room behind the stools, but only enough space for a half dozen small booths in the back on the way to the restrooms and a tiny storage area.

Sarge, standing behind the bar, looked right at Frank and without a word spun around and examined a wall calendar. Rob had figured as much. Sarge wanted to make sure Frank's suspension had expired. Old ways die hard.

Sarge turned with a grin. "What'll it be, boys?"

"Two cherry Cokes. Two sandwiches," Rob replied. He wished he were ordering a beer, and Frank probably wanted his usual red wine, but Sarge had his rules.

The worst kept secret in law enforcement circles was, if you worked plainclothes and strolled into Sarge's on duty and asked for a cherry Coke, you'd get bourbon and Coke. Request a vanilla Coke, you'd get vodka instead. If you were on duty, Sarge cut you off after only one. The officers understood the rules, and they didn't want to face being suspended by Sarge. He had a philosophical explanation for serving alcohol to on-duty officers: "If a man can't have one drink with lunch, what's this world coming to?"

Rob and Frank grabbed a couple of stools at the bar while Sarge poured their drinks. Sarge didn't speak to Frank, and Frank didn't speak to him. Rob eyed both of them with a grin, curious to see how Frank would handle his awkward return.

Sarge slid the two glasses across the bar and Rob sipped his.

"Perfect, thanks."

Frank sipped his drink, and Rob waited for either him or Sarge to acknowledge the other. More customers drifted in, and Sarge kept busy making sandwiches and refilling glasses. Just when the tension reached a peak, Frank made his move.

"Hey, Sarge. How can you tell when a family of pink flamingos has moved in next door?"

Sarge threw the bar towel over his shoulder and leaned both hands on the bar, staring at Frank. "I don't know. How?"

Frank smirked. "They put little statuettes of Mexicans in their front yard."

Sarge broke into uncontrolled laughter. He was a big German, and his bush of gray-speckled blond surfer-style hair shook as he hooted. He didn't laugh like most people. It was more of a long, loud wheeze, like maybe a heart attack coming on. He slapped the bar and his blue eyes sparkled.

"By God, Frank, that's funny." He kept wheezing while pouring more drinks.

With exaggerated slowness, Rob glared at Frank. "That's the most racist, ethnically insensitive, and politically incorrect thing that's ever come out of your mouth."

Frank shrugged. "Sorry, I forgot how sensitive you Mexicans are."

Sarge wheezed louder from the other end of the bar.

Rob looked straight ahead. "Cracker asshole," he mumbled.

More loud wheezing from Sarge.

The quickest way back into Sarge's favor: telling him a politically incorrect joke. He loved them, especially if someone within earshot would be offended. Rob had figured out this ploy years earlier and played along with Frank. Actually, Frank was the least prejudiced officer he knew. A person had to care to be prejudiced. Frank just didn't care.

Sarge finished their sandwiches and pushed them across the bar. He'd been around long enough to know he'd never get any on-duty cops in the place if he couldn't offer them some cover. Since he kept a sliced honey-baked ham behind the counter, it could never be said his place was *just* a bar. An officer could drop in anytime for a ham sandwich and *special* Coke.

Rob crossed himself before starting, and he and Frank ate in silence as more customers drifted in. Rob finished first—he always did—and Frank spent another ten minutes nibbling. Finally, Frank wiped his mouth and sighed.

"Hey, Sarge?"

Sarge broke off his conversation with another customer and sauntered over. "Yeah?"

Frank leaned closer to Sarge and spoke in low tones. "You know you have the makings of the perfect ham and cheese here."

Rob lowered his head and, under his breath, whispered, "Shut up, Frank."

"You have great ham, good Swiss, a sweet slice of tomato, and crisp lettuce."

Rob moved closer and, as if wiping his mouth, whispered again. "Shut up, Frank!"

"But the mayo and yellow mustard do nothing but confuse the taste buds."

Rob gave up and looked down, brushing his trousers clear of crumbs, trying to ignore Sarge's growing anger. *This will not end well.*

Frank moved his hands around his plate to demonstrate. "Now, on the other hand, if you substituted the mayo and yellow mustard for

Dijon mustard, you'd enhance the flavor of the cheese and contrast the sweetness of the ham and tomato."

Sarge gawked at him and his jaw dropped. "Is that a complaint?"

Frank seemed to wake up to the thin ice. "No." He shifted on his stool. "Just a suggestion."

Sarge's face reddened. "Mr. Know-It-All, huh?" He turned to the customer sitting beside Frank, then back to Frank. "So, did the CIA teach you that?" He looked at the customer again. "You know that's where he learned to cook, don't ya? From the CIA."

The customer glared at Frank and leaned in the other direction, as if maybe Frank had a communicable disease.

Frank must have felt the need to explain. He whispered, "It's the Culinary Institute of America—CIA."

The customer went back to his lunch and ignored them both.

"I only make one kind of sandwich. You don't like it, pack a lunch!" Sarge said as he stormed to the far end of the bar.

"Well played," Rob mocked.

A flash in the mirror drew Rob's attention. Big Mike was entering the bar—a giant detective who worked auto theft. He swaggered past Rob and Frank and headed for the john. A couple of minutes later, he ambled out in their direction. As Frank downed his last swallow of Coke, Mike bumped his arm in passing. The glass emptied in Frank's lap.

Mike paused and laughed. "Oh, I apologize. Didn't see you there."

Frank dabbed the stain with his napkin and didn't answer. Mike laughed again and strolled to a stool at the other end.

Rob said, "That son of a bitch did that on purpose."

Frank didn't look up but continued cleaning his pants. "Let it go."

The bad blood between Frank and Big Mike had started years earlier when they'd worked Missing Persons. After months of trying to find a missing five-year-old boy, Mike had finally given up, written "Closed—Unsolved" on the case paperwork, and moved on. Looked like a child custody thing gone bad. After reviewing the reports, the sergeant had assigned the two-month-old case to Frank, the new guy on the squad. Rumor had it he was sharp.

On the third day, after an all-night, one-man surveillance, Frank had strolled in with the father in handcuffs and the boy in tow. Mike had never forgiven him the humiliation.

Rob eyed Big Mike. Being a couple of inches taller than Frank wasn't the only problem. He also outweighed him by sixty pounds. He was dumb as a post, but that didn't matter if he got his hands on you.

"You should slap that bastard silly," Rob murmured.

"Just let it go." Frank stood and threw a twenty on the bar. "Lunch is on me."

As they ambled past, Mike's weasel eyes watched them from the bar mirror. Rob made a point of flipping him off while Frank held the door.

Rob paused outside and pulled out a Copenhagen tin and thumped the lid twice. The sound of a mower around the corner and the smell of fresh-cut grass mixed with the scent of snuff as he stuffed a pinch of it in his lower lip. "So, ready to go to the girl's apartment?"

Frank brushed his pants. "Yeah, but I need to change first. My new place isn't far from here." He headed for the car.

Rob dusted the loose Copenhagen off his fingers. "I haven't seen your new place. Like it?"

"Lots more room. Yeah, it's nice."

Rob spat on the ground and wiped his lips.

Frank took a step back from the spatter. "That's the nastiest stuff in the world. Can't believe you're still hooked."

Rob hit the key fob, and the car unlocked. "I'm not hooked. I've quit dozens of times. So where's your new place?"

"Off McKinney. I'll direct you."

"McKinney, huh? Sounds expensive."

Frank didn't answer except to give him the address. When they pulled up, Frank pointed to the guest parking area and Rob wheeled into a space. Strolling to the front door, Rob craned his neck to eye the top of the twenty-story building. The doorman, dressed in a suit and name tag, stepped outside and held the door for them.

"Good afternoon, Mr. Pierce."

Frank nodded. "Good afternoon, Ralph."

They strolled through the plush wood-paneled lobby past another similarly dressed man seated behind the reception desk. He nodded. "Mr. Pierce." At that moment, Rob wouldn't have been surprised if the man had whipped out a silver tray with a pyramid of warm finger towels. *Never figured Frank could afford a place this nice.*

"Hello, Jerry," Frank said.

They rode the elevator to the top floor and hung a right down the lushly carpeted passageway. Frank unlocked the door and stepped in.

Rob froze as he entered, staring at the wall of windows overlooking downtown. "Holy shit."

Frank unbuckled his belt and wandered down a dark hall. "Like it?"

Rob eased in and closed the door. "I'll say."

"I won't be a minute. Make yourself at home."

Rob ambled to the ten-by-thirty-foot glass wall and took in the sights. It was a perfect location for a loft. To his left stood a bookcase. Painted white, like the rest of the room, it was head high and ran the length of the wall, all the way to the corridor. He strolled past rows of books, his fingers brushing titles. Nothing was organized, except maybe in Frank's mind. There were hundreds of books, on every topic: *A History of the English-Speaking Peoples*, *A Random Walk Down Wall Street*, *World Religions: An Introduction*. There were books on literature, art, music appreciation, cooking, and science. His fingers paused over a spine and he pulled the book from the shelf. *Basic Quantum Mechanics*?

He put the book back and entered the kitchen—and what a kitchen. Frank's stint as a professional chef had definitely influenced his choice in appliances. A Vulcan stainless steel six-burner gas range nestled between two dark-brown granite counter tops. A matching double-door refrigerator stood beside a similar freezer. The kitchen was painted in an earth-tone brown faux finish. An enormous cutting-block island was the centerpiece.

The kitchen, bookcase, and windows wrapped around a giant living area containing only a green fabric sofa and end table situated to take in either the panoramic view or the fifty-two-inch wall-mounted TV.

A single book lay on the arm of the sofa—*The Complete Works of Sir Arthur Conan Doyle*.

Frank marched back in, slipping on his jacket. "Okay, let's get going." He'd changed into an identical pair of Dockers.

Rob put his Styrofoam spit cup on the counter. "I just have one question." He spread his arms out to the sides, palms down, as if he was steadying himself.

"Don't drop that nasty thing in this house." Frank pointed to the spit cup.

Rob ignored him. "Just one question."

Frank kept walking. "What?"

Rob screamed, "Are you on the frigging take, or what?" He motioned in all directions.

Frank shook his head and grinned. "No, I'm still playing straight."

"I can't afford all this, and we make the exact same salary."

Frank opened the door. "Come on. I'll tell you on the way."

5

As they pulled out on McKinney and headed for the girl's apartment, Frank called a lady friend and confirmed their dinner date that night. He hung up and got comfortable in his usual slouch in the passenger seat. No one spoke for ten minutes.

Soon they were cruising through a trendy area of Dallas near Southern Methodist University. Several old apartment complexes had discovered gold in renovating and re-leasing at twice the price to students. A big racket, but since most of SMU's students attended school on their parents' dime, who was harmed? As Rob drove by yet another perfectly manicured lawn, the question about Frank's new digs finally popped out of his mouth.

"So, are you going to tell me, or what?"

Frank exhaled. "On my fortieth birthday, my trust money was finally released."

"Trust? You had a trust?"

"Yeah, my grandparents set it up when I was a kid."

"So, were they loaded?"

"Nope, just owned a big ranch in central Florida—lot of it swamp land."

"Sold it, huh?"

"Yeah, to an amusement park."

"Wait a minute. Are you saying Disney World is your grandparents' old ranch?" Rob wheeled into the apartment parking lot.

Frank laughed as he grabbed the door handle. "Disney World?

Don't be ridiculous . . . it was Universal Studios that bought their place." He slid from the seat.

"No shit?"

They climbed the stairs. Frank pulled out the paper Dora had given them with the apartment number scrawled across it. He nodded to the left and Rob followed him.

Rob eyed his partner, wondering if he really knew him at all. "How many books do you have? Hundreds?"

"A little over two thousand. I keep the overflow in my home office."

"You read them all?"

Frank kept walking but shook his head. "Not a one—just have them to impress guests."

"Smartass cracker. I never knew you read so much."

"I read a lot." Frank knocked on apartment 203. "Hope she answers. It'll be our shortest case in history." He knocked again, but no one came to the door. Shaking the key from the envelope, he slipped it into the lock and twisted the doorknob. No chain caught the door, and he swung it wide open.

"Police officers. We're coming in."

They strolled inside and looked around the dark apartment. Frank flicked on a wall switch.

"Not bad for a college kid. Pretty good housekeeper," Rob mumbled.

Frank scratched the front of his neck and surveyed the room. "I'll take the bedroom and bath, and you do the living room and kitchen." Without another word, he marched toward the bedroom. Rob realized Frank sensed something—he had this thing. Whenever they strolled into a crime scene and Frank scratched his neck, something bothered him on a subconscious level. Of course, Frank had so many peculiarities, it might be nothing more than an itch.

* * *

The bedroom door stood open, a sheer bra draped over the doorknob. On the way past, Frank rubbed a cup with thumb and index finger. An old, disturbing thought tickled his spine. He flipped the strap over: 36C. The living room looked nice, but the bedroom needed work. Clothes, college books, and curlers lay more or less where they had been dropped days ago. He went through all the drawers, stuck his head in the closet, and searched under the bed.

He glanced at a calendar on the nightstand. The disturbing tickle again raced up his back. Frank strolled back down the hall and flipped on the bathroom light. He searched the cabinets. A light whiff of floral perfume still lingered in the air. The prickle kept bugging him.

A minute later Rob stuck his head around the corner. "Anything?"

"Nope. You?"

"The most exciting thing I found was this dime bag of grass." Rob dangled the plastic Ziploc.

Frank opened it and sniffed. "Not bad." He emptied it in the commode and flushed, tossing the empty bag in the trash. "Ready to go?"

Rob shrugged and sauntered toward the door. Frank followed but hesitated at the threshold. That's when it hit him. He went back to the girl's nightstand and picked up the calendar a second time. She had lunches, professor conferences, and dates for tests penciled in. She'd already missed several appointments.

Frank marched back into the bath and stared at the counter.

Rob stuck his head in. "What's wrong?"

Frank pointed at the items that lined the counter. "Look."

Rob tilted his head to one side and pursed his lips. "What?"

"The makeup." Frank met eyes with Rob. "Everything's still here."

Rob didn't answer.

Frank waved his hand across the counter. "Face wash, lipstick, lotions . . ."

Rob shrugged. "Probably has an extra set of everything."

"Yeah, probably," Frank whispered. "But if she planned to be gone for longer than a weekend . . ." It still didn't feel right.

Frank slipped past Rob and went back to the bedroom. It was a little messy, but she was organized—disciplined. Perhaps she acted immature around Mom and Dad, but she had her act together. This girl hadn't planned on not returning. She'd scheduled things she'd already missed. Only taken the bare necessities for a weekend stay.

Something unplanned happened.

"What?" Rob asked.

Frank meandered back into the living area. "Everybody has it all wrong," he whispered. He stared at Rob. "She's not hiding. Someone took her."

Rob eyed him. "You serious? How do you know that?"

Frank let out a breath. "I just know." The evidence all around him was giving him a completely different picture of the "flaky teenage girl" he'd heard about in Edna's office. But even if he hadn't had that, his gut would have told him. He operated on gut and instinct more than most cops. When he got to a certain point in an investigation, he *just knew* if there was any meat on it. Sometimes it took days to determine, sometimes only hours. Rob trusted him enough to seldom quiz for reasons.

By the time Rob parked in the employee garage, it was pushing five. Frank opened the passenger door, his mind still on his abduction theory, and grabbed a manila folder he'd tossed on the floorboard. "I have to fax this stuff to the credit card folks and AT&T. Why don't you split? I'll report in to Edna and Terry."

Rob shook his head. "No way. You're the one with the date. I'll do it."

"You go look after Carmen. My date isn't until eight o'clock. I'm fixing her dinner at my place."

Rob winked. "See ya tomorrow."

Frank had real trepidation about sharing his suspicions with Terry. It wasn't as if Terry would make fun of him. That wasn't his style. But Frank had no hard evidence to support his theory except makeup and a few missed appointments. Terry was a no-nonsense guy who worked with facts, not feelings.

When Frank strolled into CIU, it was practically deserted. He scouted the place and found Terry and Edna talking in her office. Ignoring them, he stopped at the fax and scribbled out a cover sheet to AT&T Security, requesting them to locate the girl's phone. They would track its proximity to the nearest cell tower and give a good location.

He pressed the send button and filled out the second cover sheet to MasterCard Security.

"Any luck?" Terry asked from behind.

Frank dropped the page into the fax machine and hit send. "Nope. We interviewed Ms. Mayor and gave the girl's place the once-over. Nothing."

Terry nodded. "I'll tell Edna."

Frank wandered back to his desk and ran a criminal history check on the boyfriend, Ruiz. The guy came back clean—not even a parking ticket. Frank called Ruiz's cell number and got his voice mail. After leaving a message to return his call, Frank meandered around the office several minutes thinking about how to explain his suspicions. He finally stuck his head into Terry's office.

Terry was back at his desk. "Was there something else?"

Frank glanced over his shoulder before strolling in. "I don't think the girl's hiding."

Terry's expression darkened and he slowly stood. "What did you find? You said there was nothing there."

"Gut feeling."

Terry's brow relaxed. "I see. What do you think? Was she taken from the apartment?"

"No, nothing like that. No sign of it, anyway. I don't believe she made it home."

Terry strolled to Frank's side and spoke in a low voice. "Have you discussed this with anyone?"

"Just Rob."

"Okay, we'll keep it between us boys until we have concrete evidence."

Frank nodded and turned to leave.

"Hey," Terry called.

Frank glanced over his shoulder.

Terry stood with his hands together, rubbing the knuckles, a sign he was worried.

"I hope you're wrong."

6

They were in her room again—the ones calling themselves Sister Ruth and Sister Judy. Katrina sat at the small table spooning down bland wheat cereal flavored with honey and fresh strawberries. Yesterday, when she'd asked them if they were nuns, Sister Ruth had laughed.

"No, my dear," she'd corrected. "We're sisters in Christ."

That confused Katrina more. The two women refused to answer her basic questions about where she was, who they were, and who'd brought her there. They smiled and assured her she'd understand in time and not to worry.

That worried Katrina. If these two knew what had happened and condoned it, they weren't her friends. The problem was they were so sweet. Sister Ruth, the tall one, had long straight brown hair that hung to the middle of her back. It was tough to guess her age, but since she wore no makeup, the small wrinkles around her eyes and the corners of her mouth had no place to hide. Perhaps late thirties, early forties.

Sister Judy looked about five years younger. Her long hair, always in a tight bun, was black. No one made a fashion statement in that kind of high-necked cotton dress, and neither wore a bra. Both women had deep Southern accents, Tennessee or maybe Alabama. They hummed or sang songs under their breath while they worked. Katrina recognized one song from her grandmother's funeral the year before—"Amazing Grace."

Katrina ate slowly, examining her room as the women hummed and tidied. If this wasn't a basement, it was certainly doing an excellent impression of one. The concrete-walled, windowless room was painted battleship gray, and the bare bulb hung from a wooden ceiling. A large gas water heater, the size of a VW bug, sat in one corner. A small space heater hummed from the other, keeping the humidity and temperature perfect.

The place had a familiar odor. She couldn't place it at first, but as her mind cleared from the drugs, she knew she'd smelled it before. After her grandmother's death, she'd helped her mother clear out some things from Granny's house. They'd opened a timeworn trunk that hadn't seen the light of day for fifty years. That was the smell of the basement—old.

Footsteps and muffled voices drifted through the ceiling and she looked up, her spoon frozen halfway to her mouth. She'd seen no men since she'd arrived, but they were always close, coming in and out of the room above her, mixing their voices sometimes with the laughter of children or the crying of babies.

Sisters Ruth and Judy cleaned, added fresh towels, and changed the sheets. The sink, toilet, and shower had the bare essentials. Ivory bath soap, some cheap, off-brand shampoo, toothpaste, and a toothbrush.

Katrina put the spoon down and spoke for the first time that day. "Could you please leave me a razor?"

Sister Ruth smiled. "Ladies don't use razors here."

"What do you shave with?"

"We don't shave."

Katrina gawked at their legs, but the ankle-length dresses hid everything but their shoes.

They finished, and Sister Judy laid a white cotton dress, panties, and fresh nightgown on the edge of the bed.

"Here you go. We have some lovely new clothes for you."

Her calm demeanor relaxed Katrina. "Thank you."

Sister Ruth finished making the bed. She spread the multicolored quilt across the top, and as she straightened it, a quick movement of her hand caught Katrina's attention. The woman had pushed something under the quilt and then smoothed it back into place.

"Could I have a book?" Katrina asked.

Sister Judy grinned. "Why child, you already have the best book you'll ever read right here." She held up the Bible from the nightstand.

The ladies gathered the dirty clothes, sheets, and cleaning supplies and marched up the basement stairs. They locked the door and Katrina was alone again. She could only assume she'd been kidnapped by a bunch of religious zealots and taken to a health spa in California run by Daughters of the Confederacy. *It really isn't funny, Katrina. Just bizarre.* Since her earliest memories, Katrina had always been taught to think of herself as special, a step above everybody else. A live-in nanny, the best private schools, the most expensive clothes. Nothing was too good for Daddy's little girl. With the bat of an eyelid or one dimpled smile, she could get anything she wanted from the old man. And now she would trade all she had, or ever hoped to have, to be anywhere but here.

She finished her cereal and had an itch on her chin. There was a bump. Oh, no, not another zit. She strolled to the mirror. No zit; probably just a mosquito bite. Wiping her fingers across her face, she found no trace of makeup. They must have scrubbed it off the first night, although she had no idea how long ago that was. She remained disoriented about time and place. It was either Tuesday or Wednesday. She didn't know how long she'd been in her drug-induced la-la land. She figured time of day by food served, and she'd just finished breakfast number three.

The food wasn't bad: fruit and cereal for breakfast, fresh salad and a bowl of mixed nuts for lunch, and either baked chicken or fish for dinner. The best thing was the homemade bread. The aroma of it baking every morning when they opened the door to bring down her breakfast made her mouth water. They served it only with the dinner. She ate it first. When Katrina requested coffee, Sister Judy explained that they didn't drink it but could get her a cup of herbal tea if she liked. She passed.

She unfurled the dress they'd left her. It ended at her feet, just like Sister Judy's and Sister Ruth's. No bra hid in the pile of clothes. *Strange kidnappers.* Her dad had money—he'd pay, no problem. They treated her well, *almost too well*, as if she was special somehow. No one had threatened her or tried to do her harm since that first night.

I'll be okay. Just be patient and it'll be over soon enough.

Sister Ruth's sudden activity around the foot of the bed crept into Katrina's thoughts. Was she pushing something under the covers?

Katrina knelt at the corner and tugged up the quilt. Her heart skipped. She dashed to the other side and found the same thing. Fixing her gaze on the metal headboard, she slowly approached. Lowering her hand to the side, she reached under the soft, down mattress and pulled out another. She exhaled a quick breath and felt light-headed. Staggering to the wall, she slumped to the floor, hugging herself. Tears flooded her eyes.

Firmly affixed to each corner of her bed was a thick, leather loop. Dark stains streaked the leather—blood.

7

Wednesday morning, Frank got in early and found the return fax from AT&T Security waiting in the machine. "Unable to locate through electronic serial number. No GPS response to signal." The electronic serial number (ESN) should have located the phone if it was on and within AT&T's service area. It remained doubtful that her cell was still operational, especially since there was no GPS signal. Phone destroyed, dropped in water, buried, battery removed. The possibilities were endless.

Frank wandered to his desk, studying the fax. He caught up on some administrative paperwork and Rob marched in. He slipped out of his jacket and fell into his chair.

After turning on his computer, Rob asked, "How did the date go last night?"

Rob always asked about Frank's dates. In the three years they'd worked together, Rob had seen him with only one woman. About two years before, Carmen had insisted Frank come to dinner and bring a friend if he liked. He'd brought Taylor. The second they entered the front door of Rob's house, Frank realized he'd screwed up. All smiles froze in place as Rob's family shook Taylor's hand. The fact that she was only slightly older than Rob's teenage daughter was just one of the issues. Taylor's looks could stop a bull in midcharge. She'd been first runner-up in the Miss Texas pageant the year before and had shoulder-length blonde hair, vivacious green eyes, and pearly white teeth. The little black dress

43

revealed more than it covered, and although Frank appreciated the dramatic cleavage, he wasn't sure Rob's family did. Since that night, Frank hadn't been invited back, and Rob hadn't seen him with another girl.

"We had a good time," Frank said. "I prepared my signature charred lobster and pasta with a fresh spinach salad and crème brûlée."

"Sounds delicious. Did she stay the night?"

"Yeah, left this morning."

Rob grunted as a smile crept across his lips. They worked on their paperwork, and the morning dragged on until someone called across the room.

"Hey, Frank. You got a fax in the machine."

He sprang up and grabbed the papers, scanning the report from MasterCard Security. He added it to the previous report and knocked on Edna's door. She and Terry were in conference. They looked at him, and he held up the papers.

"Can't locate the cell, and no credit card activity reported since last Sunday evening in Austin."

They frowned in unison. "Thanks, Frank," she said.

Frank ambled back to his desk and Rob did a long stretch. "I'm hungry. Want to grab a bite?"

"Sure, what do you feel like?"

"BBQ, baby. BBQ."

Frank didn't have to ask where. If Rob wanted barbecue, there wasn't a choice.

They hiked out the front doors of the headquarters building into brilliant sunshine and hooked a left on the sidewalk that ran down Lamar. The smoke smell led them straight to Off the Bone Barbeque, Rob's favorite. The short walk, in fresh air, revived Frank's mind. He checked off everything they'd done and what else needed to be done. The girl and her car had just disappeared. Without something else to go on, they could do little but wait. He drew her photo from his pocket and stared at it as they walked. That old, almost forgotten feeling stirred him again.

After a pulled-pork sandwich and iced tea, Frank and Rob strolled back down the sidewalk to headquarters.

"So, where do we go from here? Looks like a dead-end case," Rob said.

Frank readjusted his sunglasses. "I don't know. We've covered all the bases."

"When you worked Missing Persons, wasn't there a certain number of hours you guys aimed for?" Rob asked.

Frank shoved both hands in his pockets and slowed his pace. "If we were notified immediately, like if someone witnessed a kid being snatched, we'd hit the bricks hard with all hands for six hours. Interview everybody, run out every lead, and check every possible location." Frank sighed. "After six hours, in most cases, we only recovered a body—not a person."

"So, this thing looks pretty crappy if she's not hiding out, huh?"

Frank raked his hand through his hair, and they exchanged glances. "She's been gone over sixty hours at this point. Yeah, I'd say if she was taken, with no ransom demands, she may be beyond help."

When they meandered into the squad area, most of the cubicles had emptied, their officers out to lunch. Edna remained in her office with the phone to her ear. She stood and leaned forward, one hand braced on the corner of her desk, eyes narrow and mouth agape.

When she noticed them, she said, "They just walked in. I'll call you back." She slammed the phone down and rushed out to meet them. "We've got her car and the guy driving it."

"What?" Rob exchanged a surprised look with his partner.

"Was she in the car?" Frank asked. But part of him already knew the answer before Edna spoke. Of course it wouldn't be that easy.

"No, but we have him." Edna's cheeks had reddened the way they always did when she got excited. She blew out a quick breath. "They just brought him up to the Auto Theft Unit. Get your butts down the hall, quick."

"How are the guys down there going to react when we barge in and demand to interrogate their prisoner?" Frank asked.

She stepped back and nodded. "Good point. I'll call Sergeant Holtz and grease the skids." She motioned toward the door. "Hurry. The mayor's on his way to the chief's office."

Frank grabbed his notebook and dropped his weapon in his desk drawer, telling himself not to get too excited now that they finally had a lead. *Sixty hours, Frank.* The chances weren't good that this evidence would lead them to anything other than a body.

"Guys," Edna yelled from her office. She was back on the phone, apparently on hold. She covered the speaker with her hand as they entered. Her brow furrowed. "We need this guy to give it up ASAP. Do I need to say more?"

Rob and Frank eyed each other and then Edna. "No, ma'am," Rob said.

On their way out, Frank leaned over the top of a cubicle and plucked an unsharpened pencil from the cup on the desk.

Rob asked, "You think you'll need that?"

Frank dropped it in his jacket. "Let's hope not."

Walking down the fourth-floor hall toward Auto Theft, Rob said, "So much for Ms. Mayor's theory that the girl's just hiding."

Frank didn't answer. His mind checked off what to look for in the interview: body language, voice inflection, eye contact, and a half dozen other traits. When they marched into the Auto Theft Unit, Big Mike's booming voice greeted them from across a sea of desks.

Mike and his sergeant were arguing, as usual.

"You've got to be shitting me," Mike yelled at Sergeant Holtz.

Mike towered over his slim sergeant, but Holtz held his ground. "Take it up with the lieutenant if you want, but you'll lose."

"I'll be damned if I'll let a couple of pencil-neck geeks from CIU conduct my interview. This is my case." Mike threw a notepad on the floor and glared at the sergeant.

"We're not pencil-neck geeks, you asshole," Rob said, strolling beside Sergeant Holtz.

Big Mike swung around to Rob and Frank. "These two? You can't be serious."

Holtz stepped forward, craning his neck to look up at the big detective. "Back off, or call it a day. Your choice."

Mike shifted his gaze from his sergeant to Frank and Rob. "Fine." Big Mike picked up the pad off the floor. "Let the pretty boys have a crack at him." He spun around and strutted off. "He's all yours."

"Did you Mirandize him?" Rob asked.

Mike swung around, his face a scarlet mask. "Of course. I'm not an idiot."

"Too bad. Missing a good chance," Frank muttered.

Sergeant Holtz scrutinized them, resting his hands on his hips. "I don't know what this is about, except this guy supposedly stole the mayor's car. Care to fill me in on why CIU is handling the interview and not us?" His eyes shifted from Rob to Frank.

The squad area was larger than CIU's, and several detectives stood watching the show. Frank wondered how many of them were already taking bets on the outcome. He scanned the group watching them and leaned closer to Holtz.

"Sarge, we were just instructed to talk to him by our lieutenant. Any additional information should probably come from her," he whispered.

Holtz's lips thinned. "Okay, here's his rap sheet." He handed Rob a handful of papers. "Mostly small stuff: several shopliftings, trespass, burglary of motor vehicle." Holtz shrugged, "Never served any serious time. The guy's a thief."

"How did the arrest go down?" Rob asked.

"Uniforms spotted him make a turn without giving a signal."

Rob grinned. "Slow day, huh?"

"Hey, you see a young guy in a high-crime area driving an Audi worth over fifty grand, you take what you can get," Holtz said.

"So, what happened?"

"They popped the lights, and he ran like a scalded dog. Didn't get far before he wrecked out. Really screwed up the ride."

"Any crimes against persons?" Frank asked.

Holtz narrowed his gaze. "No, why do you ask?"

Rob interrupted. "Any gang affiliation?"

Holtz maintained the suspicious glare. "Not that we know of."

Rob finished thumbing through the papers. "We won't be long—just a question or two." He handed the rap sheet back to the sergeant.

As Frank strolled into the interview room, he held his breath for a second as that familiar smell hit him. The small, windowless chamber, with three straight-backed chairs and a table, reeked of body odor, dirty clothes, and fear. They all blended together into a sickening stench. It was impossible to get that scent out of the walls.

A young kid sat behind the desk and glared at them, his right hand cuffed to a metal eyelet screwed into the top of the wood. But Frank reminded himself the guy wasn't a kid. His rap showed him to be almost twenty-two. Long dreadlocks hung limp to his shoulders. He had that belligerent air Frank often saw in young people who'd been caught on the wrong side of the law.

Rob pulled out his key ring. "Here, let me get these off." He unlocked the cuff from the suspect's wrist and pocketed the keys. "Is that better?"

The guy rubbed his wrist but didn't answer. Rob took a seat across from him and Frank followed suit, eyeing the kid. *Could this guy actually be involved in Katrina's kidnapping?* He searched his gut for an answer and came up dry.

Rob opened his notebook. "Tyro, we'd like to ask a couple of questions about where you got the Audi. Think you might help us out?"

The kid rolled his eyes and gazed at the wall to his left.

Rob continued. "We've got you by the short hairs on this one. You could really help yourself by telling us what we want to know."

The guy only smirked.

"When you go to court, you're going to be looking for a break. We could give you that break. Might make a difference on whether you do county time or state time. What'll it be?"

The kid stared up to his right, apparently finding something interesting on the ceiling. Finally, he shifted his stare to Rob and shook his head, as if he'd been asked to explain Fermat's last theorem. To Rob's credit, he tried every avenue to gain cooperation. He asked the same

48

question in a half dozen ways, offering enticements for some response. After twenty minutes he gave up.

"Give me that hand." He grabbed the guy's right wrist and again cuffed it to the table and then walked to a corner. He motioned with his head for Frank. Frank ambled over and they whispered while studying Tyro.

"What do you think?" Rob asked.

Frank shot another glance at the kid. "Well, he's not denying it, but that's not good enough."

Rob rubbed the back of his neck and met eyes with Frank. "You want to give it a shot?"

Frank shook his head. "If he won't talk to you, he won't talk to me."

"When we walk out that door, we might just find the chief and mayor waiting. What do we tell them?" Rob asked.

Frank considered the question. "I don't care about them. I care what happened to the girl. The fact that she wasn't in the car doesn't bode well. If she's still alive, she can't be in a good place. Time's not on her side. If this guy asks for an attorney, talks but won't give up her whereabouts, or anything else that kills time, she may be dead before we locate her."

Rob grimaced and gnawed his lip. "So, do we twist him?"

Frank pulled the pencil from his jacket and handed it to his partner.

Rob held up his hands in surrender. "Whoa, I don't want to do it."

Frank grunted and glanced at Tyro. "You think I do? Besides, it's your day to ask the questions."

Rob also eyed Tyro and frowned. "Flip you for it."

"Okay."

Rob dug a coin from his pants. "Call it in the air."

"Yeah, go ahead."

Rob flipped it almost to the ceiling.

Just before he caught it, Frank said, "Heads."

Rob slapped it on the back of his hand and lifted his palm. "Tails."

"Great." Frank stuffed the pencil in his jacket pocket and glanced at the suspect, who was still watching them. The poor bastard had no idea what was coming.

Rob casually picked up the second chair and strolled to the door. He fitted the back under the knob and tested it. Satisfied, he sauntered to the opposite wall, crossed his arms, and waited. Frank dug a hand-kerchief from his pocket and draped it over the video camera lens in the corner. The camera wasn't even activated, but the kid didn't know that.

Tyro's belligerent look now became a little less convincing. He swiveled his head from Rob to Frank. Neither smiled—the pleasantries were gone.

Frank assumed Rob's old chair at the desk and removed the pencil from his jacket. He smiled at Tyro while tapping the pencil on the desk. "You know the difference between softball and hardball?" Frank asked.

The kid gawked but didn't answer.

Frank lowered his gaze to the pencil and spoke in a menacing whisper. "When you play softball and you accidentally get hit, it hurts, but it doesn't sting as bad as when you get hit by a hard ball." Frank looked up into Tyro's eyes. "Right?"

Tyro stared at him but remained silent.

Frank toyed with the pencil and grinned. His looked up at the kid. "If you want to play hardball with me, I'll make sure you leave the field with the bat stuck up your ass."

The kid's head snapped to the right when Rob pushed off the wall and quickly paced to his rear. He swallowed hard, his lips tight, watching Frank with suspicious eyes. The kid tried to keep them both in sight, but Rob was already behind him.

Frank bounced the pencil on the desk several times, letting the eraser rebound it to his fingers. He studied it and looked up at the suspect. "Last chance. Where's the girl?"

Tyro showed the same disinterested gaze, just before Rob slapped his right hand over his mouth and pinned his other arm to his body. Quick as a snake, Frank grabbed the cuffed hand and shoved the pencil between the guy's index and middle fingers. Frank clasped his left hand around Tyro's fingers, holding as tight as he could.

In his crazy voice, bugging his eyes, Frank whispered, "You've made a serious error in judgment. I bet you thought we were like all the other cops. That we'd get tired of asking questions and just go away, huh? Well, it's not like that with us—we're crazy. There's no good cop, bad cop. We're both evil."

Tyro struggled to move, his eyes filling with fear, but Rob held him in a vise grip.

Frank twisted the pencil several times, keeping the fingers locked tight. The guy stiffened, then jerked and shook with each twist as if electricity rushed through his body. Frank knew how it felt: the six-sided hard object ground the skin, nerves and bones of the two fingers it rested between. Tyro's eyes widened as the pencil twisted. A muffled cry tried to escape his lips, but Rob's hand remained clamped. Tears streamed down the guy's cheeks. Frank stopped twisting just before it looked as if Tyro might pass out.

Frank pulled the pencil from between the fingers and tapped on the kid's forehead with the eraser. "Hello, anybody in there?"

The stench of urine wafted from below the table. The guy eased open his eyes and gawked in horror at Frank.

"Now that we understand each other, we can get down to business. My partner's going to let go of your mouth. Okay? And in return you're not going to shout or make any noise. The only thing you're going to do is tell us what happened to the girl who was driving that car. After that, we're out of here, and you can explain all about stealing it to the auto theft detectives. Nod if you agree."

Tyro nodded so hard he almost broke loose from Rob's grip.

"Good. Now, in your quiet voice"—Frank placed his index finger to his lips—"tell us about the girl."

Rob slowly slid his hand from Tyro's trembling lips. He gulped in a lungful of air and shook. He sucked in quick breaths as sweat rolled down his face. He had that near-death-experience look.

Frank waited a few seconds. "Enough already. Too much oxygen's bad for you. What about the girl?"

"What girl?" the suspect asked between breaths.

Rob's hand slid toward Tyro's mouth as Frank brought the pencil back into view.

Tyro jerked his head away from Rob. "I swear, there's no girl. I found the car."

Rob pulled his hand away from Tyro's mouth.

"Do we look stupid to you?" Frank snapped.

Panic set in as the kid babbled about finding the car abandoned in a parking lot in South Dallas.

Frank scrutinized him. "Tell us about it."

Tyro licked his lips. "I was walking around the Walmart late one night flipping handles when I sees a nice car sitting at the far end of the lot."

"What night?" Frank asked.

A pause. "Sunday, I think."

"Which Walmart?" Rob asked.

"You know that supercenter off Lake June Road?"

"You idiot, that's not in South Dallas—that's in Balch Springs," Rob said.

"I meant in south Dallas County, not South Dallas." Tyro said. There was a tremor in his voice.

"Go on," Frank ordered.

"Anyway, I sees this nice car, so I check it out, you know, to see if there's anything I could use. When I flip the handle, the thing opens."

"You saying you didn't bust in?" Frank asked.

"Naw, naw, nothing like that. The door was unlocked, I swear."

"Okay, then what?" Frank tightened his grip a little and the kid winced.

"So, in the ignition was a set of keys. Just like someone walked off and forgot 'em."

"You see anybody around?" Rob quizzed.

"Naw, nobody. That's why it was so sweet."

"I'm having trouble believing this," Frank whispered.

"I swear, I swear, just like I said. Nice car, unlocked with keys. I had no choice."

"His story's easy to verify," Rob mumbled.

The kid twisted his head. "Yeah, yeah, do that verify stuff—do that."

Frank gave Tyro his ice-cold stare again. "You sure there was no girl in or around the car?"

"I swear to it on a stack of frigging Bibles."

Frank slipped the pencil into his pocket. "We're going to check it out. If we find you're feeding us a line, we'll be back. If we discover you've complained on us, we'll see you later. You don't want us return-ing. Understand?"

The kid's head bobbed. "Yeah, yeah, I understand."

Frank gave his partner a little nod and Rob released the guy. They gathered their notebooks and stood. Frank bent down and got almost nose to nose.

"About what time Sunday night?"

The suspect thought for a second. "Around midnight, maybe a few minutes before."

Frank nodded. "Last question. Did you put anything in or take anything out of the car?"

Tyro's eyes were slits as he moved them from side to side. "I found a laptop in the seat and threw it in the trunk."

"Anything else?"

The kid lowered his head. "Found a hundred bucks in a purse. Stuck the green in my pocket and tossed the purse in the trunk with the laptop."

"That's it?"

He looked up. "That's it."

Rob unhitched the chair from the door and slid it under the table. Frank pulled off the handkerchief covering the camera and replaced it in his pocket.

"That big, ugly detective will be in here after we leave. We'll find out what you say to him. If you don't tell him the same story, we'll talk again," Frank said.

* * *

Rob had been half right. The mayor wasn't waiting outside in the squad area, but about a dozen detectives and the chief were. He and Edna stood together with two other deputy chiefs. The mob moved in their direction.

"Well?" Edna asked.

Rob answered for the pair. "Says he found the car in a Walmart parking lot, unoccupied."

"You believe him?" the chief asked.

Rob glanced at Frank. His nod was so slight he almost missed it. "Yes, sir," Rob answered, "but it needs to be checked out. I guess somebody in Auto Theft will do that."

The chief said, "No, stay on this awhile longer. You have more background information than anyone else. Don't want to waste time bringing another detective up to speed when you guys have the ball. Run with it."

Frank was too stunned to answer, but Rob managed a "Yes, sir. We're on it."

As they marched out, the chief said, "Don't lose the scent, boys. Chase it down."

Neither answered before walking into the hall. Frank was still wondering how he'd gotten lucky enough to keep the investigation. Now that the chief knew this was more than a rebellious teen hiding from her parents, he and Rob should have been off the case. By all rights it should have gone back to the Missing Persons Unit.

"You know, sometimes you scare the shit out of me with that psycho act you do," Rob said.

Frank didn't look at him but just kept walking. "Yeah, I know. Sometimes I scare myself."

They went back to CIU and retrieved their weapons and jackets.

Frank felt like he did last summer after getting food poisoning from bas sushi. On the way to the garage, he shook his head and whispered, "I'm never doing that again."

"What?" Rob asked. "Twist a guy?"

"Yeah. Better ways of doing it. If I just had a couple of days, I know I could have gotten him to talk," Frank mumbled.

Frank was king of the mind game. Frank could get into a guy's head and have a full written confession when he walked out of the interview room.

"But we didn't have a couple of days," Rob said.

Frank didn't look at him at him, only nodded.

"Yeah."

8

Rob swung the city car out of the employee parking lot and hooked a right on Lamar. Frank slumped in the passenger seat, laughing into the phone. From the tone of the conversation, he was talking to a woman.

Frank lowered his voice. "I've never had that done to me before. Is it legal?"

Frank laughed again and, much to Rob's relief, moved on to what he planned to cook her for dinner. He threw out a few suggestions, and she apparently rejected them all. He finally talked her into trying his chateaubriand and béarnaise sauce with glazed carrots and asparagus baked in butter and garlic. He said good-bye and dropped the phone into his pocket.

"Another dinner date tonight?"

"Nope, Saturday."

Rob wheeled onto the freeway. "I don't get it. If you love cooking so much, why become a cop?"

Frank stretched. "Too much work."

"Huh?"

Frank eyed him. "I enjoy taking my time and preparing something special. If you're a line cook, or even an executive chef, you're in a madhouse from six to ten o'clock every night. Not the perfect workplace." Frank yawned. "I got tired of being Mario Batali's bitch."

"Were you any good—as a chef, I mean?"

"Our restaurant won the James Beard Award when I worked there. Yeah, we were all good."

"Why cook for your dates? Isn't it easier to just go out?" Rob tried to remember the last time he'd cooked for his wife. He vaguely remembered preparing a box of macaroni and cheese, but that had been at least a year ago.

"Women appreciate having someone prepare a dinner just for them." Frank readjusted his sunglasses. "They like being fussed over. You cook them dinner, serve a good wine in a relaxed surrounding, and give them a massage—they reward you."

Rob chuckled. "Tipping the cook, huh?"

Frank closed his eyes and rested his head on the seat. "No less than twenty percent."

Balch Springs was a small community in southeast Dallas County. When they pulled into the Walmart supercenter twenty minutes later, Rob shook Frank. "We're here."

They found the manager's office and asked to speak with him. His secretary was an older lady who resembled a shorter version of Lucille Ball. When the manager stepped out his office door, she introduced them.

"Mr. McSwain, these gentlemen are with the police."

McSwain was one of those people who was born to be a manager. Tall, with wire-rimmed glasses, he spoke in short, clipped sentences. "Nice to meet you. What can I do for you today? No trouble, I hope."

Since it was still technically Rob's day to ask the questions, he decided to answer the last one first. "No, no trouble." He flashed his disarming smile. "We'd just like to take a look at your parking lot surveillance tapes."

"Don't use tapes. Everything's digital now. Been tapeless for years."

Rob nodded. "Of course, that's what I meant—the digital recordings."

McSwain looked at Lucille Ball. "Can you show them inside?" He pointed to his office. "I'll be right with you."

The cramped space left little room for extra chairs, but two were wedged between boxes stacked to the ceiling. Rob and Frank declined attempting to squeeze into the tight area and stood in front of the desk. Someone had recently eaten an orange; a citrus smell still hung in the air. The door opened and a pimply faced black kid with short hair combed straight down entered, followed by McSwain.

57

"Brian, these gentlemen want to view a surveillance video from the parking lot," McSwain said.

"No problem." The kid dropped into a chair at a workstation and powered up the computer. "What date are we looking for?"

"Last Sunday," Rob said, "whatever date that was."

The manager spun around to a calendar behind him.

"The nineteenth," Brian mumbled, and his fingers flew across the keyboard. "Time?"

"Probably between eleven thirty and midnight," Frank answered.

The kid scrolled to a menu and highlighted eleven thirty. He hit enter and leaned closer to the screen. A grainy color video of the parking area popped up. Few cars remained in the lot, and a couple of customers strolled toward the entrance, their images punctuated with intermittent static.

Rob edged toward the monitor. "This the best shot you have?"

"We're scheduled for a system upgrade this summer," McSwain explained.

Rob shook his head. He hated relying on poor-quality surveillance like this. "We're looking for a red late-model Audi S4 sedan."

"Is that an Audi?" Brian pointed to a vehicle at the far end of the dark lot.

Rob scratched his cheek and squinted. "Could be, but the lighting's so bad it's hard to tell."

The manager cleared his throat. "We're replacing those burned-out bulbs this week."

Rob turned to Brian. "Can you fast-forward closer to midnight?"

"Sure." The kid pressed a key and the video raced forward. In the upper right corner of the screen, a digital clock ticked off the time.

"Stop," Rob said. "There." He motioned to a figure loitering through the lot toward the Audi. "Is that him?" he asked as he turned to Frank. The digital clock read 11:47.

Frank stepped closer. "That's Tyro."

The figure touched the door handle and the interior light flashed on. He swiveled his head from left to right as he leaned into the car. A second later Tyro jumped in and drove off.

"Is that what you were looking for?" McSwain asked.

"Half of it." Frank moved him aside. He touched Brian's shoulder. "Reverse the video."

"Can do." Brian pecked another key and the video reversed, the digital clock counting down the minutes and seconds. When it got to 11:19, an old pickup truck with a camper appeared on the video beside the Audi.

"Stop." Frank pointed.

Brian slapped the keyboard and the picture froze. "In slow motion, ease the video backward," Frank whispered, his chin over the kid's shoulder. "Can we zoom in on this shot?"

"Not possible," Brian said.

As the video clocked back, one frame at a time, a tall, bearded man with long hair and a baseball-type cap got out of the Audi. He shut the car door and went to the passenger side of the truck. When he opened the door, the interior light revealed another long-haired man with a full beard and cap in the driver's seat. They could have been brothers.

"Is that a Dodge?" Frank asked.

"Looks like it," Rob replied. He eyed McSwain. "We'll need a copy of that video from the time the Audi parks until the truck leaves."

Frank gazed at the computer screen a long time. The two long-haired men appeared to have mesmerized him. Rob had given up trying to read Frank's thoughts a long time ago, but there was something about his expression . . .

* * *

Rob glanced at Frank. All the way to the police impound lot, he'd been silent. He wasn't slumped in the seat as usual with his eyes closed. He sat upright, staring at the photo Dora had given them. The girl in the picture looked back. She wore a graduation gown and hat, clutching the diploma to her bosom, her long blonde hair over one shoulder. She had clear blue eyes and a friendly smile.

Rob hated when Frank went introvert. These dreamlike trances didn't happen often, but when they did, there was no use hurrying them. It was as if Frank's mind had slipped into another dimension and had neglected to bring his body along.

Finally, as they entered the gate and began driving down lines of vehicles, Frank spoke. "I'm going to find her."

"Think she's still alive?"

"Yup."

"How do you figure?"

Frank assumed his slouched riding position as he slipped the photo inside his coat pocket. "Why go to the trouble of driving her car someplace to be stolen unless you calculated it would buy you time?" He gazed at Rob. "If old Tyro hadn't been caught by the uniforms, the car might be on its way to Mexico by now. Whoever those guys were, they didn't want anyone discovering she was missing. It worked. Ms. Mayor didn't even suspect anything. And if they were only going to rape and kill her, why take the chance of discovery by driving the car from the scene of the crime to the Walmart parking lot?"

Rob nodded. "Makes sense." He came to a stop at the end of the lot, in front of the missing girl's wrecked Audi. "Hey, look, Kelly's still here." He pointed at the Crime Scene Unit van parked nearby. The big man wearing a white Tyvek suit and blue plastic gloves handed a box to his assistant and strolled to Frank's side of the car. Frank rolled down the window. The smell of gasoline and car lubricants drifted in on the breeze.

"Afternoon, Kelly," Frank said.

Kelly slipped off the gloves and leaned down. "What brings you guys out here?"

Frank pointed to the red car.

Kelly wiped his brow. "I get it. Heard this was the mayor's ride. It won't be going anywhere for a while."

Rob studied the Audi, noting the collapsed front end and the wheel dangling at an awkward angle. Considering the price tag of a vehicle like that, he figured Tyro had shaved a good twenty thousand off the value.

"You finished processing it?" Frank asked.

"Yeah."

"Get any prints?"

"Lots of them."

"Any blood evidence?" Rob asked.

Kelly had his mouth open to answer, but hesitated. "Blood evidence? Whose blood? The suspect's?"

Rob didn't answer. No use in opening the circle any wider than it already was. Not when the mayor was involved. Frank also stayed silent.

Kelly's brow furrowed. "For that matter, why's Criminal Intelligence working this and not Auto Theft?"

Frank didn't move from his slump in the passenger seat, his gaze still focused ahead, as if they were still on the road.

"If you want an answer to that, you'll have to call our lieutenant," Rob said.

Kelly grunted. "Yeah, like I'm going to call Edna. Right."

"Any blood?" Frank repeated, turning to face Kelly.

Kelly exhaled. "Not a drop. Suspect or otherwise."

"Find anything of interest?" Rob asked. He opened the car door and stepped out. Frank also got out and posted his hands on his sides, staring at the wrecked car. The sound of gravel crunching filled the silence as Frank approached the Audi for a closer look.

Kelly flipped through an inventory sheet and shook his head. "Laptop, clothes, Bible, purse—the standard stuff. Once we process the contents, we might have something else."

"Give us a call if anything turns up," Frank said.

Kelly nodded. "Will do." He meandered to the CSU van, stripping off the Tyvek suit. Throwing it inside, he hopped into the passenger seat, and the van eased toward the exit. Rob and Frank strolled around the wrecked vehicle, peeking inside.

"Little rich girl's car," Frank mumbled as he walked around the wreck. He opened the passenger door and raked his finger through the fine powder on the seat. The deployed airbag had coated the interior with tiny white flakes.

"Not much here," Rob said.

"And whatever was here is now screwed up with this stuff." Frank dusted his hands.

Rob paced back to their car. "Ready to go?"

Frank didn't answer. He just stared at the Audi. After a few seconds, he eyed the lot of crashed and impounded vehicles as if he'd lost something. He had slipped the girl's photo from his pocket. He glanced at it and tucked it back into his jacket without comment.

Rob studied him but didn't ask what he was thinking. This was probably Frank just being Frank.

* * *

At about four thirty, Rob and Frank pulled into the employee parking garage.

"I'll report in. See you tomorrow," Frank said.

"Any use in me arguing the point?" Rob asked.

"Nope. Go see about Carmen. Tell her I said hello."

Five minutes later, Frank, Terry, and Edna stood around the television in Terry's office scrutinizing the surveillance video. Edna had that eye twitch thing going. She constantly cleared her throat and wrung her hands. Terry was probably on his fourth pot of the day, sipping a cup as the video played.

"You think she was in the truck?" Edna whispered.

"Good chance," Frank said.

They watched until the truck pulled away. Terry leaned in inches from the screen. "Can't read the plate number."

Frank shook his head. "Nope, truck's driving parallel to the camera angle." He pointed. "Notice when it makes a right on Lake June Road. There's no license plate light."

Edna cleared her throat again. "Either burnt out or conveniently removed. Do we have another camera shot on the lot?"

"No, this is it," Frank answered.

The video ended and Terry said, "So, we're looking for an old, dark-color Dodge pickup with a camper shell occupied by two rednecks in Dallas. That narrows it down." He smirked. "Wish we had a clearer picture of those guys. As it is, not even their mother could recognize them."

Edna appeared lost in thought. She checked her watch. "It's almost five. Got to make a call to the chief's office." She trotted out, checking her watch again.

Terry sat in his chair. "You were right."

"Huh?"

"You were right about the girl." Terry's brow crinkled. "How did you know she'd been taken?"

Frank didn't answer for a few seconds. He shrugged. "Sometimes I just feel things more than know them."

"Sixth sense? You're blessed."

"She's still alive, Terry. I know she's alive." It was Frank's gut, not hope, talking to him.

Terry stood. "Perhaps, but don't put that in any official report. For that matter, don't even say it outside this office. The last thing we need is to get people's hopes up and then have them crushed when a body shows up. Edna says the chief has instructed us to return the girl's personal property to the mayor after Forensics is done. Shoot them a call tomorrow and pick it up."

"Will do."

"Missing Persons and Auto Theft are working the case now. Everything's being entered into NCIC."

"They still want us working it?"

Terry set his coffee mug on the desk and stretched his back. "Until the chief pulls you off."

"Thanks."

"For what?"

Frank looked Terry directly in the eyes. "For keeping this case in CIU."

Frank left Terry's office, his biggest fear behind him now. He'd been terrified he and Rob would have to hand over their work to the detectives in the Missing Persons Unit. He couldn't have stood that. If he knew Terry like he thought he did, he'd gone to bat for them keeping the thing. Terry wasn't above pulling a string or two. And he knew the same thing Frank felt in his gut: this was his case now, and he was going to solve it.

9

Frank arrived in CIU two hours earlier the next morning. He hadn't slept well. Now that the case belonged to him, his mind had rousted him from sleep and demanded he go to work. He flipped on the lights in the squad area, powered up his computer, and reviewed his notes from the day before. He was almost finished typing up his report when his desk phone rang, startling him. In the dead morning silence of the usually noisy squad room, it sounded like a burglar alarm. He grabbed the receiver.

"Detective Pierce."

"You're in early. Didn't know you guys came in before ten." Kelly chuckled. "We've wrapped up the forensics on the property in the car. Got hair, prints, and a few trace fibers. Let you know if anything turns up after the analysis is done."

"I'll come by and collect it."

"Huh?"

Frank lowered his voice. "If you haven't heard by now, you will soon. The mayor's nineteen-year-old daughter was in that car, and she's still missing."

"No shit?"

"Yup. They want her personal property returned to the mayor."

"Won't that screw up the chain of custody?"

Frank scratched his forehead. "Probably, but I'm guessing the chief gave his blessing or Terry wouldn't have told me to do it. Besides, it's not going anywhere. Not like the mayor's going to throw it out."

"Yeah, see what you mean. Okay, we'll hold it for you."

"As soon as Rob makes it in, we'll stop by."

Frank hung up and opened his browser. His cell rang. The caller was Rob.

"Forgot, I have court today," Rob said. "Should be out by lunch. Anything going on?"

Frank assumed his usual slouch in his desk chair. "Sorting through the case file. We have lots to do."

The thought of returning to the mayor's home wasn't something Frank found pleasant. He'd wait till after lunch and take Rob with him. Edna swished in a few minutes later, complaining about a two-hour staff meeting. She dropped her bag and armload of notebooks on her desk and made her way to Frank's cube.

"Any news?"

"They finished the forensics."

She looked around. "Where's Rob?"

"Court. Be in later."

"Go ahead and run that stuff to the mayor's house. Don't want it sitting around here if the chief calls and inquires." She marched toward Terry's office before Frank could reply.

He rode the elevator grudgingly to the fifth floor, checked the property out of the lab, and hauled it down to his car. Twenty minutes later, he pulled up to the mayor's gate. The ivy-covered mansion loomed at the end of the long drive. He pressed the call button and a formal voice echoed from the speaker on the pole.

"Your business?"

"Police, to see Mrs. Wallace."

The gate didn't open immediately. He reached his hand out to press the call button again just as it started moving. He parked in the same spot he and Rob had the other day, near the fountain. Frank slid the evidence box, overflowing with the girl's personal items, to the edge of the seat and hoisted it, making his way up the walk. He rang the bell twice before the door swung open.

Oh hell.

"Mrs. Wallace . . . I expected Dora."

She had on the same robe she'd worn on his last visit, but her face appeared to have withered. She wore no makeup, and her hair was matted as if she'd just gotten out of bed.

"What can I do for you, Detective Pierce?" Her voice had a weary, aggravated tone.

Better make this quick. Frank cleared his throat and reached into his jacket, handing her Katrina's apartment key. "The mayor requested your daughter's property be returned after we finished processing it."

She gazed at the box and snapped. "I requested it. Don't want Trina's things sitting in some dark corner somewhere. Especially a police station."

"Yes, ma'am."

She opened the door wider. "Bring it in." She led him to a large table in the center of the foyer that held an arrangement of yellow bird-of-paradise flowers. "Here." She pointed to the edge of the table.

Frank sat the box down and pulled an evidence "chain-of-custody" form out of his jacket. He unfolded it and spread it on the table. "Please, sign here."

He gave her his pen, and she shot him an evil stare before she scribbled her name at the bottom.

"Thank you." He folded the form and slipped it back into his jacket. "We're doing all we can to find her. I know how you must feel." He threw that last part in as a way of making peace. *Has to be hard on her.*

She glared at him. "Do you?"

"Do I what?"

"Do you know how I feel? Do you have any children?"

"No, I'm not married."

"I thought as much. I know your type."

Frank didn't answer. He'd said too much already. He headed for the door.

"This doesn't belong to Trina."

"What?" He stopped walking and turned.

She tapped an item in the evidence box encased in clear plastic. "I said, this is not Trina's."

Frank wasn't sure how to respond. Had the forensic techs mixed up the evidence with another case? Was this someone else's property? Crap, he should have checked it before he brought it out.

"I don't understand. That's not your daughter's stuff?" he asked.

She rolled her eyes and a condescending grin swept across her lips. "Yes, I recognize the sweater, and that looks like her laptop and purse, but this isn't hers." She kept tapping the plastic bag in the box.

He moved closer. Her finger rested on a white book, "Holy Bible" embossed in gold ink across the front.

He eyed her. "You sure?"

"Of course I'm sure." She sighed.

Frank slipped the knife from his pocket and made a neat slit in the heavy plastic evidence bag. He removed the Bible and handed it to her. "Better check it out to be sure."

Anger flashed in her face. "I don't have to check it out. It's not hers."

"How do you know if you don't look? Perhaps her name's on the inside."

She spoke slowly, as if addressing a dull child. "Trina doesn't own a Bible, doesn't attend church, and to my knowledge has no faith." Her eyes challenged him to argue. Ms. Mayor refused to accept or even touch the Bible.

"I see." He tucked it under his arm. "Better check the rest of the items to make sure they're in order."

She rummaged through the bag, pulling out things for a better look. "Everything else appears okay, although I can't for the life of me understand what possessed her to buy this purse." She dangled the red-and-white striped thing in the air with thumb and forefinger. "It's ghastly."

"I'll be on my way then." He scurried out the door.

That didn't go as planned. Who the hell screwed up in the crime lab and left me holding the bag? Wait a minute. Hadn't Kelly said something about a Bible the day before? Yeah, he'd said laptop, clothes, Bible, and a purse.

Frank opened the Bible to the dedication page—blank. He thumbed through it for anything hidden between the pages—nothing. Ms. Mayor was so certain her daughter couldn't have owned it that she refused to even discuss the matter. So if the kid had found religion, why keep a dime bag of grass in her apartment? He mulled that over and concluded that lots of people who find religion probably smoke, no big deal. But there hadn't been any sign of Christian or church literature in the apartment. Did that matter? Probably not. His cell rang.

"Pierce."

"Ready to eat?" Rob asked.

"Sure, meet you at Sarge's."

Ten minutes later, Frank pulled into the bar parking lot and Rob pushed off the wall, strolling to his car. Frank opened the door but paused, staring at the Bible in the passenger seat for a moment before picking it up. "How was court?" he asked, stepping out onto the hot asphalt.

Rob squinted in the sun's bright glare. "Didn't need me. Guy pled out."

When they wandered into the cool, dim interior, Jan looked up from the bar where she was slicing a sandwich. Jan always wore a smile. A bit surprising, because she was married to Sarge. "Have a seat, boys. We'll be right with you."

The place was hopping. They flopped onto two stools at the bar.

Sarge slapped the counter. "What'll it be?"

"Two sandwiches and two cherry Cokes," Rob replied.

"Better make mine a double," Frank added.

Sarge looked up as he was grabbing the glasses. "I don't think so."

Frank laid the Bible face down on the bar. "What if I told you I wasn't on duty?"

Sarge studied him. "So, is that what you're telling me—that you're not on duty?"

Frank hesitated a second too long.

68

"Figures." Sarge sat the drinks on the bar and shoved them to the pair. "Say, did you hear about the mayor's kid?"

Rob nodded. "Yeah, that's tough."

"Any leads?"

"How would we know?" Rob said.

Sarge gave them a sideways glance, throwing a bar towel over his shoulder. "Liar. You're the primary investigators. Don't ever try pulling any shit over on me."

Rob and Frank exchanged stares and sipped their drinks. Jan finished making their sandwiches and slid them across the bar.

Frank bit into his, glanced at Sarge, and grinned. He'd upgraded to Dijon mustard.

They ate in silence for five minutes before Frank asked Rob, "You searched the girl's living room and kitchen. Find any religious stuff?"

Rob shook his head, looking down as he searched his memory. "No, nothing. Why?"

"There was a Bible in her property when I dropped it off at the mayor's house. Just wondering if it's hers."

"Who else's could it be?"

"Ms. Mayor didn't seem to think it belonged to her daughter."

"How else could it have gotten there?"

Frank dabbed his lips with the napkin, running through the possibilities. "There is one person who might know."

10

The same odor that permeated the interview rooms at the PD also hung heavy in the Lew Sterrett/North Tower Jail, amplified a dozen times. The Dallas County Sheriff's Department didn't waste money on deodorant or comfort. With its drab colors and claustrophobic atmosphere, the place felt more like a prison than a county lockup.

Rob ran a hand over his buzz cut and leaned back in the rickety chair. "You know we're wasting our time, right?"

Frank sat in the chair to his left, resting his hand across the Bible on the table. "Probably."

A large sheriff's deputy escorted Tyro across the threshold. He was dressed in the standard jail uniform: a white jumpsuit. His eyes widened when he saw them, and he dug in his heels. "Not you guys again."

The deputy gave all 130 pounds of Tyro a shove from behind, and he stumbled forward. He quickly regained his footing, turned to the door, and ran into the bull chest of the deputy. "I don't want to talk these guys. They're crazy and hurt people," Tyro said.

The deputy spun him around and pushed him toward the interview chair.

Rob flashed a smile. "He's just a little shy."

"Shy, my ass. I'm out of here." Tyro again rushed for the door.

The deputy grabbed him by the nape of the neck and pushed him into the chair. "You want me to hold him or leave?"

"Doesn't matter," Frank said. "We're only going to ask him one question."

Tyro's gaze shifted to Frank as he slowly withdrew a pencil from his jacket and laid it on the table. Tyro's eyes bulged and his body stiffened.

"Just one question." Frank spun the pencil around on the table. He leaned closer and nodded at Tyro. "When I asked you if you put anything in or removed anything from the car, you told me you only got money from the purse. And then threw it and a laptop in the trunk. Remember?"

Tyro's lips trembled.

"You staying with that?"

"Yeah, sure. That's all I did." Tyro wiped sweat from his brow and shifted in the chair.

Frank leaned a little closer still and lifted the pencil. Tyro squirmed.

"So, you're saying you didn't leave anything in the car?"

Tyro looked at Rob, then at the deputy, as if he thought it might be a trick question. "Naw, I didn't leave nothing."

"Ever seen this?" Frank held up the Bible.

"Yeah, it was in the passenger's seat when I got in."

"You didn't put it there?" Frank asked.

Tyro scanned the faces of the group again. His brow furrowed, and he stared at Frank. "Naw. Why would I do that? I don't even have no Bible."

Frank smirked. "Now, I find that hard to believe."

"Well, you can believe it," Tyro said, looking at the door again as if waiting for a last-minute reprieve. "Besides . . . I'm Muslim."

"Oh, really?" A wicked grin crept across Frank's lips.

Rob shook his head, waiting for the inevitable to happen. Frank wasn't very good at suffering fools gladly.

"Which branch—Sunni or Shia?" Frank said, as if he were really interested in the answer.

Tyro's eyes narrowed. "Say, what?"

"We finished here?" Rob sighed.

Frank nodded. "Yup."

The deputy hauled Tyro out of the room with a contented sneer glued to his lips.

71

"Satisfied?" Rob asked.

Frank stood and picked up the Bible, examining it.

Rob hiked into the corridor to the elevators and pushed the button.

Frank followed. "You know what this reminds me of?"

Rob didn't answer.

"This reminds me of the guy driving down a country road and see-ing a turtle sitting on a fencepost, his legs moving in all directions, try-ing to get a little traction. It begs a question."

"Who put it there?" Rob asked.

Frank winked. "Bingo."

Rob dropped Frank off at Sarge's to retrieve his car, and they met at the station a few minutes later. Frank spent the afternoon reading the Bible, as if maybe the scriptures held some secret they'd give up with closer examination. Every so often he'd glance at the girl's photo and then slip it back into his pocket. Rob caught up on paperwork and didn't pay him much attention. Around late afternoon, Frank's phone rang. He answered it and sat up straight in the chair.

"Yes, thanks for returning my call," Frank said. "Can you hold one second while I put this on intercom? I want my partner in on it."

"Hey, ready to interview the last guy?" Frank asked.

Rob was deep into calculating his overtime hours for the month when Frank's question made him lose count. "What?"

Frank held up the receiver. "Got the boyfriend, Ruiz, on the line."

Rob leaned over the top of the cubical. "Oh, yeah?"

Frank tapped the phone's intercom button and hung up the receiver. "Yes, hello. Mr. Ruiz, thanks for getting back to me. This is Detective Frank Pierce, Dallas Police. I'm investigating the disappearance of Katrina Wallace. We were told you were the last to see her."

A hesitant voice answered. "Sorry I took so long to call back. Voice mail's been on the fritz again."

"We wanted to ask you a couple of questions about the last time you saw Katrina," Frank said.

There was a long pause before Ruiz said, "Do I need a lawyer?"

"I don't know," Frank said. "Do you think you need one?"

Another long pause and a deep breath. "No, I didn't do anything wrong."

"Well, I won't attempt to give you legal advice, but typically witnesses don't require an attorney to be present during questioning," Frank said.

"So . . . I'm not a suspect?"

"Not at this time," Frank said. "Feel like talking to us about this? Might help us find her."

"Sure, no problem. Is there any news?" His voice had a young, timid quality.

Frank glanced at Rob. "No, not yet. We're still looking into it."

"Oh."

"Tell us about the Sunday evening you spent together," Frank said.

"What do you want to know?"

"Nothing personal. That's your business. Just where you went, what you did."

"We left my place and drove to a restaurant for dinner. Stopped for gas on the way. After eating, she dropped me at home and headed for Dallas a little after eight o'clock."

"You rode in her car to dinner?" Frank asked.

"Yes."

"Why not yours?"

"My roommate borrowed it."

"Who drove?" Frank asked.

"Trina did. Why?"

"Just a couple more questions," Frank said, crossing his arms and staring down at the speaker. "So you rode in the passenger seat of her car?"

"Right."

"Where did you put her Bible before you sat in the seat?" Frank asked, exchanging a quick glance with Rob.

"What Bible?"

"The white one she has."

"Trina has a Bible?" the voice stammered.

Frank paused and then smiled. "You sound surprised."

"I am. Never knew she owned one. She wasn't religious or anything like that."

"You sure?" Frank cut his eyes to Rob, who frowned at the phone.

"Yeah. She was the least religious person I know."

"Okay, Mr. Ruiz, that's all for now." Frank uncrossed his arms. "Oh, by the way. Did she say anything about making a stop on the way to Dallas?"

"Like where?"

"Like maybe a Walmart to pick up some things in Balch Springs."

Ruiz chuckled. "No, that's not possible."

"Why do you say that?"

"Trina wouldn't be caught dead in a Walmart." Right after he said the word *dead*, he paused. A deep shuddering breath followed. "And she doesn't know anyone in Balch Springs, to my knowledge. She's an SMU, uptown girl. Balch Springs isn't her style."

Frank pointed to the phone and lifted his eyebrows, his way of asking if Rob had any questions. Rob shook his head.

"Okay, thanks," Frank said. "We'll let you know if we need anything else." Frank clicked off the speaker.

Rob motioned at the phone. "Ruiz thinks she's still alive. Did you catch what he said at the end?"

Frank closed his notebook and nodded. "Yup, he's talking about her in the present tense. If he had anything to do with it and knew she was already dead, he wouldn't have phrased it that way. I don't believe he has a clue what happened after she left Austin."

Frank lounged in his chair the rest of the afternoon, reading the Bible, using the photo of the girl as a bookmark. As four o'clock approached, he tucked the Bible under his arm and headed for the door.

"I have some more reading to do." He didn't say good-bye, see you later, or anything else. From the look, he needed a quieter place away from the hustle and bustle of the squad area.

Rob finished his work and stuck his head into Terry's office an hour later to give him a rundown of what they'd found in the car, including the appearance of the mysterious Bible. The fact that no one could explain how it got there didn't seem to bother Terry.

"Probably belongs to the girl—no other explanation. Ruiz must have missed it when he rode with her to dinner. Kidnappers don't leave Bibles at the scene of the crime."

Rob shrugged. "Yeah, probably." He wasn't in the habit of contradicting supervisors, but he didn't believe it had happened that way. He was pretty sure Frank didn't either. Sometimes little things mattered, especially when they were inexplicable.

Rob eyed Frank's empty chair. His partner liked things wrapped up nice and tidy. Loose strings bothered him. And that Bible was a loose string.

11

Friday morning when Rob entered the CIU area, Frank had resumed lounging in his chair, Bible in hand.

"So, what do we do today?" Rob asked.

Frank snapped out of his trance. "Can you check all the social media sites for any activity or news about the girl?"

Rob draped his jacket over the chair and took his seat. "Sure. What are you going to do?"

"Read." Frank turned back to the Bible.

"You're reading the whole thing?"

"Yes."

"Well, can't say it'll do you any harm," Rob remarked.

When Frank didn't answer, he ignored him and logged onto his computer. The Criminal Intelligence Unit maintained covert accounts on all social media sites. They often used them in tracking the movements and activities of suspects who were foolish enough to post their whereabouts. Rob took his time checking each in detail. He hated computer work. Frank was better at that kind of stuff, but today he was mesmerized by the Bible. The case had hit another dead end, and they both knew it.

After two hours, it became evident that the girl had posted nothing on any social media site since the previous Sunday afternoon. Rob ran Katrina's name through several state and federal missing-persons indices but came up blank. She had dropped off the grid.

Rob stood and stretched. Frank hadn't moved. He looked painted in the chair. The only sign of life was the occasional turning of a page. *Is he even breathing?*

"You hungry yet?"

Frank lowered the good book and peered at him. "Yeah, I could eat a bite."

"Sarge's?"

Frank made a face. "We ate there yesterday."

"I know, but after a couple of hours of dealing with the morons on Instagram and Twitter, I need a cherry Coke."

Frank stood. "Okay, Sarge's it is." He picked up the Bible.

Rob snatched his jacket from the chair and followed Frank to the garage. As they got in the car, he pointed at the Bible. "So how far are you?"

"Just got into Revelation."

"Wow, you've just about finished the New Testament."

Frank eased low in the seat, his usual riding position. "No, I just about finished the Old Testament and New Testament."

"You've read the whole thing? Impossible," Rob said.

"I read most of the night at home."

"I didn't know you could speed-read."

Frank slid his sunglasses in place. "It's a gift."

Rob parked a half block away. Sarge's had become so popular you needed to get there by eleven to get a good parking place. Jan, Sarge's wife, poured drinks at one end of the bar while Sarge made sandwiches at the other.

"Hey, boys, grab a seat," she called.

They worked their way to Sarge's end and found two stools.

He looked up. "What'll it be?"

"Two cherry Cokes and two sandwiches," Rob said, leaning on his forearms. Exhaustion hit him, although he wasn't sure if it was from too much Twitter or too little movement on the case. Probably both.

Sarge wasn't subtle. "Was your last sandwich to your liking, Detective Pierce?"

A grin swept across Frank's lips. "Perfect, thanks."

Sarge's gaze stayed on Frank. "That a Bible?"

"Yup."

"I know you, Frank. No matter how much you read that thing, it won't matter when you hit the pearly gates."

Frank glanced up. "You're probably going to hell for that remark."

Jan slid two Cokes to Sarge, and he sat them in front of the pair. "Maybe, but I'm not the one reading a Bible in a bar."

Rob took a long swallow and smacked his lips. "Can't argue with that logic." He needed *this* Coke. Especially today. They'd covered all the bases and turned up zero. Frank must have also felt the frustration if all he could think to do was read scripture. When you run out of leads in an investigation, you hit up your informants or offer rewards for information. Neither was an option in this case.

Sarge finished their sandwiches and slid them across the bar. Rob quickly crossed himself and dug in. Frank was in no hurry. He took a bite between pages. Jan strolled over and dropped off another loaf of bread and began wiping the counter.

After twenty minutes without saying a word, Frank mumbled, "Wormwood." He flipped several pages and then fanned farther back. He went to the original page and studied it, his lips moving as his finger traced the scripture.

"Wormwood," he whispered again.

Jan turned and dropped the bar towel over her shoulder. "What about it?"

Frank's head shot up. "You know Wormwood?"

She leaned on the counter. "Sure, it's an herb. We have a neighbor from the Middle East who uses it in her cooking."

Frank's eyes pinched. "Oh, yeah, cooking."

Jan rested a hand on her hip. "Yeah, bitter as hell. I hate the stuff. Why you asking?"

Frank spun the Bible around and pointed to the verse.

She lifted the glasses held by a gold chain around her neck and slipped them on. "And the name of the star is called Wormwood: and the third part of the waters became wormwood; and many men died of the waters, because they were made bitter.'" She removed the glasses and let them fall on her chest. "So what does it mean?"

Frank pursed his lips. "End-times prophecy, I guess."

He reclaimed the Bible and kept reading.

Rob finished his lunch and slipped into the toilet to wash up. He splashed some water on his face, wondering when Frank would come out of his Bible-induced coma. Drying his hands and face on a paper towel, he reminded himself that when Frank had a hunch, it usually paid off.

When he came out, he touched Frank's arm. "Ready to go?"

His partner marked his page, and Rob threw a twenty on the bar. On the way to the station Frank was silent, and Rob let him be. When they returned to CIU, Frank took his chair in the cubicle next to Rob's and continued reading, and Rob forced himself to check the last two social network sites until his back was stiff. Rolling his neck, he looked up from his screen. Frank had stopped reading and was now just gazing into space. Rob knew that look. No use talking to him when he was in the zone.

Frank's phone rang and he answered it. "Hi, Kelly." He listened a few seconds and said, "That's it?" After another pause, he said, "Thanks," and hung up.

Frank returned to his space-gaze expression. After a minute or two he spoke. "Do any good on the social sites?"

"Nope, nothing since last Sunday afternoon."

"That was Kelly on the phone," Frank mumbled. "Lab finished processing the car and property. Got prints belonging to the girl, Ruiz, and Tyro. That's all."

Rob continued rubbing his neck, trying to brainstorm a way out of the blind alley they were trapped in. The sound of his partner tapping on a keyboard drew his attention. Rob leaned over to see Frank Googling something. His printer whirred and hummed a minute later, shooting out a sheet of paper. Frank grabbed it and studied the page for a moment.

"I knew I'd seen it before," he said.

"Seen what?"

"Wormwood." He held up the paper. "It's mentioned seven times in the Old Testament, but only once in the New Testament—the verse Jan read."

"So what?"

"Look." Frank handed the Bible across the low cubicle wall that separated their desks. "Read it."

Rob read the verse and returned it. "So?"

"See anything that caught your eye?"

"Same verse Jan read at Sarge's, with Wormwood highlighted in yellow," Rob said.

Frank shook his head. "I didn't highlight it."

Rob leaned forward and grabbed the Bible. He read the verse once more. "Well, if you didn't—who did?"

"Turtle on a fencepost," Frank whispered.

Rob asked, "How many other words were highlighted?"

Frank held up the Bible. "Zero. Out of three hundred and fifty-two pages, only one word. And only highlighted once in eight references."

Rob reclined in his chair. A knowing grin crept across his lips. "In our business, we call that a clue." He jumped up and watched over Frank's shoulder while Frank typed the word "Wormwood" into RMS, an in-house search index for Dallas Police to track addresses, suspect and victim names, and anything unusual officers found during an investigation. Its problem was the same that plagued all search indices: if the name had never been indexed, it never showed up.

Terry wandered up and Rob explained what Frank had found. Terry leaned over his shoulder as the computer did its work. One hit on "Wormwood" popped up on the screen. Frank clicked the link and waited for the offense report to load.

"How in the hell did you find that needle in the haystack?" Terry asked.

"Just caught a break," Frank said.

Rob snorted. "Break, my ass. He read the whole Bible in one day and night before he found it."

The computer screen flashed a copy of a DPD offense report from 2014. Offense: Criminal Trespass. Suspect: Eddie Lee Jones. An attached photo showed a disheveled white male in his midtwenties. The short report outlined how Jones had been spotted inside the fence of a trucking company in South Dallas in December 2014. He had been arrested and charged with trespassing and had served a short stint in the county jail. The report showed a couple of prior arrests for public intoxication and some minor drug offenses. The only reason this obscure crime had been indexed stemmed from the unusual tattoo Eddie Jones carried.

According to the report, his whole back was tattooed with one large mural, and the word "Wormwood" inked just above his waist.

"Sweet Jesus," Rob whispered.

"Do we have an address or phone on this guy?" Terry asked.

Frank scrolled down. "He gave an address off Elam Road in Dallas." Frank hit the print button and stood. He grabbed his jacket with one hand and the pages off the printer with the other. Rob swung around to his cubicle for his jacket just as Edna entered.

"Where you guys going?"

"Got a new lead and they're going to check it out," Terry replied, the relief evident on his face. Rob didn't have to ask. His boss wore the look of a man who had had one too many conversations with the mayor's office that morning.

"Great, but hold up a second," Edna said. "I was just informed that the Texas Rangers have been brought in on this. Their lieutenant will be over in an hour expecting a briefing. Once the state gets involved, you know how things are. We have the lead at this point. Don't want the Rangers snatching the rug out from under us." She pointed at Frank and Rob. "Beat feet on that lead. If you get anything, call me."

Rob glanced at Frank. Having the Rangers in the mix might complicate matters. Frank hated sharing investigations. The only sure way of minimizing the Rangers was to stay so far ahead of them that they could only follow. The clock was ticking.

By the time Rob pulled out on Lamar, Frank had looked up the address on his phone. They took 175 south, and the homes and buildings on either side of the highway took on a less well kept appearance. The Elam Road address turned out to be a rundown trailer park. Rob slowed and coasted down the line of mobile homes, looking for the right number. Old cars on blocks, with the tires removed, sat in every other drive.

Trash blew across the deeply gashed blacktop road. Stray mongrel dogs roamed the place. A few pit bulls and shepherds lay in the heat near the doors of several trailers, chained to railings or whatever else was heavy enough to hold them. None of the animals paid them any attention.

Number twelve was a blue, forty-foot double-wide that had seen better days. Faded, with pieces of duct tape stuck on the sides and on cracks across several windows, it listed to starboard. A satellite dish mounted on the front had a bird's nest in one corner.

Rob parked and Frank opened his door to a chorus of barking. Apparently this was the event the dogs waited for all day: someone new pulling up and opening the car door. A small black mutt ran from under the trailer and nipped at Frank's heels. He kicked at it, and the creature retreated back into the darkness of its lair.

"Looks like we've found the garden spot of Dallas," Frank said.

Rob kept his eyes open for other raiders as they ascended the rotten stairs. Frank knocked on the trailer door and sniffed. He made a face.

"Do you smell something?" Frank asked.

"Sewer connection probably needs adjustment."

Frank glanced over his shoulder, sweeping the entire park with his gaze. "This whole place smells like a septic tank, if you ask me."

Rob knew how much his partner hated foul-smelling places and people. Hell, he couldn't even stand to smell Rob after a workout, so this place had to be torture.

Frank knocked again, grimacing. The rumble of a TV blaring vibrated the trailer.

After the third knock, a female voice inside screamed, "Will someone frigging answer the door?"

Moments later the volume dropped, and the door eased open. A teenage girl leaned against the frame. She had dirty blonde hair and wore a black Lady Gaga T-shirt with a pair of skimpy red shorts.

Rob and Frank produced their identification. "Does Eddie Jones live here?" Frank asked.

She leaned forward, studied the IDs for a second, and then turned and hollered, "Mama, the police are here to arrest Eddie again."

"We don't want to arrest him, just talk," Rob said.

"Mama, come here." she shouted.

"Did you say police?" an older woman's voice called from a back room.

"Yeah," the girl shouted.

"Shit. What's he done now?"

"Y'all can come in, I guess." Skimpy red shorts opened the door and stepped aside.

If Rob had blinked, he would have missed it, but Frank's nose actually twitched as they ventured further into the living room. Rob couldn't blame him though. The combined smells of dirty diapers, a litter box in need of cleaning, and cooking odors mixed with the pall of low-hanging smoke from a cigarette still smoldering in an overflowing ashtray made Rob's stomach turn.

A skinny woman scooted around the corner carrying an infant on her hip. A half-smoked cigarette hung from her shriveled lips. She eyed the girl. "Come and get her. She's yours."

The girl lifted the baby from the woman's arms and strolled down a dark hall.

"Are you Mrs. Jones?" Rob asked.

The woman took a long drag and exhaled smoke through her nose. "Yeah. Which police are you?"

Rob and Frank both displayed their credentials. "Dallas," Frank replied.

"Figures," the woman said. "Have a seat."

There was no doubt in Rob's mind that the last thing Frank would do was sit on anything in that house. Dirty clothes and trash were everywhere. Children's toys, half broken, littered the room, and dirty plates with bits of what looked like old tacos lined the coffee table. Flies munched on the remains.

"No, thanks. We've been sitting all morning," Rob said.

"You after Eddie?" the woman asked.

Mrs. Jones looked as if her lower jaw had retreated into her neck. The weak chin, three to four missing teeth, and limp blonde hair sent chills through Rob. She probably wasn't over forty but looked sixty--plus. Some referred to people like this as white trash. A sad generational curse of ignorance and poor decision making. But Rob still took issue with the name.

"Yes, ma'am. Is he here?" Frank asked.

"Is he in trouble for anything?"

"No, ma'am, we just wanted to ask him a couple of questions."

She lit another cigarette from the butt of the one she was smoking, then snuffed the first one out, as well as the one smoldering in the ashtray. Rob was about to choke on the atmosphere. He tried breathing through his mouth, but that left a nasty taste. He moved to one side in an effort to escape the direct drift of the smoke, but it followed him.

She blew out a long breath. "He ain't here."

"Does he live here?" Frank asked.

"Hasn't in several years."

"Can you get in touch with him?"

"Don't have no phone—lives on the street, homeless."

Frank studied her for a second and jammed his hands in his pockets. "We still need to talk to him. Know where we can find him?"

"He's in the jungle somewhere."

Rob asked, "You mean under the overpasses downtown?"

She took a seat on the sofa and rested her scrawny frame against a cushion. A sneer spread over her weathered lips. "Only jungle in Dallas—ain't it?"

"It would help if we had a recent photo," Frank said.

She motioned to a ledge above the sofa. "Take your pick."

A line of pictures rested on the wobbly shelf. A baby photo was nestled next to a high school graduation photograph. Rob picked up a picture, which showed a young man in desert camo posing in front of a tent.

"Was Eddie a Marine?" Rob asked.

Mrs. Jones took a drag and exhaled before answering. "He had problems before he joined. After Iraq he was really fuc—screwed up. You sure he's not in any trouble?"

"No, ma'am," Frank said. "We only wanted to ask about a tattoo he has."

She perked up. "Oh, you mean that big one on his back?"

Frank stepped forward. "You know about it?"

"Not much, except that preacher man he lived with paid to have it done."

"Preacher man?" Frank asked.

The hairs on the back of Rob's neck rose. *Preacher man. Bible. Wormwood.*

Mrs. Jones crossed her legs and nodded. "Yeah, Eddie lived with him and his flock for a while."

"What was the preacher's name?" Frank asked.

She paused, looking at the floor. "Brother something or another. I can't recall."

"Where's the church?" Rob asked.

"Don't know, somewhere in South Dallas."

"You recall the denomination?" Frank asked.

"Naw, it wasn't a church like that. Don't have nothing to do with any regular church."

"Okay, thanks." Frank headed to the door.

"Hey, police."

They glanced over their shoulders.

"Tell him to call me . . . so I know he's still alive."

After they closed the trailer door, they pulled in a long breath of fresh air. Even the odor of sewage that permeated the trailer park was better than the stench in that place. Rob hit the key fob and the doors unlocked. The little black mutt charged Frank again. This signaled the rest of the park's kennel into a spasm of barks and howls. Frank kicked, getting closer this time, but still missed. Once safely inside the car, he looked at Rob.

"What kind of preacher pays for a full-back tattoo?"

Rob cranked the car and maneuvered onto the street. The case was alive again, that was for sure.

Frank checked his watch. "Let's swing through the jungle and see if he's around." Frank's eyes had that old sparkle. He was back on the scent.

12

Katrina finished lunch that Friday as Sister Judy and another woman cleaned up her room. The other woman was new. She was more of a girl than a woman—no way had she seen twenty yet. She resembled Katrina: same build, same light blonde hair. She hadn't spoken since coming in except to introduce herself. Said her name was Annabelle. Sister Judy kept a close eye on her while they worked, and Annabelle seldom looked up and never made eye contact.

Sister Judy strolled over and looked down at Katrina with a motherly countenance. "Would you like to move upstairs tomorrow?"

Katrina didn't answer for a moment, still suspicious.

"Brother John said since you are doing better, he'd like to have you join us for services tomorrow, and we can move you to an upstairs bedroom after dinner."

Behind Sister Judy, Annabelle's eyes widened. She shook her head.

Katrina got the hint. "No, thanks. I'm fine here."

Sister Judy pouted. "It's much nicer upstairs. Just ask Annabelle." Sister Judy posted her fists on her hips, waiting. She gawked at Annabelle while she leaned over the commode with a toilet brush in her hand. "Isn't it much nicer upstairs?" Sister Judy asked Annabelle.

A forced smile parted Annabelle's lips. "Yes, much nicer."

"See?" Sister Judy said. "We'll get you moved tomorrow afternoon. By the way, do you need any feminine hygiene products?"

Katrina looked up into the kindly eyes. "What kind?"

"Well, when's your next period? You'll need something then."

"Not for a while," Katrina answered.

Behind Sister Judy, Annabelle shook her head, and her frightened eyes sent a tingle up Katrina's spine. A sick doubt enveloped her.

"We'll make sure you have what you need when you need it, dear," Sister Judy said.

From upstairs there was a crash of metal on wood, and then a scream.

"Judy, help. I've scalded myself," a woman called. Loud crying, like someone in horrible pain, bled through the wooden ceiling and the door the two women had left open when they'd arrived. Sister Judy scrambled up the stairs and disappeared. Annabelle ran to Katrina, knelt, and grabbed her hands.

"You shouldn't have told her about your period," Annabelle said. She kept her gaze on the stairs.

"What . . . what are you talking about? I don't understand."

Annabelle held her hands tighter. "He'll come for you tonight."

Katrina's gut tightened. "What are you talking about?"

From upstairs Sister Judy's voice rang out, "Ruth, come here. I need you. Karen's hurt. Bring the first aid kit."

Katrina broke loose from Annabelle's grip. "What do you mean? Who'll come for me?"

Annabelle kept her head turned toward the stairs and whispered, "When he comes, and he will, the only way to stop him is to do something disgusting. He's a clean freak. They'll drug your supper so you won't resist him—don't eat it."

Footfalls from upstairs announced that a crowd had gathered. Steps sounded from the stairs, and Annabelle ran back to the toilet. She gathered her cleaning supplies and placed them in the basket as Sister Judy reached the bottom of the steps. Her eyes narrowed as she looked at Annabelle and Katrina.

"We're finished here, Annabelle. Come help out upstairs. We have a mess to clean up."

Annabelle kept her head low and eyes down as she left.

Sister Judy picked up the tray of lunch dishes, smiled her gentle smile, and followed. The sound of the door shutting and the lock being set sent Katrina into uncontrolled weeping. She hugged herself, rocking from side to side, and shook, staring at the cold concrete floor. Tears streamed down her face, but she fought making any sound that might tell them Annabelle had done more than clean her room.

*   *   *

The jungle was that area of Dallas where I-30 and I-45 met and the downtown freeway overpasses provided acres of coverage from the elements. Its proximity to Deep Ellum, a neighborhood of arts and entertainment venues, had always made it a popular place for the homeless. They could walk a few blocks and panhandle or, if they were lucky, catch some scraps from one of the many restaurants. The city had gone to great lengths to fence off the area under the overpasses, but the homeless always found a way back in. It was just too sweet a deal.

Rob parked the car on Dawson Street, and they walked toward the massive highway complex. Few people milled around this time of day, but the population would increase as the evening progressed. You could smell the jungle as you neared it. As the weather heated up, it only got worst. Frank's nose twitched a little more with each step. Places like this always creeped Rob out. There were basically two types of homeless: those who avoided the police and those who wanted to fight the police. Lots of mental illness, alcohol, and drug use. The guy who wouldn't give you a second look today might be the same guy who would jump you tomorrow. You just never knew.

"Excuse me, sir." Frank motioned to an old man with a shopping cart. "We're looking for someone. Perhaps you can tell us if you've seen him."

The old man ran a hand through cotton hair and leaned on the handle of his cart, which was piled high with black plastic garbage bags. "I'll try. You police?"

"That's right," Frank said. "Know anyone named Eddie? Young white fellow, about six feet, weighs around one ninety."

"Naw, sir, don't ring no bell. You say his name's Eddie?"

"Yeah," Rob answered.

The old man lowered his gaze and shook his head. "I knows a fella called Ed, but he's not near one ninety."

"Is he here?" Frank asked.

"Naw, but Pete might know where he stays."

"Who's Pete?" Rob asked.

The old man pointed. "He's the mayor here. Knows everyone. That fella in the black overcoat against the concrete pillar."

Rob considered the figure sitting on the ground in the distance, an old brown fedora pulled low over his eyes, his chin resting on his chest during the afternoon siesta. Frank led the way under the overpass. The rhythmic sound of traffic passing overhead and cool shade made a comfortable setting for a nap.

They walked in a sea of trash. Crushed cardboard boxes for sleeping and hundreds of wrappers, cans, bottles, and dirty clothes littered the ground. The odor of rot drifted through the breeze. Several jungle residents scurried away as the pair approached. If they'd had a big neon sign flashing "Cops," they couldn't have been more obvious.

They made their way through a narrow passage between a stretch of ragged tents and blue tarps and a couple of burned-out fifty-five-gallon drums, finally stopping in front of the man with the fedora.

"Mr. Mayor, we need to talk." Frank nudged the bottom of the man's work boot with the toe of his shoe.

The black man pushed up his hat with an index finger and eyed them. He appeared to be in his midforties and had short, well-kept hair and a thin mustache. "You police?"

"Yes," Rob said.

The man stood and brushed the dust off his pants. "I'm Pete." He didn't offer to shake hands. "We have a problem?"

"Nope," Frank said, "but we're looking for someone. Hoped you'd help us find him."

"Who?"

"Eddie Jones. Young white guy, about six feet, weighs one ninety or so." Frank flashed a photograph of Jones.

Pete's surveyed the photo with suspicious eyes. He removed his hat and wiped his headband with a handkerchief. "What's he done?"

"Nothing. We don't want to arrest him—only talk," Frank said.

Pete leaned against the concrete pillar. "About what?"

"We have a message from his mama, who lives off Elam Road," Rob answered.

"What's the message?"

"We'll tell him when we see him," Frank said.

Pete smirked. "We have a guy named Ed who hangs around sometimes, but he's not one ninety. Looks a little like that picture. He'll probably be here this evening."

"Thanks," Frank said.

More people drifted down Dawson toward the shade of the overpasses as Rob and Frank strolled to their car. Few of the folks made eye contact with them, at most giving only furtive glances.

* * *

They parked in the employee garage and Frank led the way into the CIU area. Terry stood near Rob's cubicle, reading a folder. He looked up when they entered.

"Well, have the Rangers solved the case yet?" Frank asked, sitting on the edge of his desk. If the expression on Terry's face was any indication, something good had happened.

"We furnished the Rangers all the information we have," Terry replied, closing the folder and tucking it under his arm. "You two are hot stuff with the chief."

"What?" Rob asked.

"He said he couldn't think of anyone else he'd rather have on the case."

Frank grinned. "In other words, the chief doesn't want the Rangers pissing in DPD's sandbox?"

"Pretty much, yeah," Terry replied.

Edna stuck her head out of her office. "Anything?"

Rob said, "Not yet. Interviewed the guy's mother, but he doesn't live there. Stays in the jungle."

Her brow rose. "He's homeless?"

"Looks like it. We checked, but he wasn't there. Going to try again in a couple of hours."

"Stay on it," she said, and ducked into her office again.

Terry motioned them to his office and closed the door. "Edna's holding on to the case for us," Terry said, "but as soon as the Rangers get up to speed and throw manpower at it, they'll start pulling ahead." He looked at Frank. "If you want to keep it, don't let them catch you.

"I understand," Frank said.

Terry cracked his familiar grin. "Okay, get to work."

On the way back to their cubes, Rob said, "What say we have an early dinner and then wait for Eddie for as long as it takes?"

"I thought Friday was date night for you and Carmen," Frank said. Those two hadn't skipped date night in years.

Rob was in his cubicle shuffling through a stack of folders. He glanced at Frank. "She left town today to see her parents in San Antonio. Be gone several days."

Frank searched his partner's face for any hint of trouble, hoping Carmen hadn't gone into a bout of depression. But Rob was busy rifling through papers on the edge of his desk, his expression neutral. The Marine in Rob refused to convey emotion, so God knows what was going on at home. Damn aggravating.

"Fine," Frank said, "but I want Chinese tonight."

"Okay, flip you for who picks it up." Rob reached into his pocket and pulled out a coin.

"Hold on. Is that the dammed lucky Kennedy half dollar?" Frank asked.

Rob showed a hurt face.

"Well, is it?"

Rob shrugged and opened his palm. The Kennedy fifty-cent piece rested there.

Frank eased into his chair. "Sneaky dog. I won't bet if you're using that thing."

Frank dug a quarter from his pocket. "Here, use this one."

Rob flipped it. "Call it in the air."

"Tails," Frank said.

Rob caught the coin and slapped in on the back of his hand. It was tails.

"Finally," Frank sighed.

Terry watched this time-honored tradition with a smirk.

Frank leaned back into his chair. "I'll have the usual, and a giant cup of hot green tea."

"Got it." Rob swung toward the door. "Be back before five."

Frank assumed his favorite slouch position, propping his feet on the desk, and beamed. "I finally won a flip."

Terry shook his head and turned to leave. "No, you didn't. He stole your quarter."

13

Within the next few minutes, the work area emptied as officers slipped out one by one, offering excuses for leaving early on a Friday afternoon. Terry even left to stop by Missing Persons and talk to the sergeant handling the case up there. As the noise level dropped, Frank found it easier to concentrate on the report update he typed. When he wasn't in deep thought, he loved the background noise of the squad area. But now, as he did a mental organization of the facts, he just enjoyed the silence.

Several minutes later, he felt the presence of a malevolent being. He looked up into the weasel eyes of Big Mike.

"Hey, asshole," Mike said.

"What do you want?"

Mike's brow furrowed. "I want you to stay away from my business."

"What are you talking about?"

"You know what I'm talking about." Mike's voice rose.

Frank stood. "Get out of here."

Mike grabbed the top of the cubicle between them with his giant paws. "Or you'll do what?"

"What's going on here?" Edna asked, staring from around the corner of her office.

Both their heads snapped in her direction. Frank had forgotten she was still there.

"Nothing. We were just discussing a case," Frank said.

Her forehead tightened. "Yes, I overheard part of your discussion." She advanced on Mike like a shark. "So, you have so little work that you have time to traipse down here and threaten my people?"

Mike's eyes widened. "No, Lieutenant."

Edna closed the distance. "That's what it sounded like to me. Are you saying that my hearing's defective?"

Mike retreated several steps. He looked as if he might wet himself. "No, ma'am."

Edna pointed at Mike. "I sent Frank and Rob to your area at the direction of the chief's office. Perhaps I should give Lieutenant Holmes a call and tell him about all your extra time. Bet he could find work for you. Whatcha think?"

Mike stumbled while retreating faster. "That won't be necessary, ma'am." He spun toward the door and left.

Edna turned her gaze on Frank. "Any other problems with him—let me know."

"Thanks, Edna."

She shot him a glance. "That's Lieutenant Crawford to you." She stalked toward her office.

"Thanks, Lieutenant Crawford."

She didn't reply or turn around but held up her thumb and index finger in the okay sign as she passed through her door. Edna would never admit it, but she loved busting the balls of jerks like Big Mike. Frank liked having her on his team.

Frank pulled his attention back to the report. If Eddie had some worthwhile information, they might have something concrete to start working for a change.

At five o'clock, Rob wandered into CIU with two plastic bags. He'd gotten Frank a whole quart of hot green tea and spicy shredded pork with lo mein noodles. Rob set out the feast and they dug in. He forked a piece of General Tso's chicken. "You really think she's still alive? Been missing a long time," Rob said.

Frank shoved a rogue noodle in his mouth with the chopsticks and considered the question. "It's *has* been a long time, but that could play both ways." He looked up. "Yeah, I think she's alive."

They ate in silence until Edna strolled from her office, flipping off the light on the way out. "Well, it just officially hit the news wire—Dallas mayor's daughter kidnapped. Now the sixth floor's gearing up to catch hell, and so should we. Oh, that smells good."

Frank held up his plate. "Want some? We have plenty."

She meandered to his cubicle. With delicate fingers, she lifted a small piece of broccoli from the edge and popped it into her mouth. "Oh, that's so good. Get that from Bo's?"

"Yup," Frank said.

She got another piece, comfortable with him, as if they picked food off each other's plates all the time.

Frank caught Rob eyeing the two of them. He quickly looked away.

"I know what I'm having for dinner. I'm calling in an order on my way home." She headed for the door, but stopped short. "You guys get anything good tonight, shoot me a call. I don't care how late."

She was talking about both of them but looking at Frank.

"Yes, ma'am," Rob answered.

With her departure, the place went quiet. They finished eating and Frank swilled the hot tea with pleasure, finishing the whole quart. "You know what?" Frank asked.

Rob sipped the last of the cola. "What?"

"You made a good point."

In an uncertain tone, Rob said, "I did? About what?"

Frank dabbed his lips with a paper napkin and said, "When I worked Missing Persons, we didn't refer to the missing people by anything but their names. We've been calling Katrina 'the girl' all this time. We should start referring to her as Katrina or at least Trina. What'd you think?"

Rob nodded. "This one matters more to you somehow, doesn't it?"

Frank didn't answer, his gaze fixed on the bottom of his glass.

"Okay," Rob finally said. "Let's call her Trina."

"Deal," Frank agreed. "It's a quarter to six. Think we should go."

"Yup." Rob stood, pulled out the Copenhagen can, and got a pinch. "Let's ride."

*　*　*

Rob parked closer to the overpass than he had earlier and they strolled toward the pillar where the mayor stayed. He wasn't there. The crowd had doubled from a couple of hours before. Many men, and a few haggard women, had found suitable areas to bed down for the night. All eyes followed Rob and Frank as they wandered through the mob looking for Eddie Jones. He wasn't there either. Someone had built a small fire in one of the fifty-five-gallon drums and was roasting some meat. Smoke drifted through the compound, and several denizens craned their necks to catch the aroma.

Frank shoved his hands in his pockets and swiveled his head. "He's not around. What do you think?"

Rob checked his watch. "A few minutes after six. Let's wait at the hole in the fence. He's got to go through there if he's coming."

Frank followed Rob to the street, and they stood to one side of the fence, checking each person. A small crowd gathered about fifty yards up the street as people who were heading for the entrance stopped and just milled around, whispering.

"You're disrupting traffic flow," a voice said from behind.

They spun around to find Mayor Pete, still wearing the overcoat and fedora. He motioned toward the crowd. "They're afraid to come in because of you—think you might hurt them."

"Why would they think that?" Rob asked.

Pete eased closer. "Because you're different. Homeless don't like different." Pete pulled off his hat and waved. "Y'all come on. They ain't going to hurt y'all."

The crowd whispered among themselves a moment and cautiously made their way to the hole in the fence. Pete kept waving his hat, directing them in. Most dropped their heads as they passed, but a few gawked at Frank and Rob as if they were watching a strange species of animal in a zoo.

Rob felt self-conscious under all the scrutiny and a flush crept up his face. Frank didn't seem to like the attention either. He crossed his arms and directed his gaze at the grimy freeway above them.

Pete motioned toward the underpass. "Come on. We'll wait for Ed in my office."

The pillar where Pete slept was still unoccupied. "Rank has its privileges. Don't nobody sleep here but me." Pete dropped down beside the pillar and pulled a soiled white paper bag from his overcoat pocket. He opened it and yanked out a baked chicken leg. Looking up, he said, "I'd offer you some, but it's all I have."

"We've eaten," Frank said.

Pete tried a bite. "Is this Eddie or Ed guy you looking for a veteran?"

"Yeah," Rob replied.

Pete spit out the corner of his mouth. "Thought so."

"Same guy you know?" Frank asked.

"Probably." Pete scanned the street and pointed. "Is that him?"

Rob and Frank swung around. The scrawny stick of a man had just stepped into the shade of the overpass. He wore jeans and a dirty desert camo field jacket, his blue wool stocking cap pulled low on his brow.

"What do you think?" Rob asked Frank.

Frank studied the guy a moment. "Kind of looks like the photo."

Pete nibbled another bite. "That's the guy we call Ed. Don't know if it's the one you're looking for."

Rob shifted his gaze to Pete. "Thanks."

Pete gave them one more suspicious glance. "You sure you ain't going to arrest him?"

Frank shook his head. "Only a few questions—promise."

They followed Eddie as he stumbled deeper into the shadows of the overpass. The man was unsure on his feet, as if he might take a tumble any second. He found a place far away from the rest and collapsed to the soft dirt, mumbling to himself and then laughing. He didn't seem to notice Frank and Rob's approach. He tugged a bottle from his field jacket, twisted off the cap, and finished it in one gulp.

"Are you Eddie Jones?" Frank asked.

The emaciated figure, with dirty blond hair spilling from the sides of his wool cap, looked up and smirked. "No, Edward Thomas Jones."

"That'll do," Rob said. "Okay to talk to you for a minute?"

The hollow-eyed creature chortled. "I don't seem to have my daily schedule on me right now, but I could probably spare a minute." His lips formed into a crooked smile. His teeth were heavily stained, and one in front was missing. The guy had that beaten-down look common in the homeless or drug-addicted.

Frank produced his identification. "We're with the Dallas Police. Need to ask you some questions." Frank's nose twitched. The guy hadn't bathed in a while.

Eddie's expression never changed. "Okay." He reached in his jacket pocket and Rob lunged, grabbing his hands.

"We don't like people reaching for things while we're talking to them—makes us nervous," Rob said, holding the hands in a strong grip and staring into Eddie's eyes.

Eddie relaxed and grinned. "Don't blame you. When we used to bust a door in Iraq and couldn't see the people's hands, it made us nervous too."

Rob patted him down. "He's clean."

"Okay to get a smoke?" Eddie held up his hands in surrender.

"Go ahead," Frank said.

Eddie fumbled again and produced a bright yellow Zippo lighter and half a cigarette. He lit it and inhaled deeply. "So what you want to ask me?"

Frank squatted down so that he was at Eddie's eye level. "Do you have a tattoo?"

Eddie coughed out a lungful of smoke and laughed so loud people shot him glances in surprise. "You came all the way out here to ask me that?" He slapped his leg and continued laughing. He coughed up a wad of phlegm and spat it on the ground. "And people call me crazy." The guy surveyed Rob and Frank and must have realized they were serious, because he stopped smiling. His gaze narrowed. "You real cops?"

"Yup," Frank said. "You have a tattoo?"

Eddie wiped his nose with his sleeve and stroked his filthy blond beard. "Yeah, got a couple." He took another long drag from the cigarette.

"Where?"

"Got this one right here." He pulled up the jacket and shirt sleeve, revealing a Marine eagle, globe, and anchor tattoo on his left forearm.

"And the other one?"

He gaped at Frank a second. "On my back," he whispered.

"Mind showing us?"

All humor left Eddie's countenance. He swallowed and studied them. "I don't show that to folks."

"Why?" Rob asked.

Eddie pulled his coat tighter. "'Cause, it's private."

"Then tell us how you came to get it." Rob knelt beside Eddie. "Your mama told us you were a Marine." Rob pulled up his jacket sleeve and displayed his own tattoo—identical to Eddie's. "*Semper fi*, brother."

Eddie's broad smile returned. "You in Iraq?"

"Yeah, but in 1991, Desert Storm. Fourth Marine Expeditionary Brigade."

Eddie pulled another drag from his ragged cigarette. "That's a good unit, brother."

Rob lowered his sleeve. "One of the best."

After one final puff, Eddie threw the butt aside. "So what do you need to know about my other tattoo?"

Rob clasped his fingers together and rocked forward. "Just where and why you got it."

Frank remained silent. Rob knew he wouldn't say a word, because a rapport had been established.

Tears formed in Eddie's eyes and he dropped his head. He sniffed. "I've screwed up my life." Eddie wiped his eyes with dirty palms. "Is my mama okay?"

"She's fine. Says for you to call her."

Eddie looked up at the dark underside of the overpass and shook his head. "When I was in high school, I used to get screwed up on alcohol. When I went into the Marines, I'd get screwed up on drugs. And when I got out, I got screwed up on religion." He laughed a shallow laugh and wiped his eyes again. He sat straighter and stared at Rob. "No, that's not fair. The religion was the best thing ever happened to me. I was just too stupid to know it, that's all." He dropped his head, and his shoulders shook as he wept.

Rob had seen this before, in others who had come back from the war. Some men had lost a limb; others had lost something more essential, as Eddie had. But Rob didn't have time to play counselor. "What about the tattoo?" he asked.

Eddie drew in a long sniff and spat. "After the Corps, I knew I was in trouble. Went looking for help. The VA didn't do much, so I turned to God. Found a pastor preaching the True Word and decided to follow him. Moved in with him and the rest of the congregation. Sleeping was tight, but we all worked. Some in the home; others, like me, on the outside. Pooled our money and lived a happy life for a couple of years.

"Brother John held nightly services, and I felt myself turning around. He didn't even allow alcohol or drugs in the place. Hell, he wouldn't even let us have tea or coffee. Only herb tea was allowed." Eddie chuckled. "Always hated herb tea." He coughed and drew another deep breath. "But I dried out. I sure as hell did. Best thing that ever happened to me."

Rob exchanged glances with Frank. Rob reached over and laid a gentle hand on Eddie's knee. "So what happened? Why are you here?"

Eddie cranked up another bout of crying. After a few seconds, he whispered, "I sinned, and threw it all away. The devil tempted me. Too weak to resist him. Always been too weak."

"What happened?" Frank whispered.

Eddie looked up at Frank. "Brother John trusted me, and I let him down. Said he wanted me to be one of his disciples." Eddie shifted his stare to Rob. "You see, God came to Brother John in a vision. After that day, he was no longer just Brother John. He was Brother John—the Prophet."

Out of the corner of Rob's eye, he caught Frank's grimace.

Eddie didn't seem to notice, lost in the story. "God told him to go forth and choose six disciples from earthly sinners. These six would be ordained and marked by Brother John. They would assist him until he was called by the Father to heaven. Then he would return to earth, after the third angel sounded."

Rob rested one hand in the other and placed his chin on them. "Not sure I understand."

Eddie's eyes brightened. "Don't you see? Brother John would be called back to the Father—to God."

"Yeah, I got that part," Rob said, "but—"

Frank spoke, quoting scripture from memory. "'And the third angel sounded, and there fell a great star from heaven, burning as it were a lamp, and it fell upon the third part of the rivers, and upon the fountains of waters. And the name of the star is called Wormwood.'"

Eddie leaned away from Frank and his mouth gaped. "Did Brother John send you guys?"

"No," Frank said.

"But you know about Wormwood. How?"

"Revelation 8, verses 10 and 11. It's in the Bible."

Eddie lowered his head and whimpered. "I let the devil tempt me away from that great man. I'll go to hell because of it." A sob escaped his lips.

"Were you ordained and marked as a disciple?" Rob asked.

Eddie sniffed again, wiped his nose on his sleeve, and nodded, but didn't speak.

Frank leaned closer. "Was the tattoo on your back the mark?"

Tears flooded Eddie's eyes. "Yes," he whispered.

"Can we see it?" Frank asked.

Eddie thought for a second and then removed the jacket. He pulled the shirt over his head, spun around, and lay on the clothes, exposing his full back. Rob snatched out his Maglite and shined it on him, feeling a tug of pity at the sight of Eddie's body, which looked like a skeleton with skin stretched over it. The man didn't move as Rob scrolled the beam across his back.

The tattoo could have been a scene out of a sci-fi movie. The artist had created a night sky filled with stars, and a large, red, glowing sphere hung above a settlement with some kind of vapor or gas radiating down. Under the picture, in three-inch letters, was the word "Wormwood."

"Good God," Rob muttered.

Frank pulled out his cell camera and snapped a shot of the mural. "Thanks, Eddie."

Eddie sat up and tugged his shirt down, his face calm now, as if his anger and grief had slipped back into its hole.

"What does the tattoo mean?" Rob asked.

Eddie eased his jacket back over his shoulders. "The mark of the Prophet."

"But what does it signify?" Frank asked, crouching down to look Eddie in the eye and resting his forearms on his knees.

Eddie shifted and raked his long hair into place. "That red planet is Wormwood poisoning the earth's water."

"Tell us a little about Brother John," Frank said.

Eddie leaned forward. "He's God's messenger on earth. Sent to spread the warning to all that'll listen of Christ's return. You know, during our nightly meetings, he could quote the Bible? We'd play a game sometimes. We'd give him a phrase, and he'd tell us what scripture it came from. Or we'd just give him a scripture, and he'd quote it to us verbatim." Eddie looked up in the darkness. "He could take a verse and talk for hours about what it meant."

"So where is he now?"

Eddie lowered his head. "The house we rented burned one night. Everyone got out, but we scattered for a while until he could find another place. That's when I drifted back into the devil's temptations. By the time they found another house, I was too far gone. They wrote me off."

Frank patted Eddie's knee. "I'm curious. Does each of the six disciples have the same tattoo?"

Eddie wiped his eyes. "Yeah, and so does Brother John—the Prophet."

"Where was the house?" Rob asked.

"Corner of Camp Wisdom and Houston School Road, but there's nothing left now."

"Where did they relocate?" Frank asked.

Eddie shrugged. "Don't know. When they found out I'd gone astray, they disowned me. I never saw the other place."

"Where did you guys get the tattoos?" Frank asked.

Eddie sniffed and wiped his nose. "Head shop in South Dallas."

"Think they'd know where the others are?" Rob asked.

"Not likely," Eddie said. "Besides, shop's out of business."

"How many people occupied the old house, and what were their real names?" Frank asked.

Eddie raised his head in thought. "Never knew anything but first names. Let's see, there was Brother John, and Brothers Luther, Marshal, Turner, Lee, and Evan."

"Where are they now?" Frank asked.

"Don't know where any of them are anymore." Eddie doodled his fingers in the dirt, not making eye contact.

"Were there any women?" Rob asked.

"Yeah, Sisters Ruth, Judy, and Karen."

Rob jotted down the names in a pocket notebook. "Any way of finding Brother John or the rest?"

Eddie shook his head. "I heard they'd left Dallas, but don't know where."

"Okay, Eddie. I think that's all for now." Frank stood.

Rob dug for his wallet. He plucked out a twenty and handed it to Eddie. "Here, brother. Take this and get a meal and a bus ticket to the VA. This rough life on the street isn't working for you anymore." He stood and dropped his notebook back into his pocket.

Eddie looked up, said, "*Semper fi*," and slipped the money into his jacket.

"Just one last clarification before we go," Frank said.

Eddie shifted his gaze to him.

"Brother John *is* Wormwood. Right?"

Eddie gaped at Frank as if he were the dumbest person on earth. "Of course."

On the way to the car, Rob whispered, "I can't believe he believes in all that. He has real problems."

Frank kept his voice low. "Eddie isn't the problem."

Rob edged closer. "What do you mean?"

"The problem is, there's a nutcase out there acting on what he thinks is God's word."

14

More people straggled into the jungle, keeping a wary eye on the pair as they worked their way to the hole in the fence. The melody from a harmonica floated in the breeze as they passed a group of men and a woman sitting on collapsed cardboard boxes. Laughter erupted from another bunch behind them. Although sunset wasn't for another hour, long shadows fell on the street from nearby buildings. A low rumble of thunder and clouds boiling in from the north carried the smell of rain.

Frank eased into the seat. A grimace crossed his face.

"What's wrong?"

"I have to piss like a baby racehorse."

Rob chuckled. That was Frank's favorite line when he needed to go. "Too much green tea?"

Frank settled himself in the passenger seat and fastened his seatbelt, shaking his head at Rob. "Don't be silly. You can never have too much green tea. Let's stop at Nellie's. We haven't seen her in months."

Rob pulled out on the street, drove past the miserable collection of people assembling for the night, and hooked a right onto Cesar Chavez Boulevard. Nellie's sat down the block on the right. The hole-in-the-wall convenience store was run by an elderly Chinese woman Frank had developed as an informant years earlier. Nellie knew everyone and everyone knew her. Information circulating around the neighborhood always found its way to Nellie.

As they strolled in, she scolded them. "Where have you two been?"

The harder she tried to appear mean, the funnier she looked. She stood less than five feet and had a tangled mop of thinning gray hair. The glasses perched on her nose wobbled with each word. No other store in Dallas had so many things in such a small space. The narrow aisles were over-flowing with anything you could imagine to snack on. Rob sniffed—tacos.

"Hey, Nellie," Frank said. "Is the bathroom still in the same place?"

She scowled. "Never come to see me unless you want something. Sure, help yourself." She pointed to the rear of the store.

"Hi, Nellie. Where's your son?" Rob asked. "Thought he worked the evening shift?"

She waved away the question. "Late class today. Be in soon. Hey, I got some more of those big bags of spicy jerky you like. Haven't had time to unpack them. They're in the storeroom before you get to the john."

"You're the best. I'll check them out," Rob said, and followed Frank through the back storeroom door. Rob located the case of jerky as Frank opened the restroom door.

Rob sorted through the box and found the best-looking package just before Frank left the tiny bathroom and squeezed into the tight hall.

Rob looked up. "Wow, looks like you weigh five pounds less."

Frank had his mouth open, probably for a sharp comeback, when a scream sounded from out front. They pulled their guns, and Rob peeked out the storeroom door.

A young Hispanic man with a shaved head, jeans, and white T-shirt shouted at Nellie, waving a pistol in her face. "Empty it." He motioned toward the register with the gun.

Rob pointed to himself and then straight ahead. He signaled for Frank to circle left. Frank sucked in a deep breath, and they silently slipped from the storeroom. Rob stayed close to the racks of merchandise, keeping his head low. By outflanking the guy, he and Frank stood the best chance of taking him by surprise.

"Hurry, you old bitch." the man yelled, pointing the pistol closer to Nellie's head.

As he closed the distance, Rob studied the tattoo on the guy's neck. The number thirteen—Mexikanemi street gang, one of the worst. Rob raised his pistol, trying to bring the guy into his sights, but he didn't have the angle. Any shot might also hit Nellie. Rob waited for Frank to get into position. He'd have a better angle. What was taking so long? Rob glimpsed over the rack of chips, and Frank stood there like a statue. Gun out, arms extended, pointed at the hijacker. He had the perfect shot. *Why wasn't he taking it?*

Nellie dropped the cash on the counter and the gang member grabbed her by the hair. He twisted it, and she howled with pain. "Where's the safe?" he asked.

"No safe," she sobbed. "Please don't hurt me."

Rob kept his weapon trained on the gangster, waiting for Frank, but he never fired. Frank had a look that disturbed him. It didn't seem normal.

"Give me the rest, or I'll kill you, now."

A hollowness invaded Rob's stomach. *Frank is out of it.* Whatever was going to get done, he'd have to do alone. *Shit.*

At that moment, Nellie shifted her stare to Rob. The wild kid noticed her gaze and jerked his head around. His eyes widened, but instead of dropping his gun, he turned it toward Rob.

"Nellie, get down." Rob yelled, and fired twice.

Both rounds hit the guy's upper chest. He fell back and released his grip on Nellie before sliding down the counter to the floor. His eyes remained open, and he still held the gun. Rob dropped to a kneeling position and tightened his finger on the trigger, ready for a third shot if necessary. When the kid's eyes closed and his grip on the pistol released, Rob exhaled. Nellie screamed and ran for the register, pushing a button. A high-pitched alarm wailed inside the tiny store.

Rob stood and advanced with his weapon trained on the guy. The smell of burnt powder hung in the air as he kicked the pistol from the man's hand. Rob's ears still rang from the shots. Two crimson stains on the man's shirt merged and pooled on the floor. Rob looked for Frank. He stood where he'd last seen him—frozen. Gun extended, ready to fire—expressionless.

"Frank."

Frank acted as if he hadn't heard him, looking straight ahead. Not even blinking.

"Frank!"

Frank jerked his head to Rob.

"Help Nellie." Rob shouted over the alarm. He pulled his cell and dialed 911.

Frank ran to Nellie as Rob stepped outside to hear what the operator was saying. Two minutes later, the street looked like a police car show. Red and blue lights whirled in the gentle rain. The ambulance collected the suspect as patrol officers established a police line with yellow tape. Detectives from the Special Investigations Unit arrived, and CSU personnel showed up to ask questions, take photographs, and collect spent shell casings and weapons.

Rob's phone rang.

"You okay?" Terry asked.

Rob blew out a breath. "Yeah, we're both fine." He glanced at Frank, whose deadpan expression was hard to read.

"I just spoke to Edna," Terry said. "We'll meet you guys in Homicide when you get to the station."

"Thanks, Terry."

Gary Carson was the Homicide detective on the scene. Everyone knew him. Nice guy. Rob waived having an attorney present before giving a preliminary account of what had happened and surrendering his pistol to Gary for evidence.

Carson eyed the pair. "Don't discuss this, okay?"

Frank and Rob nodded.

"You guys wait outside. We'll give you a ride to the station in separate cars."

"Right," Rob said as he and Frank exited the store.

They stood under the eaves while rain splattered the tops of their shoes. Neither had spoken since reinforcements had arrived.

"You okay?" Rob whispered out of the corner of his mouth.

Frank nodded.

Rob wanted to talk but wasn't sure where to start. The most decorated officer in the Dallas Police Department had just frozen in the face of danger. Rob kept his voice low. "Look, I don't know what happened, but it'll be okay. We'll talk it out later. For now, I plan to tell Homicide I had a better angle than you and that's why you didn't shoot."

Frank didn't answer or look at him.

"Hey. You hear me?"

Frank nodded but remained silent. He kept his gaze on some point in the distance, as if he were watching the rain sweep the street clean.

Rob's stomach gurgled. This was going to be tougher than he'd thought. Frank had gone into silent mode. He often did this when he was in deep thought, blocking out the rest of the world to work through some kind of puzzle or problem. Was that what he was doing now? No use pushing it. He'd open up when he was ready.

Rob ran his palm over his head and eyed his partner, knowing neither of them had the luxury of waiting for him to be "ready." Frank had to settle this tonight.

An hour later, when they finished up in Homicide, Terry and Edna met them.

"You guys okay?" she asked.

"Yeah, no problem," Rob answered.

"You're looking at a week administrative—at least," Terry said, "but take as much time as you need."

Rob shrugged. "I'm okay, Terry. This isn't the first guy I've smoked. I shot one while working SWAT, and God knows how many in Iraq."

Edna's gaze was focused on Frank. "You should also take some time."

Frank gave her a half grin before his face fell back into a stoic mask.

Rob was issued another pistol and scheduled a time to give a formal statement the following Monday. As they strolled down the hall, Terry placed a hand on Rob's shoulder and said, "Do something to unwind. I'll call you."

"Thanks," Rob said.

Edna and Terry kept walking, but Rob touched Frank's arm. "We need to talk."

Frank's gaze darted from one end of the hall to the other. "Okay, but not here."

15

Ten minutes later, they meandered through the door of Sarge's. The crowd was light on this rainy evening, mostly couples whispering quiet words in each other's ears and sharing a drink. Rob knew Frank liked rainy evenings, especially at Sarge's. Sarge always worked late on Fridays, and he spotted them as they entered. He stepped from behind the bar and laid a hand on Rob' shoulder.

"You two okay? Word's already out about the shooting."

"Yeah," Rob said. "Just another day at the office."

"I have a booth open." Sarge grabbed Rob's arm and led him to the rear. Frank followed but didn't say a word.

"You guys have a seat," Sarge whispered. "Drinks are on the house. What'll you have?"

"Beer," Rob said.

"I'll have the house red," Frank mumbled, his gaze on the cardboard coaster near his hands.

"Coming right up." Sarge rushed toward the bar.

Rob laced his fingers together and scrutinized Frank. "Can we talk?"

Frank sighed and a grin swept across his lips. "If we have to."

"We have to," Rob said.

Sarge put a beer and glass of wine on the table. "You guys need anything else, just holler." He marched to the bar, welcoming a group of new arrivals.

Rob tasted his beer and eyed Frank. This dark rear booth was the most private, usually occupied by cops meeting girlfriends and/or hiding from their wives. More than one officer had ducked into the men's room at the sight of his better half hiking through the front door. Rob kept his gaze on Frank until he finally looked up.

"Talk to me, Frank," Rob said.

Frank's sipped the wine and appeared to gather his thoughts. He stared at his hands. "I'm not what I appear to be. I'm a fraud."

Rob leaned toward him. "What are you talking about?"

"After that incident in Vice, everyone believes I'm this cold-blooded, badass shooter, but I'm not. That wasn't me."

Rob shook his head. "Frank, you killed four people in less than ten seconds."

Frank fiddled with a paper napkin, finally meeting eyes with Rob. "What if I told you it was my evil twin."

"Then I'd say you have a badass evil twin."

Frank had never talked to Rob about the incident, but it was legend around the department. Rob had never asked, probably believing Frank would tell him someday when he was ready.

Frank ran his finger around the top of the wineglass for a moment before speaking. "I was working Vice one night and pulled an old queen out of a show when he poked his junk through a glory hole. He told me he had some good information if I'd cut him some slack on the charges. What he said had the ring of truth, so I called Sarge. He was my sergeant at the time, and we agreed the information was worth more than a stupid Vice charge."

Rob sat back in the booth. "What was the info?"

"A lot of johns in South Dallas were getting beaten and robbed by a gang of Crips operating a prostitution racket. The old queen said he knew all the players. Could put us right in the middle of them."

"So, what happened?"

"Because I turned the guy, I got to be the bait," Frank said. "We had Vice cars all over the place as cover. All I had to do was pick up a whore and allow her to direct me to the place her pals were waiting to jump me. The Vice officers would move in and bag the lot. Anyway, that's how it was supposed to go down."

"I take it things went sideways?" Rob whispered.

"Yeah." Frank grinned. "Real sideways."

"What happened?"

*　*　*

Frank had relived the event so many times in his mind he didn't really have to remember anything. It all flooded back into his memory as clear as yesterday. No matter how much he tried, he couldn't forget.

It had been a frigid February afternoon with a howling north wind, and heavy clouds hung over Dallas. A nasty light freezing rain had blanketed the city for hours. All the weather forecasters were predicting a hard freeze that night. Frank and the backup team had met with Sarge in a vacant parking lot off Grand Avenue. They stood shivering under the rusty, dilapidated overhang as Sarge went over the details.

"Frank," Sarge said, "you cruise Malcolm X between Oak and Hatcher. That's the operational area." Sarge turned to the other officers. "You guys position yourselves up and down the street so he's always in sight. I repeat—always in sight." Sarge ran his finger across a wilted paper street map on the soggy hood of the car. "If he picks up a whore, she might be one of the suspects we're looking for. She'll jump in and direct him to drive someplace to turn the trick." Sarge pointed at Frank. "Keep your eyes open for tails. These Crips won't let your truck get out of sight before they're right behind you. They might even be waiting where she takes you." He nodded to the other officers. "But we'll be right behind them." He wadded up the map. "Any questions?"

No one said a word. They were shaking too much to talk. They just wanted to get out of the wind and inside a warm car. Sarge blew on his hands and rubbed them.

"Okay, hit the street. I'll let you know when Frank starts his ride."

Everyone broke up, two to a car, and rolled out of the lot.

"Frank, come with me." Sarge motioned.

They sat in Sarge's car. He opened a green thermos, poured coffee into two Styrofoam cups, and handed one to Frank. Sarge blew the edge of the cup for a second and tried a sip.

"Damn, that's good." He inspected Frank. "You got everything?"

"Yeah, I think so," Frank said.

"We'll see you when you pick her up. Don't hurry to whatever place she's directing you. Give us a chance to get into position. Okay?"

"Okay." Frank tried his coffee.

Sarge studied him. "If anything feels bad—abort. Don't push it if it doesn't feel right. We can get them tomorrow, or the next day. Know what I mean?" Sarge nodded his head.

Frank really didn't understand what the big deal was. Sarge was acting strange today, and this wasn't even a high-risk operation. Frank had been in a lot worse situations with Sarge before but had never seen him this worked up. Something was different about this deal.

"I got this." Frank sipped his coffee.

After the fact, Sarge told him he'd known something was going to go haywire but couldn't put his finger on what. Sarge had the gift most supervisors dreamed of: a sixth sense. The thing about having a gift like that—you had to listen to it.

"Okay, watch the bitch's hands. If you can't see her hands, then your shit's about to get real flaky," Sarge said.

Frank finished his coffee and touched the door handle.

"Hold up." Sarge grabbed his arm, then keyed his police radio. "All units report."

All six cars confirmed they were in position and had an eyeball on the street.

Sarge patted Frank's shoulder. "Go get 'em, Tiger."

Frank climbed in his undercover pickup truck and switched the heater on high. His feet were freezing. The windshield fogged and he waited until the defroster cleared it. Everyone but him had left the lot. A nervous churn rumbled through his midsection, but he put it out of his mind.

He eased onto Grand and crossed under the I-45 and Central Expressway interchange. When he got to Malcolm X Boulevard, the light was green, so he turned left. He drove well below the speed limit in the right lane. The rain had almost stopped, but the wind blew hard from the north.

By the time he got to Oak, he'd not seen one pedestrian, much less a whore. He did a U-turn and started down the other side of Malcolm X. This had to be the biggest waste of time in his career. As that thought cleared his mind, he crossed Martin Luther King Boulevard and saw a girl standing at the favorite hooker stop on the street. Any gal out in this weather had to be starving, or have a pimp who'd threatened her with death. Or maybe—

She looked as if she were in her early twenties, but with all the clothes and hood, she might have been older.

Frank pulled to the curb and rolled down his window. She lowered her umbrella and her brown eyes sparkled. She was very young, just out of her teens.

"Need a lift?" Frank asked.

"Sure." She jumped into the seat beside him, and he pulled into traffic.

He asked, "You a working girl?"

She lowered her hood. Her mahogany skin glowed. "Sure am. Interested?"

"How much for a half and half?" Frank asked.

She shook her head. "If you want me to drop these jeans in this weather, it'll cost you a hundred."

"Lot of money for just a half and half."

She frowned. "I might do it for ninety, but no lower."

Frank glanced in his rear mirror. No sign of a vehicle following. If this was a Crip girl, they wouldn't let her get too far away. It didn't matter. He already had his prostitution case made. Once she'd agreed to perform a sex act for money and set the price, she'd crossed the line. He didn't see any of his guys following either, but if he saw them, they weren't covert enough.

"I can spend ninety if it's good," Frank said.

She reached over and caressed his crotch. "Mine's like honey." She nudged closer. Her hands circled his waist in a sweet embrace, but there was nothing sweet about it. She had experience and used the hug to make sure he wasn't armed. Frank had hid his pistol, badge, and radio under the seat before leaving the briefing site.

"You have a place we can go?" he asked.

"Uh-huh." She pointed. "Keep going straight. I'll tell you when to turn."

Frank searched his side mirror. If he was being followed, he didn't see them. They drove to Hatcher Street and she motioned left. As he made the turn, he still saw no one tailing them.

She waved her finger. "Turn right just past this school."

When he made the turn, a sign welcomed them to Butler Nelson Park. Dozens of old headstones on each side of the one-lane dirt road, now muddy from the steady rain, seemed a bad omen.

"We're going to do it in a cemetery?" he asked.

She laughed. "Why not? Nobody out on a day like this to disturb us. Drive all the way to the end."

Frank didn't see a soul in his rear or side mirrors. *Where is my cover?* This thing wasn't going as planned. Sarge had said if it felt wrong, abort. He had to make a decision soon—he was running out of road. Most of the trees were stripped clean of leaves, with a few live oaks and pines giving what little color there was to the drab place. The whole park was surrounded by a black wrought-iron fence. *Has a prison feel.* No other cars or people ventured into one of the oldest cemeteries in Dallas in weather like this. When Frank hit the dead end, she opened her purse and removed some tissues and a rubber.

She held it up. "You need this, or did you bring your own?" She slid out of her raincoat and unzipped her jeans.

"We'll use yours," he stammered.

It's time to end this. One last look through the rear mirror—nothing. *Okay—here goes.* While she eased off her jeans, he reached under the seat and grabbed his pistol and badge. This wasn't a Crip girl. She was just a common streetwalker.

She watched him retrieve the items without emotion. "What's this shit?" she asked.

"You're busted, babe. Put your jeans back on and your hands behind your back. Time for a ride downtown."

She pouted and shrugged. Most whores realized that what they did was a business, and in business, there were times things didn't go as

planned. Getting picked up by Vice every so often came with the terri-
tory. She struggled with the tight jeans, and Frank grabbed the hand-
held. What had happened to his backup? From the side mirror, the
reflection of a dark sedan speeding toward them caused him to relax.
His team had at last found him. As the car got closer, he noticed there
were three black guys in it. None of them looked familiar.

Crips!

The girl's head whirled to the rear and a grin crossed her lips. Her
salvation had arrived. Frank had to get out of the truck and find cover.
He opened the door, but she grabbed his arm.

"Where you going, cop?"

Frank's stomach flipped and fear crept in. He jerked his arm free
and reached for the door handle again as the car closed the distance.
She grabbed her purse and reached inside.

Oh, no. Didn't check the purse.

She drew out a knife, a small dagger-looking thing with an orange
handle. She lunged. He swatted it away, but she came from a different
angle and caught him between the ribs.

The sensation of being stabbed was one thing Frank had never
considered. Numb at first, then searing pain. He pushed away from
her and brought up the pistol. She shoved it down with her free hand
and lunged again with the knife. The dagger slid into his gut. He again
pushed her away and brought the pistol up, firing twice. One round hit
her in the lower throat, the second under the chin. Blood and brains
splattered against the passenger window and headliner. With the shots
still ringing in his ears and blood blooming on his shirt, Frank checked
the side mirror.

The car with the three Crips slid to a stop. They bailed out and drew
their guns. Frank couldn't stay in the truck, but getting out now was sui-
cide. If he was going to die, he'd do it on his terms. He'd take the bastards
with him. Weakness flooded Frank's limbs. A cold tingle raced through
his body. He was passing out. Shock, loss of blood—he didn't know.

He opened the door and swung himself to a standing position with
one hand braced on the roof of the truck. Shots rang out, but he didn't

feel the impact. The three Crips were clumped together no more than fifteen feet away when he fired. His vision faded with each shot, and by the time the pistol's slide locked back on an empty magazine, he had collapsed. His last conscious thought: *Now they'll just kill me.*

When Frank came to, he thought he heard the voice of an angel. He cracked open an eye. If this was heaven, the angels weren't all that attractive. In fact, they looked like Sarge.

"Assist the officer. Officer down—Nelson Park. I need an ambulance ASAP. Stay with me, Frank." Sarge pushed something hard against Frank's stomach with one hand and screamed into the radio with the other.

The pain hurt like hell. Frank tried shoving Sarge's hands away, but the more he tried, the harder Sarge pushed.

"Damn you, Frank, you're still on duty. You're not checking out until I say so and I don't say so." Sarge's voice was an octave higher, and his face had twisted into a worried grimace.

Frank just wanted the pain to stop—to just go to sleep. His eyelids drooped and a cold sensation invaded his legs and arms.

Big tears ran down Sarge's cheeks, and he screamed out an order. "By God, you're not going anywhere, boy. Keep those eyes open. Keep looking at me—stay awake."

Frank forced his eyelids up, but he only wanted to sleep. Sirens drew nearer, and he kept his gaze on Sarge. Other voices drifted in along with the fuzzy outline of several men. His face and neck tingled, and the last thing he saw was Sarge standing and talking to someone. Sarge's mouth moved, but no words came out. Strong hands grabbed Frank. He woke up in ICU with a nurse checking some tube above him. She had nice breasts.

Sarge came in the next day, after Frank had been moved to a private room. He told a bad luck/good luck story. The bad luck was that Frank's primary cover vehicle, the one with the eyeball, had been T-boned by another car as they went through an intersection. They'd lost the eyeball on Frank's truck after that and only figured out where he was after hearing the shots.

The good luck had to do with the accuracy of the Crips. They'd gotten off five shots and missed Frank every time. Frank had made some good luck of his own. He'd fired all thirteen rounds before passing out. Only three of his bullets missed. And the last good news—a fire department ambulance, on its way to the station, had responded to the officer-down dispatch. It had been only two blocks away when the call went out.

*　*　*

Frank finished his story and swallowed the rest of his wine, slouching in the booth and looked at Rob.

Rob let out a breath. He'd heard pieces of the story for years, but never the whole thing. "Shit, dude. You *are* a badass."

Frank shook his head. "Not really." He leaned back in the booth. They stared at each other for a moment.

"You guys about ready for a refill?" Sarge grabbed the glasses and headed for the bar.

"What do you mean, 'Not really'?" Rob asked. "You killed four people after being stabbed twice? In my book, that's badass."

"Yes, I did that, but it was all luck. It couldn't happen that way again in a million tries."

Rob leaned forward and put both palms on the table. "Frank, you're an idiot. Don't you see? Luck or no luck, you found yourself in a shit storm and got out of it alive."

Sarge slid a fresh wine to Frank and a beer to Rob before retreating to the bar.

Frank shook his head. "I'm just an analytical thinker who likes solving things. I have no interest in arresting people or getting into shit storms. I just enjoy the mental exercise of investigations."

Rob sipped his beer. "Perhaps you could transfer to K-9. You could become a dog whisperer."

Frank pursed his lips. "You know, I never really considered that. Great idea."

A grin swept across Rob's lips. "That still doesn't explain about tonight."

"Yeah, I know," Frank said.

"What happened?"

Frank eyed him. "After Nelson Park, I haven't been the same. It's true, I killed four people that day, but something inside me died as well. When I pointed my gun at that guy tonight, I froze."

Rob paused before asking. "Should you talk to the shrink? I have a mandatory appointment next week." He laughed. "We could go together. Walk in holding hands. That would freak Dr. Price out."

Frank stared into the depths of his wine glass and shook his head. "No, thanks. If this gets out, I'm through as a street detective. They'll put me behind a desk and let me rot."

Rob didn't want to ask the question, but he had to. "You think this is still the right career for you if you have this problem?"

Frank sampled the wine and thought about the question.

"Tell you what," Rob said. "We'll figure it out. I know you're an excellent shot. You can shoot better than me—and I'm damn good. We'll work up some scenarios where we'll plan what we'd do in different situations."

Frank studied him. "Like what, for instance?"

Rob thought for a second. "Okay, here's an example. If one of us ever gets taken hostage, it's the other's job to free him."

"How?" Frank asked.

Rob held his forefinger to his head, simulating a gun. "So let's say I'm the hostage. I say, 'Do what he says. I don't want to die.' The first time the nonhostage—in this case, that's you—hears those words, 'I don't want to die,' that puts you on notice that I'm going to make a break. The second time I say it, you get ready, and the third time I drop down and you take the shot."

"Sounds complicated. What's the chance of that working?" Frank asked.

"A lot better than doing nothing."

Frank lifted his glass and sipped the wine. "Rob?"

"Yeah."

"Don't ever get taken hostage."

"Well, isn't this a cute scene."

They looked up to find Big Mike towering above them. His tie was loose and a food stain streaked the front of his shirt. He held his balance by grabbing the top of Frank's seat. "All cozy with a booth for two," Mike hooted. "Heard you got into a little scrape earlier."

Rob's brow furrowed. This was not a good day to mess with either of them. "Beat it," Rob said, and motioned with his thumb.

Mike laughed. "Anyway, just wanted to say what a nice couple you were." He stumbled down the hall toward the men's room.

Rob finished his beer and pushed the glass aside, deciding to be blunt with his partner. "You have to work through this in your own way. Anything I can do, I'll help, but don't ignore it. It'll get you killed."

Frank finished his wine. "Thanks. Let's have one more and call it a night."

"I could do another round," Rob answered.

Big Mike strolled out of the men's room, and Frank called to him. "Hey, Mike."

Mike stopped and whirled around. "What do you want, asshole?"

Frank shifted in the booth to face him. "Is it true what they say?"

Mike's eyes pinched. "What do they say?" he slurred.

"That you carry a picture of your wife in the buff in your wallet?"

Rob groaned. He knew exactly where this was going.

Mike let loose a booming laugh. "No, asshole. I don't have a naked picture of my wife."

Frank casually reached into his jacket and pulled out an envelope. He thumbed through the contents a second before asking, "Would you like to buy one?"

There was about a three-second delay as Mike processed the information through his alcohol-soaked mind. Then he went bat-shit crazy.

Mike screamed and lunged at Frank, swinging a big fist at his head. Frank jerked his face out of the way in the nick of time, and the big paw ripped through the sheetrock beside the booth. Mike howled with pain. There was a two-by-four behind the drywall. Rob leaped and wrapped his arms around Mike from behind, but he couldn't hold him. Sarge joined the fray, cussing and dragging Mike toward the door with Rob still holding on. Frank never moved, watching the brawl with a disinterested expression.

Sarge yelled at Mike, "Have you lost your frigging mind? Get out of here. One-month suspension."

Mike cradled his injured hand and left as Sarge stormed toward Frank.

"What did you say to him?" Sarge demanded.

Frank allowed his jaw to drop and he placed his hand over his heart. "Who? Me? Nothing."

"Bullshit!" Sarge said. "You said something. I know you. You got inside his brain, didn't you?"

"I don't know what you're talking about." Frank sat back in the booth, resuming his usual slouch. "Besides, only you think that."

Sarge's face was scarlet, and he shook with rage. "What the hell does that mean?"

Frank brushed a few crumbs of drywall from his jacket. "Only you believe Mike has a brain."

A smirk flashed across Sarge's lips, the anger draining out of him.

Frank held up his empty glass. "Could we have a little service here?"

Sarge snatched up the glasses. "Coming right up, Detective Pierce." Sarge could do sarcasm better than anyone.

Rob reclaimed his seat and gawked at Frank. "You know Mike probably broke his hand, don't you?"

Frank picked at the crumbling drywall, pulling out loose pieces and lining them up on the table. "Yeah, that's a shame."

They laughed as Sarge returned with their refills. Sarge looked from one to the other and pointed at Rob.

"Frank has become a bad influence on you." Sarge eyed Frank. "And you're still a sneaky little bastard." Sarge wheeled around and headed to the bar.

Frank tested his new wine. "Wonder if this means the drinks are still on the house?"

16

Katrina had spent the afternoon in a near panic. Annabelle's warning still rang in her ears. *He'll come for you tonight. They'll drug your supper—don't eat it.* Who was *he*? During their conversation, Sister Judy spoke of only one male, Brother John. Could that be who Annabelle meant? And what did "come for you" mean? They had been talking about her period when Annabelle signaled her. That had to be it. Whoever *he* was would rape her tonight. What else could she mean? But if Sisters Judy and Ruth were in on it, then they condoned and lived with a sexual predator. That didn't make any sense. Not if they referred to the Bible as "the best book you'll ever read" and sang or hummed religious songs while working.

She put her face in her hands as she ran through the possibilities, concluding that this madhouse would fit perfectly into a Stephen King novel.

As evening approached, Katrina got hold of her senses and began making a plan. There were too many of them to resist. She'd have to use her brain and wit to beat them. Annabelle's words, *he's a clean freak*, came back to her. That gave her an idea.

But what if Annabelle was wrong? What if nothing she did could prevent the attack? If he didn't kill her, she might still escape. She examined the leather straps on the bed. Touching them made her skin crawl. Whose blood streaked the sides? The amount of courage needed to carry out the plan might be too much for her. Could she fool them into thinking she was drugged? Would they fall for it?

She let the leather strap slip from her fingers and took a deep breath. When you didn't have any other choice, the only choice left suddenly made perfect sense.

Sister Ruth brought down Katrina's supper a few hours later. A radiant smile encased her face. "And how do we feel this evening?"

Katrina had enjoyed acting in high school. She'd been in several plays her junior and senior year, and drama had always been her favorite. Tonight she would give her best performance.

Katrina stood, raking her hair over her shoulder. "I feel wonderful. I'm moving upstairs tomorrow." She watched for any sign from Sister Ruth that might give away what they had planned for her.

Sister Ruth sat the tray on the table. "Yes, I heard." Her relaxed expression confirmed her satisfaction. "It's very nice upstairs. We have a lovely bedroom all ready for you. Are you hungry?"

Katrina paused before answering. If Sister Ruth was in on it, she gave no sign. Everything seemed normal.

Katrina strolled to the table. "Starving."

"Good, then I'll let you get started."

Sister Ruth turned to leave but looked back. Her brow had pulled in. Katrina's heart fluttered. Had she accidentally given something away? Did Sister Ruth suspect—

"By the way, dear, do you say grace before eating?" Sister Ruth asked.

Katrina nodded but found it hard to speak. The old hag had just scared her half to death. Katrina finally found her voice. "Grace, oh, yes—every meal." *Why did she ask that question?* And why now?

Sister Ruth beamed. "That's good." She hiked up the stairs, and the sound of the basement door closing signaled Katrina to act.

She eyed the plate. What was safe? She picked up her fork and pushed the stewed squash around and lifted the mashed potatoes. She sniffed. Couldn't smell anything. The baked chicken looked delicious, but she didn't want to tempt fate. Katrina sniffed the bread. It smelled the same as always. Thinking logically, what would be the easiest or hardest things to spike? A drug could easily be dropped into a single serving of squash or potatoes. Not so easily baked into bread. She'd eat only the bread. But they knew the bread was her favorite. It could be a trick. She could outsmart herself if she wasn't careful. Katrina pushed the tray aside and carried the glass of water to the sink. She dumped it down the drain and washed it. Refilling it from the faucet, she drank several large glasses. She'd stay with the original idea.

After about fifteen or twenty minutes, Katrina raked the food in the toilet and flushed. Then she lay on the bed and waited. If she was right, they'd creep in to check on her in the next half hour.

Katrina didn't know how much time had passed when the sound of footsteps eased down the stairs. The creak of the second stair from the bottom told her to shut her eyes. Soft whispers from Sisters Ruth and Judy.

"She ate it all," Judy whispered.

"Good. Help me," Ruth replied.

Katrina kept her eyes closed but moaned when they removed her dress and shoes. Her stomach had butterflies the size of buzzards when they slipped off her panties. *Keep cool. If they figure out you are conscious—the game's up.* The bite of the leather straps fastening around her arms almost caused her to bolt, but she willed herself to remain still. When they spread her legs and attached the straps, Katrina shook with fear. She covered it by mumbling, "Cold. I'm so cold."

"Hand me that quilt," Sister Judy ordered.

Katrina cracked open one eye. The women spread the quilt over her nude body. Sister Judy smoothed it on the side.

"Leave that be. He's just going to pull it off anyway," Sister Ruth said.

Katrina's mouth went dry. That confirmed it. Everybody was in on the plan. They were all guilty. Sister Judy turned on the lamp in the corner, and the sounds of them easing up the stairs brought as much relief as anxiety. The overhead bulb switched off and Katrina waited. For what . . . she wasn't sure.

Several minutes passed without a sound. Katrina's mind filled with dread, but she forced the thoughts away. "They won't kill me . . . they won't kill me," she whispered over and over as a mantra. The sound of the basement door opening put an end to the chant. She froze, straining to hear the next sound. The footfalls were so soft she wondered if a small, barefoot child was walking down the stairs.

Whoever it was approached her bed. She kept her eyes closed, but her heart almost pounded out of her chest. She felt his presence without actually seeing him. He pulled off the quilt, and a soft hand caressed her breast. His touch made her skin crawl. The wet warmth of a mouth sucked her nipple and she held her breath, gritting her teeth. Fear overwhelmed her. She couldn't finish this—*it's too much*. She almost screamed. Just before she broke, the sucking stopped, and there was a noise in the corner by the lamp. She cracked her right eyelid enough to watch him. He faced the wall, removing a pair of jeans while balancing himself.

He wore no underwear. He had a swimmer's build, small muscles and good definition, and across his whole back was one large tattoo. A weird one, like a full moon rising. There were words inked below the mural, but she couldn't read them. Other than the tattoo, the brown shoulder-length hair defined him. He spun toward the bed. She shut her eye, but she'd seen enough. He had the long beard of a sixties rock star, but he looked to be in his midthirties. The small, almost delicate face had a strange expression. The eyes weren't right. They were crazy eyes. *Oh, my God.*

She prayed. If this didn't work, if she'd miscalculated, he might kill her. Someone with those eyes was capable of anything. The bed shifted as he crawled between her legs. She got ready. *Come on, cleanness freak. I have a surprise for you.* His soft hands ran up each leg and he kissed her stomach. His tongue drifted to her navel and lower. The soft brush of his hair tickled her inner thighs as his head rested between her legs. *Show time.*

Katrina released her overfilled bladder in a gush. A wild animal–like scream broke the silence, and the bed rocked as he fell to the floor gagging, spitting, and swearing. She wanted to laugh but continued playing possum. If she moved, or presented him with any reason to believe she'd done it on purpose, he might harm her. He must be able to hear her heart pounding. It was so loud even she could hear it. Water ran, and she cracked an eyelid. He had his face in the sink and was splashing and rinsing his mouth.

Hope you enjoyed your golden shower, asshole.

When the water turned off, she closed her eye. The next couple of minutes were the scariest of her life. What would he do? Did he even know, or was he still deciding? The initial warmth of the urine soon turned to a cold chill. She shook but tried to remain absolutely motionless. Could he tell?

The sound of the squeaky bottom stair served notice. He'd had all he wanted from her tonight. She tried relaxing, but the shaking continued. When would he return?

17

Frank didn't sleep well. Rob's words kept interrupting his rest.

You think this is still the right career for you?

Frank rolled over and stared at the Saturday sunrise. If this wasn't the right career, what was? He knew guys who'd quit or retired and went to work for insurance companies or banks. Some became private detectives, but that held little interest for Frank. The higher the stakes, the more interesting the investigation. He couldn't handle mundane financial crimes cases.

Frank got up and did his morning yoga poses in the living room and then sipped coffee on the balcony. The sounds of early Saturday morning in the city drifted up to greet him. The breeze whipped an ivy that hung from the ceiling on the patio. Frank pulled his robe tighter.

He hated drama. Last night Rob could have been killed. He could have gotten both of them killed. But he loved the work too much to quit.

Frank turned his attention from the patio view to the photo of Trina that lay on the end table. He stared at it a long time, finishing the coffee and thinking about the case. The visit with Eddie had left him wanting more, but without any additional leads, what could he do? Restlessness enveloped him. He got bored too easily. If he didn't have a big case to keep his active mind occupied, he fell into a funk. If the case stalled, like now, he fell into a funk. When he thought too much about the past and all he'd lost, he fell into a funk. Sometimes having a hot beauty

127

over for an evening of expensive wine, a gourmet meal, and wild sex did the trick. Sometimes it didn't. He needed to get out and do something—anything.

There was shopping for dinner tonight, but he wanted a question answered first. He made an omelet and ate breakfast. After a shower, he got in his city car and headed for south Dallas County. When he got to the intersection of Camp Wisdom and Houston School Road, he pulled into a bus stop parking area and studied the intersection. He opened the car door and strolled toward the light, hoping for a sign. He wasn't sure what. Traffic buzzed through the light, the yellow signal only encouraging them to speed up.

He ambled back to his car. An older man walking a terrier wandered to the bus stop sign, and the dog sniffed the metal post. Gray stubble outlined the guy's cheeks and chin.

"Live around here?" Frank asked.

"Over twenty years," the man said.

Frank leaned on the car. "Was there an old house around here that burned a few years ago?"

The fellow said, "Sure was." He pointed to Frank's left. "Just across the street."

Frank scanned the empty lot. Weeds and road trash littered the area. "Nothing left, huh?" Frank asked.

The dog hiked his leg on the post.

The man nodded. "Burnt up pretty good—old, pier-and-beam, two-story."

"Know the folks who lived there?" Frank asked.

"Are you with an insurance company?"

Frank dug out his identification. "Nope, police."

The man jerked his dog away from the post. "That's enough, Cedrick, the cops are watching." The guy looked at Frank and frowned. "The folks that lived there were weird."

"Like how? What did they do?"

"They just looked strange. Had strange ways. Long hair, long beards—redneck looking."

"Anybody around here know them—know how I could get in touch with them?" Frank asked.

The old man shook his head. "Kept to themselves. Like I said, weird ducks."

Frank wasn't going to get any specifics from this guy. He either didn't know or wasn't saying. "Okay, thanks." Frank got in his car and made a U-turn across the road. He craned his neck as he drove past the weed-covered lot, checked his GPS, and copied the address and location into his notebook. He'd contact the tax office Monday morning and get information on the owner. Whoever this Brother John character was, he wasn't going to be easily found.

Frank swung by Central Market on Lovers Lane for lunch and shopped for dinner. He drove home, poured a glass of red, and again dropped into his favorite chair on the balcony. He dug out the photo of Trina and eyed it. Frank knew something nobody else knew, and he couldn't tell a soul, except maybe Rob and Terry. *She was still alive.* He'd felt it from the moment he'd set foot in her apartment—*alive*. He mentally retraced every step in the investigation, refilling his glass several times, and made notes on the pad he kept by the chair.

The mandatory administrative leave after the shooting kept Rob off the investigation for the next week, so Frank would be on his own. He made a list of questions, and beside them, another list of where he might find the answers. As usual, the questions list was longer. At about four o'clock, he called it a day and tossed the empty bottle in the recycle bin. He showered, dressed, and donned his chef's apron. Jen would expect dinner on time. And, with a body like hers, she wasn't someone he wanted to keep waiting.

* * *

Rob lounged in his patio chair and admired the excellent job he'd done. He brushed loose grass from his shoes and dabbed the bead of sweat tracing a line down his neck. Mowing his yard in the cool April afternoon wasn't bad. August was another thing altogether.

He missed Carmen. They were seldom apart, and even after calling her this morning, he still longed for her. He downed half his beer. The sun dropped a little more each minute. He didn't want to spend the night with the TV. Frank had a date; besides, they never saw each other socially. If only Frank would get married. Then they could get together as couples. But that guy would never get married. After he'd brought that girl to dinner, Carmen had put foot her foot down. No more evenings with Frank and his bimbos. A rather harsh commentary on Frank's taste in women, but probably a fair one.

Rob put it all out of his mind, dragged himself from the chair, and swept the sidewalk and patio before showering. He'd eaten a late lunch and wasn't especially hungry, but he could stand another beer. He hated drinking alone, so he decided to go to a fun, familiar place—his own personal bar. He'd go to Sarge's.

* * *

Frank uncorked another bottle of red and decanted it before Jen arrived. He opened the balcony door. A cool, sweet breeze filtered in, and he stood there a while looking at the lights in the distance. God, he loved this loft. It was high enough that most street noise didn't disturb him, but he could catch a breeze most nights.

His navel-gazing was interrupted by a delicate knock at the door. When he answered it, Jen held up two more bottles of red. Her mischievous grin told him what she had in mind.

Jen was one of those girls who always liked things her way. Last time she'd visited, they had dined, drunk several bottles of wine on his balcony, and made love in the patio hammock with the lights out. Frank didn't like making love in the hammock. Trying a few of his favorite positions in that thing could get a guy killed. But Jen enjoyed adventure and had some special positions of her own. Doing anything that could result in a broken neck somehow appealed to her.

She leaned in and planted a deep, wet kiss on his lips. As she wrapped both arms around his neck, the bottles clanged. "I've waited all week for that," she said.

No doubt about it. Her motor was revved up and ready to go. She always beat him off the line.

"Don't torque me up too fast, girl. I still have dinner to finish."

She beamed. "Great. I'll help." She slid around him, heading for the kitchen.

This wasn't going to work. Frank had no illusions about her cooking abilities. She had a knockout body, the face of an angel, and the cooking talent of a cavewoman. Her attempt at making breakfast last time had resulted in all the smoke detectors going off. He decided a distraction was the best course of action.

"Hey," he said, "how about I finish dinner. You find some music for us. I didn't have time. Classic rock or jazz would be great."

She set the bottles on the island. "Good idea," she said, and whirled toward the entertainment center.

Less than an hour later, the night had closed in, and they dined on his bar. He liked Jen because she wasn't interested in long-lasting relationships. She was a party girl out for a little fun. Their conversation never got bogged down on heavy subjects. She knew he was police and enjoyed the fact that she had, at last, laid one.

As he poured them a little more vino from the decanter, Jen smiled at him, giving him that glassy-eyed look a bottle of wine produces. Frank also had a good buzz going and looked forward to her positions. She licked some sauce off her lips and ran her bare foot up his leg. Just then, his home phone rang. *That thing never rings.* People always used his cell to contact him—except his mom.

"Hello," Frank said.

"Mr. Pierce, this is Bob at the desk."

Frank peeked at Jen. She sipped wine and unbuttoned the top button on her silk blouse. "Yeah, what can I do for you?" Frank asked.

Bob cleared his throat and whispered, "The police are here. They want to come up."

Frank shifted the phone to his other ear and faced the opposite direction. "The police?"

"Yes, sir. The Dallas Police."

About a dozen thoughts rushed through Frank's head—everything from one of his parents suddenly dying to Jen being wanted for some reason. He paused too long before answering.

"Mr. Pierce, what do I do?" Bob asked.

Frank swallowed. "Send them up."

He disconnected and sprinted to Jen's purse. Dumping the contents on the sofa, he quickly sorted through the items. He wasn't sure what he was looking for, but he didn't want any misunderstandings when the officers came in.

Jen giggled. "What are you doing?"

Frank stared at her. "You carrying anything illegal?"

She crinkled her eyebrows. "Illegal? What you mean?"

Frank pushed the pile of items around, searching for anything that didn't look right. "No drugs of any kind?"

She let loose an intoxicated laugh, hiccupped, and put her hand over her lips. "Well, excuse me. You told me you didn't take drugs, Frank. Why do you want some now?" she slurred.

He exhaled and kept sorting. "I don't. I just wanted to make sure you're not holding anything."

She laughed and sipped her wine. "What difference does it make?"

The knock on the door interrupted them.

Frank's head snapped toward it. "Because that's the police."

She hiccupped again. "No shit?"

After satisfying himself that nothing incriminating hid in her stuff, Frank answered the door.

A young uniformed officer stood on the other side. "Are you Detective Frank Pierce?"

Frank's teeth itched with dread. No good could come of this. "Yes, I'm Detective Pierce."

The officer shuffled back a couple of steps. "Didn't realize any police lived here."

Frank couldn't tell if it was an accusation or a statement of surprise. "Well, I live here."

From down the hall a familiar garbled voice said, "That's what I frigging told them."

Frank leaned out, and sitting on the floor in the hall was Rob. A second uniformed officer stood nearby and had Rob propped against the wall. Rob's shirttail was half out, and he listed to starboard a few degrees. When he saw Frank, he waved.

The expression on Rob's face was nothing short of goofy. Rob said, "They told me no police could afford this place." He laughed. Then his eyes pinched and he pointed at Frank, wiggling his finger. "I told them, by God, my partner lives there. By God, that's what I told them."

Frank grimaced and leaned in near the uniform at the door who wore a smirk. "He's drunk as Cooter Brown," Frank whispered.

The officer shrugged. "Yeah, dispatcher sent us to Sarge's to give an overserved officer a lift home. When we got there, Sarge told us to bring him here."

Frank glanced back at Jen a second. She had undone another button on her blouse. "This isn't his home," Frank said.

The officer nodded. "I know, but he lives in Mesquite. We're already out of our district being uptown. We can't take him there. Too far."

Frank peeked around the corner again and eyed Rob, who had listed further to starboard. Carmen wasn't in town. Rob had killed a man last night. He was his best friend and partner.

"Of course, bring him in." Frank said, swinging the door open.

As the uniforms half carried, half dragged Rob through the apartment, their eyes stayed on Jen. She sat on the barstool sipping her wine, her short skirt drawing a few lustful glances. And the low-cut silk blouse with the top two buttons undone, barely containing the no-bra monster breasts, didn't help. Apparently she so enjoyed their reaction that she swung the barstool their way and uncrossed her legs. They almost dropped poor Rob. She giggled, hiccupped, and slurred another "Excuse me" as they passed.

"Bring him in here," Frank said, opening the door to the guest room. He pulled back the covers and fluffed a pillow.

Rob's eyes were closed, and he was singing under his breath—a country and western song about a love gone bad. The officers laid him on the bed, and Frank escorted them out. The younger one cut his eyes toward Jen. After Frank shut the door, laughter sounded from the hall.

"Who's the drunk guy?" Jen asked, pouring another glass.

"A friend of mine." Frank marched into the bedroom and examined Rob, who was lying fully clothed on the bed. He couldn't leave him like this. He slipped off Rob's boots, shirt, and pants and spread a light blanket over him. "Sleep it off, my friend."

Frank lightly closed the door to the guest bedroom and strolled toward the living room. All the lights were turned off. Just the ambient glow of the city showed through the wall of windows. When he rounded the corner, the outline of Jen's nude body leaned against the balcony rail. Frank paused. *Um, guess the Foster flambé will have to wait.* Dessert was on the patio.

* * *

Rob had no idea what time it was. The only thing he knew was that he had to take a leak. His head ached, and a deep throbbing behind his eyes reminded him of what he'd done the evening before. He'd made it to Frank's—he recalled that. The rest of the night was a blank.

Rob dropped his legs over the bed's edge and tried standing. A little wobbly, but nothing he couldn't manage. He felt around the dark door for the handle and swung it open. The hall lights were off, which was disorienting. Which way was the john? Smoke . . . he smelled smoke. He sniffed again. No, not exactly—candles. *What the hell?* He staggered down the hall toward the scent. At the end of the corridor, a shaft of light folded around the door.

Rob steadied himself on the wall and crept forward. A low moan floated into the hall. He froze. *Sounds like Frank.* Rob peeked through the crack and caught his breath. A dozen candles lit the room. Frank lay nude on his back. A naked woman's face rested between his legs, her black hair cascading around his stomach and hips. Rob reminded himself he needed air and drew in a slow breath. She raised her head, still holding Frank's manhood with one hand. She was gorgeous—about twenty-five, maybe a little younger. She raked the other hand through her hair.

Rob gaped. *My God, the rumors are true—Frank's hung like a bull moose.* That thing could cripple a woman. Rob's hand drifted to his shorts. He was hung like a hamster compared to Frank. The woman rose to her knees and positioned herself over Frank, easing down to a seated position. A short squeal of delight escaped her lips as he entered her. She arched her back and braced herself with her hands on Frank's shins. The hard breathing and moaning was more than Rob could stand. His desire to pee had been replaced by another. A feeling of guilt swept over him. What the hell was he doing? Spying on his friend with a hot woman? Shame and disgust flooded Rob's conscience. He pulled his eyes from the door, hesitated for a second, and had one last look before heading to the john.

Rob had a lot of trouble getting back to sleep. The vision from Frank's bedroom had been seared into his mind. Several hours later, he rolled over and sunlight slipped around the edges of the blinds. He yawned and ran a hand down his face. Had he dreamed what had happened last night? Had he seen what he thought he'd seen? Rob had no recollection of there being a woman when he'd been carried in. Had there been a woman? His mouth had that too-much-beer taste. He smacked a couple of times—thirsty. Rob sat up and pain shot across his temples. Swearing he'd never drink again, he got out of bed and gazed into the mirror on the door. Disheveled hair, boxers, and a V-neck T-shirt. *Nope, not a good look.*

Rob cracked open the door and listened. No one stirred. He slipped down the hall toward the kitchen. The aroma of fresh coffee hurried his pace. As a moan drifted from the living room, he froze and plastered himself against the wall. Rob took a slow glance around the corner. Bright sunlight flooded the living room, and Frank was doing one of his yoga stretches. With his heels together, he bent from the waist and, making a triangle with his thumbs and index fingers, rested his palms on the floor. Frank slowly rose and, keeping his hands in the same position, leaned backward as he released another moan.

Rob scratched his head and kept watching. He had definitely dreamed the lovemaking thing. There was no woman in sight.

A throat clearing from behind caused Rob's heart to flutter as he turned around. And there she was, the girl from the dream. The thong panties and see-through top left nothing to the imagination. He opened his mouth but couldn't speak.

She grinned and peeked around the corner where Frank held center stage. "He's really something, isn't he?"

Rob tried keeping his eyes on her face. "Oh, yeah. He's something."

She held up a mug. "Going to get a refill. Want a cup?"

"Sure do."

She whispered, "Frank hates being disturbed until he finishes his routine—takes about half an hour." She winked. "I'll sneak us a couple."

So much ran through Rob's mind that he couldn't think straight. She tiptoed into the kitchen without making a sound, her little bubble butt wiggling with each step. How many happily married police officers did he know who would consider leaving their families for a woman like that? He was still in his underwear, so he slipped back into the bedroom. When she traipsed down the hall, he stuck his head out and accepted the coffee.

"Thanks, I really needed this," Rob whispered.

She grinned. "You tied one on last night."

He sipped the coffee. "Yeah, well . . . you know."

She touched his nose with her finger and formed her lips into a kissing face. "I know, sweetie. Have to get a shower. See you later."

She sashayed down the hall. After a few minutes, Rob went for a coffee refill. Frank wasn't doing yoga anymore, so Rob didn't worry about making noise. On the balcony, Frank sat staring at the sunrise. Rob paced to the door and knocked.

Frank motioned him out. He wore a short beige robe over the gym shorts. Frank pointed to a chair. "Join me."

Rob grabbed a seat. "About last night. I—"

Frank waved his hand. "No apologies necessary. I can't believe Sarge let you get so drunk."

Rob lowered his eyes. "Well, Sarge wasn't there. His son-in-law and daughter ran the place last night. Sarge dropped by and found me three sheets to the wind."

A grin cracked Frank's lips. "And knowing Sarge, he found a safe place to store your truck."

Rob's head snapped up. "My truck. I forgot about that."

"No problem. We'll have breakfast and find it."

From the corner of his eye, Rob watched the young woman stroll through the living room to the kitchen. She wore a short brown skirt and tight low-cut blouse. *My God, she's beautiful.*

Frank must have noticed him staring and said, "Understand you met Jen this morning?"

Rob sighed. "Where do you find women like that?"

Frank finished off his coffee. "You wouldn't believe me if I told you."

"Oh, yeah? Try me."

Frank grinned a few seconds before setting his cup on an end table. "Okay, she's a high-end call girl."

Rob laughed. "Yeah, right."

Frank kept a straight face. "Knew you wouldn't believe me."

Rob's laugh died away and he studied Frank. "You're not serious?"

"Very serious." Frank lounged in the chair and propped his feet on a stool.

Rob looked toward the woman in the kitchen. "Why are you paying for what you can get for free? There are more women in Dallas than a single guy can handle."

Frank yawned and said, "I don't want a long-term commitment. Besides I don't pay women like Jen."

"You mean there are others?"

Frank shrugged. "I only date high-end call girls."

"When you say you don't pay them, what exactly does that mean?"

Frank chuckled. "Remember the other day I told you women like to be fussed over? That I fix them dinner and give them a massage?"

Rob leaned closer. "Yeah."

"Well, high-end call girls are women too. Everyone likes to be thought of as special—have someone fuss over them. Treat them like a regular person."

Rob opened his mouth but thought better of it. Frank had drifted into his perverse logic again. There was no use arguing with him. "When you say high-end . . . how high?"

Frank pursed his lips and stared at the horizon. "She won't show up for less than a grand. She'll stay the night for five."

Rob shifted a little closer. "Do you see any conflict of interest here?"

"No. I don't work Vice anymore, and I don't pay her. Where's the conflict?" Frank asked.

Rob shook his head; perverse logic was a hard thing to argue against.

Jen eased the patio door open and slinked over to Frank. Squatting by his chair, she ran her fingers through his hair, pushing it off his forehead. "I have to go, baby. Got a flight to Vegas in a couple of hours. Have to work tonight."

He leaned in her direction and she softly kissed him. "Okay, give me a call when you're back in town," Frank said.

Jen giggled. "Always do." She winked at Rob on her way out.

Rob clasped his hands together. "Just one last question."

"Shoot." Frank stood and grabbed his empty cup.

Rob also rose. "How many Jens are there?"

Frank opened the balcony door. "Not that many. Ten or twelve."

18

The last thirty-six hours for Katrina had been nerve-racking. After she soiled the Freak, they left her naked and bound to the urine-soaked bed until the next morning. When Sisters Judy and Ruth appeared, they had changed. The once-sweet pair were now surly and rude. They released Katrina without a word and left a tray with breakfast on the table. Katrina also didn't speak. Those two were as bad as anybody there. *Why continue the charade?*

Katrina showered and checked the breakfast. Same stuff as the day before. Was it drugged? She flushed it down the toilet. She'd been thinking half the night about her next move, and now she had a new plan. When they came to clean the room, she approached Sister Judy.

"I just started—could use some tampons," she said in an apologetic voice.

Sister Judy cut her eyes to Sister Ruth. She nodded but appeared disinterested. "I'll see about it."

By lunch, Katrina was starving. All the nervous fear had subsided during the night and morning. She hadn't been molested, and the Freak hadn't shown back up. But after missing two meals, she looked forward to whatever they served. She had to eat sooner or later, drugs or no drugs. She'd planted the idea that perhaps she wasn't as *clean* as before. That might hold off the Freak for a few days. Anyway, she expected her period soon. She scarfed down the lunch and waited. If she began feeling drowsy, she'd been outmaneuvered. After about twenty minutes, the only thing she felt was hungry again. By the evening meal, she believed she might be safe from attack. She ate the baked fish and green peas without fear. Later that evening, Sister Ruth came down.

"You're being moved upstairs tomorrow," she said before taking the tray away.

Katrina slept well that night, but the thought of what awaited her upstairs filled her with dread. One thing was for sure: if she ever expected to escape, it would have to be from someplace other than this hole.

When Sister Judy brought breakfast the next morning, she had an attitude. "What you did the other night was sacrilege."

Katrina quickly realized the trap. If she admitted to pissing in the guy's face, she'd also be admitting to doing it on purpose. She had no idea what the hell Sister Judy meant about sacrilege, but this was a setup. Katrina scowled and pointed at her.

"What are you talking about? Why did I wake up strapped down naked in a bed someone pissed in? Did you put drugs in my food?" Her rapid-fire questions had the desired effect.

Sister Judy's jaw went slack. "I have no idea what you mean." She backed away toward the staircase.

"I think you do," Katrina screamed, advancing on her. "Tell those sickos upstairs to go screw themselves."

Sister Judy's face twisted and her mouth gaped. She stumbled as she retreated. "You're being moved today. Get your things together," she stammered before rushing up the steps.

Katrina felt a hundred percent better. She hadn't intended to go ballistic, but the pent-up stress had needed a release. She might be a prisoner and they might control her body, but she'd control her mind. She must at least appear to stay strong. But why had they taken her? Did anyone realize she'd not made it home Sunday night? Had an Amber Alert or something already been issued? What she wouldn't give to be sitting in that big house in Dallas right now and listening to her mom and dad complain about the latest thing she'd done that had pissed them off. But she wasn't there—she was here. These fools that had grabbed her had just made the biggest mistake of their lives. Before she was through with these wackos, she'd make "The Ransom of Red Chief" look like a picnic.

19

After breakfast, Rob made a couple of calls and discovered his truck was in the police employee parking lot, keys under the passenger floor mat. Frank gave him a lift there.

After pulling up beside the truck, Frank killed the engine. Rob gazed around, his head still throbbing from last night's bad behavior. It was a weekend, so the headquarters parking lot was deserted.

Frank sat back in the seat. "I cruised the area Eddie told us about—the place the house used to be."

"Oh, yeah. Find anything?" Rob asked.

Frank shrugged. "Nope. Nothing left. Need to check the property and tax records."

"Give Brandy a call at the tax office. Tell her I said hi." Rob grinned. "I think she has the hots for me."

"Okay."

Rob stared out the window for a moment before asking, "Is this Wormwood thing a real clue, or just a red herring?"

Frank grimaced, scratching the back of his head. "Don't know. What do you think?"

"It's the only connection to Trina's disappearance we have."

"Yup."

Rob exhaled, changing the subject. "Say, about Friday night . . ."

"Yeah, I've been thinking about that too," Frank said.

Rob shifted in the seat so that he faced his partner. "When I made detective, I knew it would be the pinnacle of my working career." He chuckled. "As a high school graduate with a few years in the Marines, a detective job was about the best I could hope for. But you—you haven't reached your potential yet. You're smarter than the rest of us. Everyone knows you're the brain and I'm the muscle of this team. With your background and an IQ off the charts, you could be the head of security for any Fortune 500 company."

Frank didn't answer.

Rob continued. "I know you like the part of police work that solves things. But it's the other part—the violent part—that I'm concerned about. If you can't pull the trigger anymore, that's a problem."

Frank looked up. "Does that mean I can't even be a K-9 dog whisperer?"

Frank was dodging the issue. Rob shook his head and opened the car door. "Hey."

Frank glanced his way.

"Sorry again about last night," Rob said. "Didn't mean to wreck your party."

"No problem." Frank replied. "Anytime you need a place to crash, come on by."

* * *

When the basement door creaked open, Katrina jumped. No one entered at first. She waited and forced herself to remain calm. The tension hung like a dark cloud over her. What was about to happen? A move upstairs, or another visit from the Freak? As the seconds ticked by and no one came down, her worry turned to curiosity. Katrina eased to the staircase and looked up. No one there. Just an open door. *A test?*

She wandered back to her bed and sat on the edge for another minute. Finally, the sound of heavy footfalls came from the stairs—a man. She tensed as the stranger stepped from the last stair. *Not the Freak.* Medium-height guy with a full beard and jeans, the sleeves of his green cotton shirt rolled to his forearms. He didn't have crazy eyes like the Freak, but he was probably one of the ones who'd kidnapped her. She stood and stepped a few paces away. Would he attack her? Had a ransom been paid? Was she being released?

In an almost apologetic tone, he asked, "Your name is Katrina?" His long brown hair flowed past his neck, and the cap accorded him a bumpkin look.

"Yes," she said. "What's yours?"

He grinned. "Brother Luther."

"Is everyone around here a Brother or Sister something?"

Brother Luther's shy manner was disarming. He grinned and glanced at the floor. "Yeah, I guess we are."

Good, she had the upper hand. Now, all she had to do was keep it.

"We'll be eating dinner soon. You'll join us," Brother Luther said in a soft voice.

"A little early for dinner, isn't it?"

Brother Luther crinkled his brow. "We always eat dinner at noon."

Okay, so the noon meal was dinner. Yeah, country bumpkin.

"Follow me." Brother Luther turned and strolled up the stairs.

A rush of anxiety filled Katrina. She had hated this basement for days, but now the thought of leaving terrified her. Like walking from light into a dark scary room. What would happen if she refused? What was waiting above? She didn't want to go, but the longer she stayed in this hole, the slimmer her chances for escape. She threw back her shoulders and lifted her head. Choking down her fear, she took the first step. She couldn't allow him, or the rest, to know she was frightened.

Katrina looked up at the open door as Brother Luther neared the top of the stairs. He waved his hand.

"You coming?" he asked.

The aroma of baking bread drifted in through the door. Katrina followed it. At the top was a kitchen that looked like something from the eighties. Gas stove, white refrigerator, and large sink and dry rack. Sisters Ruth and Judy were busying themselves at the counters preparing the meal while another woman stirred a pot. She had long brown hair and wore an ankle-length dress like the others, although she looked younger than the rest. Her frown wasn't welcoming. Steam rose from the pot as she stirred.

"That's Sister Karen," Brother Luther said, pointing at the woman.

The young woman didn't speak. Her full concentration was on the pot she tended. It smelled like soup. The bandage on the woman's left ankle told Katrina she was probably the one who had had the accident with the scalding water a few days before.

Katrina followed Brother Luther past the women into a short hall. Beyond it was a decent-sized dining room with high ceilings and dark wood floors, its walls covered with floral wallpaper. The cut-glass chandelier surprised Katrina with an elegance she hadn't expected, and a large window to the left overlooked a parklike setting. A manicured lawn stretched out for at least an acre, finally ending at the wood line, and someone had planted petunias around the tall oaks and pines in the backyard. Brightly colored azaleas punctuated the landscape. Katrina stepped closer and brushed the window with her fingers.

"It's beautiful," she whispered.

"You'll sit here." Brother Luther stood behind a formal wooden chair at the end of the long table, his hands resting on top of the chair. He had dirty fingernails.

Katrina slid into her chair and waited. The lengthy mahogany table had room for ten, but only eight places were set. A ringing, like a church bell, sounded outside. A few minutes later, footsteps and voices drifted down the hall from the kitchen. Katrina's stomach knotted. Her anxiety grew as the voices neared. Sisters Ruth, Judy, and Karen placed pots and plates of food on the table. The two men who filed in next could have been brothers. Full beards, long brown hair, dressed in work clothes. They smelled like fish. Probably the others who'd taken her. Last came the girl she'd met yesterday, Annabelle. She kept her gaze down and didn't acknowledge Katrina.

"Catch anything?" Sister Karen asked.

One of the men grunted. "Couple of blues and about a half dozen channels."

Sister Karen smiled. "Enough for a good supper and then some."

Everyone stood at his or her place, hands on top of the chair.

Annabelle's eyes bore in on Katrina until she took the hint. She stood and pushed her chair under the table, placing her hands on it like everyone else. No one spoke for several seconds. Light footsteps sounded from the living room hall and all heads turned. When he rounded the corner, Katrina's legs went weak.

The Freak stood at the head of the table. Katrina's chair was at the opposite end. His eyes met hers, and a tingle crept up her back. The Freak looked at Brother Luther.

"Would you bless the food?"

Katrina jumped as everyone joined hands and Brother Luther grabbed hers. She tried relaxing as his rough, callused paw held tight. Her heart skipped, feeling his jagged fingernails, like those of the man lying beside her when she'd first been taken. The one who'd rubbed her breast and probed below her panties. As if he read her thoughts, a quick grin crossed his lips as his head bowed and his eyes closed.

Brother Luther spoke: "Heavenly Father, make us thankful for these and all other blessings. Keep us safe from the Evil One's temptations, and deliver us unto the light. We ask this and for your blessings and guidance for Brother John. Amen."

Katrina had bowed her head but didn't close her eyes. The Freak at the other end of the table didn't close his either. They stayed fixed on her. She had heard the old saying "blood ran cold" many times but never known what it felt like until that moment.

After the blessing, they filled their plates with green salad. One of the women served a chicken barley soup with dumplings, and everyone ate in silence. Katrina had no appetite but went through the motions. One man ate faster than the others. Katrina didn't know his name—he was one of the brothers—but he gobbled down his food and stood.

"I'll see about the children."

The children? Katrina hadn't seen or heard the small voices and baby cries this morning. *Where are they?*

"Thank you, Brother Lee," Sister Judy said.

Annabelle had an anxious expression as the man left. What was going on? Brother Lee disappeared down the hall, and moments later footsteps stomped up the stairs. Katrina had the impression everybody was watching her, even though no one but the Freak stared her way. A nervous rumble in her stomach made it difficult to eat. She picked at her food, stalling for time. As each of them finished, he or she left without a word, until only she and Annabelle remained. They didn't speak.

Annabelle stood. "We'll clean up." She began moving pots and plates to the kitchen. The house remained silent. Everyone had disappeared.

Katrina picked up some glasses and followed Annabelle into the kitchen. She grabbed her arm and asked, "What in the hell's going—"

Annabelle spun in her direction and placed her hand across Katrina's mouth. Annabelle shook her head and her eyes bulged.

Katrina's fears had been realized. They weren't alone.

Annabelle's eyes narrowed and her gaze darted in all directions. Then she cuffed her hands against the sides of her head.

Katrina understood. *The walls have ears.*

They finished clearing the table and Annabelle washed while Katrina dried. After putting away the leftovers, Annabelle threw her arms around Katrina's neck and gave her a hug. The unexpected embrace startled Katrina. What was going on? Annabelle's whispering into Katrina's ear sent waves of fear through her.

"Don't be afraid of what's about to happen."

20

After dropping Rob off, Frank drove around for a couple of hours, thinking. He stopped for lunch—some Mexican restaurant he'd never tried—and headed home. He switched on the radio and took the long way back. Just before he made the turn into his parking garage, the news reported that there was still no resolution to the Katrina Wallace kidnapping. Frank turned the radio off. He needed to find a clue. A big clue. And if he didn't find it before the Rangers, the case would be theirs.

An hour later, sitting on his balcony, he scanned the downtown skyline.

Why did this shooting have to happen now? The whole crappy incident complicated things. He worked better when his mind could focus on just one problem at a time, and the shooting had pushed him out of the zone. Everything Rob had said made sense. No use denying that. But Frank didn't have to make a decision right now. After this case was over, he could decide. The smart move would be to quit.

Frank stood and leaned on the railing, looking out over the city. There was just one problem. The job gave his life meaning.

Frank fished the photo of Trina from his pocket and made a promise to it and himself. Whatever happened, he intended to find her. Nothing would stop him this time. He'd failed once before, but not again.

* * *

Annabelle broke the embrace and motioned for Katrina to follow. After opening the kitchen door, Annabelle stepped onto the back screened porch. Katrina didn't move. The same fear that had gripped her during her exit from the basement now froze her at the threshold. Katrina trusted Annabelle up to a point, but she didn't know her. What did she mean, "Don't be afraid of what's about to happen"?

Annabelle's eyes misted. "You have to go, or they'll just come get you."

Katrina sucked in a breath and stepped onto the porch, her legs wobbly. Annabelle opened the screen door leading into the backyard and held it for her. Katrina's stomach flipped as she stepped outside. Filtered sunlight crept through the branches and the sweet smell of honeysuckle drifted on the breeze. Katrina's anxiety lessened a bit as she walked across the soft Saint Augustine grass. It felt like carpet.

"Over here," Brother Luther called.

Katrina glanced to her right. He stood in the shade of an ancient oak, holding a rabbit in his arms. She looked at Annabelle, who frowned, arms crossed, and took a step back. A feeling of anxiety coursed through Katrina. She sensed a trap. Looking in all directions, she approached Brother Luther. He was leaning back on the tree's trunk, softly stroking the gray field rabbit resting in his grip.

"You like animals?" he called.

Katrina stopped well short of him. "I guess so." No one lingered in the yard but them. Was this her chance to make a break?

"Here." He extended his hands. "Take him."

She moved a little closer and gripped the rabbit. The warmth of its body helped calm her. She cuddled it to her chest.

Brother Luther motioned. "Come on. Let's take a walk."

Katrina strolled beside him as he meandered around the house. Two huge black pit bulls bounded toward them. Katrina stopped, and the rabbit almost jumped from her grasp. Keeping a firm hold on it, she sucked in a sharp breath.

"Don't run," Brother Luther ordered. "They attack anything running."

He squatted down and greeted each with a pat on the head. The rabbit fought to get away, but Katrina didn't dare release it. Its heart pounded against her breast.

"Follow me," Brother Luther said. He tracked to the front of the house and around a bed of lavender phlox. She looked up at the white stately home with Roman columns and a long front balcony, thinking the place looked like the mansion from *Gone With the Wind*. Pink, blue, and white hydrangeas outlined the front porch, their smell filling the air. A circular gravel drive ran from the front of the house into the woods. The sound of a big truck revving up and gears shifting floated through the trees.

"County road's that way." Brother Luther pointed toward the sound.

They continued to the other side of the mansion, where a tall trestle of red antique roses climbed to the second floor. When they made the last turn, they were in the rear yard again.

I've got this, Katrina told herself. She could break out of this place without too much effort. Now that she knew where the road was, it wouldn't be that hard. But why did Annabelle stay?

"That's the garden through there." Brother Luther pointed past a group of pines to a clearing. "And that's the barn and animal pens that way," he said, shifting his finger in the opposite direction.

Annabelle remained on the screened porch where they'd left her. As they passed, she lowered her eyes. The dogs still trailed them. Each weighed probably eighty pounds, with tight muscles rippling below the skin.

"He's a nice rabbit, ain't he?" Brother Luther asked, extending his hands for the animal.

Katrina didn't answer but handed the creature to him. He scratched it behind each ear. "Did you enjoy your tour?"

"Huh?" Katrina asked.

Brother Luther motioned. "Your tour of the place?"

"I guess so." Katrina shrugged. What was he getting at? Who cared about a damn tour?

Brother Luther scratched the rabbit again and his gaze met Katrina's. "Don't ever try leaving."

"What?" Katrina returned the stare.

"The yard, garden, and barn are the only safe areas outside. Stay where it's safe when you're out here," Brother Luther said.

Katrina took a step back. *What's he talking about, safe areas?*

Brother Luther tossed the rabbit to the ground and it raced across the lawn. He yelled, "Strike," and slapped his leg.

The dogs bolted in pursuit. The rabbit zigged and zagged, fleeing toward the safety of the woods and bushes. Katrina held her breath as the lead dog caught the poor thing in its massive jaws. The second one jumped and clamped its teeth on the head. A sickening squeal escaped the rabbit before it was torn in half. Katrina's stomach churned watching the beasts growl at each other and wolf down the defenseless bunny.

When she glared at Brother Luther, he squinted at the dogs, not making eye contact with her. His brow wrinkled and he gave her a hard, menacing stare.

"If you ever venture out of your safe area, you'd better be able to run faster than that rabbit." He whistled and the monsters trotted to him and sat. Blood and traces of fur stained their mouths. He pointed toward the porch. "They live under the house. Any sound, any movement, causes them to alert. They know your safe areas."

Katrina could have puked from disgust and fear, but she refused to give this son of a bitch the satisfaction. She ignored the dogs and marched to the back door. Her stomach bubbled with terror as a low growl followed her, but she didn't slow her pace. She'd seriously underestimated this Luther guy—escape looked impossible.

When she entered the screened rear porch, Annabelle was waiting. A tear slid down Annabelle's cheek. What she said shook Katrina's confidence further.

Annabelle's sorrowful eyes met hers. "Welcome to hell."

21

Rob moped around the empty house. He still missed Carmen. Since the kids had gone off to college, he and Carmen had seldom been apart, and their quiet, lonely home wasn't comfortable without her. Too much time alone. Too much time to think. About the gangster he'd killed a couple of days ago. About the incident with Big Mike. About the possibility of working with a new partner if Frank quit.

Rob twisted the top off a beer and settled on the couch. He was under no illusions. All the success he'd enjoyed the last few years had been Frank's doing. Hanging onto Frank's coattails had rocketed them to recognition by their supervisors, and now even the chief. And working with Frank held its own intrigue. He didn't always follow the book, but he always got results. That's why the chief had selected them to investigate this case. That's why the chief had more faith in them than in the Texas Rangers.

Rob glanced at the plaque on the wall for the Walker case investigation. It would never have been solved without Frank's keen mind unraveling the dozens of clues and figuring it out. If Frank left, Rob would end up partnering with God knows who.

Rob took a long swallow of beer as the realization hit him. One thing was for sure—without a smart, dynamic personality like Frank, Rob would fall back into that mass of great unwashed, unremarkable detectives. What he'd said to Frank yesterday, about how he should quit . . . A hot flush crept up Rob's neck and spread to his face. Stupid.

Damn stupid. That's what he was. He sat there in the dim light until he finished the bottle, and the next one.

* * *

"You'll sleep with me," Annabelle said. "Come on. I'll show you to our room."

Katrina's gut rumbled. *Welcome to hell?*

She followed Annabelle through the kitchen and dining room into the long hall. The whole place had an old bookstore smell about it, and the furnishings and decor had the antebellum feel she'd seen in the dining room when she'd first come up from the basement. Old black-and-white photos hung in a neat arrangement on several walls. Rocking chairs and wooden stools were scattered around the living area. In the middle of the room, some kind of altar had been constructed with pinecones, rocks, and sticks on top. A few leaves were scattered among the items, giving the altar a nature feel. The staircase wasn't as grand as the one in *Gone With the Wind*, but its red carpeted steps had a sort of old elegance.

Going up, Annabelle looked around and placed her finger against her lips. "The children are sleeping."

When they reached the top, she opened the second door on the right. Katrina followed her inside, and Annabelle softly closed the door. Bright sunlight filled the room and accented the antique furniture. A double bed, dresser, chest of drawers, small writing desk, and chair bordered the room. The dark wooden floors creaked underfoot.

Annabelle strolled to a window, and Katrina peeked over her shoulder. The whole group, all seven, stood in the side yard as the Freak addressed them.

Annabelle turned to her. "It's safe to talk now. If we keep our voices down, we can talk in here anytime, but nowhere else."

Katrina had so many questions she didn't know where to start. "Where are we?"

A quick grin flitted across Annabelle's lips. "That was my first question when I came. I'm not sure, exactly. But I also listened from behind closed doors. From their conversations, I believe we're somewhere in

East Texas, near Louisiana. I've heard them say Sabine County and Hemphill, but I'm not real sure where either is."

Annabelle strolled to the bed and Katrina sat beside her. Annabelle said, "They talk about running over to Louisiana, so we must be close. There's a big lake in that direction." Annabelle pointed to the opposite wall of the room. "They go there and come back with fish and talk about the lake level."

Katrina held her hand. "How long have you been here?"

Annabelle lowered her weary eyes, her gaze falling to her lap. "This is my second spring. A little over a year, I guess."

Katrina studied the front of Annabelle's dress. Two wet spots soiled it where her breasts touched the material.

Annabelle must have noticed her stare. She flashed an embarrassed frown and tugged at the front of her dress. "Sorry, I'm lactating. They won't let me wear a bra or pad."

"You have a baby?" Katrina asked.

Annabelle nodded, but there was no joy in her acknowledgment. "Almost three months old."

Katrina didn't really want to ask but couldn't help herself. "Who's the father?"

Annabelle bowed her head and began to weep. "Brother John," she said.

Annabelle leaned her head on Katrina's shoulder and Katrina wrapped her arms around Annabelle's neck. The weeping continued and Annabelle's shoulders heaved with each sob. A hundred thoughts raced through Katrina's head that she didn't want to consider. A new fear gripped her. *Will this be me next year?*

* * *

Monday morning Frank got in early and caught up on the case reports. Frank wasn't used to racing another agency to solve a case. In CIU, things were pretty laid-back most of the time. Except when the president had visited Dallas and Frank had to work with the Secret Service—a very serious bunch. If he couldn't get something going soon on the kidnapping, he'd be watching from the sidelines as Rangers took the lead.

Edna and Terry arrived at the same time, discussing a new department policy. Edna turned right into her office and Terry stopped at Frank's desk.

"Good news and bad news. Rob returns tomorrow," Terry said.

"What?" Frank sat up from his slouched position.

Terry grinned. "The chief pissed off a bunch of Homicide detectives Friday night after the shooting. He informed them they had to conclude their investigation and have the final report on his desk by closing time today. At least a half dozen worked all weekend."

"Sounds like the chief doesn't want to split us up," Frank said.

Terry tapped the side of his head with his finger. "He's sharper than most give him credit for."

"What's the bad news?" Frank asked.

Terry spoke under his breath. "Well, it's just that the daughter's boyfriend, Ruiz, has just started a social media campaign to find Katrina. Could help locate her, but more likely to just increase the pressure on all of us. News agencies have been calling the sixth floor since it broke. That's just what this investigation needs—more pressure." Terry's ringing desk phone sent him scurrying for his office.

At last, a break. With Rob's return, Frank hoped to recover some of his lost karma. Rob always brought him good luck. Frank thanked God he didn't have to meet with all the other agencies involved in this investigation or attend one of those goofy news conferences. Having to stand beside a tearful Ms. Mayor, begging for her daughter's safe return, in front of a dozen cameras would push Frank over the edge. He was too close already. This case gnawed on his gut like a hungry ferret. Liaisoning with the other law enforcement types and doing news conferences was Terry and Edna's job. They had to explain everything and cover the heat with the higher-ups, allowing Rob and Frank to do their jobs.

Okay, down to business.

Frank dialed the tax assessor's number and asked for Brandy. He told her the address of the burned house and requested information on the owner. She asked about Rob and giggled when Frank told her Rob had said hello. She complained that the computers were running slow and she'd have to call him back in a minute.

Terry eased up to Frank's desk and lowered his voice. "Thought you should know. The mayor has just requested the chief to contact the FBI. They'll be joining the investigation. All your reports are being furnished to them for review."

Frank shrugged. "Guess I better check my spelling and punctuation."

Terry leaned on Frank's cube. "This thing grows by the day. First us, then the Rangers, and now the Bureau." Terry lowered his voice. "Remember what I said about the Rangers throwing manpower at this?"

Frank nodded.

"Well, you haven't seen anything yet until the feds jump in," Terry said. "Just be glad they don't care to work with the locals. The last thing you want is them tagging along on your leads."

"The kidnapping doesn't seem to have hurt the mayor's standing in the polls. He's up four points since it became public," Frank said.

Terry glanced around and dropped his voice. "Yeah, he's cashing in on the sympathy vote. His daughter getting snatched might just push him over the top."

Frank nodded. That was an ice-cold way of looking at it, but it was true. *Wonder if the mayor would trade those four points for his daughter's safe return?*

Terry whispered, "Higgins called Edna up to his office after the big joint news conference. Don't know what they talked about, but when she returned she'd been crying and was fighting mad. I hope she reminded the old son of a bitch that Missing Persons, the Rangers, and the FBI haven't done shit so far. Only CIU is making any progress."

That pissed Frank off. It wasn't fair it should all fall on Edna's shoulders. When he'd been a new cadet in the police academy, every morning they'd stand inspection. The place Frank was required to stand, with eyes pointed straight ahead, was directly across from a poster on the academy wall. He must have read that thing a couple of hundred times. The quote on the poster was from Mother Teresa of Calcutta: "We the willing, led by the unknowing, are doing the impossible for the ungrateful. We have done so much, with so little, for so long, we are now qualified to do anything with nothing." That's the way police work sometimes felt to Frank. Edna was holding up, but Frank saw the strain it put on her more every day.

Frank's phone rang and Terry drifted toward his office.

"Detective Pierce," Frank said.

"This is Brandy. I have that information."

Frank copied what she told him, but it didn't help much. The person who had owned the house before the fire had sold the lot after it burned, and the new owner lived out of state. She provided the last known address of the previous owner in Dallas. Frank hung up and stared at the paper a moment before slipping on his jacket and heading for the parking garage.

Frank knew the general area: it was in the Kessler neighborhood of Oak Cliff, south of the Trinity River. He parked under the shade of a giant oak that hung over the street. The home was a Craftsman and sat on a small rise, a nice lawn stretching up from the street and flowering shrubs bordering the walkway and the wraparound porch. He caught a whiff of gardenia as he rang the doorbell. A moment later, an elderly woman with gray hair in a tight bun opened the door. She studied him through the screen.

Frank held up his credentials. "Good morning. Dallas Police. Does Gerald Fellman live here?"

The small woman leaned forward and scrutinized the identification. "Mr. Fellman is deceased."

Frank pocketed the ID. "I'm sorry. You his wife?"

"Yes, I'm Grace Fellman."

Frank asked, "May I have a moment of your time? I'm conducting an investigation and believe you might be able to help me."

Asking for someone's assistance using this technique always worked for Frank. Almost everyone but criminals secretly wanted to assist the police, whether they'd admit it or not. The thought that they might crack a big case excited the average person. Mrs. Fellman apparently didn't share this excitement.

"How do I know you're a real policeman?" she asked. Her sweet smile and suspicious eyes sent Frank back to the drawing board. "I showed you my identification."

"Could have been made on any good computer," the petite woman answered.

This wasn't the first time Frank had found himself in this dilemma. He had a fail-safe protocol ready.

"Okay," Frank said, "call the Dallas Police Department and ask to speak to Detective Pierce in CIU. When it goes to voice mail, dial the cell number on my recording."

Mrs. Fellman's eyes narrowed. "Don't move." She shut the door and clicked the bolt into place.

A couple of minutes later, Frank's cell rang as the door opened.

"Hello?" Frank said.

Mrs. Fellman stood at the threshold staring at him through the screen door. She spoke into her phone. "Come in, Detective Pierce."

She led Frank into the living room. The furniture was Old English and showed gentle wear. Lots of dark wood and heavy fabrics. A slightly frayed Persian rug adorned the floor.

She pointed at the sofa. "Have a seat."

He laid his notebook on the coffee table and dropped onto a soft cushion.

"Now, how can I help the police today?" she asked.

Frank was impressed by her cool, relaxed manner—not at all normal. Probably the result of a clear conscience. Everyone's pulse rose and heart rate increased when a policeman showed up unannounced. But not this calm little lady's. He could just as easily have been her minister, dropping by for a chat on this beautiful spring day.

"I'm looking for the previous owner of a house in South Dallas a few years ago. It burned," Frank said.

She perked up. "Was it at Camp Wisdom and Houston School Road?"

Frank leaned closer. "As a matter of fact, it was."

She grinned. "Mr. Fellman and I owned it."

"Were you renting it to someone at the time?" he asked.

She folded her hands and her face changed as if she'd just had a terrible thought. "Yes, several people lived there." She lowered her head. "Several strange people."

He leaned still closer. "Strange, like how?"

She wrung her hands and looked away briefly. "Like religious fanatics. Maybe a cult." Her voice became a whisper. "Long hair, long beards, strange."

"Oh, really? Tell me about them," Frank said.

"That's the only business deal Mr. Fellman ever made I didn't agree with." She shook her head. "I told him that bunch wasn't any good."

"Tell me why you thought that," Frank said.

Her gentle smile returned and she interlaced her fingers in her lap. "We owned the house for several years and leased it to large families. It was a grand old thing. Built in the twenties. Never made a lot from the rent, but it always covered the loan. When the previous renters moved out and that last bunch inquired about leasing it, I had a bad feeling. But they paid the deposit, signed the contract, and kept up on the rent."

"So did you ever meet them?" he asked.

Her smile faded. "Yes. That's how I knew. We escorted them on the initial walk-through and came once a year to inspect the house."

Frank's spine tingled with that feeling he always got just before a big clue broke. She seemed uncomfortable discussing it. Frank was a master of silence, his patience endless. At last she turned his way.

"I believe they were worshiping false deities. They had erected some sort of shrine in the living room. Mr. Fellman asked the man about it. He said they worshiped and prayed nightly."

"Prayed?" Frank asked.

She wrung her hands again. "There wasn't a cross, any Bibles, or anything else which indicated Christian beliefs, just a large red globe hanging from the ceiling and an altar with flowers, rocks, and sticks on top." Her forehead creased.

"The fella you rented the house to. Do you remember his name?" Frank asked.

"Oh, yes . . . John was his first name." She looked up at the ceiling, tapping her chin with her index finger. "But I can't recall his last."

Frank gave her a few seconds before providing a prompt. "I bet Mr. Fellman kept pretty good records, didn't he?"

Her eyes brightened. "He sure did." She rushed out of the room.

A minute later, she returned carrying a large black binder. After taking her seat, she opened it, licked her finger and thumb, and skimmed several pages. "John Warren," she read.

Frank held out his hand. "May I?"

She handed the binder over. On the front, a label read "Baker House." He raised an eyebrow and pointed at the name.

"That's the man we bought it from," she said.

Frank flipped the pages. Everything relating to the house was there, all indexed. The contract to buy, copies of the loan information, inspector's reports, appraiser's reports, and tax and insurance information. Under a tab that read "RENTERS," Frank found rental contracts dating back twelve years. He flipped to the last contract, signed by John Warren. Frank ran his finger down the lines. At the bottom he found the Holy Grail of identification: John Warren's Texas driver's license number. Frank removed the paper and laid it on the table. He snapped a photograph with his phone and slid it back inside the binder.

"Know what became of them after the fire?" Frank asked.

"No idea," she said. "Just glad to be rid of them."

Frank was sure of one thing. Brother John and his crew had scared the old lady, and she didn't look as if she scared easily.

* * *

Since he was already in Oak Cliff, Frank decided on an early lunch at Hattie's. He loved their smoked turkey–and–Swiss. A couple of years ago he'd given the executive chef his secret recipe for sweet potato fries. Now they had the best in Dallas. The guy had won a cooking award with that recipe. When Frank strolled in, he always got the royal treatment and no check to spoil his meal.

An hour later, he slid into his office cube. The place had cleared out for lunch. Frank rushed to power up his computer. Did he have a real lead or not? He crossed his fingers. The first solid piece of information so far. But as many times as not, leads ended up going nowhere after closer examination.

By the time the squad area was again teeming with full-bellied detectives, Frank still didn't have an answer. Warren went by the first name John, but that was really his middle name. His first name was Vernon. Frank pulled up a copy of Warren's expired driver's license. He'd never bothered to renew it. The Texas Workforce Commission reported no employment in the last six years. The utilities indicated he had no current phone, gas, or electric service in the Dallas metroplex, and criminal checks showed no arrests. The last known residence was the burned house in Dallas, and the post office showed no forwarding address.

Had the guy moved? Left the state? Died?

Terry sauntered up. "How's it going?"

Frank shuffled through some papers and handed Terry the Department of Public Safety photo taken of Warren when they'd issued him a driver's license. "Meet Brother John."

Terry eyes widened when he examined the picture. "Think he's one of the guys in the Walmart video?"

Frank lounged in his chair as Edna approached. Terry handed her the photo.

"Brother John," Terry said.

Edna glanced at the photo, caught a sharp breath, and handed it back to Frank. "What do you think?"

Frank eyed the picture and then Terry. "Remember what you said when we saw the video from the Walmart parking lot, the guys in the old Dodge truck?"

"You mean about them looking like rednecks with their long hair and beards?" Terry asked.

"Yeah," Frank said. He studied the photo of Warren—the long-haired man with the bearded and dour face. Frank held up the photo at Edna and Terry's eye level. "This guy looks like he's auditioning for *Duck Dynasty*."

22

On Monday morning, Katrina helped Annabelle prepare and serve breakfast to the group. Annabelle's revelation the day before had haunted Katrina's thoughts and dreams. The three-hour sermon from the Freak she'd been subjected to the previous night hadn't helped much either. Everyone was there, but his haunting eyes had remained fixed on Katrina, as if the sermon was personalized. He had preached from Ephesians 5:22 and Colossians 3:18—"Wives, submit to your husbands." He could kiss her ass if he expected her to submit to him. This group didn't appear dangerous on the surface, but the deeper you dug, the more terrifying they became. Whatever their beliefs were, they weren't in Katrina's best interest. She had to get out—fast.

After the sermon, Annabelle had gone into the children's room and breastfed her baby while Katrina waited in their room for her return. Katrina needed to know more about the house and the people to formulate a good escape plan. But by the time Annabelle returned, she had become so depressed she refused to discuss anything. Katrina had lain awake most of the night, trying to figure the whole thing out. Had they even made a ransom demand? Was anyone looking for her? Doubt crept in around the edges of her confidence. If no knew where she was, how could they find her?

The next morning, after breakfast, Katrina and Annabelle were assigned housecleaning chores by Sister Ruth. When they finished lunch, Sister Judy sent them to the garden. The tomatoes, peas, and squash needed hoeing. On the way to the barn, Annabelle drifted into an excited babble. In whispered tones, she explained how she'd been kidnapped from Lake Charles the year before and raped by Brother John in the basement. She had given birth to a daughter. Her confession was heartfelt, as if she were finally admitting to a great sin and at last ridding herself of the shame. They found two hoes and hiked toward the garden. One of the pit bulls followed in the shadows of the tree line.

Katrina leaned closer and whispered, "How many others?"

Annabelle must have been deep in thought, because she said, "Pardon?"

"How many other girls?" Katrina asked. "I've heard several children in the house."

Annabelle glanced in all directions as she walked. She kept her head low and mumbled from the corner of her mouth. "Four others that we know of."

"We? Who's we?" Katrina asked.

Annabelle lowered her head again and spoke just above a whisper. "Each girl passes on the names of the ones who came before to the next girl. Sooner or later one might make it out to tell what's happened to us."

Katrina's stomach flipped. *What the hell? So where are the other girls? What happened to them?*

Annabelle opened the gate to the garden, and Katrina followed her to the rows of vegetables. Weeds sprouted in the rich loam soil.

"Have you ever used a hoe?" Annabelle asked.

Katrina shook her head.

"Watch me. It's easy." Annabelle chopped at the edges of the vegetables, hoeing the weeds to the side. "See?"

Katrina followed her example. "So, where are the other girls—the ones who came before you?" Katrina asked.

Annabelle's lips pressed into a thin line and she didn't make eye contact. She paused before saying, "Everyone says they release them, but I can't believe that."

Katrina took a breath, unable to speak for a moment. Annabelle's earlier statement, "Welcome to hell," had just taken on a new level of horror. "Each has a child by the Freak?" Katrina asked.

Annabelle nodded and whispered, "A few months after giving birth, after the child's breastfed for a while, the mother disappears." Her last words were choked with emotion.

"What are you going to do?" Katrina asked.

If Annabelle intended to make a break, Katrina didn't want to be left behind.

Annabelle swung her head in all directions and answered, "I have to try. My time's almost up. If I don't leave soon, they'll come for me." Annabelle glared at the dog in the woods. "I'll have to take my chances."

Katrina edged closer. "I'm coming too."

Annabelle shook her head. "No, you're not. You're safe for the time being. I'll go alone."

Katrina's voice rose higher than she intended. "Safe? I don't call waiting to be raped and murdered safe."

When she said *murdered*, Annabelle leaned on the hoe. Tears dripped from her cheeks, and her shoulders heaved from silent weeping.

Katrina moved closer and wrapped an arm around her. "I'm sorry. I shouldn't have said . . ." Katrina held Annabelle a minute longer.

Annabelle raked her eyes with the back of her hand. "I overheard the men talking this morning. They're going after another girl tonight. Be gone until well after midnight. That's the best chance I'm going to get. I have a plan." Annabelle eyed Katrina. "You have to stay. The time will come for you as well. Perhaps between now and then you'll be rescued, or escape. If I make it, I'll bring help." Annabelle paused before saying, "If I don't, at least you'll have a chance later."

Katrina fought the emotion. Of all the anxiety she'd known since being taken, this was the worst. The knowledge that this might be her only friend's last day filled her with dread. How could she stay in this insane asylum without Annabelle? She had no doubt that sooner or later the Freak would rape her every night until he impregnated her.

After that, it was only a matter of time until she'd be in Annabelle's predicament. Could she just stand by and wait for that to happen? Did she have that kind of courage?

Katrina took a breath and looked at Annabelle, who was still fighting back tears. *No, definitely not!* Katrina would make a break before then. But that's probably what Annabelle and the others had also thought. Once you were with child, what happened to your strength and energy?

Annabelle swiveled her head again and caught Katrina's eye. "Before I leave, I have to show you something. And you must show it to the next girl."

Katrina stopped hoeing. "What?"

Annabelle opened her mouth to speak as a voice yelled from the barn.

"Get back to work." Sister Ruth pointed at them with an accusatory finger.

Katrina made a decision—a promise she'd keep no matter what. Before she left, she intended to bitch-slap that woman.

* * *

Frank spent the rest of Monday afternoon amassing all the information he could on Warren, which wasn't much. Given that he had no criminal record or recent work history, Frank was reduced to Google and Facebook to catch a glimpse of the guy's past. Warren had no social media presence. No accounts meant no inside information. The Texas Department of State Health Services offered nothing. No birth certificate, no census information. The guy must have been born outside the state. But Frank had one thing he could use: the Social Security number from the lease.

He picked up his phone and dialed a number he seldom contacted. When the man answered, Frank asked the question.

"Yes, is this the person who posted a reward for the lost dog?"

The familiar voice hesitated a second before saying, "You have the wrong number."

Frank hung up and thumbed through some paperwork, waiting for the call. Five minutes later, his cell rang.

"Hey, Frank. How's things?" Chet asked.

Chet had been a Dallas detective until about eight years before when he'd gone fed and gotten assigned to the Dallas Social Security Office working for the Office of the Inspector General. He owed Frank more favors than could ever be repaid. Best fed contact he had. There was one problem, though. Chet couldn't officially release information on a Social Security number.

"All's good, buddy. Working the missing mayor's daughter case," Frank said.

"No shit? Any leads?"

"Yeah, and that's why I'm calling. Got a number I need checked out."

"Let me have it," Chet said.

Frank read the number and Chet repeated it for conformation before saying, "Give me till tomorrow and I'll call you."

Frank stood and did a quick yoga stretch. Too many questions and not enough answers. How much time did she have? He dropped into his chair, and when his butt hit the cushion, it was as if something shook loose in his brain. Of course. Why had it taken him so long? He began typing.

Fifteen minutes later he stood in front of Terry's desk watching his boss read the paper he'd handed him.

"Can't say we've ever done this before," Terry said, "but I don't see why not." Terry initialed the bottom of the page and handed it back to Frank. "Walk it over to Edna for final approval, and have them send it out today," Terry said.

Frank snatched the paper from Terry's fingers on his way out the door. "Halfway there already," Frank said.

23

Katrina and Annabelle worked in the garden until Sister Judy called them in to help with supper. The afternoon had cooled, and the sweet fragrance of honeysuckle floated through the air. A whippoor-will called in the distance. In the shadows of the trees, the rustling of grass signaled the dog's presence.

That thing scared Katrina more than she let on. She'd been attacked by a dog as a young girl. It had latched on to her right knee and wouldn't let go. Her dad had come to her rescue, beating the thing off with a rolled-up newspaper. The attack had frightened her to the point of hysteria. She still had the physical scars, but the mental ones were worse. The thought of an attack sent waves of fear through her, and she knew she'd never be able to escape as long as the dogs watched her.

Annabelle had worked in near silence since telling Katrina about her escape plans, as if she were making peace, or coming to terms with a situation she had no control over. She was calm as she strolled in the lush grass beside Katrina.

Katrina whispered, "I don't want you to leave."

A crooked grin crossed Annabelle's lips. "I'll be leaving one way or another. Either I'll wait for them to come get me, or I'll take my chances tonight." She lowered her head and mumbled, "You'll have the company of another girl, anyway." She shifted her gaze to Katrina and a tear raced down her cheek. Annabelle wiped it away as they neared the porch door. A low growl from under the house greeted them.

After washing up, Katrina received a lesson in the preparation of turnip greens. Sisters Judy and Ruth worked on the roasted chicken and sweet potatoes. Field peas and cornbread were Sister Karen's job. Men's voices echoed from the dining room as the women finished preparing the meal and served the food.

Katrina paid careful attention to everyone at the table that evening. During their time alone in the garden, Annabelle had given her the skinny on the group. Brother Turner and Brother Lee were literally brothers. The tall, hard-faced men seldom smiled, or even spoke. They appeared to be completely devoted to the Freak. What hold he had on them she couldn't imagine.

Brother Luther, on the other hand, had somewhat of a personality and a cherub look. He had convinced her to come out of the basement, but he was also the same one who had fondled her in the truck that night. He had allowed the dogs to kill the rabbit and issued her a warning against escaping. He seemed a bit Forrest Gumpish with his shy, disarming smile, but he was as dangerous as the rest.

Sisters Ruth, Judy, and Karen were pretty much alike. They could be charming one minute and vicious the next. Their devotion to Brother John was total. Sister Karen, being the youngest, showed deference to the two older women.

As for Brother John, the Freak, he almost never talked except when giving his marathon nightly sermons. His alpha-male status seemed to give him the confidence to control with just a look or motion of his head. His intense stares froze Katrina. *A man with eyes like that could just as easily kill you as look at you.*

She stole a glimpse at Annabelle halfway through the meal. This was her last supper. Katrina would have given anything to go with her, but Annabelle had forbidden it. After eating, Katrina and Annabelle were sent to the basement to put sheets on the bed and tidy things up for "the new guest."

Twenty minutes later, they sat side by side on their bed and talked.

"When do you plan to make your break?" Katrina asked.

Annabelle took a deep breath. "As soon as they leave to kidnap the next girl. Everyone will be at the rear of the house, and I'll slip out the front."

"I have a question," Katrina said.

"What?"

"Why are they doing this? What possible reason could they have?"

Annabelle's eyes drifted to the nightstand and she picked up the Bible. She dropped it into Katrina's lap. "Here, read Revelation. It's hidden in there somewhere, according to Brother John. You see, he considers himself a new age prophet. He believes he is the manifestation of the death star, Wormwood." She tapped the Bible. "Described in Revelation. According to John, God instructed him to know seven girls, who would bear him seven children. Once the last is born, John will ascend to heaven and return to earth as Wormwood. That will signal the end of the world. The only survivors will be the people in this house—his followers and children."

"What a bunch of bullshit," Katrina said, a little too loudly.

"Of course it is, but to answer your question, the reason we're here is to provide the children," Annabelle said.

"How many are there now?" Katrina asked.

"Counting my baby, five."

Katrina shook her head. "I'm not staying here, Annabelle. Not with these nuts."

Annabelle grabbed Katrina by the shoulders. "Haven't you heard a word I've said? You're safe until you give them a child. They may threaten and be mean to you, but they won't dare harm you until well after your baby's born."

"No, I can't do it . . . I won't do it. I'm coming with you." Katrina said.

"One person has twice the chance of escaping as two. If you go, neither of us will make it. I need you to stay and cover for me. Give me a little extra time. Please, I can't do this alone," Annabelle pleaded. Her eyes were sorrowful as she begged for Katrina's help.

Poor Katrina had never done a courageous thing in her pampered life. She'd never had to. Annabelle's plea hit her hard, like a slap across the face. She swallowed her fear and held Annabelle's hands in hers. "Okay, I'll stay and buy you as much time as I can." Tears filled the corners of Annabelle's eyes, and she picked up a small flashlight off the nightstand.

"I told you I'd show you something. Are you ready?" Annabelle asked.

Katrina licked dry lips. "I hope so."

* * *

Frank sat on his balcony and stared into the darkness. It was late, but he knew it was going to be one of those nights. Sometimes investigations stuck in his head and he couldn't sleep. He sipped the red wine and thought. Since interviewing Eddie under the overpass, Frank had held a suspicion that the Brother John character played a major part in the case, but it wasn't until his interview with Grace Fellman that he was sure of it. But why?

Edna had liked his idea of sending a NCIC/TCIC query to all criminal justice agencies regarding the Wormwood tattoo. That might shake things up. And then tomorrow Rob would return, and they could reinterview Eddie. With the new information from Mrs. Fellman, Frank wanted to clarify a few things. There wasn't much else they could do.

Frank rolled his wrist and checked the time. *Got to get some sleep.* The Rangers, FBI, and Missing Persons were batting zero for zero. Frank didn't have much confidence in that bunch. He and Rob were leading the pack; everyone else only followed. Frank dropped his fingers inside his shirt pocket, touching Trina's photo.

"Hold on a little longer," he whispered.

* * *

Annabelle slid a small pair of scissors from the nightstand drawer. She got on her knees by the bed as if she intended to pray and motioned for Katrina to do the same. Lying on her back, Annabelle eased her head and shoulders under the edge of the bed and clicked on the flashlight. Katrina followed.

"Hold the light right here," Annabelle said, passing the flashlight to Katrina. It illuminated the inside of the wooden bed frame, well out of sight of anyone changing the sheets.

Annabelle began scratching the wood with a scissor point. Katrina's eyes widened. Not at her friend's strange behavior, but at the other scratches. In a neat list were the names and hometowns of the others: "Donna Willis—Houston, TX. Cindy Pullman—Alexandra, LA. Mary Billings—Beaumont, TX. Janet Farmer—Austin, TX." Annabelle finished inscribing her name and added "Lake Charles, LA." She brushed off the loose shavings and dabbed a tissue on her tongue before wiping them up. Annabelle and Katrina scooted from under the bed.

Katrina's stomach twisted, and she leaned against the wall.

Annabelle raked her hair into place and reached under the bed frame. After a moment, she pulled out a gold ring with a small emerald in the center.

"They stole this from me the day I arrived," Annabelle said. She slipped it on her finger and held it out, admiring it. "But I found where they hid it in the women's bedroom and stole it back. They've never missed it."

"So, how are they all connected?" Katrina asked.

"From what I can see, they're all married to each other. It's a commune in the truest sense," Annabelle replied.

Katrina's mind kicked into overdrive. "You mean they all sleep with each other?"

Annabelle shrugged. "Best I can tell. John takes one of the women each night. He likes Karen the best. He considers them his spiritual wives."

"Ugh. He *is* a freak." Katrina said. "Do any of them have children by him?"

Annabelle shook her head. "No, but I don't know why."

They stood and wandered to the door. Annabelle swallowed hard and hugged Katrina. "I'll spend the last few minutes with my baby." She broke the embrace and wiped her eyes.

"Good luck," Katrina said.

Annabelle's lips stretched with just the hint of a grin. "Good luck to you." She slipped out the door, and Katrina closed it without a sound. She drew slow, deep breaths. Annabelle wouldn't be around for her anymore. How could she stand this place without her? Katrina's eyes misted and she choked off a sob. Everything needed to look normal until tomorrow.

Katrina leaned her back against the door and closed her eyes, saying a silent prayer for Annabelle. Katrina had never felt so alone. Before she opened her eyes again, she added a prayer for herself.

* * *

Emilie Moore wiped sweat from her brow and pushed the button on the treadmill. The elevation increased five degrees. She had another three minutes before the cool-down cycle. The eight-mile pace and elevation increase gave her the burn she enjoyed at the end of a long run. A warm, satisfied feeling rushed through her.

Most nurses who worked the ER evening shift hit a bar or rushed home to their husbands after midnight. That's why they looked the way they did. Not her. She wasn't going to widen out and get lazy. Her routine consisted of aerobics on Monday, Wednesday, and Friday, with strength training on the alternate days. She always took Sundays off. The Anytime Fitness gym was just around the corner from her apartment off Westport Avenue. She drove past it every day going to and from work. Besides, at this time of night, she never had to wait for a machine or waste time chatting with someone who was more interested in talking than working out. Shreveport was full of chatters.

The timer beeped and the speed decreased. She pushed her short blonde hair away from her eyes and lowered the incline. After walking five minutes, she drank a bottle of water and grabbed another before heading for the wet sauna.

* * *

In the parking lot, Brother Luther sat in the back seat of the old Dodge truck and thumbed through the Bible. The two brothers—Lee and Turner—were up front, as usual. The dim glare of the streetlight was enough for Luther to see. Brother John had dictated that after each girl was taken, a Bible must be left at the scene to honor God's will. They used only new Bibles. It was Brother Luther's job to leave them while wearing plastic gloves. At each kidnapping he'd done his job, plus a little extra. To further honor God, he'd used a highlighter to mark the word

"Wormwood" once in each Bible. Luther was pleased with himself. No one else had thought of such a thing. He wasn't as dumb as they thought. This would remain his little secret.

"She'll be coming out soon," Lee mumbled. "Always between one and two after she finishes the workout."

"Always alone?" Turner asked.

"She was the last two times. You ready to get in the camper, Luther?"

Luther set the Bible on the seat. "Ready."

"When we see her head to the car, we'll drive to the apartment complex. By the time she arrives, we'll be set up," Lee said.

Luther didn't mind riding in the camper with the girls. He liked it. The women at the house never wanted to be with him. The only time he got to touch a woman was on the rides when he lay beside them on the old, stinky mattress. He had ample time to explore their private parts during the trip. He became excited at the thought.

* * *

Katrina had no inkling what time it was when Sister Judy stuck her head in the door. It was early morning, judging from the soft light drifting through the drapes.

"Where's Annabelle?" Sister Judy demanded.

Oh, no. They'd realized she was missing. There was nothing Katrina could do for her friend now but buy her as much time as possible.

Katrina sat up and rubbed her eyes. The old comedian Flip Wilson had a saying her father loved to quote: "A lie's as good as the truth if you can find someone to believe it."

Katrina stared at Sister Judy. After giving a long yawn and stretching her arms, Katrina said, "She rolled out of bed a minute ago. Said she was going to look in on her daughter. I must have drifted back to sleep. Have you checked the nursery?"

Sister Judy frowned and her eyes pinched, but she didn't say a word. Her footsteps down the hall provided Katrina a chance to get dressed. Once they confirmed Annabelle missing, it would hit the fan for sure. Things were about to get ugly.

172

24

Tuesday morning, Frank beat everyone into CIU. He started the coffee, switched on all the lights, and checked the fax machine. Coming in early gave him a chance to settle in and relax before the mob arrived. He loved the office, but the noise distracted him when he had something to sort out mentally. Terry came in about ten minutes later.

"Anything?" Terry asked.

"Nope," Frank said.

Frank's cell rang and he snatched it up.

"Got that information for you," Chet said. "According to our records, the Social Security number you gave me is issued to Vernon John Warren. If he's working, he's not having Social Security taken out of his check. Hasn't in several years. Last known location is off Houston School Road. You need the address?" Chet asked.

"No, thanks," Frank said, rubbing his face with one hand. Another dead end. "He doesn't live there anymore—hasn't in years."

"That's about all we have on him. Sorry," Chet said.

Twenty minutes later, Rob strolled in.

"Welcome back," Frank said.

Rob draped his jacket over the chair. "Hey, cracker. Must've been the quickest shooting investigation on record."

Terry stepped out of his office and motioned to Rob. A moment later, Rob disappeared inside and Terry closed the door.

Frank finished the report on his computer and hit save just as Rob emerged.

"Well, I'm officially on duty again." Rob said, flopping into his chair and powering up the computer. "What have you been doing? Having any luck?"

Frank filled Rob in on the drive out to the burned house, the interview with Grace Fellman, and the request for NCIC/TCIC to check the name *Wormwood*.

"Good to hear you weren't sitting on your hands the last few days," Rob said.

Frank stood. "We need to talk to Eddie again. I have some new information from Mrs. Fellman I want to run past him."

"Okay, before lunch or after lunch?" Rob asked.

Frank scratched his neck, thinking about Katrina. "Before."

* * *

Annabelle fell to the ground, exhausted. She could hardly catch her breath. Her legs bled and stung from briars and thistles she'd run through during the night. Her face was scratched and her hair disheveled from low-hanging branches and vines. Annabelle's carefully crafted escape last night had been foiled by the unexpected appearance of one of the dogs. Now she was lost somewhere behind the house in the vast woods.

A steep hill loomed ahead. Annabelle staggered toward it. A shallow, clear stream seemed to guide her to the entrance of the cave. She fell to her knees and scooped handfuls of cold water to her dry lips. From the top of the hill, a menacing growl caught her attention. She stood and backed away.

* * *

As soon as Rob had walked into CIU, his desire to finish a six-pack by himself had dissipated. So had his obsessive thoughts about whether he was going to lose Frank. As detectives filed in, each one wanted a blow-by-blow account of what had happened at the shooting the previous Friday night. He had given his official statement at eight o'clock that morning, so he felt safe restating what he'd just told Homicide a couple of hours earlier. Frank's shooting angle was all wrong—didn't want to chance hurting the clerk—so Rob took the shot.

Rob glanced over at Frank working on his computer, apparently not paying much attention. It was hard to tell how he was handling the stress of what had happened on Friday. But Rob knew Frank would take care of things, one way or another.

Just before eleven, Frank looked over the top of the cubicle. "Hey, let's see if Eddie's in the jungle before grabbing a bite. Have a new place I want to try."

Rob snatched up his jacket. "Suits me. Don't want to go to Sarge's'?"

Frank led the way to the door. "I think maybe Sarge has seen enough of both of us for a while."

Fifteen minutes later, they strolled through the hole in the fence at the jungle. There weren't a lot of people about at this time of day—it was kind of quiet and peaceful. A few folks lingered in small groups, but most were out foraging for something to eat. Rob scanned the area. No sign of Eddie. The poor bastard wasn't in the spot they'd left him Friday night.

Frank pointed. "There's the mayor. Maybe he knows something."

Mayor Pete knelt over a man sprawled on the grass and whispered something into the guy's ear, looking a lot like a mother tucking a sick child into bed. Pete patted the man on the back and stood. When he saw them approaching, Pete's nostrils flared and his eyes blazed. Then he made a beeline in their direction, taking long strides.

"What do you two want?" Pete asked. His hands had formed into a fist and the knuckles were white.

"Whoa, what's wrong?" Rob asked.

Frank spoke up. "We're looking for Eddie. Have a few more questions."

"Well, you're looking in the wrong place." Mayor Pete almost spit the words out.

Rob held his palm up as if trying to stop a car from plowing over him. "Want to tell us what's going on?"

Pete cooled down a little and shifted his feet a few seconds before speaking. "Eddie's dead."

"What happened?" Rob asked.

Pete glared at them. "Not rightly sure. Happened the night you two talked to him. He slipped away after you left—returned in the pouring rain and settled down in his usual place. We found him the next morning. Still had the needle in his arm. Gave himself a hot shot. Never knew what hit him."

No one said anything for a few seconds.

Frank broke the silence. "Why?"

Pete shook his head. "Don't rightly know. Must have been something you talked about is all I can figure. Still can't imagine where he got the cash for the smack."

Rob's stomach turned as his mind drifted to the last thing he'd said to Eddie as he handed him a twenty. *Here, brother. Take this and get a meal and a bus ticket back to the VA. This rough life on the street isn't working for you anymore.*

*   *   *

Sister Judy kept Katrina busy the rest of the morning. For the first time, she was allowed into the nursery. Five fair-haired children, ranging in age from Annabelle's infant to a three-year-old, played on the floor, supervised by Sister Karen. Katrina scrubbed the bath and emptied the trash. Sister Karen kept an overprotective eye on the kids and gave Katrina wary glances from time to time. The nursery had a strange feel. The thought that all the children were fathered by Brother John but had different mothers kept seeping into Katrina's mind. Different mothers who were now missing. After a brief search for Annabelle earlier in the morning, no one now seemed to care. *Also strange.*

Katrina's next job was working in the kitchen. She washed the morning dishes and assisted Sisters Judy and Ruth in getting lunch, which they all referred to as dinner, ready on time. No one said a word except to issue an order or give a command. Still, no one mentioned that Annabelle was missing or even spoke her name. *It's like she never existed.* Katrina whispered silent prayers all morning for her safe escape.

Katrina set the dining room table and began pouring each food item into individual bowls for serving. Sisters Judy and Ruth had been whispering all morning about something. Katrina couldn't hear—they kept their voices low—but they'd glance in her direction every once in a while. They'd just walked out the back door, saying they were heading to the garden to fetch some fresh tomatoes, peppers, and onions for dinner. *Must be going to get a lot if it takes both of them.* They continued talking as they walked. Katrina watched them from the kitchen window until they disappeared into the garden.

When Katrina turned around, she bumped into Brother John. He'd been standing no more than a foot behind her as she gazed out the window. She let out a yelp and caught her breath. He didn't move, blink, or speak.

Katrina leaned back against the window and put her hand to her bosom. "You startled me."

He still didn't speak but continued staring at her through those tiny black creepy eyes. For a reason she couldn't explain, she released a nervous laugh and felt a blush cover her cheeks. "I didn't know you were behind me. I . . ."

He leaned to within inches of her face. "I don't like it," he whispered in a menacing voice.

Katrina's stomach rumbled and her legs weakened. She had never been so frightened. Even that night strapped down in the basement couldn't compare to this. That night she'd kept her eyes closed, pretending to be unconscious. But now, as she stared into those crazy, haunting eyes of Brother John, she knew. She might very well be gazing into the face of the devil.

They stood there for what seemed like five minutes, although it probably wasn't longer than five seconds. Slowly he lifted his hand, revealing a fork from the table she'd just set.

"It still has food on it," he said, shoving it so close to Katrina's face that her eyes crossed trying to focus.

Katrina croaked, "What?"

He pushed it closer. "I said it still has food on it."

Katrina leaned her head back a little and stared at the fork. On one tine, at the very tip, was an almost microscopic speck of something brown.

"I don't like it," the clean freak said. "Wash it again." He tossed the fork in the sink, spun around, and marched away.

Katrina couldn't move. Her body had locked up. After a few seconds, she willed her legs to carry her to the table, where she collapsed into a chair. Her heart raced a thousand beats a minute. She felt faint, as if she wanted to throw up. The sound of the screened porch door slamming drew her out of her anxiety attack. She staggered back into the kitchen just in time for Sister Judy and Sister Ruth to bitch at her about not having finished her work.

Katrina wasn't invited to join the group for lunch. Sister Judy informed her she would be dining alone in the kitchen from now on. Nothing could have suited Katrina better. No more stares from the Freak. Finally, a chance to relax during the meal. The smell of cabbage still hung in the kitchen as she sat at her small table in the corner and lifted her fork. From the basement door, only feet away, a mournful cry drifted out.

The new girl.

Who was it? Where had she come from? Why had they grabbed another one so soon after taking her? Something felt wrong.

Katrina's appetite vanished. Annabelle had said that of all the girls who'd come and gone, not one had ever sent help. If no one had made a big deal about Annabelle's disappearance, that could mean only one thing. *They already know she'll never be able to send help.* Katrina rested her face on her hands and tried to hide the sound of her weeping. The idea gnawed at her gut. *My friend is dead.*

* * *

Rob and Frank had lunch at a soul food place in south Oak Cliff. Frank wanted fried chicken, and Rob never argued when Frank had a food craving. Better to just let him satisfy it.

By the time they made it to CIU, Terry was darting from his office in a state of nervous excitement. He waved a sheet of paper.

"Guess what?"

"What?" Rob asked.

Terry thrust the paper at Frank. "You got a hit on your request for the Wormwood information. There's a guy in a Texas state prison with that tattoo."

Frank scanned the paper as Rob looked over his shoulder. "Skyview Unit. Where in the hell is Skyview?" Rob asked.

"It's a psychiatric facility near Rusk," Frank said, still reviewing the document.

Rob and Terry shot glances at each other.

"Guy's name is Marshall Woodard. Doing life for double homicide," Frank said, handing the paper to Rob. "Pull up all you can on him. I'm giving the prison a call."

Rob dashed to his cubicle and woke his computer while Frank punched numbers into his office phone.

* * *

A half hour later, Frank sat next to Rob on the sofa in Edna's office while she read the information on Marshall Woodard. Terry leaned against the doorjamb, arms crossed, waiting. Edna sat behind her desk, her brow rising and falling from time to time, her lips moving while reading the report from the Texas Department of Criminal Justice. Frank knew a trip to Rusk might be a tough sell, but he couldn't afford to let her say no.

She looked up. "You think this guy is connected?"

"When we interviewed Eddie, he said there was a Brother Marshall living in the house with him and that he also had the same tattoo," Frank said.

Edna continued reviewing the papers. "Okay, I get it. Since Eddie's dead, you want to interview this Marshall guy." She tapped the page with her finger. "But how sure are we that this isn't a wild-goose chase? Do we have anything concrete yet?" She looked from Frank to Rob.

Frank exchanged a glance with his partner, but neither spoke.

Edna dropped the papers to her desk with a sigh. "Pretty slim, if you ask me."

Frank had been admonished more than once not to say what he now intended to say, but he felt the case slipping out of his grasp. He had no choice. "She's alive," Frank said.

Edna snapped her head up. "Who says?"

"I say," Frank answered.

Terry ran a hand down his weary face, and Rob tried to hide in the sofa.

"How do you know that?" she demanded.

"I just do, and Wormwood is the key." Frank met her stare without blinking.

A sly grin cracked the corners of Edna's mouth. "Okay, go to Rusk and interview this guy. See what he knows." She pointed at all three. "But we have to turn up something fast. This thing is reaching stall speed. None of us wants to be on board when it crashes."

Frank couldn't blame her. Everyone was pulling heat on this one, and it started at the top. Edna wasn't going to let a little thing like the kidnapping of the mayor's daughter stand in the way of her next promotion.

Rob and Frank spent the rest of the afternoon preparing for their trip the next day. Frank locked down an interview in the late morning, while Rob created a folder with all they knew about Marshall Woodard, Eddie Jones, and the mysterious Vernon John Warren, aka Brother John.

According to Texas Department of Criminal Justice records, Marshall Woodard's incarceration was the result of a trip to the beach. The year before, he'd hitched a ride to the Bolivar Peninsula, on the upper Texas coast. While waiting for the ferry to take him over to Galveston, he'd met two middle-aged women out for a little fun. They must have liked his looks, because they persuaded him to join them at their Crystal Beach house for the weekend.

That night, after copious amounts of alcohol, drugs, and foreplay, Marshall made a decision. The devil had sent those harlots to test him, to test his chastity. By stabbing one seventeen times and the other fifteen times with a butcher knife, he'd thwarted the devil's attempt and rebuffed him once again. Marshall offered no defense at trial other than that he was proud to have survived the enticement.

Frank tucked the report back into the folder. *Oh, yeah. This one will be a charm to interview.*

*   *   *

Katrina's depression deepened with each passing hour. Annabelle was dead. There would be no ransom demands for her. These nuts didn't care about money. They had a religious agenda. Once they were through with her, she'd be discarded like yesterday's garbage.

"*Katrina!*" Sister Ruth's shrill voice screamed. "Bring that mop and bucket in here. You missed a spot."

Katrina reached for the bucket and glimpsed the calendar on the kitchen wall. April thirtieth. Her birthday. She was twenty years old. She paused and gave silent thanks.

"*Katrina!* Did you hear me? Get in here, now!"

Katrina hated that rotten bitch.

25

The next morning, Frank dozed in the passenger seat as Rob drove to Rusk. Rob hated when Frank slept, especially on long drives. They'd left Dallas at eight o'clock and had just passed through Athens—a little over halfway there. Frank didn't mean to be rude, but being in a moving vehicle made him drowsy, a tendency that had probably started when he was a baby.

Frank napped peacefully, arms folded, knees against the dash, head cocked to the side by the window. An eighteen-wheeler topped the hill about two hundred yards out, going in the opposite direction. Rob put both hands on the wheel at the ten and two positions and steadied his nerves. When the eighteen-wheeler was about a hundred yards away, Rob eased his left wheels across the white stripes. The truck was now only fifty yards out. Rob waited for the truck driver to make the next move. Sure enough, the truck blared its loud horn. Simultaneously, Rob cried out as if he were being crucified and jerked the car back into his lane as the roar of the rushing truck blew past.

Frank jumped two feet off the seat and screamed like an eight-year-old girl. His sunglasses flew off and his eyes were as big as melons. He slapped his hand against his chest as if he were checking to see if his heart still beat. He jerked his head toward Rob. His mouth gaped, but he appeared unable to formulate words.

Rob wasn't sure he could keep a straight face, but if he didn't play it to the end, Frank would sleep again on the next trip. "Sorry, I don't know . . . I mean, I was looking at the road and there wasn't anyone in sight. Then the horn blew and a truck just appeared in my lane," Rob stammered. "I must have dropped off."

"Must have dropped off? You can't just drop off—you're driving," Frank screamed. He had an incredulous expression, as if he'd just learned that Bigfoot was real.

Rob threw up his hands. "Hey, I'm sorry. But with no one to talk to, I get sleepy sometimes."

Frank still clasped his chest, but he had stopped taking deep, panicked breaths. He sipped his bottle of water, and they drove in silence for a few minutes.

"Talked to Roger Wells last night," Frank said.

"Roger Wells? I know that name."

Frank slid down in the seat and propped his knees on the dash while adjusting his sunglasses. "Used to work Burglary and Theft. Resigned a couple of years ago."

"Oh, yeah, I remember. Nice guy," Rob said.

"Yeah."

"Why were you talking to him?" Rob asked.

"He works corporate security for Bank of America."

Rob's stomach tightened. "So how's he doing?"

"Good. Making a lot more money . . . better hours, company car, expense account."

Rob didn't say anything. He already knew why Frank had made the call.

After a minute, Frank said, "I asked him about life on the outside—you know—what it was like. We talked for a while, and he asked when I was thinking about pulling the plug. I told him probably by the summer."

The world dropped out from under Rob. He took a slow, deep breath but didn't want to show surprise. "Wow, that soon, huh?"

Frank cut a sideways look at him. "If I don't have a future here, why stay? Better to leave now."

This was all happening faster than Rob liked. He'd expected Frank would drag his feet about resigning and probably talk himself out of it in the end. But he was serious and already making contacts. "Summer, huh. Gee, that's right around the corner," Rob mumbled.

"Roger said they had a VP job in security opening up in Charlotte. He'd put in a word for me if I wanted."

Rob's skin tingled and he dreaded to ask, but did. "What did you tell him?"

Frank stared at the road for a couple of seconds before answering. "I told him to do it."

"That's great." Rob's tone didn't mask his disappointment.

Frank muttered, "Yeah, great."

*   *   *

At exactly 10:30 AM, Rob and Frank rolled up to the gate of the Sky-view Unit. The Texas Department of Criminal Justice prison nudged up against another: the Hodge Unit. Texas liked to keep its rotten apples in a tight cluster. Skyview, a fifty-eight-acre cogender facility, had opened in 1988 and held only psychiatric inmates. Frank had been instructed to enter through the rear gate and check in at the visitor's center.

As Rob pulled up at the intercom box outside the ten-foot chain-link fence topped with double razor wire, Frank said, "Let's make this quick. I hate these places."

Rob agreed. All prisons gave him the willies, but this place was especially creepy. Just knowing about the sick minds that dwelled within these walls caused goosebumps the size of blueberries. Rob pushed the button on the box. Several guards with shotguns strolled behind the fence, keeping their gaze on the car.

"State your business," a voice said.

Rob leaned out the window. "Detectives Soliz and Pierce to see Deputy Warden Hightower."

There was no answer. Rob looked at Frank and he shrugged.

After a minute, the voice asked, "Are you armed?"

"Yes."

"You have to check your weapons at the visitor's center. Stand by."

A small pedestrian gate opened and a guard carrying a shotgun strolled toward them. Two other guards meandered around the catwalk on the fifty-foot tower beside the gate, also dressed in gray and carrying shotguns. They watched with increased curiosity as the corrections officer approached Rob's car.

"Morning," the sergeant said. "Identification, please." The man looked middle-aged but could have been younger. Rob had always noticed that places like these aged people faster than nature.

They handed over their credentials.

The sergeant studied them briefly and pointed. "Drive through the gate, and they'll direct you." He waved to the guys on the catwalk, and they nodded. The metal gates slid open and an armed guard waved them inside.

After checking their weapons, Rob and Frank followed the sergeant outside to the administrative wing, passing inmates in white shirts and pants. The prisoners stopped weeding the flower bed and gawked at Rob and Frank. A tall black prisoner swept the sidewalk with a cavalier motion. His lazy swipes with the broom left as much dirt and grass as he swept off. He smiled as if someone had just told him a joke that wasn't all that funny. The man stopped sweeping and stood motionless. He didn't look at them but whispered something to the handle of the broom. When he turned, only a dark hole outlined where his right eye should be. The other eye was a dull, lifeless gray.

The sergeant pointed at him. "Benny, either put it back in, or wear the patch, or the sunglasses. Okay?"

A scary grin crept over the man's face. He mumbled something else to the broom and slipped on the sunglasses.

"Don't mind him," the sergeant said. "Old Benny is harmless."

"What's he in for?" Rob asked.

"A few years ago, voices told him his infant daughter was possessed," the sergeant said. "That if she wasn't sacrificed, she could never enter the kingdom of God. Benny waited for his wife to fall asleep, slipped the baby from her crib, and laid her on a meat chopping block. After he finished and saw what he'd done, he must have had a flash of sanity, because he ripped out his eye and ran from the apartment screaming. Likes to carry his glass eye in his pocket."

Rob glanced at Frank to get his reaction, but his partner stared straight ahead, avoiding eye contact with the inmate as though not acknowledging the guy would mean he wasn't really there. Rob couldn't blame him. He'd developed a pretty thick callus over the years to what human beings did to each other, but this place held the worst of the worst.

The sergeant unlocked a door on the next building, and they filed in. He relocked it and led the way to the office at the end of the hall. The place had a hospital smell, sparkling tile floors, and cinder block walls painted bright white. The sergeant knocked on a door and a voice said, "Come in."

Rob and Frank sauntered into a small office with institutional furniture, and a man greeted them.

"Good morning. I'm Deputy Warden Tim Hightower." He was a football-coach-looking guy, short, with a salt-and-pepper flattop and welcoming smile.

Another man sitting on a sofa against a wall also stood. He extended his hand. "I'm Doctor Poe, the unit psychiatrist." He wore a suit, whereas Hightower had on only an open-collar shirt and dress pants. Dr. Poe could have been Steven Spielberg's twin, except he stood a head taller.

After introductions, Hightower reviewed Marshall Woodard's arrest and incarceration history. He showed them a photo of the Wormwood tattoo on the inmate's back. It matched the one on Eddie Jones.

Hightower dropped the file on his desk and sighed. "He goes crazy if anyone steps on his shadow, refuses to have anything to do with the other inmates, and is very manipulative. I have to ask, does your interview concern any charges he's currently serving time for?"

"No," Frank said.

"Does your interview concern additional charges that might be brought against him at a later date?"

"No."

Hightower rocked back in the chair and interlaced his fingers on a bulging stomach. "In that case, I'll turn it over to Dr. Poe for his observations."

Poe cleared his throat and relaxed on the couch, crossing his legs. "Mr. Woodard is one of the most interesting patients I've ever encountered. While I object to the use of the word *crazy*, he does make crazy seem normal." Poe chuckled at his joke. "He maintains an illusion about a living deity. He refers to him as the Prophet. According to Woodard, this prophet was sent to earth by God to warn the true believers of the Savior's return." A trace of a grin cracked the corners of Poe's lips. "And only those ordained by the Prophet will survive the biblical end-of-days event predicted in Revelation."

Poe shifted on the sofa and rubbed his knee. His voice dropped a little. "We've diagnosed him as bipolar with a severe persecution disorder. He can be lucid one minute and irrational and violent the next. Probably caught him in the nick of time. He's only murdered two people we know of. If left untreated, he has the makings of a serial killer."

Rob raised his eyebrows. "Serial killer?"

Poe cleared his throat again. "Yes, grew up lonely and isolated. Psychologically and sexually abused by his father and has admitted to acting out sexual fantasies on animals as an adolescent. Prefers autoerotic activities. Unable to maintain any kind of normal relationship."

Rob stopped taking notes. "Any hope for someone like that?"

Poe's brow furrowed. "We've tried all the standard psychotropic drugs and counseling. But until he lets go of the fantasy, we can't move forward in the treatment."

Rob wrote a mile a minute in his notebook and flipped the page to a new sheet. Frank hadn't asked one question. His face had a blank expression. Rob wondered if he was thinking about the case or about the VP job in Charlotte.

Rob turned his attention back to Poe. "This deity that he talks about . . . does he have a name?"

Dr. Poe shifted again and leaned an elbow on the armrest. "He refers to him as Brother John," Poe chuckled, "but also calls him—"

"Wormwood," Frank said.

Poe sucked a sharp breath between his teeth. "How in the world could you know that?"

Frank stood. "Because it's not just a fantasy."

* * *

Dr. Poe led Frank and Rob into an interview room in the maximum-security unit of the prison. After Frank's disclosure, Poe had practically begged to join them in the interview. Neither saw any harm, so they agreed. Poe was chatty on the way, wanting to know everything about the man called Wormwood. Rob kept his explanation short. The doc probably had only a clinical interest, but Rob wouldn't be forthcoming about a case still under investigation.

The sparsely furnished room had all the charm of a holding cell at Dachau. Bars and wire outside the windows. A table bolted to the floor. Three straight-backed chairs with well-worn green leather seats. Frank squirmed and kept folding his hands in his lap as if he were resisting a severe case of the heebie-jeebies. When the guard led Woodard in, Frank stood, and Rob could have sworn he saw Frank's shoulders instantly relax and the wrinkles in his forehead disappear. His partner was in his element now—the inquisitor.

"Hello, Marshall," Dr. Poe said. "Please, have a seat." Poe pointed to the opposite side of the table.

Marshall Woodard could be described in one word: wiry. He was no more than five five, and his intelligent and suspicious eyes scanned everyone, seeming to immediately assess the situation. He wore shackles on his ankles and wrists, attached to chains around his waist. Although an old stain marred his left sleeve, his white shirt and pants were clean and well pressed.

He shuffled to the desk with a smile that said, "I'm ready—let's go." The guard unlatched a cuff and ran it through a metal eyelet on the table before locking it in place. Poe, leaning against the wall as far as possible from Woodard, motioned for the guard to leave. Rob and Frank sat across the table from the inmate. Woodard nodded his head, as if he agreed with something someone had just said. His mysterious smile didn't disappear until Dr. Poe spoke.

"Marshall, these men are with the police."

Woodward gazed blankly at Rob and Frank. The hair on the back of Rob's neck rose. He had no idea what was going on in that head, but there was a big part of him that didn't want to know.

Poe crossed his arms and casually asked, "They'd like to ask you a few questions. Do you feel like talking today?"

The prisoner glared at Poe. Woodard tried pointing at the doctor, but the handcuff prevented it. In a sulky voice, the inmate said, "They took away my Bible again."

Poe flashed a defensive grin at Rob and Frank. "Sometimes Marshall gets a little worked up when he reads the Bible too often. Don't you, Marshall?"

Woodard shot a stare at Poe. "Screw you. You've damned my soul by cutting my hair and beard and keeping me in this den of sin. What's my crime? The least you could do is allow me one last chance at salvation. Now I'm as cursed as the rest of you."

Poe stepped a little farther away but maintained eye contact. "Marshall, your salvation has nothing to do with your hair and beard. And you are perfectly aware of your crime."

Rob kept as far away from Woodard as he could while still being able to use the table for note taking. Woodard didn't appear to notice.

"Marshall," Frank said.

The man's gaze drifted away from Poe. He blinked a couple of times, as if he were having trouble focusing.

"I'd like to know more about your salvation," Frank said, "about why cutting your hair and beard is damning your soul. Will you tell me?" Frank leaned forward, his forearms on the metal table.

A Cheshire Cat smile crossed Woodard's lips. "Sure," he said.

Frank sat on the edge of his chair and locked eyes with Woodard.

Marshall scanned Frank's face, then Rob's. "Because the Prophet said that only he with uncut hair could enter into the saving grace of the Father," Woodard quoted.

A cold tingle raced up Rob's back. *Echoes of Eddie Jones.*

Speaking in a soft voice, Frank asked, "Why's that?"

Marshall blinked a couple more times. "Because the Prophet said it. Don't you see? He's the mouthpiece of God here on earth. He rose to meet the Father and was sent back to earth to deliver His message." Woodard relaxed in the chair with a peaceful expression.

"Yes," Frank said. "I understand now. Tell me more. I want to know."

Woodard squinted and moved closer, rolling his head toward Poe, and said, "He thinks I'm crazy, but we'll see who's crazy when the third angel sounds its trumpet."

Frank nodded in agreement. "That will herald the rise of Wormwood."

Woodard's eyes brightened. "You know your scripture. You a true believer?"

"I want to be," Frank said.

"I am." Marshall edged even closer and dropped his voice to a whisper. "You know I only sleep two hours a night." He giggled and swatted away some imaginary insect from the side of his face. "I spend the rest of the time praying."

Frank leaned in so there were only inches between their faces. "Is that so?"

"Yeah, and I tell you something else," Woodard said. "God opens his salvation to everyone—even women—but they can't be harlots and whores. They must remain pure. Can't expose their skin, stop painting their faces, and can't cut their hair. They can't even wear undergarments . . . except, you know, on their private areas, down there." Woodard's eyes lowered to his crotch.

"Yes, I see what you mean," Frank admitted. "But I want to know more about Wormwood's teachings. Or should I just call him Brother John?"

Woodward giggled and winked. "Don't matter none. One and the same." He grinned. "I'll tell you a secret not even Dr. Poe knows." Woodard glanced at Poe, who was still leaning against the wall. "You can't kill the Prophet," Woodard whispered.

"Really?" Frank asked.

"Yup, he'll just resurrect himself. He's immortal."

"Is that a fact?"

"Yeah. The day he claimed the gift of prophecy, God instructed him to go forth and take seven flaxen-haired spiritual brides. They will bear him seven children, who will be the ruling elders of earth, after he departs unto heaven," Woodard said.

Rob's skin almost crawled off his bones. *Seven flaxen-haired brides.* Trina had blonde hair. Did this mean she wasn't the only one missing?

* * *

Rob and Frank relaxed on the sofa as Edna clicked the ballpoint pen with one hand and held her stress ball with the other. She reclined in her chair and stared at Terry, who was sitting across from her, his usual easygoing demeanor absent. Rob wanted to ask her if she had another stress ball in her desk, but he was pretty sure that would piss her off.

"So, what do you think?" she asked.

Edna always requested Terry's sage advice before making a major command decision. It might be hers to make, but it was also her head on the block.

Terry crossed his legs and glanced at Rob and Frank. Rob leaned forward, holding a hand in a fist, his arms resting on his knees. Frank slumped to one side, yawning.

"We have to look at what we have and not what we wish we had," Terry said. "If the guy at Skyview is to be believed, then the mayor's daughter is probably still alive and being held somewhere. We don't have any better lead than the Wormwood thing. The Rangers, FBI, and our Missing Persons Unit aren't getting anywhere. It's not perfect, but it's probably the best we've got."

Edna stopped clicking the pen and tossed it on her desk. "We know the guy's raving mad. The warden even told you he was manipulative. How do we know he's not just leading us around by the nose? Have you ever met a nutcase whose information you trusted?"

"It had a ring of truth, Lieutenant," Rob said, remembering Marshall's expression as the guards led him out. He had seemed at peace, as if he was waiting for something wonderful to happen. "I believe him. You had to be there."

Edna picked up the pen again and twirled it through her fingers. She shifted her gaze to Frank. "You've been pretty quiet. Have any thoughts?"

Frank scratched his neck before answering. "I agree with Rob. Staying on the Wormwood angle is the only sensible course."

She exhaled. "Okay, but where do we go from here? We don't have any forensics or witnesses to link this Brother John character to anything. We don't even know where he is."

She was right, Rob thought. They didn't have much to go on.

Frank sat upright and pursed his lips. "We could be missing the forest because of the trees. The mayor's daughter may be the first of seven, the last of seven, or anywhere in between. We have no way of knowing. I say we canvass regional police agencies to determine if they have any 'flaxen-haired' young women missing from their jurisdictions in the last few years," Frank said. "And if they do, was there a Bible found at the scene? Especially one with the word *Wormwood* highlighted. If so, we might be able to triangulate the approximate location of Brother John."

Rob's insides unwound as it became clear from Edna's expression that Frank's argument was winning her over.

She exhaled. "Okay, make it happen."

Frank spent the rest of the afternoon assembling information for the agency notifications. Rob tried talking to him but only got a distracted mumble for a reply. Just before five, Frank pulled off a sheet of paper from the printer. "Let's talk to Terry."

Terry had already logged off his computer and turned off the coffee maker when they traipsed in. "What do you have?" he asked.

Frank passed the sheet to him, and Terry spent a minute reviewing it. He looked up. "So, why did you choose these towns?"

"I figured whoever grabbed her had to go by road. Probably not more than three hundred miles," Frank answered.

Terry nodded, his brow pinched.

Rob pointed to the page. "And snatching girls from a small town wouldn't be smart. Too much publicity. Everyone would make a big deal over it. So we're searching only cities."

"Twelve cities from San Angelo to Alexandria and Beaumont to Hot Springs," Terry said. "Jeez, that's three states."

Frank shrugged. "Cast a wide net."

Terry switched off his office light and said, "Okay, I'll run it past Edna."

Rob strolled to his desk and grabbed his jacket, but Frank plopped into his chair and stared straight ahead.

"What's wrong?" Rob asked.

Frank looked up. "I dread what I have to do next."

Rob slipped on his jacket. "What's that?"

"Wait," Frank said.

Rob made his way out of CIU, thinking about Marshall in his grimy cell, waiting for Judgment Day. That's what all of them were doing now—him, Frank, Marshall, and Katrina. Waiting. And he wasn't sure how much time Katrina had left.

*   *   *

Katrina listened at the door leading to the basement. The wails of the girl below pulled pity from her, but there was nothing she could do. Had the Freak *visited* her yet? She'd been down there a day and a half, and no one had said a word about her. *Does that mean something?* Only Sister Judy and Sister Ruth had keys to the deadbolt lock on the basement door; each of them carried one on a ribbon tied around her neck. How could Katrina get one?

Voices sounded from the screened-in porch, and Katrina rushed to the sink, immersing her hands in soapy dishwater. When Sisters Ruth and Karen strolled inside, Sister Ruth wore a smirk. They continued through the dining room, and the voices faded. Katrina rinsed the plates and silverware and stacked them neatly in the drain tray.

She had never washed dishes before coming to this freak show. Growing up, maids had collected the dishes at the end of meals, and the next time she saw them, they were set on a fine linen tablecloth with knives, forks, and spoons. This crappy place didn't even have a built-in dishwasher. No. She was the dishwasher.

"Katrina," Sister Ruth yelled, "we're starting."

If being their slave wasn't bad enough, she had to endure the nightly sermons from the Freak. The guy hardly ever spoke, except in whispers to one of the brothers or Sister Ruth or Sister Judy. But give him an altar and the silly bastard went on for hours about a bunch of gobble-goop that made no sense, unless you already had mental problems. Katrina untied the apron and hung it on the hook by the wall clock. Yup, seven o'clock on the dot. He always started then, and they'd be lucky to get out by ten.

She wandered into the living room and sat in the usual chair facing the altar. *Altar? What a crock. A bunch of sticks, leaves, and rocks. Signifying what? Mother Earth or some shit.* She looked around, and all were present except Sister Karen and the Freak. It must have been her night to watch the children. More than once Katrina had decided not to attend the nightly sermons but chickened out at the last minute. Better to lull them into believing she went along with them until she could figure something out for escape. If they threw her back into the basement, she'd never get that chance.

When the Freak walked in, he carried his well-worn Bible and stood behind the altar. He raked the long hair behind his ears and examined the group. "God just spoke to me about tonight's teachings. We'll read from the Book of Isaiah. Turn with me to the thirty-forth chapter and the sixteenth verse."

Bibles opened and pages flipped.

He cleared his throat. "Seek ye out of the book of the Lord, and read: no one of these shall fail, none shall want her mate: for my mouth it hath commanded, and his spirit it hath gathered them."

He lifted his eyes after reading the verse, and they rested on Katrina. Her skin became cold and clammy, and goose bumps sprang up like weeds. What did he mean, *none shall want her mate*?

26

From the time they'd visited Marshall Woodard in prison, Frank's obsession with the case had grown each day. He spent most of his time checking either the fax machine or his email. The notifications sent to the police agencies to canvass their records for missing blonde girls, especially where a Bible was involved, had *his* email and fax number at the bottom as primary contact. It was no surprise to anyone, except Frank, when by Friday afternoon not one agency had called. Police departments honored requests from each other, but few broke their necks to get them done in a hurry. They got pushed around for a few days, finally landing on the junior guy's desk. If he happened to be sick, busy, or on vacation, the request tended to drift beneath the pile.

By Friday afternoon, Frank's mood had grown so black that Rob figured they needed to drink it out at Sarge's after work. Rob ran an errand, and when he returned to CIU, he found Frank slouched in his cubicle watching some YouTube video. The sound was so low only Rob and Frank could hear. Rob leaned on the cube's low wall, and Frank shot him a look before turning back to the screen. The video was of an older preacher dressed in a white suit, with silver hair and rings on all fingers. His hazel eyes sparkled as he held the mike and admonished the audience.

"Do you love God?" the preacher asked.

A timid "Yes" rose from the congregation.

The man whirled in a different direction and pointed. "If I can't hear you, what makes you think God can? I said, do you love God?"

A louder "Yes" echoed from the people.

The preacher held up his free hand and started to speak but instead collapsed on the floor. He put his head against the carpet and moaned. "Yes, Lord . . . I hear you . . . yes, Lord." After a minute, he rose and wiped sweat from his brow with a silk handkerchief. He slipped it into his coat pocket and drew in a deep breath.

"God just told me something, folks." He laughed and looked up. "Praise God . . . yes, Lord, I'm going to tell 'em right now." He scanned the gathering and spoke in tongues. He closed his eyes and lifted both hands to heaven and continued declaring the mysterious foreign words. The congregation joined in. After a moment, he again wiped his brow and mouth with the handkerchief.

"God told me that tonight he wants his children to give him a special love offering, above and beyond your tithe. He said for those who will bless his church with this special offering, he'll bless you a hundredfold."

The color had drained from Frank's face, and he wasn't breathing. His hand gripped the chair's armrest—knuckles white.

"Frank, you okay?" Rob whispered.

Frank twisted his neck and met eyes with Rob. His mouth had a look like he'd just eaten a lemon. He paused the video. "Yeah, I'm good."

"Who is that guy?" Rob asked.

Frank sat up. "That's the quite reverent Truly Fischer. A full-faith minister from Florida."

"Never heard of him," Rob said.

Frank chuckled. "You're Catholic. He doesn't run in those circles."

"What's he famous for?"

Frank sat up straighter, suddenly more animated than he'd been in days. He raised his hands and moved them in some kind of mystical wave. "Oh, he heals the sick, raises the dead—you name it, he'll do it. But he's mostly famous for having the most scandal-ridden ministry in the country. Several attorney general probes, two IRS investigations, and more sexual escapades than Jim Bakker and Jimmy Swaggart put together. But you know what?" Frank grinned. "The true evangelical believers still flock to his BS sermons." Frank shook his head and mumbled, "They still come."

From the corner, the fax machine hummed as a page rolled into the tray. Frank pushed out of his chair and sprinted in that direction. After a moment, he sauntered back empty-handed.

"Not for you?" Rob asked.

Frank shook his head and collapsed into his chair. The fact that some old heads in other departments still used a fax machine probably frustrated Frank. But old guys had old ways.

Rob checked his watch. "It's close enough to getting-off time. Let's go to Sarge's."

Frank shut down his computer and stood, his shoulders hunched. He'd fallen into a serious funk. "Yeah, let's go."

* * *

By the time they arrived at Sarge's, the Friday after-work crowd was in full party mode. Rob and Frank squeezed past a wad of people congregated near the door and wormed through the mob to the last two empty stools on the far end. Country and western music filled the room while Sarge mixed drinks and Jan pushed them to the customers and took new orders.

"Be right with you guys," she yelled above the noise of the voices.

Frank shuffled behind Rob. Frank's face had a vacant look. He got that way when things didn't happen as fast as he liked, and it put people off who didn't understand. Rob referred to it as his melancholy stare.

Just then a booth opened up and Rob touched Frank's arm. They transferred their headquarters to the booth, and Jan cleared the table.

"What'll it be, boys?"

"Mic for me and house red for Frank," Rob said.

She scurried toward the bar, and Rob looked at Frank. "Why were you watching that video about the preacher?"

Frank squirmed in the booth as if trying to decide if he wanted to sit or slouch. He finally decided and sat upright with his hands gripping the edge of the table.

"My grandparents took me to hear him when I was a kid in Florida." Frank gazed in the distance, remembering. "This was before they hit it rich on the land deal. Reverend Fischer preached out of a big tent then. My grandma said when we finished listening to him, we'd get a hamburger and fries."

Jan slid a cold beer and glass of red wine to them. "Cheers," she said before retreating.

Rob tasted the beer and studied Frank. His partner didn't touch his glass but glared at the table with a sour face.

"So you got a hamburger and fries . . ."

Frank seemed to wake up and glanced his way. "No, I didn't. After Reverend Fischer passed the plate for the regular offering and my granddad almost emptied his wallet, Fischer passed a canvas bag for a 'special love offering.' I'll never forget the look on my grandma's face as she and my grandpa stared at the last few dollars in his wallet. He dropped them into that bag, and we went back to the ranch and ate leftovers."

Rob chuckled. "So Reverend Fischer screwed you out of your burger and fries?"

"No, the old bastard screwed my grandparents out of their last few bucks," Frank said.

"So, was that an old video, or is the guy still preaching?" Rob asked.

"Yeah, still cheating people—on cable and the Internet now."

"You down on religion in general, or just that guy?" Rob asked.

Frank didn't answer, but he was thinking.

"I'm not so sure I believe in the whole Jesus thing," Frank mumbled.

"Holy shit." Rob crossed himself. "A heathen. You serious?"

"The more I think about it, the less I'm convinced." Frank got into his lounge position: back against the wall and legs stretched across the seat. He looked at Rob and lifted an eyebrow.

"How much do you believe?"

Rob stammered, "What my parents, wife, and priest believe . . . I guess."

"Okay, quote John 3:16," Frank said.

"Well, I don't exactly have the Bible memorized."

"Have you ever read it?" Frank asked.

"Sure, you know . . . parts."

Frank quoted. "'For God so loved the world that he gave his only begotten Son, that whosoever believeth in him should not perish, but have everlasting life.' That's the King James version." Frank said. "There are numerous versions and translations of the Bible—over a hundred. Plus, when you consider who actually wrote the scriptures, that opens another bag of worms."

"Like how?" Rob took another swig of beer.

"Well, take the Synoptic Gospels, for instance."

"The what?" Rob asked.

"The gospels of Matthew, Mark, and Luke. They're filled with contradictions. One guy says one thing and another guy says something else. You know why?" Frank had that look that dared Rob to ask.

"Huh-uh?"

"Because they weren't written by the evangelist who is attributed as their author. The books come from other written and oral sources. All the gospels were written by who knows who. The writers weren't apostles or even eyewitnesses, and the text was written a long time after their deaths. Whether someone wrote the books with divine inspiration or just made it up as they went, we have no way of knowing," Frank said.

Rob spun the empty glass around with a finger. He looked up. "How many times you read the Bible?"

Frank's grin was lopsided, as if he was embarrassed by what he was about to say. "Five, but I'm more confused with each reading. It's like trying to figure out the US tax code. There are a hundred and ninety-four inconsistencies in the New Testament alone."

"When you say 'inconsistencies,' give me an example. Are you talking about dates, or some spelling differences?" Rob asked.

Frank finished his wine and lifted his glass at Sarge while also pointing to Rob's. "Nope, bigger. Like the fact that of all the writers of the New Testament, only Matthew and Luke seemed to be aware of the virgin birth."

"What?"

"Yeah," Frank said.

Rob squirmed. "Wow! You saying you don't believe Jesus was the son of God in the Bible Belt? Shit, I could go to hell just sitting next to your ass."

Jan brought another beer and wine and scooped up the empties.

Frank slid the wine in front of him and shrugged. "That's just one of the many inaccuracies."

"Okay, Frank, stop. You're scaring me," Rob said.

Frank gestured with his hands, getting deeper into his lecture. "During the times of the early church, many of the writers wanted to show Jesus was the son of God by having him fulfill prophecies from the Old Testament. Today we call guys like that spin doctors."

Rob drank half his beer in one swallow but thought he needed more.

"Peter is said to be the first pope, right? 'Upon this rock I will build my church'?"

"Where you going with this, Frank?" Rob asked.

"Most think the Lord's Supper was created by Peter, but he appropriated it from Mithraism."

"What?" Rob asked.

Frank tested the new wine. "It was an established religion well before Christianity and up until the time of Constantine, a close competitor. Mithras was the central deity who died for mankind's sins and was resurrected after death. It was said if you believed in Mithras you would have eternal life. Sound familiar?"

Rob ran a hand over his short hair before whispering, "Shit, I wish I went to mass last Sunday."

"Hey, the gospel writers aren't any worse than people today. We rewrite history all the time to suit our purposes. Add to that, the texts were extensively edited to reflect evolving church dogma, and you get a wad of contradictions. Everyone—yesterday, today, and tomorrow— has agendas they're pushing. What we have to ask ourselves is how much do we believe, or do we believe any of it?" Frank said.

Rob looked into his glass. *Definitely stopping by church on the way home.*

"The Catholics canonized the books of the Bible. But what about the ones that weren't canonized? Could the lost books shed any light on things, or were they left out because they didn't tell the story the right way for the times?"

Rob eyed Frank. "So now you're blaming the Catholic Church?"

Frank's jaw dropped and his brow rose. "Who? Me? Blame the folks who gave us the Holy Inquisition and the Crusades?"

"You argue like a criminal defense attorney. You know that?" Rob said.

Frank's lips pursed. "Please, Rob, there's no need for name-calling." Frank paused and looked into the wine glass, as if he was expecting to find some answers there. Finally he spoke. "My point is, people like Marshall Woodard never ask themselves any of these questions. Wormwood. Reverend Fischer. They're all the same. It's just a matter of degree."

"I'll have one more round with you if you'll stop talking religion," Rob said. He didn't know how many Hail Marys he already owed after listening to Frank's ramble, but he wasn't going to incur any more.

"Deal, but just two more questions. Okay?"

Rob shrugged. "Only two?"

"You believe in a literal translation of the Bible?"

Rob dropped his head in his hands and moaned as he considered the question a moment. "Yeah . . . yeah, I do."

"You believe dinosaurs once roamed the earth?" Frank asked.

Rob's eyebrows furrowed. "Of course," he said.

"Why were they never mentioned in the Bible, or on Noah's Ark?"

That was three questions, but at this point, what difference did it make?

27

For two days Katrina had been getting her nerve up and waiting for just the right moment. She stood in her bedroom and watched all the brothers and sisters, except Ruth, being lectured by the Freak under the big oak in the front yard. They did this every so often for an hour or so. This Saturday morning was the time Katrina had waited for. The time she'd try to make contact with the girl in the basement. The locked basement door remained the problem. There was probably a spare key somewhere. She had to find it.

Katrina had been fighting a bout of homesickness all morning. Were her parents looking for her? Did her boyfriend still care about her? She needed something to take her mind off what she didn't have. Talking to the other girl might be just the thing.

Annabelle's words about the emerald ring came to her. *They stole this from me the day I arrived. But I found where they hid it in the women's bedroom and stole it back. They've never missed it.* The bedroom where the sisters slept was upstairs. Right beside the nursery. Could Katrina get in and out without being caught? Sister Ruth would be alerted to any sounds coming from the empty room, but Katrina had to try.

Something had happened to her. She'd never expected to feel empathy for a stranger. But the thought of the girl in the basement stuck in her mind. Or was it just her own loneliness? All her life Katrina had been the center of the universe and everyone had doted on her every desire. That wasn't happening here. She was merely an incubator for the Freak's seed, when he got around to her. After that, she had no more use.

Whatever the reason, she needed to talk to that girl. Tell her not to be afraid. Tell her she had a comrade in the same predicament. That's what Annabelle had done for her. Katrina owed a debt.

Katrina slipped out the door and tiptoed down the hall. As she passed the nursery, she leaned her ear to the door. The sound of Sister Ruth's voice filled the room as she read a Bible story to the children. Katrina opened the door of the sisters' room and eased inside, closing it without a sound.

The room was furnished much like hers, except a thick green rug covered the hardwood floor. There were two double beds. Where did the third sister sleep? And then she remembered. Annabelle had said the Freak claimed one for himself every night, usually Sister Karen. *Figures, she's the youngest and prettiest.* Katrina turned, looking for a place that might hide the key. The chest of drawers looked like a good starting point.

After five minutes of searching under and behind each pile of clothes, she gave up. The dressing table was a possibility. She searched each drawer and found nothing. The nightstand in the corner was the last place she'd have time to look.

Bingo. The top drawer had a cardboard tray filled with watches, rings, and necklaces. Even Katrina's rings were there. The temptation to take them caused her to hesitate, but she stayed focused. A key was what she needed. A key to a double-cylinder deadbolt lock. It wasn't there. *Shit.* There were keys, but none fit a double-cylinder deadbolt. She knew what they looked like. That's all her parents had at home. She closed the drawer as a thought raced through her mind. She slid it back open and lifted the cardboard tray.

Yes! Found it. She slipped the key into her pocket as footsteps in the hall alerted her. When the doorknob turned, she pushed the drawer shut and dove for the floor. She gazed under the bed at the legs and shoes of the person entering—women's shoes. If they took a few more steps past the bed, she'd be spotted. Katrina held her breath. The sound of her heart pounding on the floor was a base drum. The shoes halted at the dressing table, and the grind of a drawer sliding open floated in the air. The drawer slammed shut, and the feet twisted toward the door. A moment later it closed, and Katrina breathed again. *It doesn't get any closer than that.*

Katrina rose to her knees and listened for a full minute. Finally, she crept to the door and laid her head against it. No movement outside. Was the meeting still going on? Had she been missed?

"Katrina," a voice called, scaring her senseless.

She jerked her head from the door and panicked. It was Sister Ruth yelling from the hall. What did she want? Katrina cracked the door and peeked outside at Ruth traipsing down the corridor toward the stairs, still bellowing her name. As Ruth's head disappeared from sight, going down the stairs, Katrina broke for the hall bathroom, closing and locking the door.

"Katrina," the voice cried as Sister Ruth marched back up the stairs. After checking herself in the mirror and straightening her hair, Katrina flushed the toilet and opened the door. She was greeted by Sister Ruth's suspicious glare.

"Where have you been?"

Katrina had had just about enough of this woman—caution be damned. She rolled her eyes. "Bermuda. Had a nice lunch—returning for dinner later."

Ruth pointed an accusatory finger at her and scowled. "Don't you sass me, girl."

"Did you want something, or were you just checking on my kidney and bowel movements?"

"Time to start cleaning that chicken for supper. I'll be down as soon as I'm relieved up here," Sister Ruth said.

Katrina spun toward the stairs. She glanced over her shoulder just before going down. Ruth stood with her hand on the sisters' bedroom doorknob. Trying to act normal, Katrina sauntered through the living room on the way to the kitchen and looked out the front window. The outside meeting was breaking up. She hurried to the locked basement door, fitting the key into the grooves and turn it. A snap sounded from the lock. She tried the door and it opened a crack. Katrina closed and relocked it.

She had the right key. Now all she needed was a chance to use it. A sense of profound satisfaction washed over her—such a small victory. But any success in a place like this made her feel on top of the world. Katrina held her shoulders a little straighter as she made her way to the kitchen counter to begin her evening's work. If she could score a small victory, perhaps she might also escape.

* * *

Frank sat on his balcony and had an after-dinner glass of red. He'd shocked Rob with his revelation about doubting Jesus. What he didn't share was that he even had doubts about God's existence. How could a loving God allow horrible things to happen to *his children*? Frank had lost the last vestiges of faith a long time ago in New York and saw no way or reason to recover them. He put all thoughts of God out of his mind and had another sip.

Frank liked these early spring evenings, the way the horizon glowed just before dark. The city took on a different look when the shadows closed in. Rush-hour traffic had died away, and only the diners and partiers ventured out. Others were home with their families watching TV and picking up kids from after-school activities. He could have had a life like that. He'd still be living in New York and cooking if he and Carly were still together. Would he be happier? Their romance had been full of the fire of youth, but they had been just kids, people who didn't know or care where their lives would lead. *Yeah*, he thought as he had another sip. *You would have been happier—much happier.*

Frank wasn't much of a navel-gazer. The past was fixed. Long-ago mistakes and sins needed putting away in a dark place of the mind, a place you didn't visit too often. With all the distractions of the case, he hadn't been there in weeks. *But when old ghosts scratch on the walls, sometimes you just have to look around the corner.*

* * *

Brother John rocked in the chair and enjoyed the whippoorwills in the field, the owl behind the barn, and the tree frogs. No one ever disturbed him on the front porch this late. He'd left orders.

He rose and scanned the area before stepping into the yard. One of the dogs rustled behind a bush as it slipped around the house, but he paid it no mind. A northerly breeze sent a strong whiff of pine through the trees while he meandered in the shadows toward the Farm to Market Road. Lighting bugs flickered in the dark woods, signaling their mates. Every so often Brother John stopped and checked. No one followed.

He dug in his pocket and slipped out a joint. Lighting it, he pulled in a long drag and held the smoke until he needed air. So relaxing. He kept the joint cupped in his palm and strolled as if he didn't have a care in the world. But he had more cares than anyone knew. The weight became more pronounced each year. Only his spiritual adviser kept him from slipping off the edge. Without him, Brother John was lost.

As he neared the road, a silhouette emerged out of the darkness, becoming sharper as he approached. It leaned against a tree and waited. Brother John hadn't expected him this close to the house. They usually met at the entrance of the county road. He'd have seen the joint by now. *No use trying to hide it.* John had another long pull before halting. The quiet voice welcomed him.

"John, you don't need that anymore, you know. You've got the spirit."

28

By Saturday morning, Frank had received no phone calls or emails about kidnapped girls. He took his time going through his yoga routine, drank coffee on the balcony, ate breakfast, and resisted the urge to check the office fax. Few agencies used fax anymore for basic communication anyway, so he piddled around the house for a couple of hours until he couldn't stand it any longer.

CIU wasn't open on weekends, except for a duty officer to take emergency calls from home. When Frank sauntered into the work area, it was dark. The only light shone from Edna's office. As he walked past, they made eye contact and asked the same question at the same time: "What are you doing here?"

She laughed and leaned on her forearms. In jeans and a casual blouse, with her hair down, she looked years younger.

"Just catching up on a few things I didn't have time for on Friday. You?" she asked.

"Checking the fax," Frank said.

She nodded and went back to typing. He ambled through the quiet space, usually filled with laughter and conversations, and found no fax for him. He sorted and stapled a few for other detectives and dropped them in their boxes on the way out. After wandering in the hall for a bit, Frank checked his phone and email for messages. Ready to give up, he smacked the down button next to the elevator. Just as the doors slid open, Edna's voice stopped him.

"You have a fax—just rolled in." She stood wedged in the door to CIU, a small smile on her face.

Frank sprinted past her. "Thanks."

The cover sheet was from the Shreveport Police Department. Frank scanned it and held his breath. *Emilie Moore—W/F, DOB 7/16/1991, reported missing by family last Tuesday. White Bible discovered with Wormwood highlighted in her vehicle. Full offense report enclosed. Detective Harold Bibbs SPD—Missing Persons.*

"Gotcha!" Frank said.

Edna reviewed the cover while Frank dug into the report. Same MO as Trina. He finished reading it and called Detective Bibbs. Ten minutes later, Frank slammed the phone down triumphantly and turned, only to find Edna hovering nearby.

"Now we know we've been on the right track," he said. "Wormwood *is* the key."

She leaned against his desk. "But what does that get us? What does it mean?"

"Nowhere, unless Shreveport gets something else, or we have another agency report come in. If we could just have at least three kidnap locations, then we could triangulate the anchor point of the suspect. We need at least one more."

Edna's shoulders relaxed and she flashed one of her rare smiles. "I'm happy things are panning out. You can't believe how much pressure I've been getting from the sixth floor." She looked especially pretty today. With the tight bun released and long black hair cascading around her shoulders, Frank again wished she wasn't his lieutenant.

He slid into his lounge position and folded his hands across his stomach. "How bad does the sixth floor want this?"

Edna squinted and her lips pressed flat. "Why?"

"If we rescue her but have to crack a few eggs, how much support could we expect?"

Edna scrutinized the empty room a moment before answering, but still lowered her voice. "I know you, Frank. And I've pulled heat for you in the past. But if you bring her home in one piece and don't commit any first-degree felonies, I've got your back."

Frank considered the deal. "Probably won't come to that, but good to know I have an ace in the hole."

Edna showed that smile he liked. "Give me time to close out my computer, and I'll buy you lunch. We deserve to celebrate a little," she said.

"I'd like that, Edna. I mean Lieutenant—"

She shot that look again. "Edna's fine. We're off duty."

An hour later Frank checked the office one more time before going home. The fax machine sat cold and lifeless. He spun around and headed to the parking garage. On the way, his phone rang.

"This is Pierce."

A hesitant voice said, "Yes, I'm Detective Grover, Houston PD. We had a Donna Willis go missing a couple of years ago. Fit the general description you outlined in your alert."

Frank froze and braced himself against a wall. "Was there a Bible?" He figured he sounded excited but didn't care. Could he be lucky enough to get two confirmations in one day?

"Yeah, but it got returned to the next of kin with the rest of her stuff."

Frank calmed down. "I see."

"But we just finished reinterviewing the relatives, and I'm holding the Bible in my lap as we speak."

Frank sucked in a sharp breath. "Is the word *Wormwood* highlighted?"

A chuckle drifted over the line. "Oh, yeah. Right where you said it'd be."

That was number three. The triangle was complete.

*   *   *

Sunday morning, Katrina helped with breakfast and cleaned up the dishes. Sister Judy carried a tray of food to the basement and came up a minute later. Katrina fingered the key in her pocket and eyed the lock.

Sunday morning services were about to start, so everyone made their way to the living room. Sister Ruth ran her finger around the inner edge of a frying pan in the drying rack and frowned.

"This still has grease on it. Wash it again and be quick about it. We're starting."

Katrina dropped the pan in the hot, soapy water and wiped it once before rinsing it. The sound of the group milling around and sliding chairs into position in the living room floated into the kitchen. Katrina was alone at last. The temptation to open the basement door and slip down the stairs became overpowering. That crazy thought drew her to the door, and her hand went for her pocket. She was about to ease the key into the lock when Sister Ruth stuck her head around the corner.

"You coming?" she asked.

Katrina jumped. She hung the dishtowel on the rack while slipping the key back into her pocket. "Yeah, be right there."

* * *

Frank checked the fax machine that Sunday morning, but nothing new had arrived. He picked up a copy of *The Dallas Morning News* on his way home. He'd always enjoyed reading the news instead of listening to some moron recite it on TV like a trained parrot.

Last night, Frank had played around with the triangle theory of the kidnappings. While it wasn't an exact science, it at least offered him an approximate area to cue on. It was basically an inverted triangle. According to Google, the distance from Dallas to Shreveport was 188 miles. From Dallas to Houston, 239, and Houston to Shreveport, 240. A big area of rural East Texas—real big.

State and federal missing-persons records could help only so much. If you had a specific geographical area and looked for young blonde women, you'd receive a lot of hits from a database inquiry. Too many for investigators to run out quickly. But when you specified only those cases in which a Bible had been left at the scene with the word *Wormwood* highlighted, you narrowed them down fast. Problem was, that was too specific for most indices. Calling the different cities and talking to the missing-persons detectives who worked the cases was how you handled it.

He dropped on the sofa and opened the paper. After scanning the headlines, he flipped to the second page. On page five, the story of Katrina Wallace's kidnapping appeared again, complete with photo. It dominated the sheet. She had been missing two weeks. When the news broke, there had been several days of coverage. As time passed, it fell back to the Sunday edition—page five. It would probably never appear again unless a body was found. Frank read the article and grunted a couple of times about the misstatement of facts. It ended with, "Sources say the FBI and Texas Rangers are no closer to locating the missing mayor's daughter than the day she disappeared."

Not a word about the Dallas Police Department or the progress they were making. *Figures.* Frank studied the photo of Katrina. It wasn't the same one he had. This was a more relaxed girl. Dressed in a T-shirt and sitting in a patio chair. A wide smile and her hair not quite perfect.

A sense of warmth spread through him. "I know you're out there." Frank brushed his finger across the photo. *Hold on just a little longer.*

*   *   *

Rob walked into the office Monday morning after his workout and found Frank typing a hundred miles a minute, leaning into the monitor.

"Got your message about the triangle," Rob said. "Anything else happen?"

Frank pushed away from the desk and draped a leg over the chair arm. "Nope."

Rob took his seat, thinking that was a whole lot of activity for nothing else happening. But that was Frank. It was either feast or famine with him—hours of frenetic typing or a day of staring into space.

Terry emerged from his office and made his way toward Edna's, running a hand through his thinning hair. Once he spotted Frank and Rob, he halted and leaned against Frank's cubicle.

"Edna told the chief about your theory, Frank."

"And?" Rob asked.

"He wants to know how you're going to find the girl in seventeen thousand square miles of real estate," Terry said.

Frank yawned.

Rob's frustration level rose a notch. "It's just a theory, a premise. We need a starting point," he said.

Terry shrugged. "Yeah, I know." He whirled around and headed to Edna's.

Rob threw up his hands. "What do they expect?"

Frank seemed unperturbed by the whole conversation. He was about to say something when his office phone rang. Caller ID showed Beaumont PD. Frank stared at Rob for a beat, his eyes filled with anticipation, as he answered the call and put it on speaker. "This is Pierce."

"Hi, I'm Sergeant Snider, Beaumont PD."

Frank grabbed a pen. "Yes, Sergeant."

"Don't know if this helps, but we had a gal go missing about a year or so ago. Her name was Billings. Mary Billings—sort of fits the description you put out."

"Did anyone find a Bible?" Frank asked.

Hope rose in Rob's gut. Just one more and they could start really zeroing in.

"She disappeared from her apartment. Looking at the crime scene photos, there *was* a Bible on her pillow."

Frank looked ready to pop. "Did it have the word *Wormwood* highlighted?"

"Never checked at the time. But it was a white Bible like you described."

"Can we get our hands on it?" Frank's question sounded more like a command than a request.

"Not likely. Relatives cleaned the place out, and they've since moved."

Frank's shoulders sagged and he glanced up at Rob. "Sergeant, I can't tell you how important it is that we get in touch with them and see if they still have that Bible. *It's the key.* If the word *Wormwood* is highlighted, that proves she is one of the girls in my case, and that will help me locate them. Will you try?" Frank asked.

There was a pause. "We'll do what we can, but no promises." The sergeant's tone had that doubtful quality Rob had heard too often in cases like these.

"Thanks. If you turn up anything, call me at the cell number," Frank said, and hung up.

Frank marched to the wall map of Texas and pointed. "Houston, Shreveport, and now Beaumont. Still in that eastern Texas/western Louisiana corridor—that's three for that area."

"You don't know that for sure yet," Rob said. "You won't know until Beaumont reports back."

Frank stepped away from the map, crossed his arms, and studied it a moment. "Okay, two and a half."

Rob stood next to his partner, eyeing the map, wondering where, in all those lines and dots, Trina was hidden, and if any of the other girls were still alive.

* * *

Brother Luther drove Sister Karen into town every Monday morning to pick up supplies. They never bought much since they caught, killed, or grew almost everything they needed at the farm and lake. While she shopped, Luther usually wandered around the store. He didn't mind going with her. She was nice, pretty, and always ready to talk when she was away from the house. As Brother John's favorite wife, she held a special place in Luther's heart as well. They chatted all the way to the store because they shared a special secret: a love of candy.

Luther would buy several pieces, as he did every trip, and he and Sister Karen would eat them on their way home. Brother John never allowed such worldly things at the house. But they'd laugh and gobble down as much as they could before turning into the driveway. He always drove extra slow.

One of the store clerks pushed a cart to the candy stand. The newspaper rack sat beside it. The clerk bent down, grabbed a stack of yesterday's papers, and dumped them into the cart. A page from *The Dallas Morning News* slid from his grip. As it fell open on the floor, Luther stooped and picked it up, intending to help the guy out. His gaze fell on the photo of Katrina.

"Thanks, buddy." The clerk reached for the loose page.

Luther's breath caught. He could hardly speak. He pulled the page away from the clerk. "Could I please have this, mister?"

The guy shrugged. "Sure, don't matter none to me."

Luther read what he could about the missing girl. He didn't understand too good, but from what few words he could figure out, it seemed just about every law enforcement outfit in the world was looking for her. Who knew this girl was some politician's daughter? He rushed to find Sister Karen.

She lingered in the spice department, comparing two kinds of cinnamon.

He touched her arm. "We have to go."

She ignored him and chuckled. "I'm almost through, Luther. Just a few more—" She stopped talking when he pushed the photo in her face. Her jaw dropped. She shoved the basket aside and they raced to the front door.

29

After the call with Beaumont PD, Frank felt like celebrating, so he and Rob headed over to Sarge's for lunch. A crowd sat at the bar and there were a few couples in the booths. Sarge gave them a friendly nod as they entered.

"Better make mine a double today, Sarge," Frank said as he took his place at the bar. He tapped his fingers on the wood, unable to sit still. Frank tried to name the feeling he was experiencing today. Giddy. That was it. He was ready to crack this case.

Sarge sneered. "Are you starting that crap again?"

"We had a couple of good breaks over the weekend," Rob said. He slid onto a stool.

"Oh, yeah—great." Sarge nodded.

"Sandwiches and cherry Cokes. I'm buying." Frank slapped the counter.

Rob shot a look. "It's your turn to buy."

"I know; that's why I'm buying," Frank said.

Rob rolled his eyes and checked his email while Frank tapped a beat on the bar. Sarge's stare fixed on Frank's fingers as he passed the Cokes to them.

"On the house, boys. You're going to solve this damn case, aren't you?"

"That's the plan," Frank answered, and drank half the Coke in one gulp. *Absolutely. We're going to solve the damn case.*

Sarge eyed Frank's fingers again. "The drinks are free, but the music has to go. Know what I mean?"

Frank quit tapping but was still finding it hard to sit still. Jan handed them their sandwiches. The TV over the bar showed the midday news. A picture of Katrina flashed on the screen. It was the one from the Sunday paper.

Frank pointed. "Turn that up."

Sarge grabbed the remote and pointed it at the TV.

". . . may have been found. According to our sources, she was seen at the WinStar Casino over the weekend in Oklahoma. The caller saw her photo in the paper and called the police. No confirmation as yet, but authorities are investigating." The newscaster looked to his left. "Dan, tell us how long we're going to hang on to these mild temperatures."

Sarge pressed the mute button. "She's in Oklahoma?" he asked.

Frank grinned and attacked his sandwich.

"Yeah, she and Elvis are playing blackjack with Jimmy Hoffa," Rob said.

Sarge threw the bar towel over his shoulder and leaned to within inches of Rob before saying, "I had great hopes for you at one time, but Frank's turned you into a first-class smartass."

Frank wiped his mouth and fingers. "He's just—"

His ringing cell interrupted his quick comeback. "This is Pierce."

A deep voice said, "Yes, sir, I'm calling about that NCIC notification you sent."

Frank stood and gave the sign for quiet. "Who's this?"

"Sheriff Richard Lewis, Sabine County Sheriff's Office."

Frank waved his hand again for more silence. The place got quiet.

"Yes, Sheriff. Do you have a missing girl and Bible?"

The line went hushed for a moment. "No, I'm sorry. I must have the wrong information. We don't have anyone missing."

The knot in Frank's stomach relaxed. "How did you get this number?"

"It was on the notification about people with that tattoo."

Frank tensed. "You know one of those people?" He shot a glance at Rob.

"Yup, sitting in our jail right now," Lewis said.

"Sheriff, I'm not familiar with Sabine County." Frank turned to Sarge, who knew Texas better than anyone. "What's the county seat?" He said it loud enough for anyone in the bar to hear.

"Hemphill," Sheriff Lewis said.

Frank mouthed the word to Sarge and Rob. They shook their heads and shrugged.

"Still no help," Frank said.

A chuckle echoed from the phone. "Didn't figure you big city boys would know. I reckon it's on a line between Houston and Shreveport. Know where they are?"

"Sure do."

"We're about a hundred miles south and a little west of Shreveport. Beside Toledo Bend Reservoir."

"That would put you in East Texas," Frank said.

"Nope," the deep voice chuckled again. "Deep East Texas."

Frank didn't dare to hope, but he had to ask. "Is the guy in your jail Vernon Warren?"

"Naw, sorry. It's another guy," Lewis answered.

Frank let out the breath he'd been holding. "Okay, that's fine, Sheriff."

"But I know Vernon Warren," the deep voice said.

Frank had only passed out twice in his life. Once, as a kid, being popped with a penicillin shot—turned out he was allergic—and the second time when he got stabbed. This came close to being the third. Frank steadied himself on the bar and squeezed his eyes shut.

"You know Vernon John Warren?" he slowly asked.

"Yup, lives just outside Hemphill."

"Sheriff, I've been waiting to hear that for days. It's essential I interview your prisoner with the tattoo. When could I come?" Frank asked.

"You got a three-and-a-half- to four-hour drive ahead of you. When do you want to come?"

Frank glanced at his watch. "How about late this afternoon? Say, around five o'clock."

"I'll be here," Lewis said.

Frank pulled a small notebook from his pocket. "What's the prisoner's name?"

"Evan Rhodes. Got him on public intoxication, disturbing the peace last night."

"Sheriff, I have to talk to him. Can you hold him until I get there on just those charges? Don't want him bonding out and getting in the wind."

The deep chuckle again. "Son, this is East Texas. Don't worry, he'll be here."

An hour later, Frank and Rob were blowing out of Dallas. After packing a small suitcase, Rob had grabbed a six-pack of beer from his refrigerator and dumped every cube from his icemaker into a cooler over the bottles. Rob drove the speed limit down I-20 while they sipped Michelob.

Terry's last words still rang in Frank's ears. *If you find her, don't take any unilateral action until you've notified the Rangers and FBI.*

Edna was more to the point. *Remember what I told you Saturday morning. If you locate her and don't commit any first-degree felonies, I've got your back.*

Frank didn't care if he committed a felony, no matter what degree it was. If he found her he'd grab her—that was that. He owed her that much.

* * *

Katrina wasn't sure what was going on, but the Freak had called another meeting in the side yard under an ancient pine tree. Only Sister Ruth was missing. *Must be with the kids.*

Katrina fingered the basement key in her pocket. She might not ever have a better chance. She could slip in, talk to the girl, and be out before they were the wiser. It was a chance worth taking. It wasn't pure empathy. Katrina needed—no, craved—someone to share her feelings with. She thought she'd go crazy if she couldn't at least meet the girl.

Katrina knew everyone's location. Now was the time.

She eased through the silent old house into the kitchen. Fitting the key into the grooves, she unlocked the basement door. A loud *click* sounded. Katrina quickly entered and relocked the door. No sound from the girl. Was she still down here? Katrina braced herself on the handrail and eased down the stairs. She craned her neck and listened, straining for any sound. When she reached the creaky stair near the bottom, she scanned the room. Nothing. Where was she? Oh, no. They'd already moved her—but where?

"Hello," Katrina whispered, turning her head in all directions as she neared the bed. "Hello, is anybody—"

She didn't finish the sentence. The sound of the shower curtain ripping open, combined with a blur to her right, made her stumble backward. The air was knocked from her as Katrina tumbled to the floor. The wild girl with short blonde hair straddled her, and a pair of strong hands clamped around her neck. The woman pressed her thumbs into Katrina's trachea as if ready to punch a hole right through.

Katrina boxed the attacker's ears and she let out a scream, but continued trying to choke her. The feral eyes were fixed and the lips had a determined grin. Katrina's vision blurred and she realized she had only one chance. With her last breath she croaked, "Friend."

The woman's expression changed. She kept the tight grip on Katrina's throat but stopped trying to crush her windpipe.

Katrina repeated, "Friend," and went into a coughing spasm.

The girl allowed her to cough it out but stayed on top of her with her hands loose on her neck. "Who are you?" she asked.

Katrina cleared her throat. "Katrina Wallace from Dallas. Who are you?"

The girl examined her with suspicious eyes. She released her grip and pushed hair from her face. "Emilie Moore. Why did your people kidnap me?"

Katrina caught her breath. "It's not my people. It's *those* people. I was kidnapped too."

"How do I know you're telling the truth?"

"Well, if you'll get off me, I'll explain," Katrina said.

Emilie stood and offered her a hand up. Katrina rubbed her throat and moved toward the bed. Emilie was still in a fighting stance. She flinched as Katrina turned.

"Let's sit down and talk," Katrina said.

"I'm fine right here."

This was going to be harder than Katrina expected. "Okay, then I'll sit, if you don't mind."

Ten minutes later, Katrina had convinced Emilie they were in the same boat. Katrina never asked if Brother John had raped her. She didn't want to know.

"So we're allies?" Emilie asked.

Suspicion still laced Emilie's voice. Katrina couldn't blame her. "Yeah, we're definitely allies," Katrina said.

Emilie lowered her head. "Sorry I jumped you. I was scared and just decided I wasn't going to take it anymore."

Katrina laid her hand on Emilie's. "That's okay, but we don't stand a chance trying to fight them—too many."

"Are there any guns in the house?" Emilie whispered.

"I've never seen any, but I know they hunt."

Emilie rested both palms on the bed. "You have to find out where they are."

"Okay, I'll snoop around."

Sister Ruth bellowed from upstairs. "*Katrina!*"

"I have to go," Katrina whispered. "I'll check on you when I can, but they watch me like a hawk."

Emilie's face softened. "I'm glad you came down. Sorry about jumping you."

"I'm glad I came down too." Katrina hugged Emilie. "Don't worry, I'll find a gun or some kind of weapon."

Katrina broke the embrace and headed for the stairs. Just as her foot hit the first step, she froze as the scraping noise of metal on metal rushed down from above—the sound of a key in a lock.

* * *

Brother John finished talking and studied the group. "You've all heard the news Sister Karen and Brother Luther brought back from town."

Sister Judy scowled. "Why'd we have to take the mayor's daughter?"

Brothers Luther, Turner, and Lee looked down.

Brother John said, "Well, it wasn't like she had a sign around her neck. We didn't realize it until today. We shouldn't blame them."

Sister Judy sulked at the rebuke.

"The question is what to do now," Brother John said. He scanned each face and waited.

Sister Karen pouted. "Get rid of her as fast as we can. Take her out back. If the police are looking for her, it's too dangerous for her to be here."

Brother John leaned against the tree and again examined each face. "Is that what you all want?"

Everyone nodded in agreement except Brother Luther. He lowered his gaze and kept quiet.

"Okay." Brother John held up his Bible. "I'll pray on the matter and give you my decision tomorrow." He strolled away, knowing what needed to be done. Katrina hadn't worked out—wouldn't cooperate. If she wouldn't submit to his husbandly authority, what kind of mother would she make? She might even harm the children. Too big a chance. Yeah, better to get rid of her and concentrate on the new one. The sooner the better.

* * *

Katrina didn't move—didn't even dare breathe. She watched from her hiding place in the shower as Sister Ruth edged farther into the basement, toward the bed. Ruth scanned the area, looking for who knew what. Katrina peered through the thin crack between the curtain and shower wall as Sister Ruth approached Emilie. Crazy thoughts raced through Katrina's head. Rush the old bitch, hold her hostage, and make the others let her and Emilie go. No—hold her hostage, find a gun, and force their way out, killing those dogs if necessary.

"Has there been anybody down here?" Sister Ruth asked.

Katrina's knees weakened. *For God's sake, say no.*

"Yeah, why you asking?" Emilie answered.

Katrina tensed. *No, don't tell her.*

221

"Who?" Sister Ruth marched closer to the bed.

Katrina eased the curtain closed and prayed.

Emilie's voice echoed through the basement. "Santa Claus. Got my Christmas list. Said he'd see me in December."

Katrina slapped her hand over her mouth to keep from laughing. *Yes! A girl after my own heart.*

"You'd best keep your sassy remarks to yourself," Sister Ruth said.

The clip-clop of her footsteps sounded up the stairs. The basement door slammed shut and the lock clicked. Katrina eased the curtain open and Emilie smirked.

"I hate that bitch," Emilie said.

Katrina rushed to her and gave her a hug. "Me too. Listen, the Freak, Brother John, might try and attack you. They'll drug your food so—"

Emilie's lip quivered and her eyes misted. She dropped her head in her hands and wept.

Katrina embraced her. Was it her fault? If she'd had the courage to unlock that door a few days before, maybe Emilie wouldn't have been attacked. Katrina held her until Emilie finished crying.

Emilie looked into Katrina's eyes, searching for answers. "Who are they? Why are they doing this?"

Katrina pushed her to arm's length. "There's too much to explain now, but I'll come again. If I don't show, they'll get suspicious."

Emilie wiped her eyes. "Promise you'll come back?"

"Promise," Katrina said.

She crept up the stairs and put her ear against the door leading into the kitchen. Silence. She inserted the key and twisted it. The click sounded like a gunshot going off. She peeked out and the coast looked clear. She quickly closed and relocked the door, dropping the key in her dress pocket. Voices sounded from outside, and the screen porch door slamming sent her scurrying for the sink. She began washing the last few dishes as the group filed in. The way they stared at her made her uncomfortable. *What had they discussed?*

Sister Ruth was nowhere in sight, but Sister Judy said, "Start peeling those potatoes. We'll be eating soon."

30

A little before five o'clock, Frank and Rob rolled into Hemphill, Texas. The clouds made it seem darker, and the long shadows of evening weren't far behind.

"Let me handle the sheriff," Frank said, thinking back to their phone call. "I think I've got a good read on him. Not exactly the brightest light in the chandelier."

"I'll take the lead with the suspect," Rob said.

"Good idea."

Hemphill was one of those sleepy little East Texas towns that hadn't changed much since being incorporated in the thirties. Surrounded by the Sabine National Forest and nudging up against the massive Toledo Bend Reservoir, it remained a quiet place to raise a family. Hemphill had become the epicenter for the Columbia Space Shuttle recovery when tons of debris fell into the thick forest and nearby lake. Not that long ago, shuttle pieces ranging from thumbnail to car-hood size had littered the area.

The sheriff's department was located off the town square on Main Street. Its official name was the Blan Greer Law Enforcement Center, and the county jail was housed within. Rob parked in a space marked "Police Vehicles Only."

Frank led the way inside.

A deputy greeted them at the desk. "Can I help you?" She was young and cute, but her short red hair was a tangled mess.

"Yes, we're here to see Sheriff Lewis," Frank said.

She crinkled her brow. "You're from Dallas?"

Rob nodded.

"The sheriff said we should expect you. He's just pulling up behind the station—been to a meeting. He told me to have you wait in his office. Would you like some coffee?" she asked.

"No, thank you. We're fine," Rob said.

She led them into the hall and motioned inside an office. Frank surveyed the room. Not a bad setup. Desk with bookshelves and photos. Certificates and more pictures on the opposite wall.

"Just have a seat. I'll let him know you're here," the young deputy said.

Frank made a beeline for one of the chairs in front of the desk while Rob meandered to the wall of photos and certificates. Frank opened his case file and organized his reports, getting ready for the meeting. He scratched his neck and thumbed through the papers, his gut telling him Hemphill was the right place to be.

"Hey, Frank. You might want to take a look at this guy's credentials. Might change the way you approach him," Rob mumbled, still scanning the wall.

"Huh?" Frank looked up.

"I said you might—"

"Well, you boys made better time than I figured."

Frank craned his neck, and in the doorway stood one of the biggest guys he'd ever seen. Everything about him was big. His ears, nose, and hands seemed better suited to a giant than a mortal.

"Howdy, I'm Sheriff Richard Lewis." The deep bass voice echoed off the walls.

He towered a foot over poor Rob and stood several inches taller than even Frank. They introduced themselves and shook hands, and Frank had the distinct impression that the man had the ability to break his fingers with an ill-timed cough. The sheriff was one of those people who wore a perpetual smile, as if he knew something you didn't and wasn't about to let you in on it.

"My deputy offer y'all coffee?"

"Yes, but we're fine, thanks," Frank said. He and Rob dropped into the chairs.

Lewis removed his felt Stetson and threw it on a hat rack as he strolled to his desk. He wore khaki pants, a western-cut white shirt, and a belt buckle only a bull rider could appreciate. The guy was seventy if he was a day.

"Why don't you run down all the details? You said this concerned the Dallas mayor's missing daughter?" Lewis reached in the drawer and pulled out a pack of chewing tobacco. He stuck a small wad in his jaw, fell into his chair, and propped his size-fifteen Tony Lamas on the edge of his desk.

"Yes," Frank said, eyeing the giant's feet. Frank spent the next ten minutes explaining the case to the sheriff and showing him photos of others with the tattoo. "Ever seen any of these guys around here?"

Sheriff Lewis shook his head. "Nope, can't say as I have, except Vernon. You reckon he has the same tattoo?"

"Yes, sir, and we believe he's connected to the girl's disappearance. What do you know about him?" Frank asked.

The sheriff interlaced his fingers across his chest. His Masonic ring, outlined with small diamonds, caught the light. "He lives just outside town, near the lake, in the old Chandler house."

"Chandler house?" Rob asked.

"Thelma Chandler was his aunt. She never had any kids. After she died, Vernon and his bunch showed up."

"Did you know her?" Frank asked.

Lewis smirked. "Know her? Hell—graduated from high school with her. When we were kids, we used to roam all over those woods behind her house. Even sweethearts for a while. When her husband passed about five years ago, she started a downward spiral. Finally gave up the ghost three years back."

Frank leaned forward, his spine tingling. "You mentioned 'his bunch.' How many are there?"

"Don't rightly know for sure. Heard there were a half dozen or so," Lewis said.

"So you've been to the house?" Rob asked.

"Yeah, got a call about poachers several months ago. I went out and spoke to Vernon."

"How did he seem?" Frank asked.

Lewis screwed his face into a frown. "Oh, he's a weird duck. Hippy-like and quiet. Don't have much of a personality, if you ask me. Hard to imagine him as the leader of anything."

Frank scribbled in his notebook. "What about this guy you have locked up?"

"He's another weirdo."

"Like how?" Rob asked.

"Better if you see for yourself. Want to talk to him?"

"You bet." Frank stood.

Lewis rose and picked up the photo of Eddie Jones's back. "This is the same tattoo our boy has. What you figure? Some kind of cult?"

"Perhaps," Frank said.

They made a right out of the office and strolled farther down the hall.

"I expect we'd better leave our guns here," Sheriff Lewis said.

Lewis halted in front of a line of metal boxes embedded in the wall and unlocked one. Dropping his .357 Magnum Colt Python in, he unlocked another for Frank and Rob. They dropped their pistols inside, and Lewis handed Frank the key. The sheriff looked up at the closed-circuit camera and flashed the high sign. The steel door unlocked with a dull snap, and they entered the cell block. A strong whiff of Lysol hit Frank, but it didn't last long. They went to the last cell on the end. The man sat on his bed, leaning forward with his forearms on his knees and one hand in the other. He had a bandage on his left hand.

"Evan, there's some folks here wants to talk to you," the sheriff said.

The man looked up. He had hard features. The gray stubble on his balding head and chin were misleading. Probably an early grayer—couldn't be over thirty.

"I don't know 'em." Evan lay on the bunk with his hands behind his head.

Rob took the lead. "We'd like to ask you some questions."

The man glared at him with sullen eyes. "Just because I'm in jail don't mean I have to talk to no greaser."

"Nice," Rob said. "A redneck and racist. Two for one."

Sheriff Lewis leaned a hand on the bars. "Now Evan, you should try and get along. These guys are police out of Dallas." He pronounced the word "police" like *po-leese*.

Evan eyed them and didn't say a word.

Frank winked at Rob, and he stepped aside.

Frank wandered up beside Sheriff Lewis and also leaned a hand on the bars. "You talk to us, we might see about getting you out early."

Evan smirked. "Lost my job, lost my room, and got no money. Why would I want to get out early?"

"Want to talk about Brother John?"

A blind man couldn't have missed Evan's expression change. Frank had seen that exact look before. Grace Fellman, the old lady in Dallas, had flashed it when she spoke of Brother John. It was pure fear. Evan recovered and shook his head. "Ain't got nothing to say about that either." He shifted positions in the bed and turned his back to them, gazing at the opposite wall.

The sheriff shrugged and they marched back to his office. When everyone was seated, Lewis said, "After you called from Dallas, I talked to Evan. Seems he moved out here with that bunch and lived with 'em for a couple of years, then had some kind of falling out. Left a few months ago and started logging with one of the local contractors. Lived in an old trailer on the guy's land. Had a falling out with him, got fired, and was kicked out of the trailer. According to Evan, that bunch in Miss Chandler's old place pretty much lives off the grid, and off the land. Of course, lots of folks around these parts do that." He propped his boots back on the desk. "What else can I help you with?" Lewis asked.

"You said Vernon, or Brother John, or whatever he's called, lives just outside of town?" Frank asked. He spread a map on the desk. "Could you show us?"

Lewis nodded and stared at the map. "He stays in his Aunt Thelma's old mansion in the woods. Fine place; looks like a park in there. She was awful proud of her landscaping. She could afford it. Before her husband died, he leased the land out for natural gas—made millions—has a dozen operating wells." The sheriff pulled the map to him and with a red marker circled a jagged finger of land jutting into the lake.

"Take Highway 87 south, and hook a left on FM 2928. The entry's on the right, just about here." Lewis put an X beside the road. "Can't miss it. Big old eight-foot chain-link fence and gate. 'No Trespassing' signs everywhere. Got nearly three hundred acres back in there."

Frank got comfortable and cocked his head. "What say you go with us and we just take a look around the place?"

The sheriff's forehead furrowed. "You've talked to Judge Mathews about this?"

Frank spoke before he realized what he was admitting. "Who's he?"

Lewis crossed his arms. "Thought so."

"Huh?"

"You city boys wouldn't come all the way out here to run a bluff on old Sheriff Lewis, would ya?"

Frank didn't like the way this was going, but it was too late to back down now. "We just thought you'd like to come with us when we approach the guy, since you already know him."

The sheriff's eyes narrowed. "Now just wait one damn minute. We may be hicks, but I have a little concern, even out here in the country. It's called probable cause." The sheriff leaned toward Frank and raised his brows. "You probably heard about that from your academy days. Now, if you want to go out there and talk to the guy, I'm all in. But I'll be damned if I'll stand by and let you bully him into an illegal search. Hell, anything you find would be thrown out of court. Come on, guys, you know all this."

Frank bristled. "Sheriff, a young girl's safety's at stake. I don't care if it is thrown out of court."

Lewis stood, all six foot eight of him, and strolled around the office with his hands in his pockets. "Okay, let's say we go out and he tells us to pound sand. What then?"

Frank searched for a clever comeback, but nothing came to mind.

The sheriff kept wandering around his desk. "So we say, 'Okay,

never mind,' and go home? No, we do it the right way or no way at all."
The sheriff's booming voice rattled the furniture. He pointed at them.
"Now, I'm willing to help. God knows I got nothing for those fools in
Miss Thelma's house. But that dog won't hunt around here." He reclaimed
his chair. "You boys think about it and let me know if you come up with
a better plan."

"You think the local judge will issue a search warrant? Frank said.

The sheriff asked, "What's your probable cause?"

"I just explained our probable cause," Frank said.

"No," the sheriff said. "You told me an interesting story that might
have a connection to the girl's disappearance. That's not enough for
Judge Mathews to issue a warrant. He's a good judge, but a real hard-
ass on probable cause. You'll need some direct evidence."

Rob spoke up. "If a sworn Texas peace officer were to witness the
girl on the property, would that be enough?"

Sheriff Lewis slid his knife from his pocket and began cleaning his
nails. He didn't make eye contact with them, but nodded. "Probably,"
he said as a smirk formed on his lips.

* * *

When they exited the sheriff's department, the rolling dark clouds
seemed to match Frank's mood.

Rob said, "Well, that didn't exactly go as planned."

"No, it didn't." Frank sighed.

"I tried to tell you before he came in. The guy retired after forty
years on Houston PD. Left as a lieutenant in Homicide Division. Also
served in Nam. Ranger, won the bronze star and has two purple hearts."

Opening the car door Frank released a long breath and said,
"Yeah, that would have been good to know going in. Wasn't the hick
I'd hoped for."

Rob slid behind the wheel. "And another thing. We were in his
office, what? About a half hour?"

"Almost," Frank said.

Rob looked his way. "He never spit once after taking that chew."

31

Frank had called ahead and gotten reservations for a two-bedroom cabin at the Harborlight Marina and Resort, just northeast of Hemphill, right on the lake. He was tired and hungry but wanted to check out Brother John's place before dark.

He and Rob drove with the windows down and followed the state highway to the turnoff. Sweet pine and flowering shrubs scented the car, even at seventy miles an hour. They followed the sheriff's map until they came to an eight-foot-high wire fence on the right. After a half mile, a white gravel road guarded by a gate came into view. Looked like the kind of place that didn't care for visitors.

"He has a regular compound, doesn't he?" Rob remarked.

Frank stared at the gravel road leading into the dark woods. At the end, Katrina waited for help to arrive—he knew it. *Well, you won't have to wait much longer.* Now all he had to do was figure out how to get in.

"Okay, we know where it is. We'll start surveillance first thing tomorrow," Frank said.

The first drops of rain streaked their windshield as Rob found a good turnaround spot and cruised past the entrance again on the way back to town. They grabbed a couple of rib plates to go from Hemphill BBQ and swung by a supermarket where Rob bought more beer and Frank picked up a couple of bottles of red. By the time they got to the marina and resort, it was well after eight.

The cabin on the water was well appointed, with stained pine boards on the walls and ceiling, clean and comfortable. After showers, they met in Frank's room. Rob dragged in his cooler and situated it just inside the door.

Frank sat propped on pillows with his laptop, staring at Google Earth.

"Hey, check this out," Frank said.

Rob twisted the top off a beer and studied the screen.

Frank pointed at the picture. "Once you enter that gate, you have a choice about twenty-five yards down the drive—left or right. Take a left and you're heading straight to the house. Turn right and you're driving deeper into the woods toward the gas wells and lake. See?"

Rob took a swallow. "Uh-huh."

Frank moved his finger down the road to the right. "If we could get on the road leading to the gas wells, we'd be able to cut across these woods and have a good eyeball on the house."

Rob sipped the beer. "Makes sense."

Frank closed the computer and grabbed a plastic glass and the bottle of red. They meandered through the living area to the outside porch. The rain had passed, leaving the night with a clean, fresh smell. They gazed at a starry canopy, leaned their chairs against the wall, and listened to the sound of the lake and woods. Fireflies flickering along the water's edge reflected back tiny green lights. Like fish winking at them.

"Had no idea how beautiful this part of Texas is," Rob said. "Never been here before."

Frank took a long sip of wine and then motioned to a light in the distance on the other side of the lake. "Know what that is?"

Rob eyed the light. "Nope."

Frank brought the glass to his lips again. "Louisiana."

* * *

Brother John stepped from the porch and looked at the house. No one stirred—all silent. He strolled in the tree shadows down the drive, stopping once and listening. After he was sure no one followed, he marched down the road. He always met him a little after ten o'clock. The dark outline of a person appeared from the woods.

"Nice evening, isn't it, John?"

Brother John fell on the man's shoulder, sobbing. "I don't know what to do. Help me?"

The man embraced him, but remained silent.

"I'm tired of this charade," John said. "It's gone on too long. I want to just tell them. I'm no prophet—you're the prophet. You have the blessing, not me." After a minute, John stepped back and wiped his eyes. "Mama knew our strengths and weaknesses. She knew what she was doing, but I don't. You take over now. I've done enough."

The man leaned against a tree. "Yeah, she knew what she was doing. Always said you had the gift of gab, and I had the gift of prophecy. She knew that together we'd make a fine pair. It won't be long before the last trumpet sounds. When this little piece of earth is all that's left, that's when the hard work starts. We still have lots to do."

Brother John didn't want the responsibility anymore, but he understood it was his and his alone. He'd taken them this far. Like Moses leading his people through the wilderness, John needed to finish God's calling. He straightened up and threw his shoulders back.

"Okay, tell me what you want me to do."

Brother Luther put a firm hand on John's shoulder. "First thing is to decide what to do about Katrina."

32

Frank woke early with too much on his mind. He made coffee and opened the porch door to the new sunrise. The pine air had a crisp feel.

Is she still alive? Are we too late?

His questions unanswered, he strolled into the kitchen with an uneasy feeling in his stomach, leaving the front door open. After refreshing his cup, he switched on the local news.

"Nice morning, huh?" Rob said, staggering into the living area.

"Yeah. You hungry?"

"Sure, we can swing by McDonald's on the way to the compound," Rob said.

"Nope."

"Why not?" Rob asked.

"'Cause there's not one in Hemphill."

Rob glared. "A town without a McDonald's? Are we still in America or what?"

An hour later they sat in their car at the entrance of a park service road and gazed in the direction of the compound. Rob finished off his cold ham-and-cheese sandwich and downed the last of his coffee. "We need a better plan for breakfast tomorrow," he said. "Two-day-old sandwich from a convenience store is no way to start the day."

Frank leaned forward and squinted, looking down the Farm to Market Road. "What we need is a better setup location. We can't even see the entrance. Any ideas?"

233

"We could go overland, through the woods." Rob grinned. "Or rent a boat and try an amphibious assault."

Frank didn't bother looking at him. "You love that Marine talk, don't ya?"

"What do *you* think, cracker?" Rob asked.

"Let's drive past the gate again."

Rob drove slowly toward the entrance of the gravel road leading to the house. The gate was open this morning. As they neared, a white pickup pulled out and headed in their direction. When it passed, the driver didn't look their way. The man was young, with short hair and a yellow hardhat. A sign on the driver's door read "RemTex Energy Services."

"Who's that?" Rob asked.

"Probably someone who inspects the gas wells. They check pressures and volume levels every few days. Look for stuck valves and leaks."

Rob shot a glance his way. "How do you know so much about gas wells?"

"Read it in a book."

The gate was still open but they didn't drive in. Frank had a better idea. "Nacogdoches is about an hour west of here. Let's take a drive over there."

Four hours later, Frank pulled up to their cabin driving a new GMC white rental pickup truck. In the seat were two yellow hardhats and a freshly made magnet sign that read "RemTex Energy Services." Rob pulled up beside him in their city car. They emptied the bags of work clothes on Frank's bed, and each changed into beige coveralls and steel-toed brown boots.

"You look ridiculous," Rob said.

Frank stuffed his hair under the hardhat. "How about now?"

"Doesn't help."

Frank slouched in the passenger seat as Rob drove them back to the compound in the truck, watching the pine forest zip by on either side of the road, a heaviness settling in Frank's stomach that had nothing to do with the crappy sandwiches they'd picked up at the convenience store on the way. Whether Frank liked it or not, this was his baby.

Frank had called Terry on the way to Nacogdoches, and Terry had given them the green light, but he didn't sound encouraging. Rob wouldn't complain or criticize—he'd be there no matter what. Terry had told Frank the Texas Rangers were sending a man to Hemphill to meet them that day or the next. Frank could do without any outside interference. Neither the FBI nor the Texas Rangers nor the local sheriff had the emotional attachment he did to this case—*to Trina*. If she was in that house, he wasn't leaving without her.

Rob held up his nasty sandwich and made a face. "You know, we could have eaten at that Chinese buffet in Nacogdoches. Wouldn't have taken a half hour."

Frank didn't answer. When they pulled through the open gate, he pointed to the right and they cruised through the woods on the white gravel road. Traces of blue appeared through the brush as they got closer to the massive lake.

After about a quarter mile, Frank said, "Park here."

"There's no gas well. They're farther down," Rob said.

"Yeah, but this is the shortest distance through the woods to the house."

They trekked up a small hill through thick bushes and vines. Rob had a compass and kept them heading southeast. After about ten minutes, the house came into view. Rob lifted the binoculars and scanned the yard.

"No movement, but nice house and landscaping. Looks like an old plantation in the South," Rob remarked.

He handed the binoculars to Frank and slipped out his Copenhagen box. He got a pinch and dusted his fingers on his coveralls.

"Okay, we'll—jeez!" Frank jumped as a green snake slithered between his legs.

"Relax. It's only a grass snake," Rob said. "Probably more afraid of you than you are of it."

Frank moved to the left. "I seriously doubt that."

They maintained the surveillance until a little after five. Several long-haired men went into and out of the house, but there was no sign of Trina—or, for that matter, Brother John. The two large dogs presented a potential problem, but Rob mentioned that he might have a solution.

At exactly 5:17 PM, Frank's phone buzzed.

"This is Pierce."

"Sheriff Lewis here. Got someone sitting in my office wants to meet you and your partner."

"Would that someone be a Texas Ranger?" Frank asked.

"You Dallas guys must have ESP. Yeah, he'd like to say hello. Think you could drop by?"

"Sure, Sheriff. We'll be there in about half an hour."

Frank pocketed the phone. "A ranger wants to meet us at the sheriff's office."

Rob lay on his stomach with his elbows spread, holding the binoculars. He sat them down and rubbed his eyes. "Good for me. I'd go blind if I looked through these another hour."

They gathered their gear and drove to meet Sheriff Lewis.

When they strolled into his office, the sheriff's mouth fell open. "You boys decide to take on an extra job while visiting?"

The ranger, with short hair and cowboy hat, grinned while examining their clothes.

"We've gone native, that's all," Frank said.

"Boys, meet a buddy of mine. The ranger who works this county, Harold Parker."

The ranger stood and they shook hands.

"Been telling Harold about your suspicions," Sheriff Lewis said. "From your clothes, I reckon you've been snooping around."

Frank wasn't sure where this might go. He didn't want to give anything away, so he kept it short. "I reckon."

Ranger Parker nodded. "We're not trying to take anything away from you guys. It's your case. You work it as you see fit. We're all big boys here. Just don't put the sheriff and me in a position—if you know what I mean."

"You mean don't do anything to embarrass you?" Rob asked.

"It's not just that," Sheriff Lewis spoke up. "If you screw around and we get a call from them about folks trespassing on their land, that leaves us little choice but to appear, at least, to run you off. Lots of times people around these parts don't bother calling. They just take a shot at the trespassers, and that usually makes their point."

Frank glanced at Rob. "We won't screw up."

"Got a call from the FBI man who works the Lufkin area," Sheriff Lewis said. "Said he was ass deep in a bank robbery investigation. If we need the feds, he wants us to call him." The sheriff smirked. "You think we need the feds?"

"Nope," Frank said, "we got this." No one was going to stand in his way of rescuing Trina. Federal agent involvement just added an extra layer of complication. That was the last thing he wanted.

The sheriff chuckled. "Y'all are a lot smarter than ya look. Especially in those clothes." His expression darkened. "You two city boys could find yourselves in a world of shit out here in the woods. Folks disappear in those river bottoms every hunting season. Sometimes we never find the bodies. Wouldn't want to explain to your chief what happened to you. Take care you know what's in the bushes behind you."

* * *

After walking out of the sheriff's department, Rob didn't have a good feeling. "I think they just delivered a not-so-subtle message."

"Yeah, it's the same as always. Everyone's willing to share in the credit; no one wants to take the risk. What else is new?" Frank said.

Frank slipped into the passenger seat and opened his notepad. Rob started the car and pulled out of the lot.

Rob glanced at his partner, an uneasy feeling growing in his stomach. This wasn't Frank—not the one he knew. The "I don't give a damn" guy he'd worked with for years had transformed into an obsessed fool, ready to charge ahead without thought or consequence.

He searched his memory for ground zero, the epicenter of his partner's massive personality change. With a start he realized it was the day they'd interviewed Ms. Mayor about her daughter's disappearance. Was it something Ms. Mayor had said? No, that wasn't it. She'd been a bitch. Frank hated bitches. Dora, her assistant, had talked to them, but she hadn't seemed to affect Frank in any way. What he'd said when they finished searching Trina's apartment seemed to be the first outward sign.

She's not hiding. Someone took her.

Rob glanced at his partner and opened his mouth to ask, then closed it without uttering a word. Frank hovered over the notebook with his brow knitted. With him in this mood, Rob would never get anything out of him. Rob turned on the road leading to their cabin. Tonight would be a better time to talk.

33

Katrina gazed at the dark forest from her second-floor bedroom. She had looked everywhere for a gun. Guys like them hunted deer, squirrels, and quail. There had to be shotguns, rifles, and maybe even a pistol somewhere. But she couldn't find them. Of course, she hadn't checked the men's rooms. They kept them locked during the day, when she could search undetected.

If that wasn't bad enough, something strange was going on. Ever since the secret meeting outside the other day, she'd been treated like a leper. They no longer made eye contact. Their demeanor appeared different, and no one talked around her anymore. She couldn't figure it out. She hadn't said or done anything, other than being her snarky self. Maybe that was it.

No, it feels bigger than that.

They might let Emilie out any day now. When they did, she'd be ready to run. Katrina would go with her, but they needed an edge of some kind—a weapon to fend off the dogs and guarantee some degree of safe passage.

Tonight's sermon had been especially boring. The Freak wasn't up to it, she could tell. His disinterested manner of delivering "God's word" had almost put a couple of them to sleep.

The feeling of impending doom seeped into Katrina's spirit—that feeling you got walking alone through a deserted parking lot late at night, just before you heard the sound of hurried footsteps approaching. Katrina shivered and put it out of her mind. *Stay focused, think positive, and don't give in to doubt.* She took a breath and let it out slowly.

Good try, but it didn't work. She just wanted to wake up in her own bed, wrapped in her favorite blue blanket, and for this all to have been a nightmare. The prayer slipped out without her even thinking about it.

"Please, God. Send us a rescuer."

*   *   *

On the way back to their place, Rob stopped off for a six-pack and Frank picked up a couple of bottles of red. After dinner and a shower, Rob knocked on his door.

Frank answered wearing a towel and holding a glass of wine.

"Sorry," Rob said, "but I'm married."

Frank didn't take the bait. "I've finished. Just hadn't got around to dressing yet." Frank motioned. "Come in and sit a while. I've been looking over the case file."

Rob grabbed a beer from the cooler and meandered inside. Frank had disassembled the file and had each report, photo, and statement stacked in neat piles on the extra bed.

"What are you doing?" Rob asked.

"Just rereading everything. Making sure we haven't missed something."

Frank's eyes looked sleepy. One of the bottles of red lay upside down in the trash and the other was half empty.

"So, come up with anything?" Rob pulled up a chair.

Frank dropped to the edge of the bed and sipped his wine. "No. Nothing."

No one spoke for what seemed like a long time. Finally, Rob asked the question he'd been holding for days. "What is it about this case?"

Frank raised his head. "Huh?"

"What's different about this one? You're letting it get to you. That's not your style. You've worked dozens of missing-persons cases—some involving young girls. But this one's become personal. I don't believe it's because Trina is the mayor's daughter."

A twisted grin formed on Frank's lips. He stood with a slight wobble, refilled his glass, and strolled to the chest of drawers. He rifled

240

through his wallet and pulled out a small photo. After inspecting it a second, he glanced at Rob. Frank's pondering look lasted another couple of seconds before he ambled over and laid the picture in Rob's lap. Frank lay on his bed while Rob examined the worn and tattered photo.

"Pretty girl," Rob said. "Friend of yours?" Before Frank could answer, Rob pulled the picture closer. He shuffled through the photos on the bed, finding one of Trina. He held them side by side.

"These two could be twins," Rob said, staring at Frank.

Frank sighed. "There is a remarkable likeness."

"Likeness, my ass. They must be sisters. Who's this?" Rob held up Frank's photo and tilted the beer bottle for a long swig.

Frank flashed a wandering smile. "My wife."

Rob spit the beer halfway across the room, and a little dribbled out his nostrils. "Whoa! Your what?"

Frank took another big swallow of red and laid his head on his pillow. "My wife."

Rob's mind vapor-locked. So many questions he couldn't process in the order he wanted to ask them. "You're married?"

"Used to be. Not anymore."

"Never figured you for the marrying type, Frank. How come you never said anything when we first met and I asked you?"

"I did. I said, 'No, I'm not married.' You never ask if I'd *been* married," Frank answered.

Rob took one last look at Frank's picture and laid it on the nightstand. "Things didn't work out, huh?"

Frank gazed at the ceiling. His voice cracked when he whispered, "No, they didn't."

"Hey, it happens. Takes a lot to hold a marriage together these days. Don't beat yourself up over it. Have any kids? Still stay in touch?"

Frank closed his eyes. "She was two months pregnant when she died."

Rob's gut tightened. "She's dead?"

Frank talked to the ceiling. "We met in high school. Had to wait for her to graduate before getting married. When I got accepted to cooking school in New York, we found a studio apartment in Hyde Park. Best years of my life. She was funny, and sexy, and witty. We'd talk all night sometimes about all sorts of stuff. Never owned a TV, but had plenty of old Billie Holiday and Miles Davis records and rock and roll CDs. She worked; I got my degree in culinary arts and cooked dinner for us every night. She was my best friend and top food critic." Frank chuckled. "Hated my gumbo."

Rob wasn't sure what he should say. Frank had never spoken at length about his past. All people knew about him was that he came from Florida and used to be a chef. That was all Frank wanted them to know.

"How did she die?" Rob asked.

Frank opened his eyes and pulled in a deep breath. He kept his gaze on the ceiling. "We moved to Queens when I graduated. She disappeared from our apartment one night while I was at work. They found her a couple of days later. Been raped and murdered."

Frank's hollowed-eyed look sent another uncomfortable tingle through Rob.

Frank stood. "Excuse me." He stumbled to the bathroom and closed the door.

At that moment, it all fell into place for Rob. Frank's life could have been just like his if things hadn't gone wrong. They'd both married their high school sweethearts, both started with nothing, both wanted families. His wife's death threw Frank into a different trajectory. No more serious commitments, only young beautiful girls who wanted to have fun. But Frank's karma had been interrupted by this investigation. That day, as they were sitting in the car in front of Mrs. Mayor's house, when Dora had come out and handed him the envelope with the key and *a picture of Trina.*

"Holy crap," Rob said to himself.

Frank hadn't been able to be there for his wife. She had died terrified and alone. And now he had no intention of letting the same thing happen to Trina.

The sound of the shower drifted from the bathroom. Rob had no more taste for beer or conversation. He left, closing the door softly behind him.

* * *

Brother John rocked on the front porch. The night sounds filled the air, and he thanked God for his blessings. He might have remained a wandering soul if not for God's grace and mercy. Growing up in the woods of Alabama, he and Luther had dreamed of getting out. The Christian rock band he'd formed had played at picnics, weddings, and other special occasions but never cleared enough to provide a living. Always trying to make ends meet, while still at home and listening to his father's crap, had finally forced John out. The day he and Luther left to find construction jobs in Texas felt like breaking free from a small, dark box. John's mom had told him that while Luther wasn't the smartest, he still had much to offer. Listen to him. Listen to his prophecies. He had the gift—the blessing.

John had listened and followed Luther's teachings. Luther had told him to recruit men, whom he'd ordain and mark with the sign of Wormwood. These would be his disciples to carry out God's word in Revelation. When the angel sounded its final trumpet, *they* were promised salvation. Then John would rise to the heavens and return as Wormwood. Mankind would take its last breath—except for their little congregation.

They'd survive, and thrive, and the children that sprang from John's loins would become the elders of the new earth—just like Adam and Eve's children. John would be the transformed Messiah, dying for his congregation.

And, just as Luther had said, three of the chosen had betrayed the faith and returned to their earthly ways of sin and degradation. When John became discouraged, Luther propped him up. Luther said God had shown him a beautiful cool garden and a great house where they'd live during the coming tribulation. A place they'd be safe and food would be plentiful.

A light breeze brushed John's face, and he stood, leaning against the tall porch column. They'd found their Garden of Eden. The only hitch to their plan had been Katrina. She still troubled John. It wasn't what he'd hoped. He'd wanted her as a spiritual bride. A woman of Godly virtue who could raise his child to understand its life was ordained by God and prophesied by Luther. But this new revelation about her being the Dallas mayor's daughter only complicated an already complicated issue. If she refused to submit, then getting rid of her was the next best thing.

34

Rob awoke Wednesday morning to some loud bird squawking. He staggered to the front door with malice in his heart, ready to lob an empty bottle at anything he saw. As he opened it, the first rays of the sun were creeping over the horizon. The bird was a pelican. It sat on the rail of their porch. A crumbled cookie also lay on the rail near the intruder.

"Morning," Frank said.

Rob leaned out a little farther. Frank sat on the porch in his underwear with a cup of coffee.

Frank held up his cup. "Have a full pot inside. Help yourself."

Rob grumbled a little and wiped his eyes, staggering to the kitchen. The pelican flew away and continued its protest as it soared out of sight. A few seconds later, Rob dropped into the chair beside Frank.

"You're up early," Rob mumbled.

"Sunrise and sunset are my favorite times of day."

Rob tasted his coffee. "Hey, I've been thinking about last night."

Frank didn't face him, keeping his eyes on the sun.

"Could I ask one more question, about that?"

"If you must," Frank said.

"Did what happened to your wife cause you to stop being a chef?"

"Yeah, guess so."

"So being a cop in Dallas was the opposite?"

Frank grinned, but didn't answer.

"One last question," Rob said.

"I thought I just answered your last question."

Rob faced him. "Did what happened to your wife change your views on religion—on God?"

Frank finished his coffee and stood. "I need a refill." A minute later he sat down and again eyed the horizon. "My feelings about religion changed when I was a kid. Remember I told you about that day at the tent revival with my grandparents in Florida?"

"Uh-huh," Rob said.

"During that same service, the evangelist said that the world was only six thousand years old. He said atheists had snuck into anthropological digs and seeded them with fake dinosaur bones to make people turn away from God. And believe it or not, he got half the tent to say amen. Thank God my grandparents didn't. I would have walked out on 'em."

"So the guy's a nutcase?" Rob said.

Frank nodded. "Even an eight-year-old kid like me could figure that out. He wants us to completely suspend reality in favor of faith. Totally disregard radiometric dating, potassium-argon dating, and radioactive decay—throw science and reasoning out the window."

"I see what you mean." Rob tried another swallow of coffee. "You should join me and become Catholic. We don't discuss those types of things."

Frank rolled his head in Rob's direction. "And that would solve all my doubts about Jesus being the son of God?" Frank asked.

"Oh, no, but you wouldn't think about them so much."

Frank chuckled.

"Or, you could just get around the whole 'son of God' thing by accepting Judaism," Rob said.

Frank stood and downed the last of his coffee. "There are three reasons I could never do that."

"Oh, yeah. What?"

Frank walked toward the door and smiled over his shoulder as if last night's conversation had never happened. "Bacon, sausage, and ham."

*   *   *

Katrina helped with breakfast, and everyone's attitude toward her remained the same—cold. She cleared the table and had just started washing the dishes when Sister Ruth entered, smirking.

"We'll be bringing that gal up from the basement this evening. You best make sure your area's ready for a roommate. Go ahead and wash the sheets, make sure there are clean towels in the bath, and straighten the place a little. I'll finish cleaning up here."

Katrina had mixed emotions about Emilie's release. She wanted the company, but Emilie wanted to get out *too* bad. She might try something stupid, before they were ready. Besides, they still had no weapons. Katrina had looked everywhere, but no luck. *Listen to yourself.* Katrina was making excuses about why they should stay in this joint another minute. But these were dangerous people, whether Emilie believed it or not. Katrina needed to think it through. If they were going to escape, they had to make it happen soon.

A chill moved over Katrina's skin. For some reason her situation had just started to feel a lot more dangerous.

*   *   *

As they pulled out of the cabin's parking lot, Frank's phone rang.

"This is Pierce. Hold on, I'm putting you on speaker so my partner can hear."

". . . Sergeant Snider—Beaumont PD. We found the Bible that belonged to the missing girl. It was just like you described. *Wormwood* highlighted in Revelation."

Frank cut a sideways look at Rob. "Thanks, Sergeant. Hold on to it for us. I'll let you know."

"So, whatcha thinking?" Rob asked.

Frank pondered the question. After a few seconds, he said, "Swing by the sheriff's office. I have an idea."

They were dressed in their work clothes and driving the pickup when they parked in front.

"Sheriff Lewis in?" Frank asked the deputy at the desk.

It was the same redhead they'd seen the first day. She gave their attire a second glance before ringing the sheriff. "The Dallas detectives want to see you, sir." She looked up at them. "Yes, sir." Pointing over her shoulder, she said, "He's in his office."

When they marched in, Sheriff Lewis stood. "Get you boys some coffee?"

"No thanks, but you could do us a favor," Frank said.

"Oh, what's that?"

"Still got Evan in jail?" Frank asked.

"Sure do."

"Wait a couple of hours, and then call Brother John. You've got his number?"

"Yeah. And why am I calling him?" Sheriff Lewis asked.

"Tell him Evan wants to talk to him—say he's been going on and on about how it's important—something about Wormwood."

"You mean have John talk to Evan on the phone, or in person?"

"In person. Tell John that Evan is raving like a lunatic—he needs to come down," Frank said.

The sheriff smiled and eyed the pair. "You're going to do something?"

"We're going to find out if she's there, if that's what you mean," Frank said. "We're not planning on identifying ourselves. Hope to get away with just a covert search. But if she's there, against her will, we're grabbing her and hightailing it to Dallas. We'll let you know either way. It's your county; do whatever you think best."

Lewis offered a sympathetic nod. "Fair enough, but don't get yourselves into anything you can't get out of."

"Okay," Frank said. "Thanks."

Lewis pointed at the pair. "Don't go thanking me. 'Cause this conversation never happened. Understand?"

"Understood, sir," Frank agreed.

"Okay, get the hell out of my office."

They swung toward the door with Rob in the lead.

"Hey, one more thing," Lewis shouted, filling his jaw with tobacco.

They turned and faced him.

A grin crept across the sheriff's lips. "Good luck."

Rob pulled into a bait and tackle shop on the way out of town. He went in and a couple of minutes later came out with a large paper bag.

"What's that?" Frank asked.

Rob threw the bag in the back seat. "Anti-dog devices."

* * *

"So how do you want to do this?" Luther whispered. He and John sat in the old Dodge pickup in the side yard.

John looked at the house. He didn't want to excite the brothers and sisters.

"They're keeping her busy this morning with chores, but we need to do it before we let the other one out," John said. "We'll take care of it ourselves—like the others. No use involving the rest."

"Don't you figure they know?" Luther asked.

"Of course they know," John answered in a more scolding voice than he'd intended, "but we don't have to shove it in their faces. You got any chores this morning?"

"Just checking the trotline," Luther said.

John ran a hand across his face. "Okay, you finish that and we'll do it while the others are cleaning the fish. Shovel still in the truck?"

"Was last time I checked, but I'll look. Who's going to do it?" Luther asked.

"This one's your turn."

Luther stared out the window and his lips stretched tight. "I'd rather not, if you don't mind. Could I just do the next one?"

"What's the matter?" John asked.

Luther shrugged. "I don't know. Guess I like her. I just don't feel right about it."

Luther was a blessed prophet, but he had trouble with basic earthly decisions. John felt bad about raising his voice to him earlier. Luther couldn't help the way he was any more than John could. John loved and respected his brother; putting him in distress seemed cruel.

"Never mind; I'll do it." John opened the door and got out.

He walked into the house and up the stairs. After unlocking the door to his bedroom, he slipped inside and opened the nightstand drawer. John removed the old .45 Long Colt and opened the cylinder, eyeing the shells before sliding the piece into the back of his waistband. John pulled his shirt over it. On his way downstairs, the phone in the kitchen rang. The sound of Karen's voice echoed around the corner. When John walked up, she held the receiver toward him and mouthed the words "sheriff's department."

"Hello," John said. They had never called the house before.

"John, Sheriff Lewis."

"How are you this morning?" John glanced at Karen.

"Locked up a friend of yours the other day—says he wants to talk to you." The sheriff's voice sounded relaxed.

"A friend of mine?" John asked.

"Yeah, old Evan had a little too much to drink and got in a fight. Didn't he used to live with y'all?"

"For a while."

The sheriff paused before saying, "Well, says he wants to discuss something called Wormwood. Don't really know what that is."

John pulled in a low, slow breath. He shifted his stance and moved the receiver to the other ear. "I see."

"If you plan on coming by, I'll leave word with the jail."

John ran a hand across his mouth. "Sure, I can stop by for a minute."

"Fine. I'll tell him you'll be coming."

"Sheriff, why didn't he call me personally?"

"Don't rightly know. He could have. We allow him use of a phone. But he asked me if I'd do it for him. Been feeling poorly lately."

John understood perfectly. "Thanks. See you in a bit."

John dropped the receiver into the cradle.

"What's wrong?" Karen asked, turning away from the counter where she was stirring something. Her hands were still covered with flour.

"Not sure," John mumbled. "Evan's in jail. Asked to see me."

"You going?" She wiped her hands on her apron.

John looked at her. "Not on your life. I haven't been off this property in almost three years. Don't plan to start now."

"What'll you do?"

John smelled a rat. A big, old, stinking police rat. "I'll send the brothers. Has Luther left yet?" John glanced out the window.

Karen motioned with her hand. "Saw him drive away on the four-wheeler just after you came in."

He kept his gaze out the window, and his mind on the cops, until Karen hugged him from behind, letting her hand slide down to his crotch.

When he locked eyes with her, a smile had formed on her lips. She'd wanted to be a spiritual wife, but he had forbidden it. It wasn't in God's plan. But she allowed him to do things Judy and Ruth balked at. She enjoyed the games and toys. He took one last peek out the window. Luther wouldn't be back for a spell. He'd send the brothers to talk to Evan and then satisfy Karen. Besides, with all that was going on, a good stress reliever couldn't be a bad thing.

35

Frank and Rob coasted up to the compound's open gate and turned right down the gravel road. They stopped at the same spot they'd parked yesterday. Frank had it worked out. They'd skulk through the woods and set up surveillance on the house somewhere between the garden and barn. They'd keep an eye on the back of the place and wait. After John left to see Sheriff Lewis, they'd make their way to the rear door and slip in. They intended to search the whole house.

Rob led the way through the thick underbrush, weaving around briars and clumps of poison ivy. It had been a long time since Frank had spent time out in the woods like this. A low ground fog clung to his knees, making an already creepy experience even creepier.

When they eased up to a large pine near the area where they'd been yesterday, Rob swung the binoculars toward the house. Frank scanned the ground for snakes.

"Looks all clear," Rob whispered.

"Let's go." Frank turned right, staying in the tree line, working his way to the back of the property. The parklike setting and soft scents of pine and blooming shrubs kept his anxiety level steady.

"You know, Brother John didn't have much luck with his disciples," Rob said. "One overdosed and died, one is in a prison for the criminally insane, and one is in jail for drunk and disorderly."

"I'm not concerned with them. I'm worried about the ones who'll be in the house when we go in. How many, you think?"

Rob ducked a limb. "Eddie said he chose six disciples from earthly

251

sinners. That would leave three in the house, unless one goes with John to the sheriff's."

"Think we can handle three guys without shooting a couple?"

Rob hesitated a few seconds before answering. "Then there are the women."

Frank's thoughts drifted to the girl he'd killed in the truck. The one with the dagger. The one who'd almost ended his life. "The odds just get better and better," Frank grumbled.

Ten minutes later, they found the perfect place. They lay on their bellies about sixty yards from the house in a shaded, hidden area.

Rob put the binoculars on the screen door just as it opened. "We got movement. They're on the porch."

"How many?" Frank asked.

"I see three. Wait, they're coming outside."

"Isn't that John?" Frank pointed.

"Yeah, looks like him. Shit."

The two tall men who resembled each other got in the truck and left. John remained on the porch, looking out over the lawn as if waiting for something.

"Old John must be smarter than he looks," Frank said.

"What do we do?"

Frank scratched his neck, thinking. "Stay with the plan. With two out of the way, we'll have one less to deal with."

"Let's give them a few minutes. Let them get closer to town," Rob said before passing the binoculars to Frank. Rob rolled onto his back, staring into the tree branches. "This *is* pretty country. Nice place to retire. Yeah, Carmen and I could sell out, come here and buy a few acres, build a cabin. I'd have a place to hunt, plant a garden, raise a few cows."

"Then you could be a real cowboy—not just dress like one," Frank remarked.

Rob rolled back to his stomach. "I could live this kind of life, and so could Carmen—you know, when she gets better." Rob pulled out his

Copenhagen can and filled his lip. Probably to further prove his cowboyness.

Frank swiveled his head toward him. "Yeah, you could live here if they'd accept you as friends and neighbors, but they won't."

Rob's brow crinkled. "Why, because we're Mexican?"

"No, because you guys still have all your teeth."

The sound of a four-wheeler floated through the trees from the direction of their truck.

*   *   *

Brother Luther pulled up to the white pickup and glanced inside. Two yellow hardhats lay on the seat. *One of the gas service trucks?* But where was the driver? The first gas well was another quarter mile down the road. Luther switched off the engine, slid off the four-wheeler, and walked around the truck. It looked okay. No flats or any reason it wouldn't run. He touched the hood—still warm, but not hot. *Must have been here a half hour or less.*

Luther craned his neck down the road for signs of the driver—nothing. If it had quit running, the guy had probably walked to the main road and called for a ride. Readjusting the string of catfish in the front basket, Luther cranked up the four-wheeler and drove toward the Farm to Market Road. If the gas guy was there waiting for a ride, that would be all right, but if not, then where was he? He'd have to tell John about this.

*   *   *

Frank kept the binoculars on the porch door and mentally worked through several scenarios. Only a couple seemed feasible, however. They'd either meet serious resistance or they wouldn't. If it turned out to be the former, how much force was he willing to use to conduct the search? They certainly didn't want to kill anyone, but what if they had no choice? If Trina was found safe and rescued, anything would be forgiven. If they came up dry and were forced to hurt someone in the process, they'd be the outlaws. All Frank knew for certain was he had to try. The thought of not trying ate at his heart. He would risk all he had or would ever have on the outcome.

Frank glanced at Rob, who held out his hand for the binoculars. Frank handed them over. It wasn't right that Rob would suffer the same punishment as he if things went tits up. He was just being the loyal partner of a nutcase, people would say. Frank could hear the comments now: *An ill-conceived notion. A stupid idea. Foolish and dangerous.* Best case would be to avoid the dogs, spy Trina through a window, and whisk her away with no one the wiser. What were the chances of that?

Frank took the binoculars again and scanned the yard for the mutts. They'd seen them the other day, but not this morning. In a locked kennel, perhaps? The song of a bird preceded a splat and warm feeling on the back of Frank's right hand. He wiped the poop off and stared at Rob. A smirk spread across his partner's face.

"Ain't nature great, cracker?"

"Yeah, great. How much time?"

Rob checked his watch. "They should just about be at the sheriff's office by now." Rob grabbed the paper bag he got from the bait shop and emptied it on the ground.

"What are those?"

Rob grinned. "Bait casting nets."

"What are you gonna do?"

Rob stood and unfolded each one. "See if I can catch me a dog."

Frank rose and Rob handed him the open net.

"Hold it like this as we approach the house," Rob said, "I'll have the other. If the dogs come at us, I'll snare them. Give us a few extra seconds to make it to the door."

"I don't know how to use this thing," Frank said.

"Don't worry about it. Just hand it to me the way you're holding it now and I'll do the casting."

"You sure about this?"

Rob got his net ready, got a fresh dip of Copenhagen, and lifted an eyebrow. "Who do you think caught all the bait for my dad, brothers, and uncles growing up in Port Aransas?"

Frank spread his feet and shifted his weight forward. "Okay, Captain Ahab, it's all yours."

Rob shook the wrinkles from his net and nodded.

"On three," Frank said, his earlier thoughts echoing in his head again. *A stupid idea. Foolish and dangerous.*

Rob spit and flexed his knees.

"One—two—three."

36

Katrina pushed the sheets and pillow cases into the washer and added detergent. It didn't take that long to straighten up her room, and she had a few minutes to kill waiting for the sheets to wash. Better make herself scarce if she didn't want another job. Sisters Ruth and Judy had been their bitchy selves today—as usual. At least they were busy upstairs and not yelling at her to do something. All the men had drifted off somewhere, except the Freak. He'd moped around all morning from room to room, giving her a stare she didn't like. He'd looked at her with his creepy eyes since she'd arrived, but today seemed different. More threatening somehow. He and Sister Karen had disappeared upstairs a while ago.

She set the water level and temperature and spun the dial for the wash cycle. As she closed the lid, some movement outside caught her eye. She leaned closer to the window and squinted. Two men ran from the woods toward the screened porch, carrying some kind of large white cloth in their hands. A dog bounded straight at them as the short stocky one whirled the cloth once and released it on the dog. It collapsed and rolled forward, kicking and biting at the cloth.

A net—it was a net, and the dog was tangled in it. The larger dog charged. The tall guy handed his net to the short one, and he again whirled it at the animal. This dog appeared smarter, and ducked its head. The net slid off its back. The beast made a beeline for the short guy. When it hit him, they both toppled to the ground as the tall man kicked the dog. A shot rang out from the melee, and the one on the ground pushed the dead dog off. The men raced the last few yards to the porch.

What the hell? Katrina ran into the kitchen.

* * *

Luther rode up and down the Farm to Market Road for a half mile in each direction before he headed home. He couldn't figure it out. The fella having truck trouble must've called for a ride. No sign of him walking on the road.

The sound of a gun going off from the direction of the house didn't particularity alarm Luther. Someone shooting a snake or armadillo, most likely. He tootled down the gravel road on the four-wheeler. Needed to get these fish somewhere cooler. He'd rather clean them than be with John when he took Katrina out back, anyway. Of all the girls, she remained his favorite. He didn't know why. She wasn't a particularity pleasant person. Had a smart mouth most of the time, but she had a quality he admired—spunk. Shame she had to go so soon. Could have produced a better-than-average baby.

* * *

Frank hit the screen door like an offensive lineman. He jumped on the porch and held it for Rob, who was one second behind him. Frank pushed opened the kitchen door in a run and came face to face with Katrina, the girl who looked like the love of his life twenty years ago. The straight hair draped over her shoulders, and the old-maid dress hid her figure, but he was pretty sure.

Panting, Frank asked, "Are you Katrina Wallace?"

Rob bolted through the door, catching his breath, his left forearm bleeding. He swung the pistol left and right.

"Clear," Rob shouted. He moved to the side, keeping the pistol trained on the next room as the sound of footsteps approached.

Katrina seemed frozen, unable to speak. Frank grabbed her arm and shook it. "I said, are you Katrina Wallace?" he yelled.

She found her voice. "Yes . . . yes, yes. Who are you?"

257

Before Rob could announce they were the police, Frank cut him off. "Two crazy guys your father sent to bring you home. Let's get out of here."

Trina pulled away. "No, wait, my friend's in the basement. We have to take—"

"What's going on here?" A tall woman with long, straight brown hair marched around the corner and met eyes with Frank. "Who are you?"

Trina looked in her direction and said, "Get out of my way, Ruth. I'm letting Emilie out."

Ruth stood in front of the basement door and spread her arms. She defiantly raised her chin. "You'll do no such thing."

Trina never missed a beat but wound up like a big-league pitcher and flattened the woman's nose. Ruth didn't let out a sound as she slid to the floor. Trina grabbed Ruth's long hair and jerked her to one side.

"That's for Emilie and the rest, you old bitch," Trina said. She dug in her pocket and produced a key, unlocking the door.

Frank was dumbfounded by the little dynamo in his midst.

"Nice cross punch," Rob muttered.

Trina swung the door open as another woman rushed around the corner. She was dark-haired and a little shorter than the woman who now lay sprawled limp on the floor, half unconscious, blood pouring from her nose.

"Ruth!" The new woman's hateful eyes scanned Frank and Rob. "What have you done?" She went to the injured woman and knelt to help her.

Trina ignored her and yelled, "Emilie, come on, we're leaving—hurry."

Footsteps pounded stairs, and a second later a pretty girl in her midtwenties with short blonde hair rushed out the door. Trina and she embraced for another second before the girl eyed Frank and Rob. The girl gave Frank a wide-eyed look, and her stare darted to Rob before coming back to Trina.

"No time to explain," Trina said. "They're friends."

"Let's go, now!" Rob said.

258

Emilie grabbed a cast-iron skillet as she walked past the stove. With-out a word she approached the woman who knelt by Ruth and slammed it down on her head. The woman collapsed on top of her friend.

"Now I'm ready," Emilie said, dusting her hands.

Frank led the way out as the growl of an engine came around the house. Trina grabbed Frank's arm. "That's Brother Luther. He's not going to let me go easily."

Frank took in the cherubic face and the dull expression of the man on the four-wheeler. Luther slowed the cycle and eyed Frank.

"Come on . . . come on." Frank motioned to the others.

When Trina stepped out, Luther screamed, "No!" He pulled a pistol and pointed it at them. He cocked the hammer.

Rob didn't hesitate. Jumping off the porch, he aimed his pistol at Luther. Rob's shot went wild. Luther didn't hesitate either. He rolled off the machine and used it for cover. He fired, and everyone ducked. The ricochet whistled past Frank's ear, and a cold dread ran through him. He forced himself to breathe and assessed the situation. The guy was between them and the truck. No way to get past without a major shootout.

"This way," Frank yelled. He sprinted for the corner of the house. They could use it for cover. The group ran around the house and flattened themselves against it. Frank peeked from the corner. The guy hadn't moved or tried to shoot again. The four-wheeler idled, and he stayed behind the fortified engine block. Nothing showed but his head—a small target. There had been no loss of life yet, and Frank intended to keep it that way.

"Whatcha think?" Rob eased beside him.

Frank pointed at the thick underbrush. "If we work our way around to the truck, we'll be okay."

"Not much of a plan, but it's the best we've got."

Frank glanced at him. A confident grin spread over Rob's lips, and he spit out the wad of snuff. He motioned at the woods. "Let's go."

37

John and Karen stood at the kitchen window and watched. He wore only boxers, and she still had the sheet wrapped around her. "Put some clothes on," he ordered.

She scrambled away as he stepped onto the porch. He opened the screen door and motioned to Luther, who ran to him.

"What happened?" Luther asked.

"Ruth and Judy have been attacked. Katrina and the other one's gone."

Luther pointed to the dog still struggling to get out of the net. "When I pulled up, Delilah was dead and Samson was tangled up. Saw them folks run out the door and shot at 'em with my snake pistol."

"Hit 'em?" John asked.

"No, they cut around the house." Luther motioned. "I saw bushes moving. Probably trying to get to their truck."

"What truck?"

Luther pointed into the woods. "Found a gas service truck on the gravel road after I ran the trotline. Nobody around. Figured they must have had engine trouble."

John's stomach soured. "If they came in a truck, they'll use it to get out." He glanced down the gravel drive. "Lock the front gate, untangle Samson, and put him on their trail. He'll keep them distracted until we can cut 'em off. Meet me here in five minutes."

"Who are they? Can't be gas folks," Luther said.

"No, they're either police or private investigators. Don't matter. Can't let them get out of here."

"Reckon they'll call for help?" Luther asked.

John shook his head. "We barely get cell service here. In the woods there's no signal at all. I'll get us some better guns. Get going, Luther."

John swung through the kitchen door and found Karen wiping blood from Ruth's face. Judy lay still beside them. "She dead?" he asked.

Karen looked up. "Still breathing."

John ran upstairs and dressed. He unlocked the closet and got the double-barrel with a box of buckshot and grabbed the Colt from the nightstand. If only the brothers had had a cell. He'd call them to return. Too late for that. He and Luther would have to handle it. By the time he got outside, Luther stood waiting for orders. John tossed him the shotgun and shells.

"You follow Samson," John said. He pointed to the right. "I'll head the other way and cut them off. Don't let them get past you. If they make it to the truck, we're screwed."

Luther's head bobbed. "Okay." He whirled around and raced toward the woods.

John stared back at the house. Everything they'd worked for, everything they'd planned, was on the line. What he and Luther did next would determine not just their future, but the future of all mankind. The intruders' trail was easy to follow. He stuffed the Colt in the waistband of his jeans. They'd find them soon enough.

38

Frank brought up the rear as the four fought through the underbrush. Rob led the way, making a wide arc that kept them at least a quarter mile from the house. It would take longer to get to the truck, but this way there was less likelihood of running into somebody.

"How many men are still at the house? We saw two leave earlier," Frank said.

Trina ducked under some vines and glanced over her shoulder. "There's only four total. Who are you guys? Did my dad really hire you to find me?"

Frank reached into his pocket and held out his badge. "Dallas Police."

Trina exhaled. "I'll never complain about the cops again—promise."

As Katrina walked in front of Frank, he noted her movements. Her delicate gait and the way she swung her arms were exactly like Carly's. Her voice even sounded the same. The way she pronounced certain words and her speech tempo sent trembles through him. Had his deceased wife been returned to him? Had his feelings about religion been misplaced all these years? *Had his prayers been answered?*

Frank shook himself out of his daze and pulled his cell phone out of his pocket. "You have any signal?"

Rob dug out his phone. "Nope. You?"

"Nothing."

"Where are we going?" Emilie asked.

"Got a truck over there." Frank motioned in the general direction they were walking. "Shouldn't be too much farther." He really had no idea where they were in relation to the truck, but he trusted Rob's Marine instincts to get them there.

"Hey, check it out," Rob called. He stared at a rise and a small hill to their left. "Might get some phone reception on top of that thing," he said, walking toward it with his phone in the air.

A clear, shallow stream led the way to the hill. Frank sprinted past everyone, jumped the creek, and scrambled up the sixty-degree incline, using clumps of grass and bushes as handholds. Rob and the girls watched.

"Anything?" Rob shouted.

Frank paced the crest of the hill, holding the phone over his head and tipping it so he could see the screen.

Emilie's voice floated up the hillside. "Hey, mister. Look."

Frank glanced down to see Rob, Trina, and Emilie disappear into the side of the hill. Frank did a double take. *Where did they go?* A moment later, Rob reappeared.

"You're standing on top of a cave," he called up to Frank.

"Seriously?" A ping sounded from Frank's phone. He stared at it. "Hey, I got a signal."

Rob held out his palm to Frank. "Don't move."

Frank called the sheriff's department and got put through to Sheriff Lewis.

"Wondering when I'd hear from you boys. Any luck?" the sheriff asked.

"We got her and another one they were holding."

"No shit?"

"Yeah, but we could use some help. During our escape, we got cut off from our truck. Working our way there now, but they may be after us. Could you lend a hand?"

"Where are you?"

"We're behind the house in the woods. There's a cave back here. With these two girls, we're going to bunker in and wait for help. Any idea how long it'll take to get here? Hello? Hello?"

Frank looked at the phone and his heart went cold—no signal. *Did the sheriff hear anything?*

Frank scanned the bottom of the hill until the top of Rob's head appeared. "I lost the signal midcall."

"Call him again," Rob shouted.

Frank hit redial, but a movement in the woods caught his attention. He studied it as the thing crept behind bushes—never fully showing itself. *An animal?* A primal fear welled up in Frank's gut. *The other dog.*

"Anything?" Rob yelled.

Frank didn't answer, instead sliding down the hill silently. "We've got bigger problems."

The pit bull emerged from behind a tree. At least eighty pounds and all muscle, it paced toward them, head, shoulders, and tail down. A deep, menacing growl hit Frank right in the sternum. The thing was twenty-five yards and closing when Rob pointed his pistol.

Frank laid his hand on Rob's shoulder. "Really want to do that?"

Rob paused a second before lowering the weapon, now realizing the same thing Frank did. The gunshot would draw Katrina's captors right to them. "Is the sheriff coming?" Rob asked.

Frank eyed Trina and Emilie huddled at the entrance of the cave. He moved closer to Rob and lowered his voice. "Not sure if he knows where we are."

Rob whispered, "I say we stay here, wait for help. If it was just us . . ." He looked over at the girls.

"Yeah. You're right." Frank kept a wary eye on the dog, which showed no sign of giving way. It growled again, baring its teeth.

"Okay, everybody inside," Rob said.

The creek flowed through the cave, so they waded into the ankle-deep cold water and followed it into the dark abyss. The dog advanced, still growling. Frank wasn't sure why it wasn't attacking. Perhaps it was intimidated by the size of the group.

A few yards inside, Rob halted. The stream eddied around their feet. "What's going on?" Frank asked from the rear. He kept his pistol trained on the dog, which waited just on the other side of the creek.

To Frank's surprise, a flashlight came to life, giving them a clear picture of what lay ahead.

"You have a flashlight?" Frank asked.

"I was a Boy Scout long before I was a Marine. Look." Rob shined the light and scanned the interior of the cavern. It was about twenty feet high and thirty feet across. Old roots showed from the sandstone around the edges, and vines and ferns cascaded down, straining toward the light. There were two paths. One followed the stream. That was the narrow one—maybe three feet across. The wider one had a sandy floor and led up a twenty-degree incline.

"I say we take this one." Rob shined the light to the right on the wider path.

"Makes sense," Frank said.

They edged into the abyss. The sand was deep, like beach sand.

"God, something stinks," Rob said. "No telling what feeds and craps in here."

Now Frank smelled it. Moving through the darkness, he had the feeling they were being watched. This wasn't unusual; he sometimes had the same feeling in his own loft. His personal paranoia, he called it. They were at least thirty-five to forty yards inside now. The entrance looked like a pinhole of light behind them. A low growl floated through the darkness somewhere to the rear.

"Hold up," Rob said. He dropped to his knees and shined the beam into a hole to the left. The light disappeared, and the darkness overwhelmed Frank. Rob pulled his light out from the hole. "Hey," Rob said, "this connects to the other tunnel. About a five-foot drop to the creek. There's another entrance about twenty yards that way." Rob pointed into the darkness.

The stench was almost unbearable. A fetid, putrid, rotting smell. Frank scanned the area. "Some critter lives here, that's for sure. Let's hold up for now," he said. "We can defend this place and evacuate out the other end if necessary." Mounds of sand were piled up along the sides of the walls. Frank strolled to one and sat on the moist earth. Katrina looked over at Rob and Emilie, then turned to Frank.

"May I join you?" she asked.

"Sure." Frank scooted over, giving her room.

"What's your name?"

"Frank—Frank Pierce."

In the dim light, a trace of a smile crossed the lips Frank remembered from years past. She extended her hand.

"Thank you for coming for us. You don't have to be here, but I'm happy you are."

Frank shook the hand. It had a familiar touch. "Are you okay? We've been looking for you since the day after you went missing."

She sat close to him. "I'm fine. I wondered if we'd ever be found." She stared at him in a strange way before the smile returned. "It was you—wasn't it? You figured it out."

Frank looked into her eyes, hoping to gain some sort of confirmation of who she really was. He'd never believed in reincarnation, but there were just too many similarities to be a coincidence. *Katrina or Carly?*

"I couldn't give up . . . I had to find you," Frank whispered.

Rob and Emilie sat across from them on another mound of sand.

"Is help coming?" Emilie asked.

Rob glanced to Frank.

"Sure, we called the sheriff," Frank said, putting a reassuring hand on Katrina's shoulder. "We'll be out of here in no time."

Rob lowered his voice. "I'm going to turn off the light now. We may need the batteries later. We should remain as quiet as possible until help arrives."

* * *

Katrina never imagined what that narrow beam of light meant to her until it disappeared. Not only did it plunge the group into darkness; it dropped her spirit into the blackest pit she could imagine. Her chest tightened and her breathing became labored. She shook and coldness seeped into her very being.

The unexpected touch of Frank's warm, reassuring hand on

hers shut down the panic attack. She relaxed and leaned her head on his shoulder. Why did she feel so comforted by this stranger? It was as if she'd known him for years. Maybe someone she'd dreamed about a long time ago—a hero she'd forgotten.

"Are we going to be okay?" she whispered.

Frank's arm reached around and squeezed her shoulder, pulling her into him. "I promise, nothing's going to happen to you. I'll protect you this time. Don't worry."

Katrina should have been confused, but strangely, the cryptic message made sense somehow. Who was this guy? They had definitely met, but while he was familiar, she couldn't place him. It didn't matter; she felt the type of love and security a newborn must feel toward its mother.

Uncomfortable on the uneven ground, Katrina shifted but didn't want to leave Frank's embrace. Finally it became too much. *Must be sitting on a root.* "Hand me the light," she said.

The Maglite switched on, and Frank let his arm drop from her shoulder.

"What's wrong?" Rob asked, passing her the flashlight.

"Don't know what I'm sitting on, but it has to go." Katrina stood and put the beam on the area beside Frank. She almost passed out. In the sand, a dirty decomposing hand curled into a claw. The tips of several fingers were missing, and gnaw marks scarred the palm and wrist. Maggots wiggled in every direction. One finger remained intact. It had a small gold ring with an emerald in the center.

Katrina screamed, *"Annabelle!"* and fell to her knees, weeping.

Frank cradled her in his arms, stroking her hair. He guided her away from the terrifying sight and held her.

Rob picked up the flashlight and waved it at the piles of sand, his expression becoming more and more horrified. "This is a graveyard—a shallow graveyard."

Emilie sobbed and held tight to Rob's arm.

Katrina couldn't stop crying, all the pent-up stress and fear from her captivity releasing at once. She shook and her insides rolled. She gagged, dropping to all fours.

Emilie screamed, and Rob shifted the light toward her. She stood wringing her hands, staring at the mound they'd been sitting on. The decomposed outline of a rotting face poked up through the sand.

Rob pulled Emilie away, and Frank helped Katrina to her feet. Her legs barely supported her. Frank led her to the dead end of the cave where Rob and Emilie waited.

"Stay here and don't make a sound," Frank said.

"Lie on the ground," Rob said. "Stay as low as you can get. No matter what you hear—don't get up."

Katrina lay in the cold sand and she and Emilie locked hands. A prayer slipped from Emilie's lips. Katrina's hand tightened on hers.

39

Rob joined Frank at another mound of sand. Frank raked his fingers around the side, and a decaying foot came into view. Rob's stomach turned. "Mother of Jesus!"

"They're all here," Frank whispered. "All the missing girls." A sadness that Rob had never heard before filled Frank's voice.

Rob had no words to answer. A threatening growl drifted from the darkness toward them.

"After all that screaming, I'm pretty sure they know we're in here," Rob whispered. "We need to shut down this flashlight." Rob pointed behind them. "Go back and guard the hole that leads to the other chamber. You're the second line of defense."

Frank rested his hand on Rob's shoulder and squeezed. "Good luck."

Rob switched off the light and lay facing the entrance. As his eyes grew accustomed to the darkness, he registered the pinhole of daylight almost fifty yards ahead. He took deep breaths, slowly releasing each, while keeping his pistol pointed at the speck. There were probably at least two guys after them and two entrances to the cave. Would they try the same one, or split up and hit them from different sides?

After about five minutes, Rob had a feeling—a bad one. The same kind he had had that night in Iraq when he yelled the challenge and had gotten only silence. He'd lobbed a grenade over the perimeter wall and killed three enemy sappers. *God, I wish I had a grenade right now.*

Rob strained to hear something—anything—but the silence of the cave was deafening. *No, this isn't right.* Rob's Marine training had taught him to be scared when things were *too* quiet. He slid backward on his belly through the cold sand until his foot bumped Frank.

"What's going on?" Frank whispered.

Rob eased up on one knee and felt for him in the blackness. He put his chin on Frank's shoulder to whisper in his ear. "Someone or something's in the cave with us."

"What are you going to do?" Frank asked.

"Switching on the flashlight for a second. Have your pistol ready. If you see a target—take the shot."

The sound of Frank slowly exhaling filled Rob with doubt. Could he do it? Or would he freeze up again?

"Okay," Frank whispered.

Rob low-crawled back into position. His eyes reacquired the pale speck of daylight from the entrance. If someone was approaching, they'd block that glow in a second—he'd be ready. With the flashlight in one hand and pistol in the other, he kept his eyes fixed on the distant speck.

The speck disappeared. As Rob's vision went black, he thought at first he'd imagined the light going out. A second later, he knew he hadn't.

Rob switched on the flashlight and came face to face with the dog. Brother Luther, behind the animal, held a double-barrel shot gun.

"Strike," Luther yelled.

The animal lunged, snarling. All fur and teeth, six feet from Rob's face. Rob squeezed the trigger, the gunshot deafening in the close confines of the cave. The dog didn't even have time to whine. It fell in a heap, half of its skull blown off. Rob turned off the beam and rolled to his left.

The blast from both barrels of the shotgun lit up the cave and sounded like a cannon going off, throwing dirt into Rob's eyes. Three shots came from the rear, and Luther grunted. Rob's heart leapt as he realized who had fired those shots.

Frank!

Rob flicked on the light, expecting to find a body. Instead, a bleeding Luther stood over him with the shotgun, holding it like a club. Rob swung his pistol up, but Luther kicked sand in his face. Two more shots from Frank and Luther staggered. Rob couldn't see. Everything was a blur. He turned off the flashlight and raked sand from his eyes. A moment later something hard crashed into the back of his head. The shotgun. Luther was using it like a club on his skull.

Rob rolled onto his back, switched the beam back on, and pointed the pistol at Luther. The wild man, bleeding like a stuck hog, swung the shotgun again, knocking Rob's weapon from his grip.

"Kill him, Frank!"

Rob's vision faded as three more shots echoed from behind. Luther wobbled a moment before collapsing. Rob exhaled and rolled on his side, barely conscious. His fingers touched the raw flesh on the back of his head. His eyes watered, his vision fuzzy from sand. He wiped his face. When the shadow strolled up beside him, he relaxed.

"You got him," Rob said.

No answer.

"Rob, you okay?" Frank yelled. The voice came from behind, not from the shadow that had appeared beside him.

Rob snapped his head up and scratched through the sand for his weapon. Brother John's revolver was already pointed at his head.

When the shot echoed through the cave, Rob flinched. How had John missed him? But it wasn't John's shot.

Brother John fell back on his butt. He looked down at his shirt, where a crimson stain bloomed. The words of Marshall Woodard came back to Rob. *You can't kill the Prophet. He'll just resurrect himself—he's immortal.*

In the dim light, Rob's fingers wrapped around his pistol. *We'll see about that.*

Brother John wasn't looking at Rob. His focus seemed to be on the dark cavern where the shot had come from. Before Rob could swing his weapon around, John squeezed off three rounds. Rob found his target, blinked his swollen eyes, and emptied the magazine. John fell to the sand and lay still.

Rob's adrenaline rush was at its height, and he shook so hard he felt weak. Pulling himself to his knees, he pointed the flashlight toward the girls. "You okay?"

Before they could answer, he swept the beam over the sprawled figure of Frank, face down in the cold sand.

Rob rushed to his side and rolled him over. The front of his worker's coveralls were soaked in blood. He was barely breathing.

40

Rob rested his elbows on his knees and his face in his palms. The waiting area of the Level III trauma center had no chairs and only a few metal benches along the wall. The constant ringing of phones and disembodied voices overhead, paging doctors and calling code blues, got on his nerves. He needed a silent moment to reflect on what had happened.

It had taken forever to get to Nacogdoches Memorial Hospital. Carrying Frank out of the woods, getting an ambulance, the long drive with red lights and siren. Not being able to stop the bleeding.

Katrina and Emilie had been checked by the nurses, and with the exception of a few scrapes and bruises, they were both fine, although Rob wasn't sure what they had endured in the house and what kind of mental scars they would have. Sheriff Lewis had left with the girls a few minutes earlier to go to the sheriff's department for statements. They had promised to come back as soon as they were finished. Lewis's deputies had raided the house and rounded up the rest of the brothers and sisters.

Rob had nothing left. They'd patched up his dog-bitten arm and the head wound Luther had given him—no big deal. After three washings, his eyes still felt gritty. He pulled up his sleeve and focused on his watch. Almost three o'clock. Frank had been in surgery over an hour. By chance, the renowned Houston trauma surgeon, Dr. Francis Adams, had been holding a regional training seminar on emergency medicine when the call had come in: "Police officer shot and in route." Adam's team had been waiting when the ambulance rolled up to the ER. That was the only break they'd gotten—other than the fact that Frank was still alive.

Those who make it to the ER usually survive, right?

A tall, skinny man with a gray-speckled beard, wearing scrubs, walked toward him. Rob stood and the man introduced himself.

"I'm Dr. Adams."

They shook hands.

"Your friend's being moved to ICU," Adams said.

Rob exhaled. "Thank God."

The doctor appeared hesitant. "Why don't we have a seat?" He motioned at the bench. "You're not by chance a relative, are you?"

"Naw, we're partners. Dallas PD." Something didn't feel right. Adams's eyes darted from side to side and he leaned forward and clasped his hands, resting his arms on his legs.

"Does he have any relatives nearby?" he asked.

"No, they're all in Florida," Rob said.

"No wife?"

"Huh-uh—deceased."

A grimace crossed Adams's face. "I believe his family should be notified."

"Yeah, sure—we'll let them know. This isn't his first close call."

"I'm not certain you understand what I'm getting at." The doctor paused a couple of beats too long before continuing. "When someone receives a very serious traumatic injury and there's blood loss, the body uses its natural defenses to rush chemical compounds to the site of the injury. You know, to clot the blood and stem the bleeding."

Rob followed the doctor's eyes as he spoke. "Yeah, I understand."

"But when there's a substantial delay in getting proper medical assistance, the body works overtime to stabilize things. If this happens, sometimes all the natural clotting chemicals get used up. The patient bleeds out."

Rob shook and didn't want to hear any more. He looked in the opposite direction. As if maybe if he didn't stare at the guy, the nightmare would end—he'd wake up. A weakness and fear crept into his gut.

The doctor cleared his throat. "We haven't been able to stabilize your friend. He's still losing blood. He's had numerous transfusions, and we're pumping all the coagulants we can into him, but nothing's working."

Rob wanted to scream, *But he's alive, in a hospital, and you're a doctor—save him!* Instead, he only nodded. He squeezed his lips and his eyes misted. He sniffed and wiped his nose.

"So, straight up, doc. What's his chances?"

Adams looked down and swallowed. "When someone gets severely injured, the body goes into shock. It's very hard to reverse sometimes. It was made worse by the delay in getting him to the ER. In cases like this, it's almost always a futile uphill battle. After this much blood loss, the patient seldom survives. One-in-ten chance, at best. If they wake up, they're usually out of the woods. Most never regain consciousness."

A dizziness clouded Rob's head. He closed his eyes, grabbed the sides of the bench, and drew long, deep breaths.

A hand rested on his shoulder. "I'm very sorry, but any relatives should be contacted as soon as possible," Dr. Adams whispered.

Warm tears skated down Rob's cheeks. He wiped them and sniffled. "How long?"

The doctor stood. "No way of knowing. Depends on how strong the patient is. Hours—a day, sometimes."

Rob stood, but kept a hand on the wall. This couldn't be happening. "Okay. I'll see they're called." He eyed the doctor. "Will there be indicators right before . . ." Rob trailed off, losing his voice.

Adams frowned. "His vitals will tank a few minutes before. We won't be able to pull him out of the dive."

An ICU nurse rushed up. "Dr. Singer needs you."

Rob grabbed Adams's arm, swallowing down something hard that had just appeared in his throat. "Hey, doc. I'm not a relative or anything, but we're closer than brothers. If he has to die in a strange place, please don't let him die alone—let me in."

Adam's expression softened. "Absolutely." He touched the nurse's shoulder. "As soon as they're finished recording vitals"—he pointed to Rob—"he's in."

She nodded and Adams walked to the ICU entrance to confer with the other doctor. Rob collapsed on the bench. He wiped his eyes and gathered his wits. This call would be hard.

When he told Edna what the doctor had said, there was silence. He thought he'd lost the signal just before she said, "I understand," and disconnected. She and Terry would soon be breaking all speed laws racing from Dallas.

Weeping from a young couple in the corner caught Rob's notice. Their kid had been brought in just after Frank. His condition didn't look good either. Death lingered around every corner of life. You never quite knew when you'd turn the wrong one and look it in the eyes.

Ten minutes later, Adams returned. "Okay, follow me."

Rob's wobbly legs barely held him. He followed the doctor through a swinging set of double doors at the end of the hall and entered the ICU. His stomach churned, and a sudden chill caused him to shake.

Few beds were occupied. Only three nurses worked the floor. One stood over a patient, blocking Rob's view. Adams stopped there, and when she leaned back, Rob drew in a breath. Frank. His sallow complexion shocked Rob. *He already looks dead.* The nurse tore off another piece of tape and secured the needle in Frank's arm. The tube led to an IV of clear liquid.

Adams scanned Frank's chart. "Still holding at two cc's?"

The nurse dropped the tape roll in her pocket. "Yes, we're on our third platelets and three hundred out of the chest in the last hour."

Adams looked her way. "Respiration?"

"Good saturation so far."

He nodded. "We'll hold off on intubation until needed."

"Yes, doctor." She moved to one side and revealed a chair. When she departed, she drew a privacy curtain around the bed.

The area had sort of a bad-breath odor. Rob had never smelled anything like it. One of those tube things for oxygen was wrapped around Frank's head and poking in his nose. Several IVs hung above him, all leading to the tube with the needle. A half-depleted bag of blood also hung on a hook, draining down into the other arm. A digital monitor pinged while displaying sets of green numbers. Under the bed, two plastic boxes collected blood from giant hoses coming out of Frank's chest. Rob had trouble processing the horror show.

"Stay as long as you like," the doctor said. "You won't be disturbed. I've left orders."

Rob shook the man's hand. "I really appreciate it. Anything I need to do?"

"No, a nurse will be around every few minutes, and the vitals are being monitored. Just spend time with him. He's lucky to have you. Most never get that at the end."

Adams pushed the curtain away and departed, pulling it back into place after he left.

Rob was afraid to sit, afraid that any change might trigger something. Finally he dropped into the chair and watched his friend's chest move up and down—not looking at his face. He'd never felt so helpless, so useless. He took Frank's hand, and the warmth felt good. Rob pulled in a deep breath and just talked.

"I'm sorry, Frank. I know you probably can't hear me, but I need to say it anyway. The last three years with you have been the best of my life. You made 'em the best. I couldn't have wished for a better partner. We had some times." Rob choked and took a second to recover.

"You drove me a little crazy with your peculiarities, but I wouldn't have had it any other way." A new thought entered Rob's mind. "I wished I'd known about your wife earlier. I would have understood a lot of the crazy shit you did. Would have been great to get to know her. Bet Carmen would have loved her." Rob drew in a breath and wiped his eyes.

"You saved Trina, Frank. No one else could have figured it out—only you. When everyone doubted—you believed. God knows how many more you may have also saved. I even doubted and made fun of you . . . shouldn't have done that. And I've picked at and harassed you about things I didn't understand. Shouldn't have done that either. Hope you'll forgive me." Rob blew his nose and shook his head.

"If this is our last time together, I want you to know that I love you. You got a bad break on this one. Could have happened to anyone. But you saved my life. Gave me a second chance to hold Carmen, to see my children marry, to play with my grandchildren someday. I can't repay a debt that big. Saying thanks isn't enough, but it's all I have. If you have to go now, I understand." Rob closed his eyes tight and drew in a breath. "Just wanted to get that off my chest."

Tears dripped to the floor, and Rob had to blow his nose a couple more times, but he was sure Frank wouldn't mind. Rob wrapped both hands around Frank's, laid his forehead on them, and prayed:

"Lord, I come to you in humble obedience. I've sinned and fallen short of your grace, but you know I'm one of your children. This man deserves to live. He's also a sinner and fallen short. He may not be a believer, but I beg for his life. He's a good person." Rob choked on his words and took a second to calm down. "His life would have been different if things had happened differently. I know your will be done, so he was set on his course for a purpose. Maybe the reason for his tragedy put him in a position to save those two girls . . . I don't know. Don't let him die, not now." Rob sniffed and wiped his eyes before crossing himself. "Amen."

He released Frank's hand and nodded. "Thy will be done." He leaned his head into his palms and breathed deep, slow breaths. Fatigue enveloped him, and he closed his eyes. He just wanted to lie down. He didn't want—

"Are you okay?" a weak, raspy voice asked.

Rob froze. He didn't even breathe. He slowly lifted his head. Frank stared at him through clear, thoughtful eyes.

Rob gasped. "Yes . . . yes, I'm fine."

"And the girls?" Frank cleared his throat, swallowed, and grimaced.

Rob began laughing and crying at the same time. "Yes . . . yes, we're all okay." He shook his head. "Only you, Frank, would wake up after being shot and start asking about everyone."

A mischievous grin crossed Frank's lips. "Well, I didn't want to piss you off by not asking. I know how sensitive you Mexicans are."

Rob broke into a satisfied smile and grabbed Frank's hand again. Rob's eyes clouded with more tears, and his voice broke. "Cracker asshole."

Epilogue

T uesday Morning Rob pushed the wheelchair down the hall of Nacog-doches Memorial Hospital. This would be his last trip to this place, and he was glad. The sights, smells, and sounds held too many bad memories. Frank had been there for almost two weeks. During his stay he'd wanted for nothing. Edna and Terry had seen to that. A CIU detective was stationed in Nacogdoches to be at Frank's beck and call. Frank had mended well and even begun physical therapy. He would fully recover.

It wasn't Frank's physical recovery that concerned Rob. During his stay in the hospital, he'd not received a visit, call, or card from Katrina Wallace. He'd asked about her a few times and Rob had assured him she was fine. He'd finally stopped asking and drifted into one of his familiar funks. Rob couldn't blame him.

When Rob wheeled the chair through the open door of Frank's room, he found him sitting by the window, staring at the vast green sea of pine forest behind the hospital.

"Ready to go home?"

Frank looked around and stood. He wore the T-shirt, shorts, and sandals Rob had pilfered from his condo a few days earlier. "Yeah," he said, and picked up the patient bag of personal items, cards, and clothes off the bed.

"You already officially checked out?" Rob asked.

"Yeah, signed the papers about a half hour ago."

Rob locked the wheels on the chair. "Okay, let's go."

Frank eyed the wheelchair a moment before saying, "Don't need that thing. Been walking the halls for over a week."

Rob thumped the top of his snuff can and got a pinch. "There's a mean-looking RN down the hall. Says this is the only way you're leaving this place."

"Whatever." Frank shrugged and took a seat in the chair. He set the bag on his lap and said, "Let's get out of here."

Rob unlocked the wheels and backed out of the room with Frank in his full-slouch riding position. As they passed the nurse's station, one attractive young nurse waved. She looked as if she might cry. Another, even more attractive nurse smiled and mouthed the words, "Call me."

Um, must be the ones who gave him sponge baths.

Neither Rob nor Frank spoke until entering the elevator. As the doors closed, Rob said, "Edna made a big pot of stew and Terry a big pot of chili and a pan of cornbread. I left them in your refrigerator this morning before driving down. At least you'll be eating well."

"Yeah, that's great," Frank mumbled. His voice had a worn-out, flat sound, like that of a cat that's just realized it's lost a couple of its nine lives.

When the doors opened into the lobby, Rob swung left toward the patient loading zone. As they approached the doors, Rob said, "Can't waste any time. Have to be in Hemphill in two hours to appear before the grand jury. They're indicting the brothers and sisters today. Have just enough time to grab lunch before then."

Frank jerked his head around. "Grand jury? I can't appear before a grand jury dressed like this!"

"Don't sweat it," Rob said. "They only need me. I've scored you a ride to Dallas."

The automatic doors swung open and a new, bright red, Audi S4 sedan came into view. Katrina stood holding the passenger door open. A full-toothed smile spread across her lips.

"Detective Pierce," she said, "we have a lot of things to discuss. Hop in. I'm driving."

Acknowledgments

Few good books are written alone. I am indebted to a number of people.

Thanks: To my daughter, Natalie Enmon Mobley, for the Christmas gift that provided the spark of inspiration and for reading the original draft.

To Allen Holtz (Ret. DPD- CIU), Anna Davis, Kelli Grant, Walt Baty, and Zana Tidwell for reading and offering valuable suggestions for various versions of the manuscript.

To my editors, Tex Thompson, Leslie Lutz, and Anne Brewer, for their magic with words.

To my agent, David Haviland, of the Andrew Lownie Literary Agency, for believing in the project.

To Jenny Chen and the staff of Crooked Lane Books for being easy to work with.

And, last but not least, to the DFW Writers' Workshop for their critiques and encouragement.